A DYSTOPIAN SEA ADVENTURE

ONERO'S HUNT

J. R. DEVOE

DARK TIDE PUBLISHING

Dark Tide Publishing

ISBN: 978-1-7771231-4-7 (hardback)
ISBN: 978-1-7771231-5-4 (paperback)
ISBN: 978-1-7771231-6-1 (ebook)

Second Edition
First Printing: February 2020

Book cover designed by MiblArt
Map art by Chaim Holtjer

www.jrdevoe.com

ANTERRA
ANNO 2722 CE
Point Bay Station
Peninsula
Isle of Arokya
Port Abersali
POLARIA
THE ARTERY
FORT CYPRESS
Alnitak
Alrelam
Mintaka
AMYRIA

N
ORTARIA
olis
Bories
Mountains
S

Onero [oh-n*air*-oh]

Modern Noun
   surname assigned to indentured servants of Polaria

Old Verb
   burden, load, overwhelm

THE ORDER

Law I:
Defend the Mother.

Law II:
Exploration into ancient culture is prohibited.

Law III:
Practice responsible innovation.

Law IV:
Public participation in council matters is essential to fair
governance.

Law V:
Consume only what is necessary for healthy living.

Law VI:
Surplus children shall be remanded to the National Service.

Law VII:
Never leave the safety of Anterra.

Law VIII:
Report any infraction of the Order without delay.

ONE

It was too fine a day to watch a man hang.

Toris wobbled in the solstice heat, suffocating under the hood of his wool poncho, but he dared not remove it. He squinted to focus on the gallows ahead, felt the burn of sweat in his eyes and resisted the urge to wipe his face. Even the slightest movement may draw the attention of the peace officers watching the crowd. Not worth the risk. Normally he'd tie back his hair, but today he let the coal-black strands obscure his face.

On the platform before him, Captain Clavilla's knee-high boots clunked across the wooden planks, his long, black slicker matched by his greasy hair and beard. A scimitar rattled at his side as he paced before the audience.

"You all know the penalties for exploring," Clavilla said. "And yet this man chose to defy the laws that have kept Polaria from destruction...*three* whole times."

Behind Clavilla, Toris's shipwright mentor Sallus stood with a rope looped around his neck, shivering despite the heat. With his chin lowered to his chest, all that was visible was the white hair atop his head.

Toris tried to swallow the lump growing in his throat.

All around, wooden shutters squeaked open and clunked

against walls of whitewashed stone as newly-arrived spectators crammed into the upper floors of the surrounding shops. Seagulls squawked from the dock at the end of the lane, indifferent.

"For centuries the Order has protected Polaria from repeating the mistakes of our ancestors," Clavilla boomed. "Bear witness to the fate of those who put *self* above all. Leave here and spread word far and wide in service to your country."

In response, the crowd turned collectively back to the statue of the Sage Abelia sitting cross-legged in the center of the square, where the words *'Society over Self'* were inscribed in its base.

Captain Clavilla pulled a black recording device from his slicker. "Are there any who wish to speak their last words to the damned?"

On the dais, Sallus looked up for the first time since the noose had slipped around his neck. In the three days since Toris had last seen him, the sixty-year-old shipwright appeared to have aged two decades. The grey hair skirting the side of his head had blanched full white, and where his eyes once hosted a defiant fire, there was now smoldering ash.

Toris felt a stirring at his side as Jayda brushed strands of her brown hair aside to give him a sidelong look with a slight shake of her head. Sunlight caught the ragged scar across her cheek as her glare shifted to Clavilla. Toris had told her that an execution was no place for a fourteen-year-old, but she'd insisted, reminding him that he'd been much younger when he'd witnessed his first hanging.

Toris stood on tiptoes to reveal himself in the fifth row to Sallus. He wished for nothing more than to go up and embrace the closest person to a father he'd ever known, but to reveal his presence on the mainland would be to declare a violation of his exile. Then he may as well wrap a noose around his own neck.

A sailor armed with a submachine gun standing to Sallus's left noticed Toris first and narrowed his eyes on him. Toris's heels lowered to the ground along with his gaze. Everyone knew that the captain's offer was not an extension of humility, but a tactic to identify accomplices and sympathizers.

At the crowd's silence, Clavilla nodded and slid his scimitar from its sheath. He pointed the curved blade at the convicted.

"Sallus Cygnus, for your repeated crimes against Law Two of the Order, you have been sentenced to die."

Sallus lowered his head.

Clavilla gripped the hilt with both hands. "May the Mother have mercy on your soul."

As the captain raised the sword high, Toris's throat tightened as if the noose were around his own neck.

Jayda grabbed his hand and laced her fingers in his.

On the dais Sallus glanced up and locked his eyes on Toris, and Toris tried to offer an assuring smile, to resist stealing a glance at the blade swinging down. He held his mentor's stare until the blade sliced the rope and the plank slid back from under his feet.

Tense silence choked the crowd like the rope squeezing Sallus's neck, making the creaking wood of the noose post all the louder.

Toris squeezed his sister's hand as the only adult to have ever shown him dignity wriggled like a fish on a hook. Watching him struggle like a cod, his face twisted in agony…It was too much. Toris turned his eyes to the ground, where a single tear spattered on the flagstone between his bare feet.

When the sounds of struggle stopped, Clavilla stepped to the front of the stage. "No bell rings for the dead on this day."

Toris's head snapped up.

Clavilla waved his sword over the crowd. "Anyone who touches that bell in the next twenty-four hours will lose their hand," the captain said. Then he sheathed his sword and marched off the stage.

The simmering tears of Toris's sorrow boiled over to rage as he watched Sallus sway from the rope in silence. Every mariner deserved their toll, whether they disappeared at sea or hit their head on the tavern steps in a drunken stupor. It was the rite of every soul who danced the tides.

The crowd receded, but Toris remained with his head down whispering a prayer. They were the same words he and his foster siblings recited for their orphan kin who had donned the uniform to fight the savages at their border, only to return to the orphanry wrapped in sheets upon funeral carts.

To live is to struggle. To serve is divine. To embrace death in life is to defeat it, for death is naught.

His gaze lifted from under his sunken hood to the brass bell hanging from the post at the back of the stage.

Death is naught.

Jayda gave his hand a squeeze. "Come, brother. It's done."

If only that were true. "Meet me at the boat."

Jayda gave him a forbidding look, but did not protest. Instead, she unlaced her fingers from his and drifted away with the crowd.

An Omniguard officer remained at the dais steps, casting Toris the occasional suspicious glare. In his boredom, he pulled the navy-blue wedge cap from his head and fanned his face with it.

Toris sauntered to the edge of the square and sat upon the stone steps of a bakery. Its doors were locked, and its windows shuttered. With the rise of inland crop failures, all Polarian food-stuffs were now held in banks and distributed by the local Omniguard.

A horn blew, long and solemn, from the harbour.

Up the lane, citizens barged from inns and tea shops and flooded across the square toward the marina, each desperate for a crack at the catch before the Port Authority took its tally. More inland folk were relocating to the coast everyday as seafood became the more reliable food source. Toris had even noticed a few new residents on his home isle, Mintaka, which was a fair distance for mainland folk to move for better access to food.

Toris sat up on his haunches. There'd be a riot at the docks. People would fall into the water, even drown. The Omniguard would have their hands full.

He didn't have to wait long for the shrill blast of a whistle to beckon backup to the marina. As the Omniguard officer watching

Sallus's body rushed down to help, Toris stood and marched across the square.

At the bottom of the steps he took a good look around, but the newly-arrived fishing boat had attracted both citizens and peace officers alike.

Still, the vacant square didn't ease his throbbing heart, which drummed loud in his ears. But there'd be no better time.

Planks groaned under his bare feet as he climbed the thirteen steps to the stage, wood that had felt the weight of many a man's last steps. The bell hung from a post at the back of the dais, for the days when the mayor stood upon this podium to read off the names of mariners who now belonged to the merciless sea.

Toris gripped the thick braided rope. He took one look at Sallus dangling from the noose, then pulled back and gave the clapper a hard whip forward.

DING!

Toris cringed as the ring rattled through every strand of his body, further splitting his already frayed nerves. Clapping wings rose from an array of solar panels atop a hydrogen motor repair shop as a flock of pigeons took flight.

They were not the only creatures to stir.

"Hey!" An Omniguard officer emerged from a food vault across the square. He pointed his baton at Toris and blew his whistle—an order for Toris to drop to his knees.

Instead, Toris ran.

Sliding from the dais and dashing to the opposite alley, Toris led the officer through a maze of white walls, the clunk of heavy boots rising ever louder. To shed some dead weight, Toris threw off the poncho and hiked up his shendyt, the band of black linen covering his waist to just above his knees. Rounding the next corner, he slammed into the alley's far wall and pushed himself along the white brick face in lieu of slowing.

At the end of the alley lined with waste bins, sunlight glittered off the harbour and beckoned him to safety.

The officer's boots skidded around the corner close behind

him. In three quick bounds he sounded as if he were within reaching distance. "Got ya now," the man huffed.

Toris hunched his shoulders in anticipation of a hand seizing his collar and drew the dive knife from his waistband, its polymer handle cold in his clammy hand.

From his left, an empty waste crate screeched over cobblestone as it slid into the alley, narrowly missing Toris. It rammed the officer at the knees and flipped him forward onto his face.

Jayda emerged from a doorway where the crate had originated and wrenched the officer's left boot from his foot. He swiped at her but missed as she darted back toward the square. Toris continued his run, and the officer looked between him and Jayda to consider which offender to chase before climbing out of the bin and continuing after Toris.

The end of the alley opened up to Finn's Marina, where three docks reached into the harbour like wooden fingers. Toris weaved through a mob to the longest dock in the center. A woman grabbed the pursuing Omniguard, pleading for his help in finding her child among the rabble, which gave Toris more of a lead. Splinters pricked his soles as he sprinted across the dock between empty boat slips. The escalating food shortage had forced the Port Authority to increase their fishing license approval tenfold, so anyone with a boat was out on the water trying to balance Polaria's crop losses—which left one vessel conspicuously tied up ahead.

The lone twenty-three-foot sailboat rocked patiently at the end of the dock, her wooden hull rubbing against the wharf pillars and peeling away more of her sky-blue paint. As the *Atlas* wrestled against the hemp rope holding her to the dock, a shriek rose from the officer's whistle.

Toris dared not steal a look back as he slid *Atlas'* fraying dock line over the cleat and jumped into her cockpit with it. His forward momentum sent the boat drifting into the harbour just in time for the Omniguard to skid to a halt at the edge of the wharf. The officer whipped out his data pad and set his thumbs to work, surely noting a description of Toris and *Atlas*. But it didn't matter. *Atlas* needed a new paint job anyway.

If only Toris could change his own identity so easily.

At the start of the dock, Jayda's black attire broke through the crowd of brown and grey shawls. She waved Toris on, then pointed to the fishing vessel that had drawn the mob, which he now saw hailed from Mintaka. Jayda could catch a ride home with the crew after they unloaded their catch.

Toris got to work, hauling on the halyard with his callused hands. The sail rose, grey patches dotting the ragged white canvas as it luffed in the midsummer breeze. When it reached the masthead, it bulged full of wind and took the shape of a triangle, towing Toris away from the mainland.

His constant, all-around search for Coast Patrol vessels was interrupted by a pot clattering in the covered cabin below.

He shot to his feet, every fiber in his body taut as a harp string. He grabbed his cutlass from under the starboard bench and stood over the slanted cabin hatch. It was only a dull antique, but a stowaway wouldn't know that at first look. "I hear you down there. Show yourself."

Silence.

A wave rocked the boat and sent someone into a stumble below.

"Come out or I'll come down swinging!" He shoved the sword point through the hatch to bolster his threat.

"Hey, take it easy!" came a girl's voice.

The stowaway appeared in the patch of sunlight below. She pulled back the hood of her brown cloak to reveal a head of stubble that glistened with beads of sweat. Her icy blue eyes watched the sword tip nervously. "For Sage's sake, is that how you always greet your guests?"

Toris lowered the sword slightly, but kept the weapon at the ready. "Who else is down there?"

"I'm alone." She spread her cloak open. "And unarmed."

Toris crouched to peer as far into the cabin as he could see.

Unless someone was hiding in the crawl space below the cockpit, she was telling the truth. Which begged the question: what was a pretty girl on the cusp of womanhood doing aboard his boat?

"Awful nice clothes you're wearing, for a stowaway." Under her cloak, the frayed hem of her purple gown did not demean the luster of the rich silk, and the narrow red welts on her scalp suggested she'd shaved her own head and was not in the habit of doing so.

He sat at the tiller and set the cutlass at his feet. "Well? You comin' up?"

The girl stuck her head up through the hatch, craning her neck to see beyond Toris. "How far are we from land?"

"Close enough to bring you back."

"You can't!" The girl scrambled up into the cockpit, her anxious eyes fixated on Port Abersali, now far beyond *Atlas'* spreading wake.

"Who are you running from?" Toris said.

"Who are *you* running from? I heard someone chasing you."

"Look here, I'm first mate—I mean, this is my boat." He swallowed, trying not to think of Sallus. "So, I ask the questions. What's your name?"

The girl pressed her right palm to her belly and gave a slight bow. "You may call me *Lex*."

"Who are you so desperate to get away from that you'd hide in a random person's boat? Do you know what kind of scoundrels take to sea around here?"

"Are you a scoundrel, Brother . . .?"

"Toris. And no, I'm a perfect law-abiding Polarian. Now answer my first question."

Lex sat on the bench opposite him. "I'm running from my father." She gripped the edge of the seat nervously. "Please don't take me back. Just drop me off wherever you're going and I'll be on my way."

Toris's grip tightened on the tiller. Judging by the fine stitch of her clothing, he didn't like where this was going. "Who's your father? Are you highborn? Will he come looking for you? *Answer* me."

"He's…well, there's no light way to put this. My full name is Alexandra Arcturus."

Toris's heart dropped like an anchor.

"You—you're lying." No way would the Chancellor's daughter stow away on a piece of driftwood like *Atlas.* "Alexandra Arcturus is supposed to marry General Aldebaran…" Toris struggled to recall the date he'd heard announced on the radio but couldn't.

"*Supposed* to marry," Lex said. "But if I'm somewhere else, like on this boat, then, well…" She shrugged and looked ahead toward the ocean horizon.

Toris felt a bad case of sea-belly swelling up, though not from the rocking motion. If this girl was telling the truth, then she had a lot of people looking for her. Powerful men with eyes and ears everywhere, people who might make improper assumptions about her relationship to present company.

He stood, leg muscles too tight to sit with, but the tiny cockpit offered little room for him to pace.

"Sit down," she said, glancing back at the port.

"I have to take you back."

Lex stood and jabbed a threatening finger at his face. "You do that, and I'll tell the Omniguard you kidnapped me."

Toris stepped back and saw from her challenging stare that she was serious. He sank to the bench and gripped the tiller. Suddenly the sea seemed like a very small place.

TWO

Out past the Isle of Alnilam, Toris swung the bow directly into the wind. The sail deflated in the warm breeze as *Atlas* eased to a stop.

He double-checked the red circle on Sallus's map, comparing the mark with his position to Alnilam's north coast.

Lex looked around. "Where are we?"

Toris leaned overboard and stared at an undulating wreck below, which he and Sallus had explored two weeks past. The arrival of a Coast Patrol ship had forced them to abandon the site, so Sallus had marked the location and vowed to return.

Toris slicked back his coal-black hair and looked at the eagle gliding over Alnilam's green shores, which sat two miles away. Surely that bird was not the only predator watching these waters.

His gaze swept out to sea, where the glare of sunlight glittering off the blue water made nature's movements difficult to distinguish from anything other. To his left, the Antarctic peninsula's grey mountain range stretched from the mainland to the horizon like a bottom row of jagged teeth. Somewhere out past its point, the Decimators had once ruled the world with their toxic machinery. But it was not the ghosts of a drowned civilization that Toris now feared.

Back toward the mainland, he could see a few scattered fishing ships casting their nets to meet county quotas. Toris had never seen so many vessels upon the water, and he was grateful for them. The influx allowed his tiny sailboat to blend in while at the same time stretching the Coast Patrol's attention.

As the lazy flapping of the sail and the gentle rocking of the boat eased his apprehension, he pulled a spyglass from under the bench and handed it to Lex.

"Keep watch," he told her, pulling off his black tunic.

Lex set the brass cylinder aside and leaned over starboard to look at the wreck. She turned back to him with eyes flared wide.

"Has the heat fried your brain? That's illegal!"

Toris pulled a harpoon from under the bench. "Yet not the most illegal thing I did since waking up today."

Lex's eyes grew wider at seeing the brand on his left deltoid. The *O* of raised scar tissue marked him as an Onero, a member of Polaria's serving class. This alone was common enough, but it was the diagonal slash through the O that damned him.

"You *are* a scoundrel," Lex said. "Why are you banned from the mainland?"

"You want to find another ride? Keep asking awkward questions."

He stepped onto the swim deck, where a coiled cable hung from the pushpit. He tied one end around his ankle and clipped the other end to the rail.

"Didn't they just hang that guy in Abersali for exploring?" Lex said.

Toris suppressed a shiver. His mentor's blood hadn't even gone cold yet and he was doing the same thing that had earned Sallus a noose necklace. And to do it in the presence of the Chancellor's daughter on top of that? Madness. But the calm water all around assured him he'd have no better chance. *Slack tide.* No water flowing either way for fifteen minutes as the ebb tide reversed to flood. Such a rare occasion to find himself above a wreck with no current to whisk away his boat while he was down under. That's why, when on a vessel with no anchor, you needed a skilled partner to keep bringing the boat back around. Toris couldn't even remember if he'd ever dived a slack tide, the occasion was so rare. He'd not get another chance, for time was running short. *Three days.* That was how much time his sister had before the Academy's admission deadline.

The prospect of getting her into school was enough to bolster his courage. And besides, the girl on his boat likely claimed to be the Chancellor's daughter to ensure no fool would dare harm her.

Such dives typically involved a tank on his back, but the Coast Patrol had seized all of Sallus's black market gear, so it was time Toris challenged his free dive record. He took a deep breath and then dove from the swim deck.

The warm water soothed his sunburnt skin. Bubbles cleared from before his face, revealing the ruins below—scraps and chunks of rusted metal that had littered the seabed since the birth days of Anterra, back when some still called it 'Antarctica'. Yet this wreck's fair condition suggested its demise had come considerably later than the first steel ships to make the perilous voyage in search of salvation seven hundred years ago.

When his dive momentum waned, a few breaststrokes and frog kicks brought him the rest of the distance to the safe that he and Sallus had been forced to drop during their last dive. He brushed silt from the box's rough surface, but there was no time to admire the prize while he couldn't breathe.

Wedging the harpoon tip beneath the box, he pried the bottom of the safe from the seabed, then removed the cable from his ankle and wrapped it around the box. Shaking hands crisscrossed it in opposite directions, ensuring a secure hold while his lungs and heart burned in their cry for oxygen. Finally, satisfied with the rigging, he launched up toward *Atlas*.

At the surface he clambered onto the swim deck.

Lex now sat on the starboard bench, hunched over a reading tablet on her lap, her bare skin red from the blazing sun. The spyglass he'd given her rolled gently across the wooden deck above the cabin, out of reach.

Toris climbed into the cockpit. "I'm glad to see you've made yourself at home."

Lex looked up from his reader. "Where'd you get this data?"

"Found it." He grabbed the spyglass from the deck and waved it before her face. "Remember when I told you to keep watch? What do you think will happen if the Coast Patrol catches us out here scavenging?"

Lex picked up the cutlass at her feet and jumped atop the cabin, where she adopted a wide fencing stance, one foot back, the jagged hem of her purple dress rising to reveal the pale skin above her sunburned knees. "When I get through with them, they'll wish they'd picked another boat to harass."

Toris held up both hands in mocking surrender. "You'd make a fierce pyrate." He grabbed the dull blade and twisted the hilt from Lex's hand, then offered her the spyglass in its place. "If only the Coast Patrol armed its boarding parties with antique swords."

She snatched the brass cylinder and jumped down into the cockpit.

"Find anything?" she said.

"Maybe."

Toris caught sight of a grey Coast Patrol battle cruiser weaving through a cluster of fishing vessels near the mainland. Its course suggested he should be safe for now, but it might not be the only patrol ship on the hunt.

Turning away, he unclipped the cable from the rail and fed it through a track of pulleys attached to a metal arm that reached astern, then wrapped the line around a small drum bolted to *Atlas'* swim deck. He cranked the winch handle, winding the groaning cable around the drum.

His arms burned as they wrestled his catch from its grave. A childhood of toiling in the fields at Lake Orion Orphanry had built up his endurance, and the prospect of securing Jayda's future provided strength enough to haul the slimy, dripping box above water. Seeing it in direct sunlight sent a ripple of hope through his heart.

He swung the hoist arm into the cockpit and lowered the safe onto the starboard bench, where for a moment all he could do was stare lustfully at it. Keeping his eyes on the safe, he dug a hammer and pry bar from under the bench. He jammed the flat end of the bar between the door edge and the body of the safe, then struck the other end with the hammer—*ting*—and the pressure of the wedged bar snapped the ancient hinges. The door hit the deck with a *thud*.

Toris's hand was inside the safe before the water had completely drained. His fingers skimmed over rusted coins and mounds of slime until they encountered a smooth object that made him giddy. He pulled the artifact from the safe and held it with trembling hands. The onyx finish of the circuit box inside the glass encasement filled his heart with lust.

Lex gasped. *"Sage's grace.* I didn't think you'd actually find anything."

He set the bounty down and tapped its clear shell with the hammer to shatter the glass. He picked up the black, palm-sized box and stroked the polymer casing. In their final days, the Decimators took to storing data from their world onto archives. The government viewed their knowledge as toxic, seeing the wrong combination of words as a sleeping virus waiting to wreak havoc across the world's last habitable land. That's why all literature predating the Decimation was forbidden, with the only exception being select writings from the Old Greeks. But the black market valued this rediscovered information higher than gold.

"If the young lady can learn to take orders, then I might keep her around," he said. "Then I'll show you a world long forgotten."

Lex planted her hands on her hips and frowned. "Young lady? I bet we're the same age."

Toris smirked. Same age in years, sure. But he had been forced to grow up faster in his seventeen winters as a serving class orphan than a sheltered highborn girl from the capital.

This wasn't the place to do this, but Toris couldn't help himself. He pulled his data harvester, a thumb-sized rectangular magnet, from under the bench and set it on top of the archive. A red light flashed as the harvester absorbed data from the larger box, sorting what corruption it could and discarding what it could not. Polarian reading devices were designed to view state-approved texts only, but this black market harvester could interpret ancient archives and translate them to readable documents.

When the harvester finished extracting, it automatically exported the documents to Toris's reading tablet. The reader's black screen flashed blue. Blocks of files popped up in a grid pattern that covered the whole screen. Jackpot.

Lex leaned over his shoulder. "See if there's a story about Achilles."

Toris flicked through photos of people driving automobiles and groups gathered in dark dance temples lit by elaborate light displays until one image stopped him. The crimson-clad king sat stiffly upon his throne, but the smiling children seated on his lap and the rosy cheeks above his snow-white beard clashed with the malevolent depictions of capitalist rulers from that era.

"Well?" Lex said, leaning closer. Her warm hand on his shoulder and her bare leg against his sent a prickle down his spine.

He cleared his throat and shifted uncomfortably, then typed an *A* into the search field before struggling for the next letter. Orphans and surplus children of the Onero serving class were expected only to interpret blueprints and orders for their National Service, so the orphanry keepers never bothered teaching them to read beyond their occupational requirements.

Lex spelled out the rest. "C. H. I. L. L. E. S. It's okay. That was a hard one."

He typed it in. No results. Lex's enthusiasm deflated, but Toris's had grown.

"Let's get out of here," he said, then set about clearing the remaining items from the safe. He'd been away from Mintaka too long already. Though he was technically out of work until they assigned him to a new shipbuilding mentor, his island's warden kept him busy gutting and salting fish to help meet the food quotas.

Toris flipped the empty safe overboard and sent it splashing toward the seabed, then pulled the tiller to swing the bow off-wind. The patched sail inflated and dragged them away from the mainland and toward Mintaka—the farthest satellite island in the three island chain that stretched out to sea in the same configuration as Orion's belt, and the place Toris called home.

He glanced over his shoulder at the mainland. Toris hadn't been allowed there since he was twelve, which was fine with him. In the five years since they'd exiled him to the islands, he hadn't once had to scrape dirt with his bare hands to plant seeds like he'd had to do at the dreaded orphanry. He'd take building ships by the sea over plowing potato fields any day. And on the Isle of Mintaka, most citizens never knew his mother was a traitor or his father a 'savage' Ortarian.

What would Lex think if she knew the identity of his mother? Surely she'd heard of Anaraxa Centaurus, the Polarian Defence Force colonel who allowed one of her barbaric enemies to seduce her during Anterra's only Peace Summit. Her arrest for treason had reignited hostilities between both nations when his father led a failed Ortarian attack against Polaria. He died in the fight and his mother immediately after Toris's birth, when they slipped a rope around her neck and hanged her for thwarting Polaria's only chance at peace. Would the Chancellor's daughter have accompanied Toris so eagerly into exile had she known what blood pumped through his veins?

"What are you going to do with the archive?" Lex asked.

"Trade it for something I can use," Toris said. His foster sister Jayda had her heart set on making the Capital Academy's admission deadline this year, which was in three days. The school only accepted Oneros who displayed exceptional promise for a vocation in demand. Luckily, Mintaka's prep school's headmaster suffered from a reckless obsession with contraband literature, of which Toris provided the most exotic kind.

Though Toris considered every Onero his brother or sister, Jayda held a special place in his heart. Back in their orphanry days, whenever a group of children attacked him because of his half-Ortarian lineage, Jayda was always eager to retaliate. Once, she led a boy into a bear trap. That earned her six weeks in the hole—the same length of time it took for his broken leg to heal. Such acts reinforced his suspicion that they had more than just Onero status in common. Her records listed her parents as *unknown*, but a lone child wandering up to the orphanry at Spring's dawn, full of fire where there should have been fear, suggested at least a taint of Ortarian blood.

Lex lounged over the cabin with her face buried in his reader, studying the new files.

"It's nice to see you're enjoying this little holiday," Toris said.

"I'm hard at work, I'll have you know."

"Is reading considered work where you're from?"

Lex turned the screen toward him. "It is when you're researching a solution to the food shortage. You know, saving lives and all that."

Toris squeezed the tiller. He'd heard the Chancellor on the radio, many times, insisting there wasn't a shortage. That food shipments to the capital were for safe-keeping and fair distribution. "Your father doesn't seem to think there's a problem. Maybe you can enlighten him when you go home."

Lex lowered the reader. "He knows. He just doesn't want to risk a vote of no confidence." She looked down at her feet and wiggled her toes. "That's why he's shifting the country's food to the capital's shelves. Amyria houses more voters than the rest of the country combined."

Toris shook his head in disgust. Of course the Chancellor would redistribute food according to a territory's voter strength. More First-Class Citizens resided in the capital than anywhere else, and each of their votes was worth thrice that of a third-class citizen. Keeping the capital happy would pay off in the next election.

Lex resumed her reading.

Toris pulled the mainsheet to trim the sail. "You really think ancient words can save us?"

Lex shrugged. "We know what the problem is. Our seeds don't have enough diversity to adapt to changing conditions. The Decimators may have faced the same problem." Lex tapped words into the search field. "But they didn't starve. Most likely they blew themselves into oblivion."

No one knew how the great infernos started, but many scholars asserted it was from nuclear war. Sallus had once told Toris this was wrong, because a decades-long winter would have followed such a catastrophe. But such knowledge was privy only to those who dared read ancient texts.

"It's just a matter of knowing what questions to ask," Lex said. "Let's try...*Genetic erosion*. I heard the council say those words a lot lately." She scanned the results and frowned. "Not that." She erased the words. "*Genetic diversity in crops*." She read the results until something on the screen caused her to inhale deeply, her wide eyes zipping side to side. She laughed in disbelief.

"All Odillian's glory, I think this could be it."

Toris leaned forward. "What?"

Lex stood, then turned the screen toward him. "This article describes a seed vault that the Decimators constructed to preserve the world's crop diversity."

Toris leaned in for a closer look at the photo of a tall rectangular doorway protruding from a snow-covered mountain slope. "If that was in the old world," he said, "then it's dust like the rest."

"You don't know that."

Lex flipped the reader back around for another look at the article.

"This says it was designed to last a thousand years, and that it was built to remain above the highest possible sea level rise. They even called it the *Doomsday Vault*. With those millions of varieties, genetic erosion will be a thing of the past. No more crop failures. If you show this to the council you could claim the Accolade. You could wipe your debt clean and become a First-Class Citizen"—Lex snapped her fingers—"like that."

"If I show that to *anyone*, I'll end up slaving in a salt mine for two years." Tempting as the reward for reversing the crop failures was, with its promise of First-Class Citizenship and one million credits, Toris would have to admit to breaking the Order to bid on it.

"Then let me show them," Lex said. "I'll give you the reward."

Toris shook his head. "You'd be admitting to breaking the Second Law. Even *your* last name won't save you from that."

"Given the circumstance, they may make an exception."

"And stick you in the mine beside me?"

Lex frowned. "That's not what I meant."

"That world is long gone, Lex."

She tapped the screen to enlarge the image of the Svalbard archipelago. "The vault was in the Arctic, too isolated to waste bombs on."

"The Arctic?" Toris stifled a sardonic laugh. "Then that vault may as well be on the moon for all the good it'll do us. You forget the Seventh Law? *Never leave the safety of Anterra.* They made that law for a reason." He nodded toward the ocean horizon. "No one has ever crossed the sea and come back. Besides, the council will never sanction a breach of the Order to go look for it."

Lex lowered the tablet and gave him a scolding look. "They might send the Defence Force if it's our only hope. You have an obligation to help your country."

"I know my obligations," Toris snapped. The sixteen years of service he owed to pay off the debt of his upbringing ensured Polaria got from him the best years of his life. He'd not risk a sentence of two years in a salt mine on top of that.

"But—"

"Just let it go."

Lex sat on the bench and crossed her arms over her chest. But she didn't stay like that for long. She rose slowly to her feet, absently grabbing the mainsheet to steady herself as her eyes grew wider. Toris followed her gaze astern, where a battleship carved through *Atlas'* fading wake like a shark on the hunt.

Toris's thumping heart almost burst. A quick look around confirmed his worst fear—that his *Atlas* was the only boat out here.

The Coast Patrol was coming for him.

THREE

Toris scrambled to lower the sail. Normally he'd never pile the lines in such a mess on the cockpit floor, but this was far from a normal situation. This was his worst nightmare.

"What are you doing?" Lex said, rubbing both hands across her shaved head in distress. "We need to outrun them!"

Behind the *Atlas*, the Coast Patrol ship was cutting a line through their wake, its long shadow creeping closer to the sailboat. The semi-circular edges of overlapping steel plates glinted in the sun and gave the hull a scaly appearance.

Toris jumped down to the cabin and dragged a hydrogen motor from the crawl space beneath the cockpit. With the hunk of metal over his shoulder, he wobbled back up the steps. He tried to ignore the pursuing ship as he slammed the outboard motor onto the swim deck at the rear of the boat. With one hand he held the motor in place while with the other he twisted its mounting clamps to secure it to the rear ledge.

"That's a G-series hydrogen motor," Lex said, "approved for Coast Patrol use only. Where did you get that?"

Toris frowned. How did she know what this was?

"Do you know how to use it?" he asked.

Lex shook her head and held up both hands.

Toris twisted the mounting clamps tight, then pressed the start button. Nothing.

"They're gaining on us," Lex said. "Get us out of here!"

He traced the hydrogen line to the primer on the fuel tank, then pressed the button for ten seconds. Sallus had kept the motor for emergency use and, though Toris had never used this relic, he'd worked on a few newer models as a shipwright apprentice.

A second try brought the old motor sputtering to life.

The battleship was within a nautical mile and chewing up the remaining distance fast. In a few quick heartbeats she came close enough for Toris to read the ship's name scrawled across the bow in white—*Sea Serpent*.

Toris sat on the bench with the handle at chest height. "Sit," he told Lex, and she obeyed with her eyes trained on the growing cruiser. Toris twisted the handle throttle. The engine revved and shot *Atlas* forward, which sent Lex tumbling into Toris as the bow lifted above the water.

Bracing her with an arm, he twisted the throttle and sent the small sailboat skipping over whitecaps. The frequent wave-launching and landing forced Lex's head down against his chest, her torso shuddering as if she were about to heave. Toris pushed her away so she didn't spew on his lap and found that she was laughing.

Ahead of them, the green Isle of Mintaka rose higher from the sea. When the rocky shores came into sight above the choppy waves, he risked a look over his shoulder and saw the cruiser had fallen behind.

He kept on the throttle, ignoring the smoke and the smell of burning rubber as the engine strained. Sitting at the helm with so much power at his command, his hair whipping back in the spray, Toris had never felt so alive. Even *Atlas'* keel scraping over the reef didn't slow him, though it did make him cringe.

He cruised past the island until there was only the distant ocean horizon beyond the bow, then swung back around to Mintaka's north shore. Only here, where shallow waters denied the battleship entry, did Toris release the throttle.

"We lost them for now," he said, the tightness in his chest loosening as momentum and the tide carried *Atlas* into Isher Cove. Here, twisted arbutus branches reached out from the rocky hills, their shadows a welcome respite from the merciless sun. Without a whisper of wind to disturb the leaves, the cove offered the illusion of safe harbour.

Toris scanned for the cruiser through the trees. Why had they chased them in the first place? Had they seen him dumping the safe? Or spotted Lex aboard *Atlas*? Without solid proof of wrongdoing, the Coast Patrol may not pursue them on land—but if they felt the need, they possessed landing craft capable of following *Atlas* wherever she went.

Toris scooted across the top of the cabin, grabbed the prow line coiled at the bow, and then splashed down into the waist-deep water. He ran the line across the stony beach and hitched it around a smooth arbutus trunk, then climbed back aboard and set about furling the sail.

"Pull up the panel at your feet," he told Lex.

She obeyed. The instant she cracked open the lid, she gagged and shot upright while pinching her nose.

Toris pulled a basket from under the bench and set it at Lex's feet. "Load the fish into this," he said, stuffing the archive and reader into a canvas sling bag.

Lex's face twisted in disgust. "You expect me to just grab them…with my *hands*?"

He squeezed past her and slipped down into the cabin. "Unless you can think of a better way to scoop them up. Besides, you know how many people would risk death to get their hands on those fish right now? Come on, princess, we need to clear out of here."

Lex gagged again, and Toris couldn't keep an amused smile from tugging at the corner of his mouth. This capital girl couldn't be further out of her element. He felt a sliver of pity for her. But only a sliver.

Down in the cabin, he gathered every contraband artifact he could see into his pack until something on a shelf stopped him—Sallus's heirloom.

Toris held the brass ring before his face, studying its anchor emblem with blurry eyes. He'd always hoped his mentor would offer his father's ring at his passing, to acknowledge him as a son in the same way Toris had seen him as a father. But Sallus had never said the words, never accepted this burden Onero as family, so Toris set it back on the shelf and wiped the tears from his eyes.

Back up top, he slung the bag over his shoulder and jumped down onto the beach. Stones crunched beneath his feet as he marched toward the jagged dirt path that zigzagged up the rocky slope in the shape of a forked lightning bolt.

"Hey!"

He turned to see Lex sitting over the starboard rail, trying to slide down to the beach. He trudged over, took the basket of fish from her, and then helped her down.

The absence of anything but the clothes she was wearing gave Toris pause. Serving class Oneros were in the habit of carrying a hammock, cutlery, and a full canteen wherever they went, as sometimes understaffed projects required the workforce to shuffle around temporarily. To see someone venture so far from home without these necessities was puzzling to say the least.

"You didn't bring any belongings?" he asked.

Lex shrugged and marched past him. He shook his head and followed, and together they scrambled up the scree.

"You do know Mintaka is without fancy shops and lodgings," he said, his feet instinctively falling into familiar footholds.

Lex continued climbing. "I can take care of myself."

At the top, in the shade of the arbutus forest, the cheerful chirping of birds drowned out the rolling surf. Lex wandered left and Toris peeled right.

"Town is this way," he said.

Lex nodded and continued left, so Toris turned and left her to it. He'd fulfilled her request of dropping her off. He owed her nothing more. A few hundred feet into his trek, however, he turned to check her progress. She was sitting on a rocky outcrop staring out to sea, hugging her knees to her chest.

Keep going, he told himself. *You owe her nothing.*

Lex rubbed a hand over her bald head as her shoulders shook, but Toris knew she wasn't laughing this time. He'd seen many new Onero cry like this at the orphanry—children who'd just become orphaned and at the same time had to accept they were now members of the serving class—*Oneros.*

His fists clenched.

"Come with me," he called to Lex.

She turned to watch him with puffy red eyes, which narrowed suspiciously.

"Or stay here," Toris said. "Makes no difference to me. But there's a storm coming in," he said, smelling a hint of fresh moisture in the air, "so you should find shelter somewhere."

Lex stood and wiped the dirt from her bottom. Toris led her uphill to a glade, where a hammock swayed between two trees and a ragged sail hung overhead for shade. Typical of the island's other habitations, Toris's private retreat sat high above the storm surges that frequented the island and offered a sweeping view of the endless sea. Even now, black clouds were rolling in from the ocean horizon.

"You can stay here," he told her, setting a cod from the basket onto a stone beside the fire pit. "You know how to prepare it?"

Lex's twisted expression was all the answer he needed.

"I'll be back later to show you," he said.

Lex nodded and hugged herself, shivering at the sight of the ominous clouds rolling in from the sea. "Feels like we're at the edge of the world out here," she said.

Toris paused and watched her watching the clouds. Odds of her getting passage back to the mainland anytime soon were slim, so she was staying whether she liked it or not. And if she was going to survive out here, she'd need some guidance. But he wasn't going to pander to her like a servant. She'd get her hands dirty like everyone else on this island. "I won't be long," he said, then marched toward town.

He zigzagged through the forest, careful to avoid stamping a path to his private retreat-turned-hideout. At the edge of town he emerged from the tree line, where the Onero Block stood alone in a field of knee-high grass. The weathered wooden building housed the island's indentured servants in communal dorms. Though most of its inhabitants were skilled tradesmen or apprentices, the cubiform building had fallen into disrepair with only scrap material allotted to them for upkeep. A six-foot hedge rose behind the Block, ensuring the community's servants remained out of sight when not needed.

Aster saw him approach and shoved through the curtain that covered the front doorway during the summer months. The wooden steps creaked under his weight as he descended to the wild lawn.

"The warden was looking for you," he said. Delight flashed in his eyes as he saw the basket of fish. "That's twice as many as last time."

"Is the brat back yet?"

Aster reached for a cod. Toris swung the basket behind his back, awaiting an answer.

Aster huffed. "She's at the tower again."

Toris bristled. He'd practically begged her not to go up there alone.

He set the basket down and said, "Save some for the others this time."

Aster panted and groaned as he carried the catch into the dwelling. In the doorway he stopped and hunched his shoulders. "You coming to Lenus's *Calling* this time?"

"I'm busy."

"You should at least get Jayda to come."

Good luck with that, Toris wanted to say. "I'll try."

Lenus had left for the border four years ago. Not a week had gone by where he didn't write Jayda until a few months ago, when the letters stopped. Many still held hope the savages hadn't skinned him alive, that his position in some remote mountain outpost had been cut off from its supply route temporarily, so the Oneros of Mintaka frequently held a *Calling* ceremony to summon word about his fate.

In Toris's experience, there was never a good reason for an Onero sibling to stop writing during their twenty-year border service. He'd stopped attending such ceremonies after the Defence Force sent what was left of their sister Layna's body to Lake Orion for her final rest, the skin peeled from her face and her eyes carved from their sockets. Rumours claimed it happened when she was alive.

Sometimes it was better not knowing.

With the threat of a Coast Patrol pursuit on land, Toris had to unload his bounty fast. So he carried on around the Onero Block and followed a dirt path to the ragged hedge-row, where he shoved through its shrinking gap. On the other side, he followed a dirt track up a hill toward the brick residence rows of the upper town, the shimmering blue harbour at his back.

At the edge of the first brick building, Kyer and Sweeney, the island's redhead Onero twins, were scouring the grass for chicken eggs, gathering them in their rolled up shirts. Neither lifted a head to acknowledge him as he passed.

Closer to the town center, spaces between the brick residences narrowed until the units became an unbroken row. Most doors were open, inviting a breeze, but no signs of life rose from within. When he reached the town square, Toris could see the citizens had gathered on the dock at the bottom of the lane to watch a fishing boat cruise into the harbour, its hydrogen motor humming across the water. Unlike on the mainland, citizens of Mintaka claimed a personal amount before the main haul went to the cannery, where many of the town folk earned their living.

Toris carried on to the public school grounds at the opposite end of town, eager to secure Jayda's letter of recommendation. Though designed for citizens, the education system allowed the occasional attendance of Oneros, so long as it didn't interfere with their civil duties.

Behind the brick administration building, a path surrounded by rows of overgrown shrubs led him to the outdoor lecture pit. There, semi-circular rows of stone benches sloped down to a flat round floor, where Miss Seraphina addressed a group of adolescents scattered across the lower benches. Behind her shimmered a holographic map of Anterra from seven hundred years ago, when it was covered in ice.

"...the thick ice sheets that once covered our home had been pushing the land mass down," the teacher explained. "As the ice melted, a process called post-glacial rebound occurred, where the land sprang upward."

On the hologram, animation showed the white ice cover melt into the sea. Without the weight of the ice, the Antarctic land mass rose higher while distant continents shrivelled from rising sea levels.

"While this was happening," the teacher went on, "the rest of the world was overcome by rising seas until all that remained was our home—the continent they called 'Antarctica'."

The hologram zoomed in on Anterra. A red line traced the Borien Mountain range to divide the southern continent into its two countries. The Polarian section on the lower left was shaded green, and the larger Ortarian mass on the upper right shaded red. A valley corridor connected the two countries through the mountains, where a heavily manned border served as a dam to keep the Ortarian hordes out of Polaria.

Toris spotted the Headmaster sitting alone at the back, following the teacher's words from the script on his reader screen. Toris slid onto the bench beside him.

"During the days leading up to the Decimation," the teacher said, "a war was fought over the remaining land as the great sea devoured their homes. The Settlers called it the Thermal War, and attributed it to society's excessive liberties. The people thought they'd won a great victory when their governments began relinquishing their power, but in the absence of regulation they lost control of themselves. This illustrates the importance of firm governance. Without The Artican watching over us, we'd be no better than the savages across our border."

The hologram shimmered, and the map of Anterra was replaced by Polaria's capital, Amyria. The city's collective of geodesic domes bubbled like foam from a sea of golden wheat, each bearing a ring of panels that stored solar energy for the six months of darkness that the polar winter promised. This was where the Sage Abelia, distant descendant of the Sage Amyria, established Polaria's first democratic government. Her words were so sacred that even those mispronounced from her deathbed carried on through the decades, including the name of the newly-established council—'The *Artican* Government', surely meant to be *Antarctican* but slurred by failing muscles.

"You ever get sick of listening to the lies?" Toris said to the Headmaster.

The Headmaster's eyes kept pace with the words on his tablet. "A sweet lie goes down better than an inconvenient truth."

Normally Toris wouldn't conduct business in the open, but the threat of the Coast Patrol storming into town at any moment inspired him to drop protocol. He offered the Headmaster his reader with the newly scavenged data.

The Headmaster checked his surroundings, then accepted the device. He scanned through several documents, head bobbing with approval. "There's a lot of material here." He skimmed over a few articles, pausing for a close read of the occasional passage.

"I told you I'd come through," Toris said.

"That you did." The Headmaster returned the reader and pulled a folded letter from his robe.

Toris handed him the ancient archive and snatched the letter. His heart fluttered with the rare thrill of success. Just like that, it was done.

"Well," Miss Seraphina said, "that's enough for today, class."

The students dropped to their knees and lowered their faces to the ground, where they recited the Order's eight laws.

The Headmaster stood, smoothed the folds from his robe, and slid to the aisle. He turned back to Toris. "Oh, by the way, Jayda placed higher in her technical scores than anyone on this island. I just thought it best for you to deliver the news." He gave Toris a sly smile and waved the archive. "But I did put in a good word for her, so I'll be keeping this."

Toris held up the letter, his chest swelling with pride. He didn't even know Jayda had taken the technical test, had no idea she really had a chance at getting accepted on her own merit.

Feeling the first raindrops on his forehead, he slid the letter into his tunic and watched the Headmaster disappear behind the shrubs.

A sparrow landed on the stone rail before him. One instant it was there, the next—*whap*—gone in a puff of feathers.

Jayda scurried before the rail and scooped up the dead bird. She held it up proudly in one hand while waving her slingshot in the other. "That's next breakfast," she said.

Her bulging cheek, with its ragged scar rising and falling with her chewing, betrayed her return to an old habit. "On the *khat* again, I see."

Jayda stuffed more *khat* leaves into her mouth. "Just until I finish my project. Gives me that extra *uumph*." Wardens kept the stimulating plant readily available so Oneros remained productive through their long days of service.

"You're wound up enough without it. I heard you were at the tower."

"Had to check in at the stables," Jayda said, eyes narrowing, no doubt wondering who'd snitched about her whereabouts. "Just came to ask Miss Seraphina a question."

Toris stood and roughed her hair. He waited at the top of the stairs while Jayda descended to see the teacher. When she returned, she led their way out through the gardens.

When the rain wet her hair and Jayda tied back the brown

strands to expose the freshly shaved side of her head, Toris noticed three deep scratches on her neck. "You were scrapping with those stable boys again."

"Show no weakness," Jayda said, reciting their childhood mantra. She looked down and kicked a rock. "They say I'm wasting my time at school."

"They're right." Toris felt the letter in his pocket. "Your mind outgrew this place long ago. Thanks for coming to Port Abersali today."

Jayda shrugged.

Toris had planned to surprise her after scraping together a nice celebratory meal, but he couldn't wait. He pulled the letter from his pocket. "Here."

But Jayda's eyes caught something past the edge of town. "Aster! You little snitch!"

Across the field, Aster was on his way into the forest for Lenus's *Calling*. He froze stiff at Jayda's accusation, and when Jayda bolted into the field, Aster did what Aster does best and fled into the forest.

Toris waved the letter. "Jayda!"

But she couldn't hear him over the bells.

Toris shivered. Each chime rattled his nerves, demanding all Oneros report immediately to the town hall. This usually only happened when an Onero ran away or failed to report for duty. But sometimes it was for something worse—like when they came to arrest Sallus for exploring.

Jayda skidded to a stop and pointed across the field. Toris followed her gaze to the harbour, where a familiar battleship cruised out beyond the reef. Four landing craft sped into the shallow waters toward Mintaka's north shore, their course dead-set on the quay at the bottom of town.

Jayda marched stiffly back to Toris, her eyes locked on the approaching Coast Patrol boats. "Did you make a stop?" she said, eyes locking onto him in a *khat* frenzy. She shoved him. "Did you? What took you so long getting back?" The tears welling in her eyes were nearly as shocking as the Coast Patrol coming ashore. Toris had never seen her cry. Her face twisted with a mix of betrayal and disbelief. "You did, didn't you."

Toris rubbed his neck but could not loosen the phantom rope squeezing his throat. Still, now that he'd traded with the Headmaster, they had no proof that he'd uncovered data.

He rubbed a hand over his hair. Should he cut it off as Lex had done? Or maybe they were actually here for her. For his sake he hoped so. Although the man she'd left at the altar was General Aldebaran, supreme commander of the Polarian Defence Force, abandoning an arranged marriage carried consequences far less severe than those that accompanied exploring.

He absently returned Jayda's letter to his pocket. He wasn't going to let a Coast Patrol visit spoil her special moment.

"Let's go," he said. "We have to report."

FOUR

A stream of Oneros garbed in black were funnelling into the town hall when the bells stopped, with more trickling in from their posts. Beside the entrance, Toris stopped to help Sweeney hold a wooden ladder against the stone wall while her twin, Kyer, raced to attach the Polarian flag—a white, eight-pointed star centered over a black background—to its post over the arched doorway.

The buzz of hydrogen motors drew Toris's attention to the curved seawall bulging in toward town, where the Coast Patrol sailors were docking their four landing craft. A dozen sailors armed with submachine guns climbed from the craft, but Toris saw only one—Captain Clavilla.

His clammy palms squeezed the wooden ladder rungs.

When Kyer hung the flag and returned to the ground, Toris joined the stragglers filing into the town hall. Warden Castor conducted a headcount from the double doorway. His glistening dome stood at least a head over the tallest Onero, his neck craning like a vulture's as he matched the names from his reader screen to the Oneros entering the hall. His handlebar moustache and the long grey hair that skirted the bottom of his bald head dripped beads of rainwater.

Inside the hall, hushed voices echoed off stone walls. The group included young faces from every territory of Polaria's mainland, from Travaria to Khartum to the scattering of islands up the peninsula. Surplus children from families who'd exceeded their one child allotment were Oneros since birth, with orphans sometimes falling into the Onero serving class later. The only territory missing was the Great Isle of Arokya, whose councillor, Rosaria, refused to transfer her Oneros off island. Rumour claimed she treated Oneros like citizens, and that once you ended up on Arokya, you were safe from being sent elsewhere. Toris had often entertained the idea of sneaking there after Jayda left for the Academy.

He found Jayda at the back of the gaggle. They stood in silence as others chattered nervously around them, speculating on the reason for the Coast Patrol visit. Complaints about trampled toes rippled toward them as Aster shoved his way to the back.

"What's going on, Toris?" said Aster. "Why are they here again?" His words sounded like an accusation.

"I don't know," Toris said.

"You better hope they're just here to take our food," Jayda said as she glared at the battleship through the doorway, her ears glowing red.

Toris hadn't even considered that possibility, and he hoped she was right. Mayor Schilla was in charge of ensuring the island met its food quota to send to the mainland, but he may have skimmed from the offering to keep Mintaka's food stores stocked. If the Coast Patrol were here to collect, Toris could always take *Atlas* for some side poaching to keep the Onero Block fed.

Since Mayor Schilla was attending a meeting on the mainland, Castor remained in the doorway to receive the envoy.

"Captain Clavilla," he stuttered, "we weren't expecting you."

"As was my intent." Clavilla brushed past the warden and entered the hall. His boots echoed loud as they clunked down the stone steps. At the bottom he paced before the tight assembly, sizing every person up. To Castor, he said, "Some Oneros on Alnilam got word of our approach and went into hiding. Are all yours accounted for?"

"All but those out fishing," Castor said. "What's this about? You said the Alnilam Oneros abandoned their posts?"

"Don't worry," Clavilla said, "we have search parties out looking."

Toris squeezed toward the front of the pack to hear better, because it sounded like the Oneros of their sister island had gone AWOL. Most of Alnilam's Oneros were dissidents posted to its salt mine as punishment, so why condemn themselves to something worse just because the Coast Patrol were paying the island a visit?

The captain stopped before one of the Oneros in front. The arrowhead tattoo on the back of his neck marked him as Gin. "Him," he said, and two sailors dragged the senior Onero from the group. They positioned Gin against the stone wall beside the entrance as his eyes darted about in confusion.

Clavilla picked three more—Kyer, Sweeney, and Aster. Sailors dragged them to the line and punched their identification numbers into a data device. Citizens watched from the doorway, holding their curious children back.

Toris's heart drummed an ominous beat. This was definitely not about his scavenging or Lex's disappearance from the capital, or even the food quota. Occasionally Oneros were reassigned to a different island or the mainland, depending on local requirements, but not so many at once. And never by order of the Coast Patrol.

He tried to discern a pattern connecting the stricken faces in line facing the crowd. Kyer and Sweeney were au pairs, Aster a carpenter and Gin a bricklayer—two housemaids and two trades-men. Aside from bearing the common last name of 'Onero', there was no obvious link between the four.

Clavilla waded through the middle of the crowd, picking more Oneros for the line. Just before reaching Jayda, he wheeled back toward the entrance, but her challenging stare drew him back. "Occupation?" he asked her.

Toris approached Clavilla from the side. "What's this about?"

A submachine gun muzzle rose to Toris's chest. "Shut your mouth, boy."

"I'm a stable hand," Jayda said.

"You ride?"

Jayda raised her chin. "Won the Khartum Junior Derby three years ago."

Clavilla nodded to a sailor and then squared off with Toris. Toris met Clavilla's stare as the sailor grabbed Jayda above the elbow and dragged her to the front of the hall. Eyes hard and cold as granite sized him up. "Occupation?"

"Shipwright," Toris said, fighting to steady the tremor in his voice.

"You build ships?" Clavilla's expression softened as he nodded with what could possibly be approval. He moved on.

Toris gave Jayda a reassuring smile, though she didn't seem to need it. She stood with her arms crossed, glowering impatiently as the captain sent a few more boys and girls to join her in the widening line.

When twenty-five Oneros stood in a straight line across the hall, Clavilla mounted the entrance steps to address the crowd of citizens gathered outside. "By order of The Artican, any Onero not on critical assignment has been drafted to defence service."

Defence service? Toris felt a tsunami of nausea rise in him as memories of funeral carts arriving at Lake Orion came flooding back.

Looking at the twenty-five stricken faces across the hall, he saw clearly what was classed as 'critical assignment' to The Artican. Greenhouse workers, beekeepers and fishermen provided food, while carpenters and au pairs, for the most part, offered luxuries.

Marching forward, Toris held up Jayda's letter and pointed her out in the line. "She's enrolled at the Academy. She starts next semester."

Jayda gave him a puzzled look.

Clavilla snatched the letter. Jayda's eyes were full of doubt, so Toris gave her a reassuring nod and smile.

The sailor who'd run Jayda's ID shook his head. "She's not registered as a student in the system."

"Even if she was," Clavilla said, tearing the letter in half, "the Defence Force needs messengers more than the Academy needs Oneros."

Toris felt his heart tear along with the paper. He clutched at his belly, where his guts twisted like a ball of snakes. He looked up to see that Jayda's impatience had melted away, her face now blanched and mouth gaping in shock.

Outside, several citizens crowded the stairway. "You can't just come unannounced and steal away our help," said Morly Prax, who managed the island's stables.

"Who's going to build our new hive?" said Mintaka's beekeeper.

Clavilla raised both hands to demand silence. "The Artican retains the right to build the Defence Force's ranks during times of uncertainty. Feel free to voice your complaints at the next council meeting."

He looked back into the hall and nodded for his men to escort the conscripts down to the quay.

A terrible idea popped into Toris's head. He barged past Clavilla in the doorway and blocked his path down the stairs.

Clavilla drew his scimitar and held it before Toris. "You must be Mintaka's fool."

Toris held up both hands, trying not to flinch as he stared past the blade that had delivered Sallus to his death. Give a bully fear and he'll want more.

"I want to make a deal," he said.

Clavilla smirked. "You have something of interest to me?"

"I do."

It was time for Toris to call in on his investment. An act of betrayal during a desperate time could be justified. And who was Lex to him, anyway? Sending her back to the capital to earn favour with the Chancellor, a favour that might save his sister, seemed easy enough. But when he opened his mouth to speak, a damning realization held his tongue firm. In retaliation for handing her over, Lex may report his exploring to Clavilla, who not twelve hours ago had hanged Sallus for the same crime. Not only that, but the chances of Clavilla helping an Onero claim a reward from the capital were thinner than the edge of the sword in his hand.

Clavilla's narrow eyes opened wide in understanding. He lowered his sword. "You're volunteering to take her place."

Toris's heart drummed a dreadful tune.

The captain sheathed his sword. "Well, too bad. We need ship-builders now more than ever."

"I'm not a shipwright anymore," Toris blurted, struggling to keep his voice steady. "I'm awaiting reassignment."

"You ride?" Clavilla pressed.

Much to his own horror, Toris said, "I taught her everything she knows."

Jayda opened her mouth to protest, but Toris's warning look stayed her tongue. It'd be too late when the recruiters discovered he'd lied. Besides, how hard could riding a horse be?

"Captain." Warden Castor stepped close to Clavilla. "The Artican expelled him from the mainland when he was twelve. He's in exile."

Clavilla looked to Toris. "What for?"

Toris felt his face and neck blaze red hot. "Exotic blood."

"Got some Ortarian in ya, huh? Couldn't trust you running dispatches anyway."

Toris extended an arm toward the conscripts in the doorway behind. "Look at them. I'll make a better soldier than any two put together. Take me."

"So you can spy for the enemy? I think not. Tag them and take them aboard," Clavilla said to his men.

Toris had Jayda locked in his arms before the sailors could stop him. She trembled in his embrace, her breath shuddering in his ear. He felt her heart slamming against his ribs, and his own pounding back in return as the pressure of fear, helplessness, and anger ballooned inside his chest. A gloved hand grabbed his shoulder but could not pull him away.

"What do we say?" he said in her ear.

"Show no weakness," Jayda said. "I'm not afraid." But the tremor in her voice betrayed her. She'd seen the funeral carts arrive at the orphanry from the border, and even helped lay a few of her siblings to rest beside the lake.

It took three sailors to finally pry them apart—two on Toris and one on Jayda. Toris struggled to free his arms from their hold, but all he could do was watch through teary eyes as Clavilla's men dragged her down to the quay.

Toris no longer cared about stamping a path to his hideout. His footsteps crunching dry arbutus leaves caught Lex's attention long before he reached her camp.

She greeted him with a smile and offered him a half-charred fish. "I wouldn't get too excited about my cooking."

"They took Jayda."

Lex lowered the fish and frowned. "Who took who?"

"The Coast Patrol. They took my sister."

He hustled past her camp and down the path toward Isher Cove. The Coast Patrol had already taken Sallus from him. To let them take Jayda in the same day…

No, not today. Not ever.

The next train departed Abersali on the mainland for Fort Cypress, the Defence Force's primary training base, in two days. Toris had to get to the Port and free Jayda before she boarded that train. Going there meant breaking exile, which carried a punishment of death by hanging, but what he had planned would earn him worse than that if they caught him. Once he freed Jayda, they'd sail up the peninsula to Arokya. The island's leniency toward Oneros made it their surest haven.

Lex ran after him. "Why did they take her? Tell me what happened."

"A draft for defence service."

Lex broke step a moment, then continued her pursuit. "So where are *you* going?"

"Port Abersali."

Lex grabbed his wrist and dragged him to a stop. "You really love pushing your luck, don't you? I seem to remember you barely escaping the mainland the last time."

"I have to free Jayda."

Toris twisted his arm free and descended the path to Isher Cove.

Lex followed. "How is hanging from a rope going to help her? Because that's what'll happen if they catch you."

"If the Ortarians catch Jayda at the border, they'll do far worse than that."

Toris tossed his sling bag onto *Atlas'* deck and unhitched the dock line.

"Even if you slip in undetected," Lex said, grabbing the line and pulling against him, "they'll keep the conscripts somewhere secure."

Toris wrenched the rope from her hands and tossed it over the prow. "I'll find a way."

He didn't tell her about the explosives packed into *Atlas'* hull. Sallus had acquired them on the black market should they ever need to destroy the floating evidence vault that was his sailboat. Toris could blast his way into any building and help Jayda escape in the confusion. Or he could blow the tracks to trap the recruits in Port Abersali until he found another way

Lex ran ahead and stood before the bow, blocking his access. He picked her up by the waist and spun to set her down away from the boat, then climbed on top of the cabin. Much to his surprise, Lex scrambled over the swim deck and into the cockpit.

"Is life on Mintaka too rough for you?" he said, sliding down to join her at the helm. Most likely she'd already had enough of exile life and saw him as her only ride back.

"If I'm to stay out here for the long haul, I'll need a boat, and this one will be free for the taking after they slip a noose over that thick head of yours."

Toris started the hydrogen motor. The engine rattled to life, and soon they were speeding away from Mintaka toward the main-land. In the distance, Clavilla's battleship was already rounding Alnilam, so Toris eased off on the motor to linger behind. When the *Sea Serpent* disappeared around the island, he then gave the throttle a twist to pick up speed.

But the spurt didn't last long. The remaining hydrogen brought them just past Alnilam, where Toris was forced to raise the sail and sit patiently while watching Jayda's transport shrink toward the mainland. The creaking stays and the odd shudder of the sail were the only sounds for a long while as they crossed the strait.

Lex sat at the prow, where she watched a halo of grey clouds swell around the Borien peaks that dominated the inner mainland. Sitting cross-legged, with her arms stacked on the bowsprit rail and her chin resting on top of them, she made for a gloomy figurehead.

"Why do you look like the one who's just lost everything?" he said.

Lex turned to face him. "Even if you and your sister pull off this escape, you'll live the rest of your lives looking over your shoulders."

"At least we'll have the rest of our lives to live. In case you haven't noticed, we weren't living the Polarian dream anyway."

The shot hit its mark. Lex scowled. "You think my life is some fairytale, don't you. I bet all the little Onero girls grow up dreaming of an arranged marriage to a man twice their age."

"Oneras have worse fates than that to fear. Many would consider a place in a highborn's bed a luxury. Your problem is that you think your last name entitles you to a fairytale life. I'm glad to see it's not just Oneros being sold off like stock."

Toris's own words shocked him. So did Lex's watery eyes.

"I shouldn't have said that," he said.

Lex shook her head dismissively. Then, in a flash, her eyes flared wide. "What if there's another way?"

Toris resisted the urge to say something sarcastic as his instinct yielded to curiosity. "Like what?"

"We make Jayda ineligible for conscription."

"She's an Onero. She meets all the criteria unless we cripple her, or she magically ends up on critical assignment."

Lex shook her head. "Not *magically*. With access to my father's database, I can slot your sister into a critical role."

"You think you can just walk into your father's office without someone noticing you?" The skepticism he'd meant to inject into his tone was overwhelmed by the hope in his voice, which surprised him.

"The council takes a two-week holiday around Summer Solstice," she said, "and I know the access code to his chambers."

Toris gave her a dubious look. "And you'd risk going back to Amyria to do this for me, for nothing?"

Lex chewed her lip. "Not for nothing. I want that archive with the Svalbard reference in return."

"Forget it. I traded it back on Mintaka."

Lex pointed to his pack. "The document is still on your reader. I don't need the original."

Toris gave her a pleading look. "Lex…"

"I can't stay on the run my whole life. I'll shoulder the risk of exposing the vault to claim the Accolade. I'm already a First-Class Citizen, and if I donate the million credits, they'll probably grant me a Sagehood instead. Then even the Chancellor couldn't tell me what to do, let alone who to marry."

A sarcastic laugh burst from Toris's mouth. "You really think they'll make you a Sage?"

Lex frowned. "Why not? You just give me that seed vault reference and see. I'll transfer both you and your sister to Arokya if you want."

This offer took Toris off guard. He studied her for signs of deceit, but her blue eyes were bright with sincerity. Yet the offer was too generous to be true. Though she seemed as trustworthy as highborns came, what highborn would go to such lengths to help two Oneros? He'd floated the idea of selling her out back on Mintaka. Surely she'd consider the same if she were cornered.

But the mainland wasn't far off. A decision had to be made.

"I'll come with you to Amyria," he said. They could make it to the capital within half a day barring no mishaps. Besides, blowing the tracks was never a real option because it risked derailing the train if the rail crew slacked in their inspections. "Is there anywhere safe I can wait while you register us in your father's database?"

Because so many Omniguard patrolled the capital—any one of whom could run his ID and discover his exile status—he would need to hide.

Lex's eyebrows scrunched as she took a moment to think about it.

"The Observatory," she concluded. "It's a hilltop garden for stargazing. No one goes there during summer."

"Okay," Toris said. "We can't afford any delays. If Jayda ends up in uniform at the border, even a letter written by the Sage Abelia's cold dead hands won't bring her back."

"Got it. Now," Lex held out a hand, "give me your reader."

Toris slid his pack between his feet. "Not until you give me a letter confirming our new posting."

FIVE

Toris ran *Atlas* aground in an unnamed inlet ten miles down the coast from Port Abersali. Standing upon the prow with dock line in hand, he surveyed the shore for an anchor point. Any one of the ash trees lining the beach would work, yet his feet remained planted on the deck.

"Having second thoughts?" Lex said from behind.

"I'm fine." Toris stared through the staggered ranks of trees. Their leaves rustled as if to spread warning that a crime was about to take place.

"I can go alone," Lex offered.

Toris glanced back to see she'd already finished furling the sail. How long had he been standing here at the prow? Too long. Jayda's situation didn't allow for delays. Who knew how long it would take for Lex and him to reach the capital and for her to access her father's database to reassign them to critical assignment on Arokya?

Lex watched the forest uncertainly, likely regretting her offer to go alone. She had to know she wouldn't make it far on her own. Even if she didn't get lost within the first hour, the bears and wolves would eventually track her down.

Toris splashed onto the rocky shore, officially breaking his exile for the second time since last waking. Rocks crunched and scraped as they shifted beneath his feet. Despite his efforts to stay light-footed, the sound of him treading across the beach seemed loud enough to reach the port ten miles away. He hitched the rope around a sturdy ash trunk and tied a triple knot to secure it.

Lex waited with his sling bag for him to return. She took his hand and, with his help, slid down from the prow. He led her into the forest. Diagonal streams of sunlight cut through the canopy of fluttering leaves, but large patches of the moss floor remained shaded.

They stopped in a glade, where Toris noticed Lex's hand still gripped in his. He released it. "Sorry, I—"

"It's okay. I don't think my betrothed has eyes out here." Lex surveyed the surrounding forest. "Though, I can't be too sure."

That wasn't a possibility Toris needed to hear, whether Lex was joking or not.

He scoured the forest floor and found two sturdy branches of roughly his height. With his dive knife he sharpened the point of each, handing one to Lex and keeping the other for himself. He hoped any predators would see two humans as too much bother to attack.

They followed a gully up through poplar forest, occasionally ducking under or climbing over fallen trees. Way back during the rapid melting of the ice sheets, the flooding water carved gullies and chasms across the lowlands as it emptied into the sea. These made inland navigation easy. Finding a side trail to Amyria, however…

Luckily, Lex wasn't so backwards outside the capital after all. When the gully slope levelled out, she led Toris from the ditch and through the flatland forest, stopping occasionally to check the sun through the tree canopy.

A dense mat of moss made for pleasant travel as they continued their trek inland, crossing logs over streams and rivers, through meadows and shrubs. But Toris's bare feet weren't accustomed to traveling such long distances over land, so he struggled to keep pace with Lex in her slippers. And that was not the only thing wearing on him.

His heart grew heavier with each step away from the coast. He hadn't been this far from the sea since they kicked him out of Lake Orion Orphanry and sent him into exile five years ago. But he dared not allow these aches to slow him.

The first sign of civilization was a set of overgrown wagon tracks carving diagonally across their route. Lex led their way inland between the ruts.

Toris yawned. A search of his sling bag for *khat* came up empty, as he wasn't in the habit of carrying the stimulating plant, but he was hoping Jayda had left some in there. To take his mind off his aching feet and itchy eyes, he turned to conversation. "How did you know so much about that hydrogen motor?" he asked Lex.

Lex stiffened and slowed her pace. "I learned about them in the Maritime Academy."

Toris stopped and narrowed his eyes, a smile tugging at the corner of his mouth.

She looked over her shoulder and said, "Are you surprised?"

Toris started walking again. "I didn't take you for the seafaring type."

"Well, my mother did. She'd arranged for me to start junior officer training on my thirteenth birthday." Seeming to pick up on Toris's lingering skepticism, she stared up at the blue sky and continued, "I spent my entire twelfth year devouring every naval training text available. By the time I started, I knew every word before it came from the instructor's mouth. That gave me extra time to practice my hands-on skills while my classmates split their time with the theory work. I was named top navigation candidate and given my lieutenant bars soon after my sixteenth birthday."

"Did the other cadets score poorly on purpose to gain favour with the Chancellor's daughter?"

Lex rubbed her arm and hunched her shoulder. Toris had meant his words as a joke, but now he realized how accusatory he sounded.

"If you'd seen me after sword practice," she said, "you'd know the answer to that."

Toris recalled Clavilla's scimitar. He'd assumed such weapons were simply for bravado and ceremony. "They taught you sword-fighting?"

"It's tradition. But no, it wasn't the academy that taught me. Not when I was losing all the time. So my brother Iggy set me up with a private tutor—a three-time Commander's Cup winner. I drove him near mad with the amount of training hours. While my classmates had their heads in their readers, I was on the fencing mat. And in sessions proper, I slacked off so my competition would write me off as a weakling for the academy's annual challenge."

Lex marched faster. Toris had to run to catch up. "So?" he said. "Did you win?"

"Never got a chance," Lex said, her shoulders tense. She nodded ahead. "I think that's the Trillium Trail up ahead."

She broke into a trot toward the end of the wagon ruts, which merged with a gravel track that he guessed was the Trillium Trail, a famous road that ran the length of the entire country. Toris watched as Lex checked her pocket watch for the time and, using the sun's position in its six month circular descent, determined the Trail leading off to the right led south to the capital.

Toris knew what it was like to face awkward questions about his past, so he didn't press Lex further as they followed the Trail's hard-packed surface. Another half hour passed before the forest opened up into the plains, where rolling grass hills stretched all the way to the foothills of the Borien Mountain Range, sporadically interrupted by patches of golden wheat. The Boriens dominated the afternoon sky with a crown of black clouds, serving as the natural border between Polaria and Ortaria—and as a reminder of where Jayda would spend the rest of her days should Lex fail to reassign her in these next few hours.

A flicker drew Toris's gaze left to where the tree line curved inland. From the forest, a train stretched into the field like a silver snake, sliding along the tracks that crossed the Trillium Trail up ahead.

"Hurry," Lex said, then dashed ahead. She pulled a scarf from her cloak to flag the coming train.

Toris sprinted after her, and together they reached the tracks as the brakes squealed to a halt. Polaria's wild and vast terrain required the service to stop for passengers wherever needed. This concept dated back to the days of Ortarian raiding parties hitting Polaria, when civilians needed an escape to safety and messengers access to the capital.

"Wrap that scarf around your face," Toris said. The last thing he needed was her getting apprehended.

The rear door of the forward car slid open, and a porter sporting a grey handlebar mustache reached down to take Lex's hand. Toris helped her up with a push from behind, then climbed aboard without the porter's help, as it was not offered.

In the car, Toris's heart pounded at the sight of men and women in uniform. He relaxed, however, when he registered their black suits, high fastened collars, and knee-high boots—a uniform that marked them as Defence Force officers. Soldiers weren't in the business of harassing civilians this close to the capital.

Double rows of violet seats ran the length of the car along both sides of the aisle. The only available pair were at the front, so Lex plopped into the aisle seat. Toris sank into the plush window chair beside her, where he surveyed the surrounding passengers. His black, salt-stained tunic and shendyt drew disgusted looks from a few of the highborns, and their condemning glares suggested he retreat to the rear where he belonged.

He ignored them and leaned his head against the glass to his right as the train launched forward at dizzying speed. Through the window, the rolling grass hills gradually levelled out to wheat fields. Spinning wind turbines grew in frequency as Amyria's geodesic domes rose like glittering bubbles from the golden sea ahead. The capital was where the Sage Amyria had successfully planted Anterra's first tree, and the point from where she dispatched her acolytes to carry on her work of cultivating the harsh land. *Star Children*, she'd called them, each group named after a star that would eventually become the members' surnames when they split up or mingled with other groups to form towns and cities. Every Polarian made the pilgrimage at age eleven to Amyria to swear fealty to the First Tree in the Mother's Womb.

With their journey temporarily in the conductor's hands, Toris allowed his heavy eyelids to sag. His head was slouching forward into sleep when a silver point gleamed high above Amyria's highest dome. When lit during the long polar night, the Central Spire served as a beacon, assuring those in the smothering darkness across the country that they were not alone. And that sanctuary was there if needed. The cluster of domes surrounding its base retained heat during the polar winter while providing an artificial environment for the six month night. Many rural folk visited the capital during winter for the comfort these domes provided.

When the train curved right for a direct approach at the capital, pillars of black smoke swept across the tracks ahead and obscured the city. Down in a valley to their right, Toris saw flames devouring piles of blackened corn as farmers looked on with folded arms. Through the car's left side window, black patches of wilted corn dotted the fields from the tracks to the distant hills, so far untouched by fire. Ahead, scattered watch towers stood from a sea of golden wheat that surrounded the capital, where Omniguard officers kept watch over the healthy plots.

As the bases of Amyria's domes came into view, solar arrays shimmered in the fields before them. Their circular arrangement around the city spread like ripples from a stone cast in water.

Toris looked away from their glare and caught sight of a bulletin streaming across the noticeboard at the front of the car:

Council Meeting - Orichalcum - 1800hrs

Lex shifted nervously, and Toris suspected why. She'd been expecting the Orichalcum—the complex that housed Polaria's center of politics—to be mostly empty for the Solstice holiday. Yet, because Law Four of the Order entitled the public to attend all council meetings, there would now be a large crowd around the Chancellor's office. Lex could use that to remain inconspicuous among the masses, but surely she thought this increased a chance encounter with her father.

In the twenty minutes it took for the train to cross the remaining distance to the capital, Toris's fatigue had given way to fluttering angst in his belly. It was one thing to escape the Omni-guard in coastal towns when he had access to a boat. Within the confines of the capital's domes, however, his chances of attracting attention were great and his chances at escape were limited.

As the train slipped into a tunnel below the city's forward dome, Toris closed his eyes. Being underground, confined by darkness... He couldn't imagine what it was like for the mine workers. That would have been his fate for two years if he were caught scavenging. Somehow the fatal punishment for breaking exile seemed more tolerable.

"Death is naught," he whispered to himself.

His eyes remained shut until the train stopped at Centauri Station, where the commotion of disembarking passengers stirred him from his nervous breath counting.

Bright fluorescent lights forced Toris to squint as he joined the crowd shuffling across the platform. He'd been here six years ago to swear fealty to the Order in the Mother's Womb, just before his exile, but the underground station now seemed smaller, more confining despite the vaulted ceiling supported by thick blue columns.

On the platform walls, murals depicting the Sages' saintly acts were alternated with scenes of Polarian bravery in the war against Ortaria during the Split.

At the end of the platform, Toris followed Lex up a stairway toward the surface, away from the station's artificial light and into the sunlight filtering through a massive dome that arched across the blue sky. As they neared the top of the stairs, chirping birds replaced the squeal from the train tracks below.

Above ground, he stepped into a grass boulevard and surveyed the long rows of glass buildings that lined both sides of the lane. Closer inspection revealed the material to be clear polymer tinted in shades of blue, green, and purple. The levels of each building rose no higher than five storeys.

High above the roofs, expansive geodesic domes loomed for miles in all directions, their round bases touching down somewhere beyond the neat rows of residences and offices. Atop the dome ceiling above, a dozen Oneros repelled across the curved surface with window wipers, cleaning the transparent polymer and repairing cracks.

Amyria - City of Plastic, Toris thought. Even the stiff grass between his toes felt fake. The Artican claimed that all of the polymer used to construct the capital came from Decimator waste pulled from the sea, but Toris found that hard to believe. He'd seen bits of plastic here and there while on *Atlas* or washed up on Mintaka's shore, but not near enough to build even one of these structures.

"This way," Lex said, and she led him up the boulevard of manicured grass in the same direction as the crowd.

Toris followed, admiring the row of royal palm trees to either side of the lane, until he stopped dead with his mouth hanging open.

Recent occurrences had raised his tolerance for shock. But when he saw the market stalls lining the main buildings stocked with food, and the citizens lounging on eatery patios with plates piled high, his fists squeezed tight and his heart even tighter. Even his vision blurred in his anger, and he realized it was from tears. While the rest of Polarians were learning to chew slower to cope with diminishing rations, it was all to keep capital bellies full.

Lex grabbed his wrist and dragged him along. "Don't cause a scene," she muttered through clenched teeth. Up ahead, two Omniguard officers stood in the shade of a royal palm.

Toris wiped the tears from his eyes and marched on.

At a park square where children played in a fountain, Lex pointed down the lane leading off to their right. The lane's residence rows ran half a mile and ended where the dome touched down, but a path continued through an arched hole in the clear wall, through which a green hill stood in a blur between this dome and three others surrounding it. "The observatory is at the top of that hill. Now, give me your reader and I'll meet you there when it's done."

"Where's the Orichalcum?"

Lex gave him a questioning look.

After seeing the way capital folk fed so shamelessly off the rest of the country, Toris wasn't trusting his sister's fate so blindly to one of them. Especially the daughter of the man who'd been siphoning food from starving territories to keep his high-class folk in good spirits for the next election. "I'm coming with you."

SIX

Three pyramids of black glass—arranged in a diagonal line and attached at their corners—marked the center of Amyria. Located at the base of the Central Spire and without the cover of a geodesic dome, the silver star atop the center apex gleamed in the midsummer sun.

Toris raised a hand to shield his eyes from the glare as he crossed the bridge over the moat. Staying close at Lex's side, they walked over seamless faux marble to join the crowd funnelling into the base of the nearest glass pyramid.

The crowd congealing at the base had Lex on edge. She gnawed on her bottom lip and drew blood.

"Relax," Toris said. "The crowd is good for us."

Hopefully the approaching meeting had her father distracted, and the crowd was perfect to allow her to slip into his office undetected.

They weaved through the mass of shuffling Polarians and into the pyramid entrance. The occasion had even attracted a few Arokyans, whose islander accent and layers of flowing robes rarely graced the mainland. Even a few Travarians had made the inconvenient journey from their impoverished territory in the Cidian foothills. Toris was glad for their presence. Their drab shawls sullied the vibrant mosaic of robes before the nearest pyramid, making his faded black garb less conspicuous. Because, without voting rights, Oneros rarely wasted their free time at such events.

Inside the first pyramid, a dense forest of vine and trees reached toward the pointed glass ceiling while the echoes of exotic birds smothered all the human chatter.

Toris followed Lex as they ambled with the crowd along a stone pathway to the center pyramid, where the floor sloped down into a sunken auditorium in the shape of an inverted cone. Circular rows of seats were already crammed beyond capacity, forcing the newcomers to stand behind the upper seat row that ringed the top of the audience stands. An Omniguard officer stood atop each aisle to ensure the crowd kept the stairway clear.

To prevent them from getting swept to the audience stands, Toris grabbed Lex's wrist and pulled her away from the crowd spilling in through the entrance.

"Where's your father's office?" he asked, watching the officer guarding the nearest aisle warily.

"Below," she said absently, frowning as she listened to the voices echoing off the slanted glass walls. She twisted her wrist free and wandered toward the sunken auditorium.

Toris followed her to the back of the crowd congealing at the top. Below, a ring of flat floor separated the bottom seat row from a raised dais in the center, around which a company of Omniguard officers stood facing the audience. On the stage behind them, eight councillors bickered around a glass-top table. One chair sat unoccupied, and its position at the head of the table suggested it was the Chancellor's.

When Sydra of Travaria slammed her fist on the glass, tense silence seized the audience.

"Enough of this petty squabbling," Sydra said. Her silver hair complimented her pale skin. Most councillors had that ghostly look about them. The only color to their faces came from the orange light reflected off their golden collars. Except for Rosaria of Arokya, who Toris immediately recognized by her black silky hair and red robe. The youngest and fairest of the council would stand out even without a dress fashioned like a rose, with its silky layers arranged like petals.

"Sydra," boomed a man's voice, "you seem eager to voice your concerns before the meeting start time."

Toris followed Lex's gaze to a tunnel under the audience stands that opened up to the ring floor before the dais. A moment later, AnaXagoras, Chancellor and High Protector of Polaria, entered the hall from the tunnel mouth.

Sydra stood and pressed both hands down on the table. "This council has waited long enough to begin its talk of concerns, Chancellor. It's time we take action. The loss of the Khartum corn plots should have initiated a state of emergency. People are already panicking."

Toris grabbed Lex's arm and leaned close to her ear. "This is our chance. Let's go."

But the muscles in Lex's arm stiffened at the sight of her father, and she resisted Toris's pull as AnaXagoras sank into his seat.

Sydra faced the audience. "Yesterday I received word from Sol-Brae that bandits raided ten percent of the territory's grain stores."

AnaXagoras shifted in his chair. "Such reports have not yet been verified, and until they are, should be treated as hearsay. It is a great distance between here and that border territory, and word has surely passed over many tongues before reaching your ears." He swivelled in his seat to face the crowd. "Rest assured that any territory experiencing shortages will soon see food from the more prosperous regions shifted their way."

Toris bristled. Surely the Chancellor didn't consider the capital one of the 'prosperous regions' that would be giving up its food. This city would suck the whole country dry before its first resident felt the pang of hunger.

"And if we lose more plots before the harvest?" Sydra prodded.

"We have emergency stores to see us through winter."

Sydra wagged a finger at the Chancellor. "These are short-term solutions to long-term problems."

AnaXagoras leaned back in his chair, arms spread in resignation. "Well, Sydra, I assume your reason for calling this meeting was to offer us a better answer?" To the audience he said, "And I must stress, these disturbances with our crops are isolated and of no threat to the nation as a whole."

Sydra straightened and faced the audience, a grave look on her face. "Even those who won't acknowledge the problem know that farming practices which rely on uniform seed strains is agricultural suicide. Our crops need genetic diversity, and if offering the Accolade has failed to turn up a solution from the public, then we must expand our search."

AnaXagoras leaned forward in his chair. "Explain your meaning, Sydra."

Sydra straightened and placed a hand over her heart. "The Mother always provides. If our salvation isn't here, it must be elsewhere. That leaves only one place."

"Even if we were foolish enough to ask Ortaria for assistance," the Chancellor said, "they'd never help us."

Sydra shook her head. "We needn't ask anything of those mongrels. Such requests are signs of weakness. The strong *take* what they want."

The Chancellor's eyes narrowed on the Travarian councillor. "For the record, what exactly are you suggesting?"

Sydra turned her back to him, faced the audience, and held out both hands. "It's time the great Polarian people came together to seize Ortaria's farmlands nearest the border."

"You're saying we should invade Ortaria?" said Councillor Catalina of Kaladia. "Have you lost your mind?"

"Our Rangers report flourishing farms across the border," Sydra said, "which suggests this crop problem is unique to us. Controlling those Ortarian plots will give us immediate access to their next harvest, while any captured seeds make their way back to our farmers. Even if you won't acknowledge a nation-wide famine, you can't deny that the very near future holds widespread food shortages if we continue down this road."

The Chancellor shook his head in disbelief. "The Defence Force's name describes exactly what is: a *defence* force. Even with the conscripts from the recent draft, we don't have the numbers to invade. And drafting more Oneros will collapse local economies."

"Then extend the draft to citizens," Sydra said.

Boos rose loud from the crowd, rattling Toris's eardrums. He released Lex's arm and watched on in disbelief.

"It seems our citizens don't relish the idea of sending their children to bleed over filthy Ortarian soil," the Chancellor said.

"They won't have to," Sydra countered. "Our citizen troops can mind the border while the Onero brigades march into Ortaria. Our predecessors drafted citizens to bolster Defence Force ranks when their numbers dwindled due to plague. Too long have we relied on Oneros and criminal conscripts to secure our border." Sydra's voice boomed louder, her passion for war growing more obvious with each word. "We should muster our strength and strike while they think us weak. The Sun sets in less than three months. That's enough time to equip and deploy a force large enough to seize Ortaria's borderlands and harvest."

Shouts erupted from the audience stands.

Toris felt as if he'd been thrown overboard at sea with no safe land in sight. But it wasn't him in danger. If Polaria went on the offensive, Jayda and countless other Onero siblings would be at the pointy end of the invasion force.

"Let's make this motion official and be done with it," the Chancellor said with a dismissive wave.

Above the council table, suspended from cables, a large cube comprised of four digital displays glowed white. Then, flashing blue letters posed a question for the audience: *Citizen Draft?*

Heads dropped as the citizens scanned their ID bracelets on the armrest scanners and punched in their opinions. On the screens above the council table, a column of *Pro* and *Con* appeared, below which double-digit numbers spun to reflect the live tally. Half a minute passed before the final numbers came in—twenty-two percent for Sydra's invasion.

Toris crossed his arms and glared at the seated crowd. How could so many vote for this? Though, approval would have been much higher if not for the Chancellor's illusion of prosperity. Most likely those in favour had come from territories hit by higher food levies.

"There you have it," the Chancellor said. "You don't get your war today, Sydra."

Travaria's councillor clutched her chest. "*My* war. We're in this fight together, and anyone who doesn't see that a fight is coming lacks the heart to sit at this table."

The council table erupted into debate. Each councillor claimed a side, but it was unclear who stood where with all the shouting and pointing.

As the shock of the high number favouring Sydra's invasion waned, Toris breathed easier. Though a high approval rating, it was nowhere near being a threat to invade Ortaria.

"Well, does anyone here have a better idea?" Sydra shouted.

Toris felt a hand burrow into his sling bag. He instinctively grabbed the invading wrist and saw Lex's hand gripping his reader.

"Let go," he hissed.

Determination blazed in Lex's eyes. When she heaved back with all her weight to rip the reader free, Toris released and sent her stumbling back.

Her behind slammed onto the floor first, followed quickly by the back of her head. The smack of her skull off the ground sent a wave of regret through Toris. He was stepping forward to help her when a man's voice stopped him midstride.

"Don't move!"

The Omniguard blocking the top of the nearest aisle pointed his baton at Toris.

Seeing Lex sprawled across the floor a few feet away, Toris realized how this must look to someone who hadn't seen what had happened. The distance she'd fallen suggested she'd been pushed, and through the blood rushing in his ears, he heard a few citizens claim that this had indeed been the case.

Toris held up both hands as the officer rushed to Lex's side. "It was an accident," Toris said.

But the officer's attention zoned in on Lex, who was rubbing the back of her head and looking around in a daze. A moment later, his eyes flashed wide in recognition. "Lady Alexandra?" he said. Then his furious stare lifted to Toris. "Captain Orysk! I need backup in the concourse."

Within a few seconds, a burly Omniguard officer with a shaved head and colourful tattoo sleeves came bounding up the stairs. Bootsteps announced the approach of more officers from around the concourse.

Lex's dazed eyes sharpened, and Toris followed her line of sight to his reader under a top row aisle seat. While she scrambled around the officer and toward the reader, Toris backed away in hopes of fading into the crowd. Lex grabbed the reader and pulled it close to her chest.

"Lady Alexandra?" said Captain Orysk from the top of the aisle, huffing from his run up the stairs.

With backup on scene, the first officer tackled Toris to the ground. Lying on his belly, the officer's weight squishing him against the floor, Toris could hardly breathe.

Lex scrambled to her feet. She either didn't notice Toris under the guard or was ignoring him.

"Captain Orysk," she said, smoothing the wrinkles from the front of her ragged gown. "I'm back, and I bring good news for the council."

Orysk's scornful eyes went to Toris writhing under the guard. "Who is this brigand you were rolling on the floor with?"

"He's nobody," Lex said with a dismissive wave. "Just someone I bumped into. You can let him go."

Her convincing tone stung, but Toris didn't have time to dwell on it as Orysk grabbed his wrist. A second set of hands seized his other arm, holding him steady while a third officer punched the number from his ID band into a data device. Toris's face flashed on the ID scanner screen, and everything—the audience and the council—faded around him.

He knew then that Toris Onero was breathing his last breaths.

The officer holding the ID pad gave Toris a sly smile. "Seems we have a celebrity here."

Orysk pried the tablet from his hands. His eyes grew wider as he read.

"This fool has broken exile," the ID officer announced to his colleagues.

"Would you expect anything less from the son of Anaraxa Whose-last-name-I-shall-not-say?" Orysk said in disgust.

This revelation drew a surprised look from Lex.

"Guess we'll be tying a noose after the meeting, sir," said the officer holding Toris's arm.

Show no weakness, Toris reminded himself. His eyes locked onto his reader tablet. He wasn't a dead man yet. Having just witnessed the Chancellor's struggle to avoid war, he'd be interested in Toris's discovery.

Toris met Lex's stare. He nodded for her to hand over the reader.

Lex clutched his reading device close to her chest, and her reluctance sent a wave of dread washing through him. Would she really condemn him to death for her own glory? Her eyes flicked between Orysk and the council table below for a good many heartbeats. Too many.

After what seemed an eternity, she offered him the reader.

Orysk snatched the device and turned away from Toris, examining it warily.

Toris burst from the officer's hold and ran to the top of the aisle.

"I know how to solve the crop crisis!" he shouted.

From the council table below, the councillors stood and strained to see Toris at the top of the stairs.

"It's true!" Lex said from beside Toris atop the aisle.

AnaXagoras stepped up to the bottom steps. "Alexandra?"

Orysk seized Toris's arm above the elbow. "This is Anaraxa's son, Chancellor."

AnaXagoras's eyes shifted to Toris and darkened.

"I brought him out of exile to present the solution," Lex said, grabbing Toris's other arm. "He really does know how to solve the crisis."

On the dais, Sydra snapped her fingers at Orysk. "Arrest—"

AnaXagoras raised a hand to silence Sydra. "How?"

"It's best I show you," Toris said.

The Chancellor waved at Orysk. "Let him down. And escort my daughter to her chambers."

Orysk handed Toris the reader and patted him down while another guard checked his sling bag. Finding only the dive knife in his waistband, Orysk seized the weapon and stepped aside to let him into the aisle.

As two officers escorted Lex back to the entrance, she looked over her shoulder and gave Toris an encouraging nod.

He took the cool marble steps down two at a time. As he approached the dais below, many citizens and a few councillors assessed his faded black clothes with doubt. When he reached the dais at the bottom, the Chancellor tried his best to conceal his revulsion, but the twist of his lips betrayed him.

"You have an idea about how to stop the crop failures?" he said.

Toris's grip on the reader tightened until his fingers tingled. He nodded.

"Well speak up, boy," said the Chancellor.

Toris pressed the power button at the top of his device. On the screen, the photo of a tall rectangular doorway flashed to life. He laid the tablet on the council table's glass top. "Here," he said. The point of no return.

The councillors leaned in. "What is this?" Sydra said.

Toris fidgeted with the bottom of his tunic. "That document tells us where to find diverse seeds," said Toris. He pointed to the image on his reader screen. "Seeds from every variety of crop that ever sprouted from the Mother are there, in that vault, in a place called *Svalbard*."

"Svalbard?" said Catalina of Kaladia, pulling the tablet across the table for a better look.

Toris looked to the Chancellor. "The Decimators created that vault to preserve the world's crop diversity." The words came easier now. "They stored over a million varieties of extinct crop species in there."

"If this was in the old world, then it was destroyed like everything else," Catalina said.

Toris addressed the crowd. "They designed this vault to withstand all forms of catastrophe—natural or manmade—for whatever event that wiped them out," he said. "They constructed it for people like us. Survivors."

Sydra swept in beside Catalina, nudging her aside for a closer look at the reference. Her brow creased as she picked up the reader and squinted at the screen, no doubt checking for the document's state-approved seal. "Where did you get this?"

"I discovered the archive by accident in a cellar," Toris lied. "I was going to destroy it, but then I saw this text. I took it as a sign from the Mother."

The Chancellor's stunned expression seemed genuine. "So you admittedly broke Law Two of the Order, then broke exile to bring the evidence *here*?"

"I did it for the love of my country," Toris said. That combination of words left the taste of bile in his mouth. But he'd been telling citizens what they wanted to hear all his life. He forced a smile and said, "I've come to claim the Accolade. You wanted a solution to reverse the crop failures. There it is."

The councillors all swarmed around AnaXagoras, where they buzzed like hornets, their eyes drifting back to Toris more than to the document that offered their salvation. All except Rosaria, leader of Arokya, who'd taken his reader to her seat.

The audience stands seemed to close in on Toris, bulging in and retreating with each throb of his heart. He stood firm, fists clenched at his side. *Show no weakness…*

Easier said than done.

Sydra broke away from the huddle. "The law is the law. It is the beacon that guided us from chaos five centuries ago, and to undermine it is the greatest of crimes. Captain Orysk, arrest this boy for breaking exile and breaching Law Two of the Order."

All around the dais, Omniguard officers whipped out their batons.

Toris's belly lurched. He stepped back and bumped into the council table.

Beside him, Rosaria of Arokya stood from her seat and raised both hands. "This young man has risked certain death to bring us a solution to a problem that threatens us all. To condemn him will only deter others from stepping forward in the future."

The circle of guards stopped on the stairs below the dais and looked to the Chancellor for direction. Sydra glared at Rosaria, but Toris could have kissed her. The claims about her territory were not unfounded.

"A *solution*?" Sydra said. "Must I remind everyone that leaving Anterra for *any* reason is against Law Seven of the Order?"

"Then it's time to amend those laws," said Rosaria.

Her words hung heavy in the silence that followed. Even the Chancellor watched the Arokyan councillor in surprise, clearly unsure how to proceed.

Toris watched as his only champion faced down the stares of her colleagues. Was such talk against the Order permitted, even by a councillor?

Rosaria tapped the table to summon graphs onto the screens overhead. Arrows showed crime statistics on the rise, while prosperity scores were plummeting.

"The Order was written by our forebearers to reflect the problems of their time," Rosaria said. "All it does now is promote misery and suffering. That's what the Sage Abelia meant to avoid when she drafted those laws. Our blind devotion to the Order will be our undoing." Rosaria pointed a sweeping finger across the audience stands. "Amend the Order! What say you?"

In the surrounding stands, heads dropped. Toris looked up to the screens directly above the dais but could not see them from this angle, so he followed the councillors' stares to their table top.

Ding-ding-ding. Large green numbers flashed across the glass top—fifty-three percent in favour of Rosaria's proposal.

The tightness in Toris's chest loosened. Approval from the audience had little weight on its own, but public pressure meant a lot to a council member. Citizens would not forget a councillor's disregard for their opinions in the next election.

Sydra's hard gaze fell on Toris, her eyes rife with disdain. "Even in death, your mother's traitorous nature continues to shake Polaria's stability. Your very presence is toxic, and a good reminder for your exile."

Luckily, the Chancellor provided a different response. He smiled at Toris and said, "Captain Orysk, please escort the Onero to my chambers."

Sydra clutched her chest and recoiled. "For a Chancellor to entertain a criminal who spits on Abelia's laws... Well, I never dreamed I'd see the day," she said with exaggerated disgust. "If that is your intent, then you'd leave me no choice but to call a vote of no confidence in your leadership."

The Chancellor's face flushed red as he shot Sydra a rueful glare. Toris saw the conflict in his eyes. From where he was standing, Sydra's smug smile suggested she knew he had no choice from here. After consideration, AnaXagoras nodded to Orysk. "Detain the half-blood."

Toris allowed the Omniguard captain to escort him from the dais, confident the Chancellor would seek him out for a private meeting. Two more officers joined them at the tunnel entrance and followed him under the stands. They turned left into a side passage, out view of the audience.

"Stop resisting," said Orysk from behind.

Toris turned to see the captain holding a baton. A blue current crackled between the two prongs at its tip—a stinger.

Toris's heart raced.

"Regards from Councillor Sydra," Orysk said, then jabbed the baton into Toris's belly.

Electricity exploded through his abdomen like a blast of lightning and sucked the air from his lungs. He dropped to a knee.

Orysk circled behind. Another blast shot through his back, quickly followed by another to his shoulder. Toris's muscles locked stiff wherever the prods touched. The bite to his back ribs was the last thing he remembered of his visit to the Orichalcum.

SEVEN

The dead man could not sit still. The chair's plush upholstery did little to soothe his wounds, and the chain around his waist to which his wrist manacles were secured sat over two swelling blisters where the stinger had scorched his skin. But it could have been worse.

Waking upon a comfortable chair in a bright lobby, rather than on the floor of a dank prison cell, had been more a surprise for Toris than the stinger attack. Sunlight flooded through floor to ceiling windows, gleaming off the seamless white floor and walls. The windows offered sweeping views across the rounded tops of Amyria's domes. Through the window on the right, the Borien Mountains spread to the south like a petrified sea. The left window offered a view of the rolling ocean under a grey sky.

A lump formed in his throat. What he wouldn't give to feel that warm water soothe his skin just once more…

It had to be done, he kept reminding himself. *Had to be.* Jayda would be in uniform soon, and claiming the Accolade was the surest chance to free her. And the Orichalcum could not have been a better venue. His public revelation denied The Artican any chance at concealing the vault's existence from their citizens.

Still, he had broken the law in the worst of ways.

As his vision sharpened, he noticed a rectangular outline in the white wall ahead that suggested a door—its flush features a work of mastery. Nothing about the room resembled the cell he deserved. In fact, the unobstructed view outside the windows suggested he was high up in the Central Spire, which housed all the government's elite. So why was *he* here?

The door ahead slid sideways into the wall to reveal Captain Orysk standing in a corridor. "Toris Onero," said Orysk, "the council demands your presence."

Toris studied Orysk's expression for any indication of his fate, but saw only a flicker of impatience. Apparently escorting half-blood Oneros was beneath him. Toris stood and shuffled through the doorway.

Once inside, he was shocked to see that it wasn't a corridor, but a room with three walls. The door slid closed and sealed them in a six-by-six-foot room. A second later, the floor pushed up into his feet. Toris wavered at the upward motion for the five seconds it lasted.

When the door opened again, it was into a massive round room. An uninterrupted window circled the entire floor as far as could be seen from the lift, over which grey shades hung to block the sun. Above, a tinted dome roof revealed this was the Central Spire's top level.

At the center of the dimly lit room, nine figures sat upon high chairs arranged in a semicircle. Soft green light from suspended orbs outlined the Chancellor's hard expression, his eyes watching somewhere from the depths of two black pits.

Orysk pushed Toris through the door. He shuffled toward the councillors, the rattling of chains announcing his approach. He stopped at Orysk's command before the semicircle. The captain retreated to the doorway.

"Toris Onero," the Chancellor said, "you've been found guilty of the following: breaking Law Two of the Order; breaking exile;

deserting your civil post on Mintaka; and one count of resisting an Omniguard officer. The sentence for the sum of these violations is death by hanging."

Toris closed his eyes and felt tears bulge behind their lids. How could he ever find peace in death knowing he left Jayda alone in this unforgiving world?

For a moment, heavy silence hung in the air. Then the Chancellor released a heavy sigh. "But times are changing."

Toris opened his eyes and looked up.

"We've sanctioned a mission to Svalbard," said Rosaria.

The words echoed in Toris's head and conjured a flurry of possibilities.

Sydra leaned forward and looked to AnaXagoras. "A decision which I am firmly against. Svalbard is a waste of time and resources. We'll need all boots on Anterran soil when food stores hit a critical level."

"Yes, we've heard at length your arguments against the expedition," said the Chancellor. "Yet the matter has been voted on."

Rosaria cleared her throat to put a stop to the exchange. To Toris, she said, "For your role in offering us this glimmer of hope, the council has agreed to spare your life."

The tension deflated from Toris's muscles to the point he felt the manacles almost slide from his wrists.

"We've arranged to return you to your warden on Mintaka," the Chancellor said, "where you'll resume your civil service in exile."

"As a finder's fee for bringing the Svalbard reference to light," Rosaria said, "we've agreed to knock two years off your debt."

"And my sister," Toris said. "She was taken in the draft."

"Then she'll do her duty at the border with her fellow draftees," Sydra said.

Toris gnawed his bottom lip to contain the words buzzing like wasps inside his mouth. If Sydra got her way, Jayda would be doing her duty well beyond defending the border. To the Chancellor, Toris said, "I brought the seed vault reference forward to free my sister. If you just release her from—"

"You are in no position to make demands, *Onero*," said the Chancellor, his eyes somehow darkening further. Apparently Sydra's threat to hold a vote of no confidence had persuaded him to take a stronger stance on criminals.

But Rosaria's dim smile and faint nod suggested that Toris *was* in a position to bargain.

"The Accolade comes with First-Class Citizenship and a million credits," Toris said.

"We're not giving you the Accolade," the Chancellor countered.

"I earned it," Toris said, tension surging back into his muscles along with a trickle of rage. "I heard your voice on the radio, Chancellor, many times. *'Any tip leading to the discovery of—'*"

"I know what I said," the Chancellor snapped, perhaps putting on a show for Sydra, "and any sensible Polarian would assume that didn't involve breaking the law. There were many ways you could have brought this solution to our attention without leaving exile."

Rosaria placed a calming hand on AnaXagoras's arm, and it quickly became evident that her grace could tame even a lion's wrath. She looked to Toris. "We cannot award you the Accolade for simply pointing us in an uncertain direction. That reward will go to whoever travels to the vault and returns with the seeds...*if* any remain, of course."

"And that's a big *if*," Sydra said.

Rosaria winked at Toris.

Was she suggesting...

"I volunteer for the expedition," he said.

"The mission we sanctioned to the vault is military in nature," Sydra said. "Only active defence service members may participate."

"And you have your civil service to resume," the Chancellor reminded.

Toris looked to Rosaria. Her mouth twitched as if she wanted to say more. Instead, she sat silently with her hands folded in her lap.

"On that note," the Chancellor said, "we've arranged for a train to take you to Port Abersali. From there, a ferry will return you to Mintaka. Until then, we've afforded you comfortable accommodation here in the tower."

The Chancellor nodded to the doorway behind Toris. Captain Orysk marched forward and removed the manacles, then motioned for him to exit the room.

Toris walked to the lift doorway without argument. The sooner he got out of there, the sooner he could search for a way to contact Lex. So long as she was in the capital, she could access her father's database to change Jayda's assignment.

Toris and Orysk stood before the door that resembled two mirrors, their edges butted against one another, waiting for the lift. In the reflection, Orysk touched the stinger on his belt either by instinct or as a threat.

Toris's neck hairs stiffened straight.

Heels clicked over the floor behind, growing louder with each step. Rosaria approached in the reflection of the doors, the tail of her scarlet silk robe seeming to glide over the faux marble floor.

"Captain, I'll escort our guest to his quarters."

Orysk gave Rosaria a quizzical look. He looked back toward the Chancellor, but the other councillors had moved to a table to deliberate over a digital map. When the elevator doors slid open and Rosaria entered, beckoning Toris to join, the conflict was clear on the Omniguard captain's face as Toris joined her. He seemed poised to slip through the shrinking space between the closing doors, but remained firm until the elevator doors sealed shut.

Despite his shabby appearance, Toris couldn't help but admire his own reflection standing beside Rosaria's in the scratchless doors. Two days ago he'd have never dreamed of holding private company with Arokya's councillor. It took everything not to beg her to do something for Jayda. She was as bound by bureaucracy as he was.

The floor shifted down and, for a second, Toris felt as if he were aboard *Atlas* rocking over the gentle sea.

"We're about to declare a State of Emergency," Rosaria said matter-of-factly. "Our aides did some digging after the council meeting, and found an old directive that will allow us to suspend certain aspects of the Order in such an emergency—such as Law Seven." She cracked a smile and said, "Are you familiar with that law?"

"Never leave the safety of Anterra," he said. The law had been enacted to prevent Anterrans from encountering destructive technologies on foreign lands, or radiation that may introduce corruption into their gene pool.

The implication of Rosaria's words hit him like a tsunami and stole his breath away. It seemed now starvation overshadowed the fear of someone returning to Polaria with nuclear arms or tainted DNA.

The elevator eased to a stop. Both doors opened into a ring-shaped corridor of rounded white walls that encircled the lift shaft. Grey doors marked the outer walls at twenty-foot intervals. Rosaria stepped out with Toris close on her heels.

"We think it best not to rely solely on one vessel to find the seeds," Rosaria said as she led him left around the corridor. "Even a Coast Patrol battle cruiser may have an unforeseeable mishap."

She stopped at a door and waved her bracelet before an adjacent screen. The grey door retracted sideways into the wall to reveal a furnished suite beyond. She gestured for Toris to enter first, then followed.

The apartment opened into a salon with crimson carpet and matching drapes. In an adjacent room, a massive bed that could sleep a dozen Oneros took up only a quarter of the space.

Rosaria ran a hand across the back of a chair as she crossed to the far window. "For that reason, we're issuing exit permits to civilian vessels. Anyone who wishes to risk their life to save Polaria will be permitted to do so. If any of these expeditions are successful, we'll award them the Accolade."

Toris could hardly believe what he was hearing. Sallus had told him about old imperial governments granting civilians the authority to act in their interests. *Privateers*, Sallus had called them, and though the idea had stirred a romantic feeling in Toris at the time, he could not wrap his head around the concept. Even now he was having trouble picturing it.

"If a ship returns with the seeds," he said, "will you award the Accolade to the entire crew?"

Rosaria stopped before the window and stared at the distant sea. "The credit reward will go to the expedition leader—the captain or his sponsor. How they split that with the crew, if at all, is up to them. However, all crew members *will* receive First-Class Citizenship. Of course, they don't have to accept the reward for their own purposes. They can bestow it upon someone else. And remember, First-Class Citizens are exempt from defence service."

Toris's heart quivered with excitement. Was The Artican really going to allow Polarians into the old world? It seemed circumstances were forcing their hand. Suspend Law Seven, or watch the country starve.

He joined Rosaria in staring out the window. One high hurdle still stood clearly in his way. "What about my civil service on Mintaka?"

Rosaria nodded faintly. "That *is* an obstacle, and one I cannot officially help you with. I only wish to inform you of the upcoming mandate. What you decide to do with that information is up to you." She turned to face him directly. "However, I *can* tell you this: for whoever goes north in search of the vault, I'll forgive whatever obligations they break to go there."

She stepped back from the window and placed a hand on his shoulder. "Wherever your heart leads you, Toris Onero, I hope the winds are in your favour."

Her hand slid from his shoulder. He listened to her clicking heels fade across the room, waited until the door slid shut, then turned to see she'd left him alone in this luxury suite.

He returned his gaze to the distant sea. Questions and doubts swirled in his head, but none concerned him right now. The only thing that mattered was the fact he was going to Svalbard. Somehow, Toris Onero was getting on a ship and going to the other end of the world.

EIGHT

Toris stared up at the Central Spire in awe. Standing on the grassy boulevard only a block away, he had to lean back to see the point piercing the blue sky like a silver stake.

He'd spent three days locked in the suite Rosaria had left him in, which was three days too long. He'd take the dusty Onero Block on Mintaka to that sterile box any day. But rather than send him straight to Port Abersali, the officials responsible for arranging his exile thought it best to hold him in Amyria to align his arrival at port with the infrequent ferry departure to the satellite islands.

Constable Gravus squeezed his shoulder. "Let's go, half-blood. The train is about to leave."

His Omniguard partner, Sergeant Stokes, waited atop the steps of the station entrance, pointing impatiently to his watch.

Toris stepped off the grass lane and climbed the steps to the platforms. Premier Station, Amyria's train hub, was the city's only above-ground station.

Apparently Toris had missed a lot in his luxurious confinement. All he had to go by were rumours and snippets of information he'd overheard between his room in the Spire and the train station, but the crowd of young citizens now gathered on the platform ahead suggested talk of the citizen draft was true. It seemed The

Artican wanted to be ready to invade Ortaria's farmlands should word return from Svalbard that the vault had perished.

At the platform entrance, army officers recorded each citizen conscript as they arrived and tagged them with a number that corresponded with their assigned cars. The amount of horseplay about the station exposed their naivety toward this assignment, as if it were a routine field trip to a solar farm. Signs of The Artican building an invasion force were disconcerting, but if this rumour were true then perhaps the second was as well.

The Omniguard officers led Toris through the checkpoint to the platform, where Amyria's youth were lining up to their assigned cars of the right side train. The Onero recruits climbed ladders to the car roofs, leaving the seats inside for their citizen comrades. Their sullen expressions indicated they were not so naive about this new assignment.

Stokes plowed through the throng of draftees to the train on the left. He pushed open a car door and nodded for Toris to enter ahead of him.

Toris marched forward but, as if reading his mind, the Omniguard sergeant stuck an arm across the door to bar his way. "You try anything stupid between here and your boat off the mainland," Stokes said, "we'll drag you straight to the hangman. Understand?"

Like many Oneros, Toris had learned at a young age what authorities wanted to see from their underlings when hearing such threats. He looked to his feet and gave a faint nod. Then, as if that were some secret password, Stokes's arm dropped to let him pass.

The empty car took Toris off guard. Then again, how many capital folk felt the need to visit Port Abersali when all the country's food was coming here?

He chose a window seat and reclined as far back as it allowed. To his discomfort, Gravus sat in the seat across from him and Stokes in the seat to Toris's left. His toes touched one officer's boots, his shoulder the other's.

The train seemed to remain motionless, yet through the

windows a smooth peeling away of the station implied they were underway. It picked up speed as it rolled through Amyria's core of shimmering buildings and slipped into darkness under the perimeter wall.

Toris crossed his arms and closed his eyes until his lids felt the heat of unfiltered sunshine. This blast of light would welcome the citizen conscripts in the following train as they raced away from the bubble that had sheltered them from the harsh world—the world they may be ordered to conquer. Toris pitied them with all his heart. But maybe they were the lucky ones. Sometimes it was easier not knowing.

He hoped the second piece of news he'd heard during his internment in the capital was true. If The Artican truly was flooded with exit permit requests from Accolade hopefuls, then he shouldn't have a hard time finding an expedition to join.

That's where the two goons crowding his personal space became a problem. If Toris ended up back on Mintaka, Warden Castor would never let him out of his sight having lost him the first time. How bad it must look on a keeper whose exiled Onero ended up in a council meeting at the Orichalcum. Even worse was if Castor hadn't reported him missing. That may earn Toris the whip as a welcome home gift.

Unable to think with the smothering presence of his escort, Toris leaned forward and said, "The motion is making me sick. I should go to the dome car."

The officers exchanged wary looks. Toris feigned a gag, and both jumped into the aisle.

"If we have to come looking for you before this train arrives in Abersali—"

Toris clapped a hand over his mouth and murmured, "Hanging and all that, I know."

The door at the back of his car led through a gangway connection and into the dome car. Its half-level rise above the rest of the train and panoramic windows offered a view of the dozen cars snaking across the plains toward the coastal forest.

Up here, Toris could breathe easier, which allowed him to think more clearly. Even if he could elude Castor's watchful stare, Mintaka's boat owners were fair-weather fishermen with little heart for adventure. Port Abersali was the surest place to join a crew. As a shipwright, sailor, and wreck diver, he'd be invaluable to one of the privateers preparing to leave. But the only ferry from Mintaka to the mainland ran at four-day intervals. Supposing he could slip back to Abersali without Castor knowing, expedition crews may have filled up or already set off before his return to the mainland. So, going to Mintaka as planned was not an option, which meant he had to ditch his escort in Abersali.

Easier said than done.

Back beyond the rear car, the tip of the Central Spire sank below the horizon into grass-covered hills, leaving only the Borien Mountains standing beyond. Ahead of the train, the glittering blue sea sent his heart skipping.

The car's rear door slid open with a hiss. A girl of twenty years climbed the steps to join Toris in the dome car. Her ceremonial Defence Force uniform matched her ink-black hair, which was tied back tight. A gold bar to each side of her fastened high collar marked her for a lieutenant.

She marched straight for him, and he stood watching her curiously as she walked a circle around him, inspecting his black tunic and shendyt. She completed her circuit and stopped before him, where her turquoise eyes lingered on his face.

"You're the half-blood," she concluded.

Toris's cheeks burned. "I am."

"Are you called anything else, or did your parents lack imagination?"

"Toris. My name is Toris."

The lieutenant gave a curt nod. "I'm Rykah."

She reached out to his chest with both hands and fastened a loose button on his tunic. Then she ran one hand down the seam to smooth the rumpled fabric.

"I'll be seeing you around," she said, then turned and left without another word.

Toris stared at the closed door a long while, wondering what the hell was up with that strange encounter. *Perhaps she's a fan of mine*, he mused.

He returned to his railcar and sank into his seat. He closed his eyes and tried to sleep, but rest would not come. His heart raced at the fear and excitement of what lie ahead. But every time he opened his eyes he drew suspicious looks from his escort, so he pretended to sleep to deflect their attention.

They arrived in Abersali three hours later.

Toris squirmed in his seat as the train squealed to a stop, his stomach roiling. Seeing the cobblestone lanes bend through rows of whitewashed buildings down to the harbour sucked the confidence straight out of him. His escape was going to require a lot of skill and even more luck.

"Wait till the platform clears," Stokes said, remaining slouched in his seat.

Toris hugged himself to hide his shaking hands. As the last passengers disembarked and bounced down the platform stairs, Gravus and Stokes stood and straightened their uniforms in the aisle.

Toris joined them at the doorway. Should he try to run even if he knew he wouldn't make it? Last time, he had a boat waiting and only one officer pursuing. One thing in his favour was the city's scarce Omniguard presence, which even allowed a black market to flourish. If Toris could lose these two, they wouldn't have much help scouring the city for him.

Gravus slid open the door and recoiled from the wave of humidity that invaded the climate-controlled car.

To Toris, the thick salty air brought a measure of comfort. After his bid for the Accolade in the Orichalcum, he thought he'd never see the water so close again, smell the salt of the sea, nor feel the humidity on his skin or smell fresh fish in the air.

Both peace officers stepped out onto the empty platform and wrinkled their noses. Gravus released an exaggerated gag.

Stokes led Toris down into the lane. Gravus followed so close that Toris felt the officer's breath on the back of his neck. They walked in single file down the lane toward the ferry terminal, where passengers were already boarding the wooden ketch that would return Toris to Mintaka.

Toris's heart quivered. Every step taken down that cobblestone street lowered his chance of escape. A quick estimate gave him three hundred paces to the terminal.

He surveyed the alleys to his right and saw most were clear of obstructions. He'd take the next. No matter what, just run.

"Halt!"

Stokes marched on ahead. But, because Toris suspected the girl who'd shouted the command had directed it at his escort, he stopped and looked back. Gravus grabbed his arm to drag him along, but then noticed Rykah marching toward them from the train platform.

Gravus released Toris's arm and watched Rykah curiously. "Can we help you, ma'am?"

She handed Stokes a folded letter with a purple wax seal, but kept her eyes on Toris.

When both Omniguard officers turned away to discuss the contents of the letter, Toris knew this may be his only chance. If Rykah wasn't watching him the entire time he might try, but something about her inquisitive stare kept him in place.

Stokes returned the letter to Rykah and said, "All yours, Lieutenant Adarah."

And just like that, both peace officers marched back up the steps to the train station. Toris watched them in amazement as they disappeared onto the platform without a second look back. He suppressed his laughter. One escort would be easier to shake than two.

Rykah cocked her head toward the bottom of the lane. "This way."

Fish carts rolled up toward the train station with mobs following and shouting their condemnation.

"Haven't we sent enough of our food inland?"

"Can't you see we're starving out here?"

"What have they ever sent us?"

Rykah pulled Toris into a shop entrance to allow the mob to pass.

Toris clenched his fists. The Chancellor's disregard for the rest of the country made him want to vomit. "You just came from the capital," he said to Rykah. "You saw how they feast away while good folk out here starve."

Rykah pulled him back into the lane.

"These shipments are going to Sol-Brae and Khartum to quell the famine riots," she said.

Toris stopped. "Famine riots?"

Rykah said nothing as she pulled him along.

Toris watched for a way to run. Though well-broken in, Rykah's knee-high boots couldn't be easy to run in. And why was an army officer escorting him, anyway?

"I have to get to Finn's Marina," he lied. "I'm to crew a ship. Didn't my escort tell you?"

"They must have left that part out," Rykah said absently. "Anyway, that doesn't matter. We have new business to discuss." She dragged him into a white-walled alley. "This way."

Toris walked beside her. "Are you sure that business is with me? You didn't even know my name when we met on the train."

"I didn't need to know your name."

Toris twisted his wrist free. "Why not? Wasn't it in that letter?"

"The sealed letter? Maybe." Rykah pushed him forward. "My job is to pry on the enemy, not on my superiors. All I know is that a civilian was arriving by train with an Omniguard escort."

She stopped and looked back toward the train station. "Unless I missed him. Did you see another half-blood Onero with an exile escort get off that train? Didn't think so."

As Rykah took the lead, Toris gave her a curious look. Nothing about this encounter made sense. Time to start digging for clues.

"What's your occupation in the Defence Force?"

She ignored him as she led him farther into the alley, away from the ferry terminal, to a rotting grey door between two waste bins. Pushing the door open with one hand, Rykah gestured with the other for him to enter. "You look like you could use a drink."

As Toris entered, he noticed Rykah take a good look up and down the alley before pulling the door shut.

It took Toris's eyes a few seconds to adjust to the darkness. The basement air was cool and musty. Candles provided the only light in the windowless space, enough to reveal that Toris and Rykah were the tavern's only patrons. With such a discrete entrance this came as little surprise. At least in here Toris could relax. This detour meant he'd miss the ferry.

Rykah signalled the barkeep and then slid into a booth in the far corner. She unfastened her high collar, then the brass buttons below, all the way down her coat to reveal a navy blue dress shirt underneath. But Rykah's opening of her coat had opened a whole new series of questions for Toris. For on the right side of Rykah's neck, a large black *V* tattoo stood out on her pale skin.

He checked his surroundings and, to his relief, saw they were alone except for the barkeep. Why was a criminal conscript escorting an exile? That was the first of many questions, because as far as Toris knew, The Artican had a policy against commissioning criminal conscripts as officers. And unlike Oneros, criminals forced into military service were restricted to the border region. Only Oneros and citizen soldiers drew domestic postings such as food security. Port Abersali was a long way from the border, so what business did Rykah have with him?

"You didn't tell me what your occupation is," he pressed.

"My team manages the Chancellor's affairs outside the capital."

Toris frowned. It was the Chancellor who had ordered him back into exile. If her intent was to see that through, she wasn't taking her mission very seriously. If the ferry to Mintaka hadn't left already then it was due to depart any minute. And why hadn't she taken over the assignment in the capital? None of this was adding up.

The barkeep set a bottle on the table with two glasses.

Rykah waved him away and poured a splash into each glass, then slid one to Toris. She held out her drink.

Toris examined the brown liquid suspiciously. What was the meaning of all this?

Rykah shrugged at his hesitation and threw back her shot. She winced at the taste, which gave Toris an idea. He took his shot, then clapped a hand over his mouth and heaved.

Rykah casually pointed behind her seat toward a door beside the bar. "Make a mess and you clean it."

Toris scrambled toward the bathroom and crashed through the door. A breeze immediately hit his face and he rejoiced. The window was above head height and barely wide enough to squeeze through, but just squeezing by was how this half-blood lived his life.

He stepped onto the wooden drop toilet and then pulled himself through the window. In the alley outside, he whispered a silent 'thank you' to Rykah, then hurried down the alley, though not so fast as to draw suspicion.

At Finn's Marina, three dozen ships of varying size and function rocked along the three wharfs that reached like fingers into the harbour. One ship caught Toris's attention above all.

Occupying a dock of her own, the sloop was crafted of dark cherry wood from keel to crown, with white nylon rope rigged to her royal purple sails. Her name, *Southern Zephyr*, was scrawled in cursive across the stern. The entire vessel, from stern to stem, exuded a stunning elegance.

"*Southern Zep-hire*," Toris said, reading the name aloud to see if the last word rang any bells. It did not, and the Omniguard officer guarding her gangway prevented him from inquiring with her crew.

At the head of the center dock, Toris noticed a young couple arguing over a posting on the noticeboard. The man said something, and his lady replied with a hiss before storming off. He followed her with pleas.

When Toris approached the board to see what they'd read, he saw a laminated page with The Artican's letterhead. The heading read: *Are you an AGRINAUT?* The following text he understood well enough to get the idea that each privateer vessel had to pass inspection—either here or at Point Bay Station up the peninsula—to qualify for an exit permit. Minimum requirements included a refrigeration unit to preserve the seeds during the return voyage, and it was highly recommended that every captain hire a security team.

"Toris Onero!"

Toris's quads tensed at the man's words from behind. But rather than spring away, the familiarity of the voice kept his feet planted firm on the wooden dock. A bad decision.

He turned to see four brown knuckles swiping for his face. The fist crashed into his cheek and sent him bottom first onto the deck, where he threw up his arms instinctively to shield against a follow-up.

Struggling to see through black patches spotting his vision, something on the man's right leg forced him to lower his hands for a better look. Bulging scars in the shape of arched teeth on his calf left little to the imagination as to who Toris's attacker was. And instead of a second fist, the next hand was open and appeared to offer help standing.

"That was for letting Jayda lead me into that bear trap."

Toris squinted a few times to focus his throbbing eye and confirmed his attacker was Drua. Even as a junior in the orphanry, none of the senior lads messed with Drua. So if he wanted to put Toris to sleep, he wouldn't need a second shot. When it came to punches, Lake Orion Orphanry's biggest bully was a one hit wonder.

Toris accepted Drua's hand, and Drua pulled him to his feet with minimal effort.

"Said I'd never get you, hey?" Drua said.

"I thought orphans gave up those games when they put on the uniform."

"Are you kidding? No one likes a good joke more than a soldier." Drua brushed the dust off the back of Toris's tunic. "What brings you here, anyway? Thought they exiled you."

"I'm on a crew," Toris lied.

"Same. Which ship?"

Toris gave Drua a quizzical look. "You are? How? I mean… I didn't take you for the seafaring type."

"Yeah, well, civilian life got pretty boring after all the excitement at the border. Figured I'd put my skills to use providing expedition security. What crew you with?"

Toris scanned the rows of ships. "It's not a sure thing yet. I'm actually thinking about jumping ship."

"I see that flaky half-blood dedication is still strong in you. Where'd you and Jayda get posted?"

Suddenly, Toris's heart hurt worse than his cheek. "She just got drafted."

Drua's expression did a fair job at concealing his concern, but not good enough. "She'll be fine," he said, rubbing his bald head. "She's a tough girl."

Toris noticed a white scar that marred the light brown skin across Drua's temple. "Tough enough to stop an arrow?"

Drua smiled. "That was a spear, actually. But you know me - always looking for a bigger challenge. It really ain't all bad there, man. She'll settle in with a good unit who'll take care of her. And she's resourceful." Drua pointed to his leg scars. "She'll do better at the border than most."

Drua's attempt at consolation didn't ease Toris's concern. It actually made it worse. The hardest of Lake Orion's orphans wasn't the type to provide comfort even in the worst of times.

Drua looked to the ships, then his eyes lit in understanding. "You're gonna use the Accolade to free her."

"*If* I can land on a decent crew. Your captain need a deckhand?"

Drua grinded his teeth. "He's pretty confident he can run the ship on his own. He's more concerned with hiring trigger fingers."

"What about a diver? Or a shipwright?"

"You know some guys?"

Toris smirked. "I know *one* guy who can fill all those roles. Less provisions required."

Drua smiled and nodded. "Follow me. I'll introduce you to Captain Antlia."

NINE

The ship Drua had volunteered to accompany to the other end of the world was called the *Barnacle,* and she sucked all the romance out of privateering.

She sat in a slip midway down the center dock but was hard to miss. And not in a good way. Across the hull, rust had bubbled through the trawler's hunter green paint, and only one section of rail remained to indicate that there had indeed been this safety measure at some point. Her mast stood thirty feet tall and Toris swore it wobbled off center with the ship's gentle rocking. No wonder the captain had difficulty attracting a crew.

Drua climbed aboard and stuck his head down the hatch. "Captain, you here?"

"Drua," came a stuffed voice from below. "How'd you make out?"

"Didn't find the provisions, but…" Drua glanced back at Toris with a sly grin and said, "I didn't return empty-handed."

A man climbed up from below, squinting toward Toris and Drua in the sunlight. Though Captain Antlia had a full head of white hair and the beard to match, he could have been Sallus had he lived another ten years. So much so that Toris had to tell him.

"I knew that crazy old sea urchin," Antlia said, smiling as his wistful gaze turned to the sea. "We were the only two sailors foolish enough to set out in the storm that smashed a Coast Patrol cruiser against the rocks. Awarded us the Order of Amyria for saving her crew." He shook his head to break his reverie. "Shame what happened to him. Artican has a short memory when it comes to good deeds." He smiled at Toris. "If you're a tenth the boat builder he was, I'd be glad to have you on my crew. There's just one problem." His smile flattened. "And it's a big one."

The captain led Toris below decks. There, they stood staring at an empty hold.

"No food," Drua said, pointing out the obvious.

That was indeed a problem.

"The Artican just imposed stricter rations," Antlia explained, wiping grease from his hands with a rag. "Even for an endeavour like this, they're not about to go making exceptions. This land will be covered in ice again before we see them risking so much food getting lost at sea."

"What about the black market?" Toris said. Due to Abersali being Polaria's port hub, and the scarce Omniguard presence in town, the town fostered a thriving community of illicit product vendors. One could buy foods like venison and lamb long before they became legal. Some of the town restaurants had even served these foods as off-menu delicacies.

Antlia rubbed his chin. "With so many nets coming up light from the open fishing season, underground prices have gone up like a hot air balloon. Without a sponsor, I'm afraid each crew member will have to provision himself for this expedition."

Toris crossed his arms and gritted his teeth. The need to provide his own food for a voyage of unknown length, coupled with *Barnacle*'s questionable seaworthiness, were not adding up to a good start. Still, it was better than the one he'd get if he ended up on Mintaka.

No, he thought, shaking his head. He couldn't think like that. When it comes to seafaring vessels, you never settle. "I'm sorry," he said to Antlia, "but my financial situation is a bit restricted at the moment."

"Of course," Antlia said with a nod, though Toris saw clearly the disappointment in the captain's eyes.

Back up top, Toris climbed onto the dock and surveyed the surrounding ships. Hadn't he noticed a few loading food crates before encountering Drua's fist? In addition to his maritime skills, The *O* brand on his shoulder provided him the opportunity to falsely add *defence service* to his experience, as it was understood that many Oneros had at some point served at the border. He'd find a well-provisioned crew about to set out. He had to.

"I'll give you my Accolade reward," Drua said from behind.

Toris turned to see Drua standing on the dock beside *Barnacle*.

"Why would you go all the way to the Arctic," Toris said, his voice deliberately rife with skepticism, "just to give me your First-Class Citizenship?"

Drua approached, but he avoided Toris's stare. "I have my own reasons for finding those seeds." He grabbed Toris's shoulders. "We'll need another shooter out there. I'll teach you to snipe like the best."

Toris shrugged out of Drua's grasp and turned away to continue his assessment of the other ships. But Drua's offer clouded his mind. Possibilities flooded his heart with hope. A life with both him and Jayda as First-Class Citizens? It didn't get better than that.

"I have a rifle," Drua said. "Pinched it from my county militia's armoury. Soaring prices be damned, we'll rob the black market for supplies if we have to."

An idea struck Toris like a storm surge. How did he not see it before? Turning back to Drua, he smiled. "We won't have to rob anyone."

If there was one thing Toris Onero was now rich in, it was black market currency.

———

Toris's heart squeezed tighter with each beat as he trotted through the forest. A few times Drua had to yell at him to slow down, which said a lot considering Drua had been a soldier. But his demands for a slower pace worked only briefly.

"You could at least tell me where we're going," Drua huffed from behind.

Toris remained silent as he raced along the coast. He'd told Drua to wait back in town because he didn't want to get his hopes up. He was already scolding himself for allowing his own hopes to rise over this prospect. And for good reason.

The light path along the coast was concerning. When was the last time someone had been out this way? Famine had no doubt drove many into the wild in search of food. Had a forager come across *Atlas* tied to that ash tree?

Toris's belly tightened into knots, squeezing tighter every time he thought of someone else at *Atlas'* helm. How could he have been so careless? He should have moored her at least thirty miles from the nearest town. Though, at the time, someone finding her was the least of his worries.

And then there was the weather. If he didn't hitch that line well, she could have blown off in a storm. What knot had he used? He couldn't recall. For all he knew he'd just whipped it around the tree and hurried off into the forest.

"That's ten miles," Drua called from behind, as Toris had instructed him.

Toris kept on for another half mile until, through the trees ahead, he spotted a pole standing unnaturally straight and smooth among the ash trunks. Drua's protests faded as Toris sprinted ahead. He kept his bearing on the mast until *Atlas'* sky-blue hull came into view below. The hemp rope that had acted as *Atlas'* leash still held her firm to shore.

He planted his hands on his hips and breathed a sigh of relief.

Drua fell in beside him. "I thought you said we didn't have to rob anyone."

"We don't."

Toris slipped through the outer row of ash trunks and onto the shore, where he kissed *Atlas'* prow and rubbed her hull's peeling paint.

"This can't be yours," Drua said, his feet crunching over the rocks behind. His skepticism was well founded. Oneros didn't own such possessions unless someone cared enough to gift them.

Toris sent high praises to the spirit of Sallus. All his scavenging was about to pay off, and may even save Anterra from war.

"This really is yours," Drua said, touching the bowsprit in amazement.

"Keep watch," Toris said.

He climbed aboard, grabbed the hammer and pry bar from under the bench, and went below.

Starting at the bow, he used the pry bar to peel away the bulkhead panels at their seams and was relieved to see his mentor hadn't lied. Behind each panel, Sallus had packed contraband documents for safekeeping. Stiff, laminated pages displayed blocks of words with related images. Bold letters summarized important events atop each document.

No Stop to the Southern Blazes . . . European Oven Jumps Half a Degree Overnight . . . Russia Claims Missile Strike An Accident . . .

These recounts of the Decimation according to different countries would fetch a high price, so Toris stuffed them into a burlap sack. Behind the adjacent panel, he found a leather pouch full of silver coins and tossed them into the bag as well. He ripped away the remaining panels in search of an overlooked archive. Nothing.

He crawled into the space under the cockpit and very carefully pried out the stern panel. With delicate fingers he removed the clay-like blocks and piled them behind. Polarians had little use for explosives outside mining operations, so their black market value had once made them too risky to sell. Hopefully the Svalbard expedition had increased demand. The name 'vault' did suggest a secure facility which may require a forced entry. Toris wrapped the eight rectangular blocks into an old shirt and crawled out. But there was one more thing.

Sallus's ring remained on the shelf where he'd left it. He shoved the heirloom into his pocket, knowing it was better in his hands than some stranger's.

Up top, he handed Drua the sack of artifacts and, with the explosives under his arm, climbed down to the shore.

Drua looked inside the bag. "What's all this?"

"Those are going to fund our mission to Svalbard."

Toris stepped back and gave *Atlas* a good look over. Her rigging and sails would sell in town, or make adequate spares for their expedition, but if taking Sallus's scavenged artifacts felt like grave robbing, then stripping his boat and rendering her unable to sail seemed like scattering his bones.

"Why don't we sail back to Port?" Drua said, shifting the sack on his shoulder while looking warily down the rugged coast.

"Sometimes the Port Authority inspects incoming vessels," Toris said. That, and the Omniguard were on the lookout for *Atlas* since Toris had used her to escape Abersali less than a week ago.

Drua nodded his understanding. Noticing grey clouds creeping in over the sea, he said, "We should head back."

Toris turned to follow him into the forest. At the tree line he stopped and watched Sallus's boat struggle against her dock rope in an attempt to float out with the tide. His heart sank. To leave her like this felt like leaving a dog tied to a tree.

With his free hand he unhitched the line and pushed Sallus's legacy out for one last voyage.

They were half a mile from Port Abersali when bells chimed loud through the drizzly air. This wasn't uncommon for a port town, and Toris thought nothing of it until the ensuing cheers.

His heart sank as he exchanged a nervous look with Drua. They dashed across the remaining distance to the bluff overlooking town, from where Toris's fear was confirmed.

Sailing out of the harbour, towed along by a purple rectangular kite flying high before her bow, was the *Southern Zephyr*. A crowd had gathered on the docks to see the crew off. Their enthusiasm left no doubt as to the ship's destination.

The cheering persisted as Toris and Drua descended the slope to Abersali's outlying neighbourhood. With renewed urgency, they raced between rows of whitewashed brick residences across town. At the far edge, where the cobblestone lane faded to wagon tracks, he and Drua grabbed a wooden cart and dragged it into the forest.

A quarter mile out of town, the wagon tracks met and ran parallel with a railway. Three-foot weeds growing between rusted rails revealed the train service had stopped using this track long ago. Another quarter mile down the tracks stood a dilapidated two-storey warehouse, inside which the rail line terminated.

The cart's squeaking wheels announced Toris and Drua's approach. Two guards wearing torn and dusty Coast Patrol slickers squeezed through a narrow gap in the sliding doors, a pistol grip sticking out from each of their waistbands. Toris and Drua submitted to a pat down under the watch of a rifleman on the roof above.

Omniguard officers had neither the manpower nor the will to raid the market, for its illegal commodities had kept bellies satisfied and the masses from rioting during previous food shortages. Even now, voices echoed loud from inside the abandoned train repair shop as citizens bartered the best deal for their valuables.

With the search complete, Toris and Drua squeezed through the double doors. Inside, twelve vendors were spaced across the massive workshop, each defending their prices to the rowdy mob before their stalls. One stand at the far back remained empty, its vendor seated on a crate picking his nails with a knife. Toris made his way straight to him.

It soon became evident why the citizens were neglecting this stand. The prices, compared to those he'd seen while passing the other stalls, were comparable, but the vendor only sold in bulk. Far from appealing to a citizen merely concerned with tomorrow's meal.

Toris spread his thirty-three contraband documents across the vendor's table. The young man looked unimpressed, even turning to his henchman nearby with eyebrows raised in amusement.

"Scholars will pay a high price for these," Toris said.

"Ain't nothing a scholar got that my bosses want," the man said, pointing to the four-pointed star tattoo under his right eye. "People are starving. It's bandits and farming folk we need to trade with, not wordsmiths."

Toris spilled the sack of silver coins onto the table. Those pieces raised the vendor's eyebrows. He grabbed a few to study their markings. "Decimator currency," he said to himself in awe. He counted them out and then scribbled his offer on a scrap of paper.

"More," Toris said.

The vendor shrugged. "What else you got?"

Toris gave Drua an annoyed look, then nodded for him to place the explosive blocks on the table.

The vendor whistled. He crumpled his previous offer and said, "My friend, you just doubled your score."

He scribbled a new list and handed it to Toris.

Considering the inflated prices, the *Barnacle* expedition could have done worse than the thirty pounds of dried venison, twelve bags of rice, six crates of canned beans, and a sack of green apples to sweeten the deal. But that didn't make the deal any less sour for Toris, so when the vendor turned his back to mark which of his inventory to take, Toris snatched a tin with an oatmeal raisin cookie from a shelf and slid it into his tunic.

"Going to draw a lot of attention to yourselves with all this," the vendor said, eyeing up the marked product. He whistled to summon two strapping lads in bloody butcher aprons from a curtained area in the back. "They'll make sure you and your food get to the docks."

One of the lads flicked out a baton and charged the stinger at its tip.

Toris nodded, satisfied that should deter a crowd.

"I need one more thing."

Finding a rifle required venturing below to the subterranean storerooms, where the angry bickering of the mob faded to a distant mumble. At a room no larger than a mop closet, an arms dealer showed Toris a small rifle that wasn't suited for killing anything bigger than a rabbit.

"A group came in yesterday and bought up all the good pieces," the dealer said. "Must be expecting the need for them soon, and I don't think it'll be out on the high sea, if you catch my meaning."

Bandits, Toris thought.

His choices were between the .22 caliber rifle and a revolver. But the vendor wanted twice as much for the pistol, and seemed pressed as it was to accept Sallus's documents even for the rifle. Luckily the material promised a good read to academics. Hard copy reports describing the Decimation were unheard of, and this guy knew it.

Toris held the rifle butt to his shoulder and stared dubiously down the barrel. He knew nothing of firearms, but this piece didn't appear as if it packed much of a punch. He lowered the rifle and felt the ring in his pocket. Sallus's heirloom would be enough for the better weapon.

"We only need something to scare off pyrates," Drua reminded him. "If it makes a bang then it should do."

The vendor snatched the rifle from Toris, aimed at the brick wall, and pulled the trigger. A deafening crack forced him to cover his ears. With ringing running deep into his head, Toris gave a satisfied nod, glad he didn't have to consider trading Sallus's ring any further.

He accepted the rifle from the dealer, then hung it across his back by its sling and followed Drua back up top.

In a courtyard behind the warehouse, they piled their food onto a wooden cart under the watch of the vendor's two security escorts.

Drua bent over to pick up a crate of beans. "Hopefully Antlia has that refrigeration unit installed by now," he said. "Wouldn't want to give our competition too big of a head start." He slammed the crate onto the wooden deck. "We'll do some target practice once we're underway."

Toris grunted and flopped a sack of rice onto the cart.

"Need some help?"

The girl's voice had come from behind and almost stopped Toris's heart dead. He turned to see Rykah standing in the court-yard exit wearing her black ceremonial uniform.

"We're fine, ma'am," Drua said, then he flopped a sack of rice onto the cart.

Rykah approached with both hands behind her back. She nodded to the rifle slung over Toris's shoulder. "Nice peashooter."

Toris gripped the sling strap. "They reserve the finer weapons for those who require more help in hitting their targets."

Rykah drew nervous stares from Drua and the security escort as she circled the wagon.

"If that's the standard they're using, then I assume you're the country's finest marksman." She cocked her head toward Drua. "Who's your friend?"

"I'm Drua, ma'am." He seemed to restrain his arm from springing up in a salute.

She gave a curt nod. "Hello, Drua. I hope you've not made any plans with my Toris here. I need him for some urgent business."

Drua's expression was a mix of confusion and betrayal. Perhaps Toris should have told him he wasn't supposed to be on the mainland. That he'd been banished into exile a second time and that they may encounter the need to execute a creative escape. Well, it was too late for that now.

Toris cleared his throat to loosen up for the lie. "I'm just going to help him bring these supplies to the marina. I can meet you somewhere when I'm done. Just name the place."

A sly smile stretched across Rykah's face. "I think I've waited long enough to make my offer."

"Offer?" Toris said, bending over to pick up the sack of apples.

That seemed too liberal a term to describe a proposal from someone of her authority to an Onero of his status.

"We have a mission going to Svalbard," Rykah said. "A colleague of mine would like to see you on it."

Toris was tossing the apples onto the cart when the words forced him to stop midswing. He cradled the sack and studied Rykah for signs of mischief, but her impassable expression suggested she was serious. Which made sense if this were a ploy to lure him onto a patrol vessel and have him shipped to Mintaka. She'd have him hanged if not for the likelihood that she hadn't reported her own mishap of losing him.

"It's a military operation," he said, setting the apples onto the cart. "I'm not allowed to join."

"I'm referring to a different expedition."

Crouching to pick up a crate of beans, Toris kept his eyes on Rykah. Did she actually think he'd fall for this? "I've signed on with another crew already." *With the promise of a second citizenship reward should we succeed,* he thought with a fluttering heart.

Rykah lifted her chin. "Yes, I've seen your *Barnacle*. Fit for scraping crustaceans from the seabed is all I reckon she's good for. Our *Polaris* is a combat-grade vessel. Which do you think has a better chance at reaching the vault?"

Drua dropped a sack of rice, his face twisted in frustration. "You heard him. He already signed on with me, so piss off."

Rykah pulled a pair of handcuffs from behind her back. "I was only saying *offer* to be generous. I'm not leaving without him."

The two butchers extended their batons and encircled Rykah. Faint buzzing threatened crippling shocks from the charging stinger tips.

Drua stepped in front of Toris. "If you were smart, you'd walk away right now."

"Funny," Rykah said as she began unbuttoning her coat, "I was about to say the same to you." She hung her black coat on the cart. "This can go one of two ways," Rykah said, rolling up her blue shirt sleeves. "Option one: You step aside and release Toris into my custody. Option two: I put you to sleep and take Toris into my custody. Both roads lead to the same place, only one is much, much rougher."

Drua smirked. He nodded to the two butchers and said, "Go easy on her, boys."

The first butcher stabbed his stinger at Rykah's chest. She side-stepped and grabbed the boy's wrist, then twisted the baton free and jammed the butt end into his face. Blood cascaded from his nose as he stumbled back in shock.

His partner lunged at Rykah from behind, thrusting his stinger at her back. She spun and batted it away with the shaft of her first opponent's baton, then caught the assailing boy's face with a backswing.

Toris stepped back as Drua rushed to join the fight. Drua grabbed Rykah before she could spin to face him. One arm wrapped around her chest while the other slid under her chin for a chokehold. He arched backwards, lifting Rykah so that her feet barely touched the ground.

With the toes of her boots, Rykah guided Drua to spin toward Toris. Once within kicking distance of the cart, she raised both knees to her chest and pressed her feet to the nearest wheel, then pushed back with all her might.

Drua stumbled backward over the first butcher and crashed onto his back. On the ground, Rykah spun out of his choke and rose to a knee, from where she delivered an open palm strike to his solar plexus. He groaned and curled into the fetal position on his side.

Rykah stood and walked toward Toris with amused fury in her eyes.

He unslung his rifle and pointed it nervously at her, hoping to give her pause, but she didn't break step at all. In one smooth movement, she grabbed both barrel and stock and spun the weapon from Toris so that he found himself staring down the muzzle.

Frightened, he stumbled back and fell onto his behind.

Rykah worked the bolt back and forth to unload the weapon. Brass rounds clinked off the ground. When the last one bounced off her boot, she removed the bolt and tossed it to her left, then the rifle to her right.

Footsteps scuffed off the ground behind. In half a blink, Rykah ducked and let Drua's fist glide free through the air, then grabbed his arm and used his momentum to flip him over her shoulder. She rolled forward with him, keeping his arm in both hands, and ended on her back with his arm between her thighs. He groaned as she pulled his wrist tight against her chest and thrust her hips up into his elbow.

Drua's eyes rattled around in panic as his arm bent up in the wrong direction.

Toris jumped to his feet. "Stop!"

Rykah looked to him. "Only one way for that to happen."

"I'll come with you."

Without second thought, Rykah released Drua's arm and rolled backward to her feet. She grabbed her coat from the cart and slipped her arms into its sleeves. "Let's go," she said. "We've already wasted enough time playing around."

Toris looked to the two boys on the ground, their heads rolling in a state of altered consciousness. Rykah considered this 'playing around'?

He offered Drua a hand and helped him to his feet. Once standing, Drua hugged him close and whispered in his ear. "Slip away first chance you get. I'll keep Antlia docked till you're back."

Toris felt cold steel snap shut around his wrist. He looked down to see one cuff on his arm, and a short chain linking him to the other cuff around Rykah's.

"Sorry to spoil the moment," she said, "but we need to make some miles."

As she led him into the forest, Toris looked back at his cart full of food. He'd be damned if he was letting all that go to Svalbard without him.

TEN

Jayda stumbled down a muddy road that separated two long rows of modular tents. As she rounded a corner to leave the main boulevard, she tripped over a pile of pots. The clamour echoed loud in the fog, made worse by her frustrated kicking that launched a frying pan into a tree stump.

A soldier squatted beside the remnants of a fire peeling a potato in the drizzle. "Watch where you're goin," he said.

Jayda hissed at him and plodded on through the mud to the secondary tent row. She pulled her shirt collar up to shield from the cold wind. The high altitude at the entrance to the Ardis Valley was always muddy and misty, and her uniform constantly damp. Despite the Borien Mountains being within throwing distance, Jayda rarely saw their peaks. But better this than the snow that accompanied the six-month night here.

She pulled open a tent flap and stuck her head inside. The stench of unbathed bodies forced her to retreat back into the fresh air. Maybe the rain wasn't so bad. The droopy eyes of the two soldiers inside told her they lacked what she was looking for anyway.

She carried on down past a half dozen tents before finding one empty. Packs under the cots suggested the squad hadn't gone on patrol. Most likely they were on sentry duty in the towers.

Jayda slipped inside and rummaged through their gear in search of *khat*. She'd been without for too long now. Between message deliveries and waiting around command posts, she'd barely managed an hour's sleep in the last two days. She sifted through cutlery, plates, moldy bread and somewhat dry socks in search of the precious plant that would make her fatigue a silly memory.

"Whatcha lookin' for?"

Jayda shot upright and jumped back from the bag.

Two men entered the tent. A short stalky man shuffled in first, followed by his lanky friend, who took a last look outside before sealing the tent flap shut. They leaned their rifles against the canvas wall.

"I asked you a question," said the stalky man, who smelled so bad of onions Jayda's eyes watered.

"*Khat*," Jayda said in as cool a voice she could muster. "You got any?"

The stalky man looked back to his partner, who stood two heads over him. "Hear that, Finn?" said the shorter man. "She's looking for a buzz. Think we can help her out?"

Finn reached into his shirt and withdrew a bundle of leaves. Black and yellow teeth flashed as he extended his hand toward Jayda. "Come on, now. Don't be shy. Ya weren't when ya came snoopin' through these lads' gear."

Jayda stepped back against the cooking table at the far end of the tent. Though these men offered her what she wanted, she wasn't willing to pay their price.

"I think she's scared of us, Orly," said Finn.

Orly's mouth twisted in disappointment. "Watch the door," he said to Finn, then marched toward Jayda.

Jayda's hands skimmed the cookware on the table behind her as Orly closed the distance between them. She grabbed the handle of a frying pan and swung wide and hard at her aggressor's face.

Orly's meaty hand caught her wrist midswing. Sausage fingers squeezed tight, drawing tears to Jayda's eyes as the pan fell to the ground. She swung her free hand with two fingers extended, hoping to find his eyes. That hand also came under Orly's control.

"Runner!" cried a distant voice.

Jayda jerked up, struggling to twist her arms free. "That's me. They'll come looking if I don't report."

"They won't think to look for you in here," said Orly. He licked his lips and leaned in.

Jayda kneed the fat man in the groin. He grunted and dropped to his side, but he pulled Jayda down with him. Finn left the door and pulled her back into a headlock. Jayda sank her teeth into his hand, biting with all her might despite Finn's howling. Orly crawled over and assisted his partner by pinning her to the damp ground. Each man placed a knee on her arm while Orly stifled her screams with his monstrous hand, which covered her nose as well. Her arms tingled and numbed under their weight, but the hand over her nose and mouth was the real worry. A few more seconds of struggle and she'd suffocate.

Baroooom! A horn blew loud and long from outside.

Orly and Finn straightened to listen. Another blast echoed loud and long. Orly's eyes filled with fear as his hand slid away from Jayda's mouth. Outside the tent, men shouted as rifle bolts clicked in a metallic cacophony.

The horn blew a third and final time, confirming everyone's fear.

Finn and Orly retrieved their rifles at the door and fled the tent without a rearward glance. Jayda followed them outside, gasping for breath and shaking like a leaf, and joined a river of soldiers that flowed from the tents toward the gap in the mountains.

Near the end of the tent lines loomed a tower of stone overlooking the trenches. Beside its base, soldiers funnelled into the trenches that stretched across the entire entrance to the Ardis Valley. Towers stood at one kilometer intervals, where sentries monitored the forested valley that cut through the mountains to Ortaria.

Jayda descended the slope into the rear trench. She bounced among the frantic bodies making their way through the communication trench to the forward line, where officers shouted orders to organize their troops. Only the towers were manned unless the enemy was reported in the area. Though every time so far had been a drill, the soldiers responded with steadfast devotion, as any stragglers would be introduced to the whipping post.

Soldiers lined up on the firestep as far down the trench as could be seen in either direction. Those with rifles aimed over the parapets at the forest beyond the barbwire. The influx of fresh conscripts had far exceeded the army's firearm supply, leaving every second soldier unarmed. Middle-class citizens from across the country flocked to factories to help increase munitions production, but it would be a while before troops at the front got to hold them.

Jayda shuffled down the line in search of Dogwood Company commander. She found Captain Sameris speaking with a soldier who wore a camouflage pattern uniform that, oddly enough, made her stand out among the olive drab line of soldiers in the trench. The captain noticed Jayda approach and said to the girl, "Here she comes."

The girl looked to Jayda and said, "You're a hard lassie to find. I'm Ivy."

Ivy's long brown hair tucked tight under a maroon beret and the hint of the orient in her eyes contrasted the black *II* inked onto her neck. And Jayda had never seen her style of uniform here at the border.

"What do you want with me?" Jayda said. The girl was only a corporal and deserved no pleasantries from her.

"Don't shoot!" cried a voice from beyond the barbwire.

Captain Sameris looked over the parapet and shouted, "Black!"

"Swan," came a rattled reply from the haze.

A soldier emerged from the fog in front of Dogwood Company's rifles. He ignored the narrow fence opening and squeezed between the horizontal rows of high-tensile barbwire, leaving shreds of his uniform behind, and plunged into the trench.

Sameris dragged him to his feet. "What's going on?"

The soldier, a man of mid-twenties, shook and sputtered: "They got 'em."

"Who?"

Jayda assessed the soldier with disdain. Of course the dregs would attack something so pitiful. Some did not deserve to wear the uniform.

Faint crying crept through the fog. The officer and soldier stopped to listen as the whining grew louder. Jayda's spine shivered.

"We were separated from our patrol."

"What's his name?" Captain Sameris said.

"Aster."

Jayda's heart squeezed tight like a fist. *Aster*? No, it must be a different one. Her Aster was a recent conscript, who wore Blue Brigade patches and was training far from here in the Borien Foothills. The troops here were Red Brigade regulars—Onero veterans and criminal conscripts.

The soldier sobbed. "He couldn't keep up and we got lost. I told him about the trip wire but he…"

"See any dregs?" Sameris asked.

The soldier shook his head.

The crying persisted, becoming louder, eventually squealing like a wailing child.

Jayda rubbed away her tears. The whining undeniably belonged to her Onero brother from Mintaka. He'd squealed like that when the Coast Patrol rounded them up.

Jayda hopped onto the firestep and jumped up the trench wall, clawing for purchase at the sandbag parapet above.

Ivy grabbed her belt and threw her back against the bulkheads.

"Let me go!" Jayda said, scrambling to her feet.

"You want to be crying next to him?" Ivy said.

Jayda stared up into the white abyss, where Ortarian warriors moved about like ghosts—unheard and unseen. The *Bloody Ribbon* on the far side of the field offered archers concealed positions to use their longbows. If Aster wasn't so loud someone could make it to him, but now every enemy was surely watching, listening, waiting.

Jayda's belly wound into knots. "I want him to stop."

Ivy closed her eyes and pressed her forehead to her rifle stock, muttering words under her breath. She then aimed over the parapet.

Jayda watched curiously as Ivy wrapped the sling around her forearm to pull the rifle butt into her shoulder, then realized what the girl was doing. "No!" She grabbed Ivy's webbing and hauled back with all her might.

Ivy steadied herself and offered Jayda a sympathetic look. "It's worse to leave him like this."

Jayda clasped Ivy's webbing, knowing to let go meant signing Aster's death permit. Yet…there was reason to this girl's madness. Aster was suffering miserably.

Jayda looked to the surrounding soldiers. "Give me your *dazies.*"

The soldiers watched her curiously as they pulled the syringes from their wound kits.

Sameris shook her head. "I won't allow it."

"What would you want done if it were you lying there, ma'am?"

"A bullet in the head," Ivy said, "five minutes ago."

"Can you guarantee to do that your first shot, aiming with only your ears?"

Ivy stared into the fog and tensed her shoulders.

Even in ideal conditions a fatal shot was never a sure thing, so Jayda gathered the dazies. She stood back and prepared to run at the trench wall.

Ivy grabbed her, then handed over her dazy. "We'll cover you."

Jayda climbed over the top with a boost from Ivy. She rattled through the barbwire fence and slid onto her belly, where she paused and stared into the white nothingness before her. Was a dreg drawing back a bowstring at this moment? Had that last meal of powdered eggs been her last? Could they smell her fear?

She pushed these crippling thoughts aside and slithered over the wet grass toward Aster's relentless cries, wishing she could sink lower into the ground.

Tall black sentinels took shape in the fog ahead, rising high toward the sky. Rumour claimed there stood a tree for every dead Polarian in this strip of forest that covered the valley between here and Ortaria.

Just beyond the first trees lay a panting lump. As Jayda crawled closer she noticed a red pyramid sprouting from Aster's belly. Blood glistened on the sharpened wood and pooled in the fleshy moat about its base.

Jayda looked away and retched, morbidly aware of her own delicate innards. Aster's cries rattled the cage where her last sliver of innocence remained, threatening to veil the rest in darkness. But the time for lamenting had passed. They couldn't stay here any longer.

"Aster, it's Jayda. I'm gonna get you out of here."

She crouched at his feet, her toes meeting the heels of his boots, and grabbed his wrists. "It'll be just like *rolling*. Remember, back at Lake Orion? Let's go… Upsy-daisy." She hauled on his arms, leaning back with all her weight. All this got from him was a petrifying scream without getting him anywhere off the ground. Though he'd lost much weight since Mintaka, she couldn't handle him alone. Yet a cry for help would summon danger first.

Aster stared at the sky, paying her no mind as he screeched.

She pulled the cap from a dazy and jammed it into his thigh. A minute passed but the crying persisted, so she did another…and then another. But still the crying prevailed, clawing away at what strength she'd managed to hold onto.

With eyes swelling with tears and a lump ballooning in her

throat, she removed all remaining caps and hit him at once to flood his body with opium.

Within seconds the force of his wailing began to fade, until finally there was only his shallow breathing.

Jayda glanced over her shoulder, toward the line, to make sure she could find her way back to Dogwood Company through the fog. A trail of matted grass showed her the way.

"Mommy?" Aster whispered.

Jayda looked at his face, but his eyes were closed. She grabbed his hand. "It's me, Aster. It's Jayda. You know, from Mintaka."

"Mommy, what was that noise?" His voice was shallow and eerily apathetic.

Jayda squeezed his hand and said, "It's Jay—" She stopped as he frowned to make sense of her words. "It was nothing," she said. "Go to sleep now."

"Okay." The word barely escaped his lips. His breathing stopped, but his grip remained tight.

Jayda stared at his face, her body trembling, waiting.

Nothing happened.

She kissed her fingers and pressed them to his lips. "Death is naught," she whispered, her voice cracking. And just like that, Aster's fight was over.

Suddenly Jayda felt very alone. Why *was* she alone? Where were the heroes like those from the stories they always told in Polarian History class? Where were the brave men tripping over each other to carry this wounded boy back to safety? This was two children lying alone in front of a trench full of men afraid of the fog. This was not how wars were supposed to be fought.

She turned around and crawled back to the line, eager to escape the lonesome fog and its appetite for children's souls.

At the parapet Ivy dragged her over the sandbags and into the trench. "Are you all right?"

Jayda nodded.

"That was very brave what you did," Ivy said. "The stars shine bright upon such deeds."

The nearby soldiers nodded their respect.

Jayda's eyes fell on Aster's partner and her stillness flashed to a boil. Her hands tightened into fists and she attacked. The boy curled as Jayda rained down punches, her rage building at his persistent cowardice. "You left him to die alone, you…you fucking coward!"

Arms wrapped around Jayda, hauling her back as she kicked and punched at the air. She needed to bust him open and leave him like he left Aster.

Ivy dragged her out of the sight of the soldiers and wrapped her arms tight around Jayda until Jayda's rage spilled over in tears. She sank to the ground with Ivy kneeling beside her, one arm across her shoulders. Jayda felt the air suck from her lungs. She took massive breaths to keep herself from passing out due to hyperventilation. Though, why bother? Worse than leaving Aster in pain, she'd taken his life. What made her think she deserved another breath? "I killed him," she wheezed.

"You ended his suffering."

Logically, Ivy's words made sense, but they provided little comfort, and the tears kept coming, flooding down her cheeks. She buried her face into Ivy's chest to muffle her sobbing and wheezing. She allowed herself this, because no amount of logic would ever convince her that she hadn't just murdered her friend and brother-by-law.

ELEVEN

The squawking of seagulls and the smell of fish had long since faded when Rykah removed the cuffs.

Toris rubbed his wrist and followed her obediently through the forest. So long as she was leading him away from Port Abersali, it was a good sign she wasn't playing him. Plus, it gave him time to read her movements to plot his escape. Her impressive hand-to-hand combat display warned that any move against her should be done with utmost care. And she knew where he'd end up going. Best to give Drua time to unload their supplies and ensure *Barnacle* was ready to set out when he arrived.

The forest thinned out to an orchard. Every tree had been picked clean, without even a rotten apple on the ground.

Toris slowly fell behind to test Rykah's tolerance, to see how far she'd let him lag behind. To know what kind of head start he'd have.

He watched her stride purposely between neat rows of bare trees, looking very out of place in her ceremonial uniform. Much of what she'd told him didn't add up. Whoever wanted him on the expedition seemed to have gone through a lot of trouble by sending Rykah, who in turn seemed willing to put half the town into a coma to get him on board.

"Who wants me on their crew so bad?" he asked.

"The less you know right now, the better. Come, try to keep up."

Across the orchard, a wall of maple trees marked the return to forest. Just past the tree line, in a small glade, Rykah crouched and dug her fingers into the ground. She grabbed hold of something beneath the dead leaves and dirt, then lifted to reveal the rotted bottom of an old door that had been covering a hole in the ground. She flopped the door over onto the ground, then pulled a canvas duffel from the hole.

From the pack she fished out pieces of a wooden rifle and mixed-pattern combat clothes. The rifle was similar in style to the one Toris had purchased at the black market, but larger. Rykah pulled off her knee-high officer's boots, then, as if Toris were not there, dropped her black trousers and kicked them away.

Toris turned to give her privacy as she slid into camouflage trousers. A few seconds later, he heard metal clicking and sliding and turned to see Rykah assembling the bolt-action rifle. In the brief time he'd been looking away, she managed to don the trousers and jungle boots, lacing each boot up from toes to shin, and placed strapped webbing over her shoulders. He'd never seen a soldier in combat attire before, but the olive tank top covering her torso seemed a casual addition to the ensemble of black and green camo stripes, which gave her more the appearance of a hunter or survival enthusiast. From a pouch in her webbing she pulled a stack of brass rounds—five held together by a clip—and slid it into the rifle.

Toris's heart raced. These rifle rounds were much larger than those that had come with his 'peashooter', and would surely put a swift end to his escape. Though, she likely wouldn't use it if he was needed on the expedition. That's what he told himself, anyway.

She slung the rifle over her shoulder and flopped a boonie hat onto her head to complete the ensemble.

"Stuff that uniform into the bag and put it back in the hole," she said, adjusting her webbing straps.

Toris obeyed, eyeing her rifle nervously. Though, more intimidating than the firearm was the blue half-moon Ranger patch stitched to her pack, which meant she'd be hard to lose in these woods.

She handed him her ruck and helped him slide his arms through the straps. It sank heavy onto his shoulders until Rykah fastened the belt, then secured the buckle with a padlock.

Toris tested the lock and gave Rykah a questioning look.

"It'll be harder for you to run off with that on your back," she explained.

He nodded to her rifle. "You take me for a fool?"

"Given your track record, I'm not taking any chances."

She nodded for him to follow her deeper into the forest. Though there was no path, Rykah's determined march suggested confidence in her direction. Toris kept pace beside her, occasionally hiking up his shendyt to negotiate the steeper slopes.

"The Artican must really like you to have dressed you in those nice new rags," Rykah said.

Toris smoothed the jet-black tunic over his belly. This new attire made his old clothes look grey by comparison.

"They don't want anyone to forget who I am," he said.

"They don't want anyone to forget *what* you are. *Who* you are is what you decide for yourself." She draped her rifle stock over her shoulder and chewed a strand of grass. "They call me a criminal, but that is not who I am. I'm simply a girl who once found herself in a less than ideal situation. They can label *what* I am all they want, but it does not change *who* I decide to be. That label can be written only by me, and it's the only one that matters."

Such insight for a criminal conscript. Toris eyed the black *V* inked to the side of her pale neck. "I didn't think your type were allowed away from the borderlands."

"My type?"

Toris's face and neck burned. He'd chosen the wrong choice of words, it seemed. But he didn't have time to worry about offending someone when his sister could be trying on the uniform she may die in.

Rykah cracked a smile. "Were you always so serious, Toris Onero? My *type* are very good at tracking people. Usually that skill is required at the border, but now Polaria has a problem with draft dodgers and deserters. Many citizens and Oneros aren't as enthusiastic about wearing the uniform as *my type*."

Toris shifted the shoulder straps. "How did you earn the honour of serving Polaria at the border?"

"You mean how did I get this mark on my neck? I was a poacher. That was back when we had the luxury of being picky with what we ate."

Toris thought he had it bad, but serving time for a crime that was recently legalized must be a briny water to drink. "How much more service do you have?"

Rykah shrugged. "Indefinitely. But if this war starts, the danger will shorten our sentences."

"You seem to consider that a fair deal." Toris couldn't imagine not knowing the length of his Onero service. The promise of one day paying off his debt was what kept him in line.

"It's the only deal they offered me," Rykah said.

Finally, Toris Onero had met someone as unlucky as him.

Rykah led him diagonally up a long slope, farther inland. Which didn't make sense for this pair going to Svalbard.

"Where is the expedition ship?" Toris asked, feigning interest.

"Our embarkation camp is away from prying eyes. We'll soon receive a special arms delivery to deal with foreign threats."

Toris slowed his pace at the mention of two words that didn't belong together. "Foreign threats?"

Rykah shifted her rifle to her other shoulder. "For years the Coast Patrol has reported contact with seafarers of non-Anterran origin. Never anything threatening, but it tells us there's something out there.

Toris stopped dead. Non-Anterrans? Could anyone have

survived out on the decimated lands this long? The idea seemed impossible until he thought about it. Everything Polarians knew about the old world came from The Artican, who never had much reason to convince Polarians there was anything out there worth seeing. If another civilization survived across the great sea, then so could Oneros seeking a new life free of service to the state.

The next sign of civilization since leaving Port Abersali was an abandoned sheep farm. Across a pasture overrun by weeds and grass stood a house whose roof was sunken and wooden barn walls slanted at a near forty-five degree angle. Only the house's stone walls remained as intended by its builders, but they were covered in moss and lichen.

Toris dropped to his knees at the collapsed fence. The farther from Abersali they marched, the harder it would be to escape Rykah. He had to make a stand somewhere.

Rykah turned back to watch him curiously.

"The heat," he said. "I need out of the sun for a bit. Haven't gotten much sleep lately."

Rykah looked to the sun as if to confirm it was indeed there.

"Wait here," she said.

Toris leaned against a wooden fence post while Rykah did a quick sweep of the buildings. Croaking frogs and twittering birds put him at ease, and he could have fallen asleep right there. It'd been so long since he'd been this removed from civilization, so long since he experienced such serenity on solid ground.

"Come," Rykah said, waving from the doorway, "we'll rest here for a bit."

Inside the house, streams of sunlight penetrated the living area through slits between boards that covered the windows. Thick cobwebs rounded out every corner of the concave roof.

Rykah unlocked Toris's waist strap and lifted the rucksack from his back. The cool air on his sweaty skin sent a shiver through him.

Rykah leaned her rifle beside the front doorway and unrolled a sleeping pad against the wall under the adjacent window. She nodded for the other roll beside the ruck. "You have two hours. Then there's no stopping, so make the best of it."

Toris yawned and tried to act casual as he spread his bedroll beside the opposite wall. By the time he set up, Rykah had pulled a rolled raincoat under her head and was lying on her side facing the wall.

Toris lay on his back staring at the ceiling. He placed an arm over his eyes and pretended to sleep, occasionally releasing faint snoring sounds.

How long could Drua delay Antlia when the slips at Finn's Marina emptied one by one, the departure of each expedition vessel chipping away at *Barnacle*'s chances of finding the vault first?

Faint whistling came with each fall of Rykah's chest, indicating she was asleep.

Toris rolled off his mat and crawled across the dusty floor, watching her at each noise made from his crawling. She remained sleeping when he reached touching distance, so he stood and grabbed her rifle. Standing over her, feeling the firearm's smooth wood and the might of its loaded bullets, all her martial arts skills couldn't stop him if she tried.

He stepped outside into the sunlight. Without the weight of the pack, he'd make it back to port in a few hours. Considering Toris had provisioned the *Barnacle*, Captain Antlia shouldn't have required too much convincing to delay his departure by a day. And this trip with Rykah into the wild wasn't for naught. Judging by the size of the rounds in her rifle, he'd have more success scaring off foreign threats than with his black market 'peashooter'.

TWELVE

Toris stopped at a rickety fence that separated the yard from the pasture. Down the line, perched upon a corner post, a falcon watched his every move.

He pulled Rykah's rifle butt to his shoulder and watched the bird over the barrel. The falcon stared at him, twitching its head side to side, indifferent. Toris feathered the trigger, contemplating. He squinted to bring the bird into focus. Border soldiers claimed that Ortarians communicated with animals like this falcon to use as spies, so they shot them all. Would he be able to shoot a person he suspected as a threat?

"Does the bird frighten you that much?" said Rykah from behind.

Startled, Toris swung around and aimed at her.

She stood in the farmhouse doorway, hands on her hips and head cocked at the sight of Toris aiming her own rifle at her.

He lowered the weapon, but not all the way. Rykah approached across the grass, undaunted.

Wings flapped from the fence post. Toris turned to watch the falcon take flight.

Rykah yanked the rifle from his grip. She slid the bolt back to expose the empty chamber.

Toris hung his head in disappointment. He hadn't even thought to ensure the weapon was still loaded.

"Think you could have hit it?" Rykah pulled a clip of five rounds from her pocket and shoved it into the rifle housing, then pushed the bolt forward.

"I can hit a shark with a speargun at one hundred meters," Toris said. He'd meant to say 'fifty', but his pride had let 'a hundred' slip.

Much to his surprise, Rykah handed him the rifle. "A shark is a pretty big target and a speargun lacks a kick." She followed the dilapidated fence line toward the corner post, stopped to pick up a clear mason jar, then placed the glass piece on the stump where, seconds ago, the falcon had rested. She stepped back. "Let's see how you do with a recoil weapon against a small target."

Toris aimed at the clear bottle over the barrel, its glass a prism of colors in the sunlight, and pulled the trigger—*CRACK!* The butt punched his shoulder and sent him wobbling backward. Half a mile behind the jar, a tree branch fell to the ground. He sensed his face burn red as he lowered the weapon.

Rykah folded her arms and gave a nod. "Again."

"I'm not one to waste. You might need these bullets out in the old world."

"You'll save ammo in the long run by learning to shoot. Now, again."

Toris slid the bolt back, ejecting the casing, then returned it to the forward position. Reluctantly, he raised the rifle and pulled off another shot. The round disappeared into the forest, leaving the jar and the trees beyond unscathed.

Rykah jumped onto the bottom fence rail behind him. "Aim again," she said, watching over his shoulder. Toris obeyed. "Don't hold your breath," she coached. "Breathe normal. Lower your elbows a bit." As his finger touched the trigger she placed a hand gently on his shoulder. "Don't pull the trigger - *squeeze* it."

He fired and missed.

"Better," she said. "Once more. Easier on the trigger, nice and slow. Steady your breathing."

Toris took a few deep breaths to settle his frustration. Then, following Rykah's advice, he eased pressure on the trigger, squeezing slow and steady with the rise and fall of his breathing.

Crack! The rifle kicked back as the bottle shattered, and with it his frustration.

Rykah jumped down from the fence behind. "The one round you have left is better than those three lodged in the trees out there."

She pulled the rifle from him and leaned it against the fence, then perched on the only top rail that had held its place over the years. "With more practice, you'll be able to kill any frightening bird that may accost you."

"Or 'foreign threat'."

"Does that possibility frighten you?"

For some reason, the thought of encountering foreigners actually excited Toris. Perhaps it was his obsession with the old world, and his desire for it to be more than just ancient words and radiation, that had sparked his enthusiasm for the mission. He was doing this for Jayda, of course, but when Rosaria had told him of the privateer permits, a burning desire beyond helping his sister had sparked in him. But he couldn't let anyone know that.

He folded his arms and leaned against the fence. "I fear anything that may come between me and the seed vault. This whole idea was to save my sister. That's all."

"You don't care about curing the famine?"

"We do well enough on Mintaka. So, no, I'd not be going if not for her."

Rykah frowned at him. "You'd just abandon your country-folk?"

"I owe them no loyalties."

"Yet you risked your life to give them hope."

Toris hugged himself tighter. "I didn't do it for them. I did it for my sister and they took her from me anyway. Why should I risk more for them?"

"Because you can." Rykah looked down at her feet. "I was in Sol-Brae not long ago. Saw starvation drive citizen folk to rise against the soldiers taking their food, and saw those soldiers gun them down. Those people don't deserve what's happening to them."

"You don't know that."

Rykah shot him a bewildered look.

Toris's cheeks and neck burned. He stepped away from the fence and stared off at the trees. Though, he couldn't let those dark words hang in the air without an explanation.

"They killed my mother," he said.

He felt Rykah's stare prickling the hairs on the back of his neck. He kept his gaze away, in case an unflattering emotion managed to slip through his defences.

"She was a member of Dardaria's envoy at the Peace Talks," he said. "Her esteemed position promised a bright future for our family. Then she allowed one of those savages to seduce her. She went to bed with him and betrayed her country." His voice was shaking now. "A civilian may have gotten away with it, but she was a military officer. Highborn, yes, but bound by oath. They hanged her for treason after my birth...in Sol-Brae's central square." He clenched his fists. "She swayed from that rope until her bones came undone."

Toris never blamed the citizens of Sol-Brae for his mother's death. She owned all of that herself. But to leave her like that, denying her funeral rites, was unforgivable.

He went on: "My father was killed leading an attack on Fort Cypress. I'm the son of both an oathbreaker and a fool." That part he'd meant to leave out, and the mention of it with such emotion was exactly what he'd meant to avoid.

Rykah slid down from the fence. "Your mother—"

"Was weak," Toris said, eyes snapping back to meet hers briefly before looking away. "But even so, everyone deserves their rites."

"What was her family name?"

"I'm not allowed to say it."

Rykah placed a hand on his shoulder. "I won't tell."

Toris checked his surroundings, then said, "Centaurus."

Her hand tightened. "A strong bloodline."

Toris lowered his head. "Once upon a time. It takes only one disgraceful act to dishonour the loyal service of every ancestor who came before you."

Rykah's hand slid to the back of his neck. Her soft skin soothed his surging torment as her forehead pressed into his shoulder. "No disgrace accompanies an act inspired by love," she said softly. "You are the result of the strongest energy from the stars. What your parents died for was the greatest of even that."

Toris turned and stared at her incredulously. Did she actually believe that, or was she just being nice? No. Most likely she was messing with him. Trying to gain his trust for some forthcoming betrayal.

When Rykah's hand fell free from his shoulder, Toris noticed the absence of an heirloom. "What's your astral name?" he asked her.

Instinctively, she spread her fingers before her face. "They introduced me as Rykah Adarah at my sentencing," she said, "so that's what I've gone by ever since." She balled her hands into fists and crossed them under her armpits. "Last names are less used where I'm from. People are more concerned with the name you make for yourself than with the actions of your ancestors."

"Where is it you're from?" Toris said, guessing the paces it would take to reach her rifle with its one remaining bullet. "I'll try to end up there in my next life."

"Sahali, way up in the Borien highlands. We trade with the Ortarians there."

Toris recoiled. "What?"

Rykah smirked. "Surprised? Imaginary lines don't keep people apart—prejudices do. Your parents knew that better than anyone."

Rykah grabbed her rifle and reloaded it. "Borders are a means used to preserve the Great Lie."

"The Great Lie?"

"That we're all different—Oneros, Polarians, Ortarians, high-borns and the lower class. Maggots in the ground don't care what blood pumped through your veins when you were alive. Nor do the flames of a funeral pyre."

Something behind Toris caught Rykah's eye. "We've got company," she said.

At the edge of the pasture, a dozen soldiers in mixed-pattern camouflage stepped out from the tree line in an extended line. As they approached the farmhouse, Rykah set her rifle at her feet and backed away. She swallowed hard, and if Toris didn't know any better he'd think she was nervous.

The soldiers covered the distance between them on high alert, their rifles at the ready. A soldier with grey hair and weathered skin led the pack from the middle. "Sergeant Sarx," he said to Rykah, hands gripping his webbing straps. "Third Ranger Battalion."

Rykah nodded. "Lieutenant Adarah - First Rangers."

Sarx cocked his head. "I hear even our side of the border is too far from the enemy for your unit. So what's a First Ranger doing so far inland? And on her own, sort of."

The patrol surrounded Toris and Rykah, assessing them questioningly. A few aimed their rifles at Rykah as she reached into her pocket, so she raised her other hand to calm them. She withdrew a folded letter and handed it to the sergeant.

Sarx snatched the paper and read it once, then again. He rubbed his chin, deliberating, then nodded to his men. They lowered their weapons. Sarx gestured toward the farmhouse. To his Rangers, he said, "Set up an operation post inside."

Rykah seemed to relax, her shoulders sagging. She picked up her rifle. "What brings your unit here?" she asked Sarx.

"Deserters—the murderous kind," Sarx said absently as he

checked a map. "They fled the border and raided Arrington's food stores. Killed two Omniguard who tried to stop them."

Rykah shifted uneasily. "You think they made it this far?"

Sarx sauntered toward the house. Rykah followed.

"A group of well-armed bandits hit another food vault in Khartum," Sarx said. "We believe they're on their way to Port Abersali to unload their bounty on the black market or find passage to Arokya."

"There's no road through here," Rykah pointed out. "Surely they'll be laden down with all that food."

Sarx stopped in the farmhouse doorway. "This is just my headquarters. I have two teams in town picking up our tracker hounds. The bandits didn't leave much in Arrington, but someone got sloppy in the Khartum raid." He held up a clear bag that contained a green scarf. "Once those dogs get here, we'll not be long finding them. You should stay with us until they're caught."

Rykah gave Toris a grave look, then to Sarx said, "Thank you for the offer, Sergeant, but we're needed elsewhere. We must be moving on."

Toris watched Rykah curiously as she gathered her gear from the living area. When she exited the house and marched toward a gap in the fence, he followed. This time she carried the rucksack.

Toris caught up to her. "What are you doing? You heard what he said—*bandits*."

"Inland Rangers are authorized to execute deserters," Rykah said. "And *exiles*. Best we put a lot of distance between us and them before they ask too many questions about you."

Toris looked back at the farmhouse. What if the hounds led the patrol to him accidentally?

He hurried to keep pace with Rykah.

In the forest, she stopped and shoved a hand against his chest. "I know you were going to run back there," she said, glancing back toward the farmhouse. "Our mission has no room for even a single half-heart, so I'll give you this one chance. You can turn around and head back to Port Abersali right now and I won't stop you. Or, you can come with me. The choice is yours. But if you're with me, it's from here until the end."

Toris didn't need much time to consider his options. This all came down to Jayda. Considering Rykah had already bested Drua, she was his best chance at securing the Accolade and setting his sister free.

Rykah offered her hand. "Well? Are you with me till the end?"

Toris grabbed her hand and squeezed. "I am."

"You're what?"

"I'm with you," he said.

"Till when?"

"Till the end."

Rykah gave him a satisfied nod and then set off in long strides with her rifle at the ready. But Toris could no longer follow her blindly.

"Who sent you to recruit me?"

"Ignatius Arcturus," Rykah said without hesitation.

Toris paused as Rykah trudged up a slope. He'd never heard of this Ignatius before, but the last name left little to the imagination. He ran to catch up.

"The Chancellor's son?"

"That's right."

Toris frowned as he tried to make sense of this. The Chancellor wanted Toris back in civil service on Mintaka, so why would his son go against that order?

"Why does he want me on the expedition?"

Rykah shrugged. "He didn't enlighten me on his motives."

Toris slowed his pace, watching the ground while he sorted the reasons swirling in his head. Did Ignatius expect him to bestow his reward onto Lex so they'd make her a Sage? Would the council even grant a Sagehood if she didn't earn it herself? Maybe this Ignatius thought Toris would go through with it in exchange for using his influence in the military to secure Jayda a safe posting in Fort Cypress. If that's what he believed, he was in for a disappointment.

Rykah stopped on the slope above. "Having doubts?"

"You know I have plans for my reward. My duty is to my sister and getting her out of uniform."

Rykah gave him a quizzical look, then nodded in understanding. "You don't know. Well, this expedition is military, with all members under orders to participate. Even our sponsor is active Defence Force. That disqualifies all of us from claiming the Accolade. Their reward will be medals and honourable discharges, with maybe a few First-Class appointments thrown in there. However, if there's a civilian among the group that returns with the seeds, well, that will qualify him for the Accolade. That means—"

"First-Class Citizenship and one million credits," Toris said in awe.

Rykah nodded. "*Especially* if that civilian happens to be the person who revealed the vault's existence in the first place. May even make you a Sage for that one. Imagine that." She punched his shoulder playfully. "Better not forget me when you're steering Polaria's future."

But this clarification only confirmed Toris's suspicions. Why would Ignatius Arcturus want Toris Onero to win the Accolade? To use on his sister, of course. Well, at least the Chancellor would give Toris the Accolade over Lex. It was a marriage that AnaXagoras had arranged that Ignatius was trying to help Lex dissolve. Should Ignatius apply pressure on Toris to bestow the Accolade on Lex, Toris could count on the Chancellor to take his side.

He continued after Rykah. The difference between joining Drua and going along with the military expedition was an extra First-Class Citizenship, assuming Drua kept his word, but The Artican's expedition had a much higher chance at cutting through pyrates and was surely better provisioned. He wouldn't even object if they raided a Polarian privateer returning south with the seeds. And in the end, there was no guarantee that Drua would give up his reward anyway. With a million credits to his name, Toris could pay off his Onero debt and become a rich third-class citizen.

He offered to carry Rykah's pack and, even with the extra weight on his shoulders, he followed her with a bounce in his step.

They stopped at a creek and surveyed its steep bank sloping down to the water. A steeper bank rose up from the other side. It didn't look like there was a way across without getting wet up to their waists, so Toris removed his shendyt and rolled it into a ball to hold above his head.

Beside him, Rykah straightened suddenly. She turned her ear toward the direction they'd just come from, then looked to Toris with eyes wide in alarm.

"Time to run," she said.

Toris opened his mouth to ask for elaboration, but the sound of barking dogs cut him off.

Through the trees behind, an extended line of soldiers led by two dogs raced toward their position.

Toris's heart slammed against the inside of his chest. When he looked back to Rykah, she was already sloshing across the creek below.

He slid down the bank into the rushing water. Fighting the current flowing against his left side, he forced his legs across the creek to the opposite bank. As he scrambled up the slope, an avalanche of loose dirt slid from under his feet, stalling his progress. He joined Rykah at the top as a Ranger led by a barking German Shepherd skidded to a halt on the opposite bank.

Each bark sent a pulse of terror through Toris. Had the Rangers figured out who he was?

"For Sage's sake, Rykah. Why are they after us?"

"Keep your head down and follow me," she said, then turned to lead him into the forest. Toris followed.

Pop! A tree branch overhead snapped free.

Toris sprawled for cover across tangled roots and dirt.

On the opposite bank, a dozen Rangers had arrived and were descending to the creek. The two dog handlers cradled their Shepherds for the waist-high crossing.

Toris sprang to his feet and bolted after Rykah.

"We know who you are!" called one of the pursuers.

"You're good as dog food now!" threatened another.

Toris recognized one of the voices from his orphanry and stopped behind an oak tree. "Wait," he called to Rykah, wrapping his shendyt around his waist.

She turned and waved. "Come on!"

"I know one of them. Just explain to them that we're on the expedition."

"Does it sound like they wanna talk? That wasn't a fucking warning shot they fired."

Crack! Bark exploded from a nearby oak.

With great reluctance, Toris left the cover of the tree and broke into a crouched run after Rykah. He stayed low until the forest opened up to a meadow, where he stood tall to lengthen his strides across the open field.

More gunshots from behind—*Pop! Crack!* Puffs of dirt exploded from a hill ahead.

Rykah led the charge into the trees and up that steep hill as the Rangers fired more rounds, these smacking trees in frightening proximity.

Toris stopped on the hillcrest to better assess his pursuers. Rykah could take out most of them from right here, but the expedition would not accept the killing of Polarian soldiers who were following orders. He turned and followed her down the opposite slope.

Thick brush rose midway up the slope. Toris crashed through without slowing, and within a few steps, bullets rained down from the Rangers who'd taken possession of the hill. Luckily, the bushes remained thick for as far as Toris could see, and it was evident the soldiers had lost sight of him and were firing blindly.

He caught up to Rykah at the base of a hill a half mile away. As they raced up the slope, the firing stopped and the crashing of feet over the forest floor signified the continued pursuit.

They ran for hours, scrambling over hills and splashing across brooks, skirting lakes and even hitting the Trillium Trail at one point. At all times the howls of the dogs haunted the two 'deserters', driving them forward.

"It's those damn dogs," Toris wheezed as he struggled to keep up to Rykah. How much longer could he maintain this pace? "Just shoot them already."

Rykah ignored him and disappeared into a ragged wall of dogwood, its low skirt of branches immediately swallowing her. Toris put his arms up and head down, then crashed in behind her, plowing and stumbling through branches for a good fifty feet until he burst clear. He fell to his knees in the opening but crawled to his feet and charged ahead without looking.

Rykah snagged his arm and hauled him back.

The sight of a chasm a few feet ahead sent him tripping backward onto his bottom, where he watched the opposite edge that loomed three hundred feet away. A fast-flowing river rushed hundreds of meters below. Toris looked up and down but saw no bridge or means of crossing.

Rykah pulled him to his feet and shoved her rifle against his chest. "Cover me," she said, then scurried along the tree line while frantically searching the underbrush.

Toris watched her in terror, the smooth wood of her rifle slick in his sweaty hands. What was she doing? *Cover me,* she'd said. Did she expect him to use the rifle on the Rangers?

She stopped at a large cedar and crawled into the shrubs around its base.

Barking rose over the rush of the river. They were close.

Toris strained to see through the thick brush and saw shaking branches. He flicked off the rifle's safety catch. The *click* was almost surreal as he prepared to make his last stand.

Leaves rustled as Rykah stumbled out of the shrubs holding a grey rope. The end was tied to the cedar trunk beside her and ran over the bank down toward the river. Upon closer inspection, Toris noticed the slack line crossed the chasm to the opposite bank. When Rykah hauled on the rope he saw the far end anchored to a tree on the opposite bank. She pulled up the slack, raising the rope from the chasm below. When the line stretched straight across at chest level, Rykah wrapped the slack around the cedar and hitched it back to the taut rope. She handed Toris a revolver and grabbed her rifle back.

"I'll go first," she said, then she jumped atop the tightrope. Belly down and with one leg dangling, she pulled herself forward, inching her way across the chasm.

The barking grew louder, closer. Toris thought he heard branches cracking a few feet away. Bushes rustled nearby. Or was it in his mind? He aimed anyway, his finger on the pistol trigger. How many shots did he have? But that was getting ahead of himself. Could he even pull the trigger? Could he shoot one of his own countrymen?

Yes. He had no choice.

Yelling startled him, but from where?

Behind.

He turned to see Rykah waving from across the river.

Toris stuffed the pistol into the back of his waistband and grabbed the rope, displaying less grace than Rykah in mounting it. It took four tries to steady himself on the line without falling over. Then, hand over hand, he pulled himself forward. As he passed the edge of the chasm he lost his balance and flipped over. He kept both legs wrapped around the rope and his hands clamped tight. Rykah's coaching was faint and indiscernible as the water rushed below and dropped off three hundred metres away. Unable to right himself, he pulled himself hand over hand across the rope upside down.

Crack! A bullet whizzed just wide of Toris's head.

He hugged the rope tighter, pulling himself close as if it offered cover. He stole a glance and saw Sarx standing on the bank. The sergeant slung his rifle and drew a bayonet, then put blade to rope and began sawing. Toris felt the vibrations as his lifeline grew thinner with each stroke.

A gunshot rang out from the opposite bank, where Rykah knelt firing. Dirt kicked up at Sarx's feet and splintered the trunk behind him. Though her shots seemed deliberately missed, they succeeded in sending the Ranger sergeant diving for cover.

Fuelled by adrenaline, Toris resumed crossing the chasm, one hand over the other as gunfire popped from both sides. The firefight became one-sided when the patrol arrived in full and their volley of bullets drove Rykah to seek cover behind a tree.

The shuddering of the rope alerted Toris that Sarx had resumed cutting.

Then he was falling.

He closed his eyes and squeezed the rope with all his might, too frightened to cry out as he fell at an inconceivable speed.

His free fall ended with a slam against the vertical dirt face of the opposite bank. The rope stretched tight above him and disappeared over the cliff edge twenty feet over his head. Puffs of dirt exploded from the bank to his left and right. One bullet struck dangerously close to the rope above him.

He dug his feet into the sloped dirt wall and climbed the rope until he crested the cliff edge. A frantic scramble brought him to the cover of a cedar tree as bullets chipped away at its trunk.

Rykah was reloading her rifle with her back to the adjacent tree. "You okay?" she said.

Toris patted himself over. When his search turned up no blood, he laughed nervously. Then the rope hanging slack from Rykah's tree incited in him riotous laughter. Sarx had unknowingly helped his prey escape.

Wasting no time, Rykah jumped to her feet and ran away from the gorge. Eager to leave the Rangers behind, Toris followed while shaking the tightness from his arms.

Though the chasm presented a challenge for the dogs crossing, he swore he heard barking drawing closer, so he ran on ahead of Rykah.

THIRTEEN

An hour after crossing the chasm, the forest ahead became a staggered row of trees standing before silvery water under a grey sky. Toris had smelled the salty air long before the sea came into view, but to see it so close inspired a sigh of relief.

"Camp is just up ahead," Rykah said.

Toris nodded absently. Ever since seeing those soldiers in combat uniforms chasing him, he couldn't stop thinking of Jayda. Was she wearing the same uniform now, learning to track Ortarians at the border? Or worse, were Rangers chasing her through the forest while she made a run for the coast?

Toris's belly clenched at the thought. Jayda was definitely the type to try her luck. If only he could get word to her, to let her know he didn't abandon her. That he'd never stop trying to see her again. Even if this seed vault thing didn't pan out, he'd go to the border himself to track her down. After going to the opposite end of the Earth for the vault, that didn't seem such a grand task. Nor as perilous. But no, that was the wrong way to think. He had to get to that vault, and it didn't matter who with.

Knocking echoed through woods and grew louder with each step Toris took down toward the sea. At a stone's throw from the water's edge, a lad of his age appeared between the trees swinging an axe. The blade sank deep into a wedge in a felled log and busted it apart. Red suspenders hung down in loops from the waist of his baggy green trousers. An *O* brand on his deltoid marked him as an Onero brother, but the wide brim of his black hat prevented a look at his face to confirm if this were a mate from Toris's home orphanry.

"Private Atilus," Rykah said. "I said you could cut wood for cooking fires—not enough to build a ship."

Atilus flipped the front brim of his hat and squinted at Rykah and Toris in their approach. Though shorter and leaner than Toris, his flattened nose and cauliflower ears suggested he'd never let his size keep him from squaring off with the big boys in his orphanry.

"Just keeping busy, ma'am." Atilus stood the axe on its head and pulled his red suspenders over his bare shoulders, then grabbed a black assault rifle and strolled out to meet them. Seeing Toris's shoulder brand with its diagonal slash, his eyes lit up. "It's really you—the half-blood."

Toris rolled his eyes. "Am I a household name where you're from?"

"No, but the troops in my unit were soiling themselves when your discovery forced the Defence Force to recruit a security team for the Svalbard mission. Probably made yourself a few enemies on that crew, I'd say." He offered his hand. "Atilus Onero. Grew up in Newfield Orphanry, just outside Khartum."

Toris gave Atilus a nod, but kept his hands to himself as he followed Rykah toward the shore. Unphased by the cold reception, Atilus settled for a squeeze of Toris's shoulder and tagged behind.

"Heard you were doing your service as a shipmaker," Atilus said. "I used to jack lumber in Cardero. Ever been to Cardero? Got redwoods there that used to take me a whole day to climb, and two days to get back down. That's till I got transferred to defence service." He scooted up beside Toris, eyes drifting up to admire the tree canopy above. "Man, those trees could grow. You use redwoods for your shipbuilding? Maybe you can show me a bit of the trade when we get back home. We'll be free men then. *If we* find the vault, of course. And assuming the seeds are still there. Think we'll come across pyrates?"

Toris gave his new companion a sidelong glance. If this were the kind of chatter he'd need to endure all the way to Svalbard, the odds of them both returning to Polaria without one going overboard were slim.

"This is it," Rykah said.

Atilus's rambling faded into the background as Toris scanned the disembarkation point. When Rykah had told him of the camp, he'd envisioned a seaside town taken over by the Defence Force with wooden crates stacked on a stone dock, food and ammunition surrounded by a fence and under the guard of a special operations troop. Instead, he saw log seats in a semicircle before a hillside cave entrance. Two ragged parachutes hung overhead for shade and reminded Toris of Lex's refuge on Mintaka, not the camp of Polaria's best chance at finding the Svalbard seeds. And instead of an organized unit of soldiers, he saw a brunette girl stooped on a log sharpening a battle axe, and two lads of early twenties wrestling within the confines of a rope perimeter strung around four birch trunks.

The mix-matched styles of fatigues hanging around the camp suggested the members of this team came from a variety of units.

"Atilus," Rykah said, "go fetch *Polaris*. Tell Skipper Domlyn we're underway within the hour."

Underway. That word plucked at Toris's nerves. Yet more than fear, he felt excitement vibrate to his fingertips and toes. Within an hour he'd be embarking on the adventure of a lifetime.

Atilus dashed off beyond the camp and disappeared into the forest.

"Jarik, Nazar," she said to the two boys sparring in the makeshift ring, "pack it up. It's time."

The soldiers hurried to pull down the parachutes.

Toris resisted the urge to grab Rykah by the shoulders to shake some answers from her. Hopefully this was merely an auxiliary section off the main camp. Atilus *was* running off to another part of the forest to fetch the ship in what Toris assumed to be the official embarkation point.

The brunette girl stood from her log seat and slid the axe into her belt. "About time you showed up," she said to Rykah. "Was gonna send a search party for ya."

"Has our special delivery arrived yet?" Rykah said, marching on past.

"Already loaded onto the ship."

She let Rykah pass, but stepped in front of Toris to block his way. She stood toe-to-toe with him and smiled wide, flashing a top row of filed teeth. "You're prettier than I was expecting," she said, then slid her tongue across the sharpened points of her hideous smile.

"Hands to yourself, Varcy," Rykah said as she pulled a shirt from a line hanging outside the cave entrance. "Or you'll get that lechery charge you've been working on."

Varcy's smile levelled. She stepped aside to let Toris pass. "Was only playing, Mama."

Toris followed Rykah to a patch of black coals within the semi-circle of log benches, watching this conspicuous behaviour with much confusion.

"How many are on this mission?" he asked.

Rykah rolled her shirt tight and stuffed it into her rucksack. "Besides us? The two men running the ship." To Toris's confused stare, she said, "You may have noticed that food is a bit scarce these days, so we have to run a lean crew. Still doing better than *Barnacle*, though, don't you think?"

She ducked into the cave, and Toris hurried after her. In the dim slit of sunlight cutting through the dark, Rykah struck a match and lit a candle. The flickering glow illuminated a desk and chair in an alcove to the left of the cave entrance, but this out of place furniture held his attention only briefly until something else drew his eye.

At the back of the cave, chunks of charred wood lay in a pile with bits of white canvas. Toris recognized the burned remains as potato crates and rice sacks. Though such provisions were expected, the black stamps on a wood strip which read '*Khartum Food Co-op*' sparked a disturbing revelation.

A silhouette appeared in the cave entrance. "They're on their way, Lieutenant."

Rykah pulled the desk out from the wall. "Go gather your belongings, Atilus."

Chair legs scraped as she sat to sort through a stack of papers. She tossed some to the floor and rolled others, which she slid into a chart tube.

Crouching for a closer inspection, Toris saw the faded black letters on the rice bags spelled '*Arrington*'. He stood with the rough canvas in hand, feeling the melted black edges where the fire had failed to completely destroy the evidence.

"You're the bandits," he said. His voice seemed to echo out across the forest, the accusation loud for all to hear.

Rykah's eyes flicked up from the page in her hands, but only briefly. "The raids were supposed to be a quick in and out," she explained. "I gave explicit orders that no one was to be harmed. When two Omniguard officers decided to be heroes, well…shots were fired."

Toris stormed over to Rykah's desk and slammed his hands down on her stack of papers—maps and charts of the old world. Wooden legs groaned under his weight.

Rykah leaned back in her chair and met his glare. "I wasn't there, Toris, but I'll find out who did the killing." She extended an arm toward the cave entrance. "But for right now, we can't be too picky with our crew."

"Why did you have to steal from civilians in the first place?"

Rykah spread her arms in resignation. "They weren't going to just *give* a crew of deserters the food for our mission."

Toris stood straight and stepped back, watching Rykah's impassive expression in the candlelight. "What do you mean, *deserters*?"

Rykah sighed and pinched the bridge of her nose. "I thought

you'd have figured it out by now."

"You said this is a military expedition."

"It is. We're military, and we're going on an expedition."

Toris shook his head in disbelief. "You deserted."

"Don't think of it like that. Think of it more as… a self-imposed leave of absence."

Seeing Toris's fist clench at his sides, she stood and nodded for him to follow her out into the sunlight. Outside, the four soldiers stopped folding the last parachute and watched her as if anticipating an address.

She pointed to the Onero in red suspenders. "You already met Atilus," Rykah said, and he waved with a smile. "Three weeks ago, his unit was ordered to raid civilian homes in Sol-Brae for scrap food to send to troops at the border. When a citizen resisted and injured a soldier, the officers ordered him shot, so Atilus dropped his rifle and ran."

Atilus's smile tightened to a frown as his eyes drifted to the ground.

"His trial was slotted for last week," Rykah said. "Major Arcturus ensured a mix-up during his transfer between brigs, so that he ended up here instead."

She then pointed to a hulk of a lad. A mat of blond hair crowning the stubble of his close-cropped temples had the sheen of a golden crown, with his ponytail in the back forming a spike. "Nazar's unit is currently training to parachute from hot air balloons into Ortaria to raid their harvest, an act that will certainly lead to full-blown war."

"Which will be fine by me," Nazar said, hefting up his assault rifle.

"What about Jarik's twin girls in Sol-Brae, Nazar?" Rykah said. "They live mighty close to the border."

The brute lowered his weapon and gave her a haughty glare.

"Nazar was kind enough to relinquish his rights to father one child so that his confidante here, Jarik, could keep both his daughters without giving one up to National Service."

Toris assessed the pair of men. A few surplus children in Toris's orphanry had ended up as Oneros by being the twin whom the parents had chosen to give up as surplus and doom to Onero Status. Sometimes a close friend or family member could relinquish their right to bear a child as a favour to the family, but Jarik looked nothing like Nazar with his black buzz-cut hair and bushy mustache.

"You already met Varcy," Rykah went on. The brunette with filed teeth gave Toris a two-finger salute. "She served under me at the border," Rykah said. "Our Ranger unit just slipped into Ortaria in search of valuable hostages to ransom for seeds. When she heard of our mission, she took her leave with me."

"Took leave?" Toris scoffed, furious he'd been duped into joining this rogue mission, and even more so that Rykah was still talking as if they were legitimate.

"Everyone here is from a family of brothers and sisters preparing to kick in our neighbour's front door for a short-term solution," Rykah said. "We all know our skills are better used in finding that seed vault. And each of us, in a way, is here under orders."

"The Chancellor's son," Toris said, trying to understand why of all the Defence Force, he'd chosen this lot.

"Ignatius, yes. Though he's not in our chain of command, Major Arcturus's position gives him exclusive access to resources most officers have never even heard of. Which reminds me."

Rykah pulled a letter from her pocket, a dab of purple wax still holding the fold closed. She peeled open the seal.

"A letter from our sponsor." Rykah cleared her throat. *'Honorable crew of* Polaris, *I, more than anyone, know the perils you boldly face when embarking on this mission, and for your acceptance of this duty I offer my sincerest gratitude. Each of you has been handpicked, either by merit or by circumstance, to partake in this endeavour. If you succeed, you will be absolved of all debts and charges. With this absolute pardon, a clean start awaits you all.*

"By now you should have a civilian among you, and though he does

not wear the uniform like the rest of you, you shall in every respect treat him as a brother in arms.

"It is with sincerest regret that I cannot be there to see you off, but duty beckons me elsewhere. I wish you a speedy journey, as the Artican's flagship, the Sea Serpent, *is scheduled to depart from Pandora Island on the fifth day of January.*

"Yours in arms, Major Ignatius Arcturus."

Rykah folded the letter with great care and slid it into her breast pocket.

"What day is it today?" Jarik asked.

"Thirtieth of December," Rykah said. "Line your gear up on the shore. *Polaris* will be here shortly."

The small expedition team clapped and patted each other's backs, obviously relieved to hear their sponsor had come through on a black hole promise *and* that they were getting a week head start on their biggest competition—the military expedition aboard the *Sea Serpent.*

As the team arranged their rucksacks and webbing, Toris sized up each of them to determine who had killed the Omniguard officers during the food raid in Arrington. On appearance alone, every one of them looked suspect.

Whoever had given the *Polaris* her name had grand delusions about the vessel. With one main deck and a raised wheelhouse that stood at one third the length back from the prow, she was a glorified swamp boat.

Atilus whistled as the ship maneuvered fifty feet from shore. "Some beauty out on the open water. How big you think she is?"

"Eighty-seven feet," Toris said. Guessing sea vessel lengths was a knack that came with his trade. As was evaluating seaworthiness. From here, *Polaris* didn't promise smooth passage in a small storm, let alone the raging turmoil of Drake's Wrath.

Rykah emerged from the cave with her rucksack sitting high

over her shoulders. She carried the chart tube in one hand, her rifle in the other.

Nazar blocked her way and pointed to Toris. "Did he run the mill?"

Rykah paused, her eyes meeting Toris's and her cheeks flushing slightly.

"I bet she's had a few tumbles with him on the way here," Varcy said with a suggestive wink.

Nazar theatrically held his ruck above his head and let it drop at his feet. "Doesn't count if we didn't see it," the brute said.

Rykah straightened. "He's ship's crew. He doesn't need to pass any soldier rites."

"Major Arcturus's letter said we're to treat him like a brother in arms," Nazar reminded. "In *every* respect." He offered a bayonet by its covered blade to Rykah. "If we see action out there, we need to know what everyone aboard is capable of."

Rykah gave Toris an apologetic shrug. She set her ruck on the ground, then placed her rifle and chart tube on top. "An old Defence Force tradition," she explained, accepting the bayonet from Nazar. "To encourage the continuous improvement of the enlisted soldier's skills, officers frequently challenge their troops in close quarters combat. Each circuit is timed. The longer it takes to pass each test, the lower a soldier's score." She twirled the blade between her fingers, testing its balance. "Squad ranks are rearranged according to each member's placement. Whoever sits at the bottom gets the undesirable assignments—both the dirty and the dangerous."

"Like latrine duty," Nazar said, folding his arms with a taunting smile.

"Or radiation testing out in the old world," Atilus said nervously.

Rykah held the seventeen-inch bayonet above her head. "Your first test is to seize this weapon from me." She shoved the sheathed blade into her belt at her lower back. "If you do that in satisfactory time, you'll move on to the next test."

"Bayonet fighting to see who draws first blood," Nazar said with a devious grin.

Toris's heart raced. He'd witnessed the ease of Rykah's defeat of Drua—a Defence Force veteran and Lake Orion's toughest bully—along with the two security goons back in Abersali. "Hardly seems fair to test someone without training," he pointed out.

"No training, true, but out there you'll face the same perils as us," Rykah said, now seeming more convinced of Nazar's push to conduct the test. "All you have to do is beat Atilus's score."

Atilus folded his arms and gave Toris a reassuring nod. "I did really bad."

Rykah held both arms behind her back and stood with her feet shoulder-width apart. "Time starts when your first foot moves."

Jarik held up a pocket watch. Rykah nodded for Toris to advance.

Toris stepped up to Rykah. Face-to-face, he wrapped his arms around her waist and seized each wrist to pull them away from the bayonet handle. His back hit the ground before he realized his feet were off it.

Rykah hovered over him as he struggled for air. "Did you really think I'd just let you take it?" she said, walking a circle around him. "An officer's rank remains firm against these trials, but our reputation..." To Jarik, she said, "Restart the time."

Jarik frowned. "Ma'am, that's not how—"

"Do it," she said, then flung the bayonet to the ground behind her. "All you have to do is get through me and it's yours. You can still beat Atilus's time."

Toris crawled to his feet and charged forward. His size and momentum would easily mow her over.

But Rykah had a different plan for his perceived advantages. She crouched just before he crashed into her, wrapped her arms about his waist, and spun around using all her weight and his to send him stumbling back to where he'd started. Toris staggered and regained his footing.

A sly smile pushed up Rykah's cheeks. "Did you not have to fight over the newest toys and the fluffiest pillows in your orphanry?"

Toris huffed and rushed again, this time looking to bear hug and plow her to the ground, hopefully landing with the bayonet within his reach. Instead, this landed him in a standing guillotine choke. The crook of her elbow cinched tight around his neck, cutting off his breathing and causing black spots to blossom across his vision.

He tapped her ribs.

Her hold loosened and she shoved him back. "Release your pride and see me as your equal," she said, pacing around the bayonet. "The biggest weakness of Polarian soldiers at the border is believing Ortarian weapons are no match for our rifles. But firearms are loud and bring much attention. Arrows are silent, and a warrior who swings two axes against a bayonet fixed to an unloaded rifle always holds the upper hand. When you see your opponent as equal you will not underestimate their abilities. But be careful not to give them more than their due, or your wavering confidence will bolster their own."

Toris approached Rykah with more caution, but it didn't matter. His third attempt ended worse, seeing him on his back with his arm in the vice between Rykah's legs and his wrist firmly in her grasp, her hips pushing up into his elbow as she'd done to Drua. Surely she'd have popped it had he not cried out.

Rykah released Toris's arm and retrieved the bayonet from the grass, then handed it back to Nazar.

Toris looked to Jarik, who double-checked his watch and shook his head. "Congratulations, Atilus," said Jarik. "You're no longer the crew canary."

Atilus bowed in relief.

Jarik and Nazar hefted their rucks and sauntered down to the shore. They waded into the water toward *Polaris*, where the crew was lowering a cargo net from her bow.

Toris glared at Rykah as he crawled to his feet. She'd told him to see her as an equal. A difficult feat, imagining an expertly trained opponent such as her as an equal. He sat on a log and flexed his elbow to soften the tension.

Rykah sat beside him with her canteen and took a drink, then offered it to him. "Sorry about that," she said. "Some traditions never die, no matter how archaic."

"Did you learn to fight like that in Ranger school?" he said.

She wiped the water from her lip. "In my labour camp, they set out only enough food to feed half the girls. Every day was fight or starve. The longer *you* go without and *them* with, the greater the divide becomes until you have no choice but to wither away." Sad eyes stared off into the distance.

"How old were you?" Toris said.

"Eleven."

Toris felt his heart melt to mush. Suddenly his childhood in the orphanry didn't seem so bad. "What happened to your parents? How are you not an Onero?"

Rykah watched Nazar and Jarik climb the cargo net hanging from *Polaris'* bow. "Never knew my mother," she said. "Papa and me lived off the land in the mountains till he died. I just carried on doing the only thing I knew how until they caught me smoking a deer at our cabin. Papa taught me to never take more than I needed, and I never did. Not once." Her voice choked and her eyes glazed. "Think those who locked me up can say the same?"

Toris grabbed her hand.

She stood and shook her head. "I'm not one who deserves your sympathy. Come," she said.

Raaap—a sound like tearing fabric had Toris on his feet, heart racing. He followed Rykah's stare to a ball of red light shooting straight above the treetops. A trip flare.

"It seems we've overstayed our welcome," she said.

She quickly gathered her gear and waded out into the water behind Atilus, her rifle held above her head and Toris almost on top of her.

FOURTEEN

Sergeant Sarx and ten of his Rangers arrived on shore to see the expedition off. When a few aimed their rifles at the deserters aboard *Polaris*, Toris's belly hit the wooden foredeck at the same time as his crewmates taking cover behind armoured plates fixed to the handrails. Fresh welds at the seams indicated the vessel had recently been outfitted with such defence means, and that this was not actually a 'combat grade' cruiser, as Rykah had claimed back in Abersali.

Gunfire crackled from the shore, peppering the plates before Toris's face and rattling his nerves. He stayed low as the bow swung clockwise to face the long grey peninsula. The deck trembled as growling engines propelled the *Polaris* forward.

Gunfire faded and tapered until the revving hydrogen motors blocked out all sounds of attack.

"We're out of range," Rykah said, jumping to her feet first. Then, as if forgetting there was a volley of bullets just trying to blow her head off, she slung her rucksack over one shoulder and picked up her rifle.

"They really scraped the bottom of the barrel putting together this lot," crackled a man's voice.

From the wheelhouse overlooking the foredeck, *Polaris'* captain assessed his crew with a shake of the head. Whether his disapproval was mock or genuine, Toris could not tell. Patches of the man's auburn hair and beard were worn gray, and the faded blue ink covering his arms suggested his weathered skin had seen a good many summers on the sea.

Nazar smiled up at the captain. "Speak for yourself, Dommy. Heard they found you in a hole nursing a bunch of rats."

"That's *Captain Domlyn* to you, boy."

"*Skipper*," Rykah corrected, a stern finger wagging at Domlyn as she carried her ruck to the rear deck. "The Coast Patrol stripped your rank when they caught you smuggling, remember?"

"Yeah, well, I'll be keeping my eye on you lot," Domlyn said. "Especially you, half-blood. You don't touch anything on this ship unless I tell you. Don't need your cursed hands breaking this already delicate vessel."

Toris ignored the jab. Old mariners had been talking to him like that since he arrived in exile to start his shipwright apprenticeship.

As he'd learned to do with any vessel he boarded, Toris took a good look at the ship that would take him to the other end of the world. Her fresh paint job and new name didn't fool him. Corrosion had long ago claimed its place on the ship like mold on bread, which rose like bubbles under the black paint and gave the overall finish a tarry appearance. Below, the rattling engines suggested the ship's problems ran deep into her heart.

But none of that mattered with the deck rocking and shifting beneath him. In fact, the sea breeze in his hair blew every doubt and fear to the back of his mind. They were actually doing it. He was going where no Anterran had gone in seven hundred years and he actually had a chance at winning the Accolade—the first Onero in Polarian history.

His heart fluttered.

He followed Rykah below decks and through the lower passageway as she inspected the berths. Varcy, Nazar, Jarik, and Atilus had crowded into a midship cabin and were jostling for who got which hammock in the tight room.

"Domlyn's wife had a taste for wine that exceeded his Coast Patrol salary," Rykah explained as she wavered up the passageway toward the front of the ship. "Just so happened that every few months, his ship was assigned to escort grape shipments from Arokya to the mainland. No one knows how long his skimming operation went on for before they caught him, but he'd been rotting in a cell for over five years when Ignatius found him."

She stopped at the forward V-berth. Her team had left her the larger quarters at the bow, where only two hammocks swayed. She dropped her ruck onto the floor and sniffed at the rising dust cloud, then nodded for Toris to take the free hammock.

"*Polaris*, she's called?" Toris said, noting the rust-streaked bulkheads. "Should have named her the *Rusty Raider*. Or the *Musty Maiden*."

"*Rusty Raider* has a nice ring to it," Rykah said, kneeling to unfasten the straps holding shut her ruck. "Did your apprenticeship involve courses in ship-naming?"

"No." Toris folded his arms and leaned back against the bulkhead. "Guess I'm just a natural."

As Rykah pulled a shirt from her ruck, a fuzzy ball of brown cloth fell onto the floor. Toris picked up the stuffed rabbit and smiled. He didn't peg Rykah as a collector of children's toys.

"Better hope the Skipper doesn't discover you hiding a stowaway," Toris said.

When Rykah noticed him holding the stuffed animal, she shot to her feet and snatched it away. "Don't touch him," she snapped. Then she stuffed the rabbit back into her pack.

Toris held up both hands in surrender. "Understood."

"There should be a bag somewhere on board with more suitable clothes for you," she said, closing up her pack. "Let's go ask the skipper where he put it."

He followed Rykah to her crew's berth, where Varcy lay in her hammock with her fingers interlocked behind her head. The three boys must have returned above, as they were nowhere in sight.

"Get some rest while you can," Rykah told Varcy. "Once we

pass the peninsula tip, we'll join the bridge watch to give the ship crew some rest. Pass the word on to the gents."

"Aye," said Varcy. "When do we get to see the new toys?"

"Keep the guns hidden until we pass Point Bay Station. Don't need to be raising Coast Patrol eyebrows."

Rykah continued down the passageway, but Toris grabbed her arm, a new doubt gripping him. All vessels were required to stop at Point Bay Station at the peninsula tip for inspection and to register their departure. "You have illegal weapons aboard? What if the inspection team finds them?"

Rykah frowned at his hand gripping her arm. "You needn't worry about that," she said, jerking her arm free of his hold. "We have a pass."

Toris gave her an incredulous look. "A pass?"

At the end of the passageway, behind the stairs leading above decks, a door squeaked open. The humming engines rose to a roar as a red-haired lad of about thirty years stepped out, then faded again as he pulled the door shut. With the palest skin Toris had ever seen, it was a wonder how he managed to remain unburnt on the sea. Perhaps by spending a lot of time hiding away with the engines.

Rykah bounded up the stairs before Toris could press her about the inspection pass.

The sailor extended a hand to Toris in greeting. When he saw his own arm covered in grease from elbow to fingertips, he withdrew. "I'm Ike - marine engineering extraordinaire."

Toris gave Ike's shoulder a friendly squeeze. "Toris. I hope you know how to keep this tiger growling."

Ike looked over his shoulder at the engine room door. "You should've seen this baby when they dragged her from the scrap bay." He held up both hands and wiggled his fingers. "They call me the Ship Witch, because these hands whisper spells to hydrogen engines."

Toris smiled and hoped the Ship Witch wasn't overestimating his abilities. "How'd you end up paired with the likes of our gracious skipper?"

"Popped out of his wife twenty-nine years ago," Ike said with a proud smile. "He's been stuck with me ever since."

It took Toris a moment to catch his meaning. "He's your father."

"I know, he's a grouch. But..." Ike shoved open the engine room door, exposing two massive engines. Over the roaring, he said, "By the time I was ten, he made sure I could strip one of these with my eyes closed and put it all back together faster than with a blueprint. Coast Patrol had me on active duty before my fourteenth birthday. Served for ten years until... well, they discovered our family's side business."

"Let's hope you don't have to prove your skills anytime soon."

Ike assessed the nearest engine with a skeptical frown. "She's got some wear and tear, no doubt, but there's not much that can go wrong with her that I can't fix. Anyway, don't judge the old skipper too harsh off first impression. Five years in a dark hole would dull anyone's people skills."

"I'm sure I've met worse," Toris said, though he'd be lying if he said he wouldn't prefer the *Barnacle*'s Captain Antlia at the helm.

Toris excused himself to follow Rykah above. He squinted in the sunlight as he took the stairs to the main deck. Above, Rykah was climbing the steep staircase to the back of the wheelhouse. As he made to follow, Atilus grabbed his arm and dragged him around to the foredeck, where Jarik and Nazar leaned over the starboard rail to watch the water breaking at their bow.

The engines rumbled louder, driving the eighty-seven foot reject vessel away from the forested mainland and toward the long grey mountain chain of the peninsula to their right, which stretched out to the horizon like a bottom row of jagged teeth.

Toris stood at the bowsprit. With hands clamping the damp steel rail, and the sea wind blowing his hair, he smiled wide. He'd never been aboard a proper motorized ship before. With propellers spinning below, building the underwater pressure that shot them forward... It was all genius. He marvelled at their speed and at how quickly *Polaris* was devouring the distance between them and the peninsula.

With a clear route ahead, Skipper Domlyn shouted his first order to the crew from above. "Deploy the kite!"

A minute later, Ike lugged a large steel cylinder across the foredeck and set it down at the prow. In the light of day, his mess of curly red hair sat atop a high forehead shaped by his receding hairline.

Toris rubbed his hands together excitedly. Work as a shipwright had taught him that winds at higher altitudes provided abundantly more towing power than winds at surface level. Not only did using a kite preserve hydrogen fuel, it also delayed engine wear and served as a reliable back-up should the mechanical systems fail.

Though Toris had never used a sky sail before, he understood the concept behind their deployment. He watched Ike set the cable hooks into a pair of deck lugs, then helped lift the tube onto Ike's shoulder. He double-checked that his feet were free of the large coils of cable on the deck, the ends of which hung from the kite launcher's forward opening, and that the deck behind him was clear for the back blast.

Ike tilted the launcher to forty-five degrees ahead of the bow and pressed the trigger—*Whoosh!*

A blur of scarlet shot like a fireball from the launcher. On the deck before Ike's feet, both coiled cables spun out and shrank until the lines tightened and jerked against the anchor lugs. In the blue sky ahead, the red ball of silky fabric blossomed like a giant flower petal. The cables securing it to *Polaris'* prow whipped as the sail's edges stretched and struggled against the wind. Once the rectangle formed fully and the sail bulged outward with air, the cables stabilized at a thirty-degree angle.

Toris gave Ike a pat on the shoulder. "Nice shot."

Ike shoved the empty launcher into Toris's chest. "Nazar tells me you're the crew canary. Go store that below."

A large part of Toris had been hoping the tradition of running the mill was exclusive to the Defence Force, and that he'd left the consequences of his failed duel back on land. He hurried below decks to stow the empty canister in the engine room. While there, the loud rumbling suddenly cut out.

When he returned above, the only noise was the occasional shudder of the full sail ahead.

Toris stood between both kite cables at the prow. A hand gripped each of the braided steel lines, jerking him side to side as the kite at the opposite end swayed and dipped, the power of the upper winds towing the ship at a speed no less than that of the propulsion system.

Off the starboard to his right, the peninsula's seemingly endless mountain range stretched beyond the forward horizon. Its end point marked Anterra's boundary—the point of no return.

Though Rykah had suggested her team rest for their upcoming watch duties, Toris couldn't sleep if he tried. Too many times he'd stared out at this glittering blue sea and wondered what treasures lie in watery graves beneath. Until now, visiting this part of Anterra had been a foolish dream. Perhaps the wind whipping his hair came from lands beyond. Lands long forgotten, places he'd see sooner rather than later.

Rykah stood at the rail to his right. With Toris's current standing on her team, she'd have no choice but to assign him the dirty and dangerous work. None of his efforts to save Jayda out here mattered if he died of radiation poisoning before returning home to claim his reward.

"I think we may have a lot of idle time in the coming weeks," he said.

Rykah leaned back against the rail to face him. "I think you're right."

Toris squinted toward the horizon. Out there, dangers beyond imagination lurked. Dangers he suddenly felt unprepared to face. "Can you train me to run the mill?"

She crossed her arms, contemplating. "To prepare you in such a short time, you'll have to work past the point of wanting to quit.

You'll have to keep going, no matter what, or you may as well not even start."

Toris wasn't going to serve anyone well by getting killed out there. "I won't quit."

Rykah stepped away from the rail. "Get some rest. When we get started, you won't be getting much sleep."

"Wait," Toris said. Something was bothering him, but had been overshadowed by bigger worries until now. "You were on the train from Amyria," he said. "Seems a foolish risk for a deserter to take."

Rykah shrugged. "Ignatius told me to meet you in Abersali, but I heard you had a record of wandering to places you shouldn't. Like I said before, I don't like taking chances."

Toris gave an amused grin. "You think I'd jump from a moving train?"

Rykah took a good look around, at the sea, the sky, and then the perilous mountains that had smashed so many vessels fleeing the Decimation.

"For your sister, I think you'd do anything."

FIFTEEN

The supply convoy of horse-drawn wagons had been traveling for two days already, moving east along a rugged track through the Borien foothills. The wheels squeaked and groaned over bumpy tracks. Crates of canned food and ammunition scraped across the damp wooden deck as far as their rope lashings allowed.

Jayda pushed her feet into the wagon's side rail and braced her back against the wooden boxes that threatened to crush her. Ivy sat beside her studying a map, oblivious to the threat of their supplies squashing them to pulp.

"Can you tell me where we're going now?"

"It's still a secret," Ivy said with sly smile.

Ivy probably thought she was being cute with her smiles and winks as she eluded Jayda's questions, but Jayda was ready to smack her off the wagon. The main deterrent from pressing harder was the black *II* inked onto her neck. Wherever prison camp number two was, it had no doubt taught Ivy a few things about self-defence.

Jayda pulled the dispatch that Ivy had given to her at the border from her shirt and unfolded it. Water splattered onto the paper from leaves above, smudging the blue ink. Though she had the letter memorized, she had to see the General's handwriting and purple wax seal occasionally to believe this unforeseen fate. What could she have done to anger the army's commander-in-chief?

She examined the letter for clues as to where she'd gone wrong and about her new assignment.

To the commander of orderly Jayda Onero (23341):

This letter is to inform you that recent transgressions have forced me to impose disciplinary actions on a soldier under your command. From this moment forward the above-named is hereby released from your authority and surrendered to the custody of the soldier bearing this letter. The nature of infraction and measures of penalization are of no concern to you, therefore requires no investigation on your end. A replacement shall be made available to you in short order.

Yours in arms,
General Tyrone Aldebaran

Jayda crumpled the letter and said, "This is a mistake. I never done anything to anger the General."

"Is that your name and service number at the top?" Ivy said absently, eyes focused on her map.

"Yes."

"Then it's not a mistake."

"But…what'd I do? You can't punish someone without telling them why. That's not how people learn."

"Ever think this punishment isn't for you?" Ivy lowered her map and met Jayda's stare for the first time in hours. "You're an Onero. You should know as much as anyone what happens when someone close to you fails in their duty."

Ivy's words stung like a slap. So this was about Toris. He must have run off or abandoned his post. Not only had he fled to a better life, but he did so knowing they'd punish her in his stead. How could he do that?

She pulled her knees up to her chest, no longer caring if the crates crushed her.

"Don't worry," Ivy said. "You may not be cut out for this punishment anyway."

"What do you mean?" Jayda said to this strange attempt at consolation. Inability to endure your punishment only made it worse.

"We started out as a disciplinary unit," Ivy explained, "but now soldiers are volunteering to join. But not all pass. It's become a badge of honour. Only, the General hasn't figured that out yet, and maybe for good reason. It's hard to say what they have planned for us. Perhaps those volunteers will soon regret their choice."

"What happens if I don't pass?"

Ivy gave a grave shake of her head. "If you go in with a losing attitude, you will do just that. Listen to what you're told, and trust that the danger you face in the coming days can't hurt you if you show it the respect it deserves."

At an interim training camp, the convoy exchanged a third of their supply for soldiers. This opened space for Jayda to stretch out in comfort. As the convoy began rolling out, three soldiers climbed into the cart with her and Ivy. Each girl bore a similar numeric tattoo on her neck and a maroon beret or boonie hat atop tightly tied-back hair.

A girl bearing a *II* on her neck crawled in close to Ivy, who welcomed the newcomer by draping an arm around her neck and pulling her close.

A blond-haired girl who sat with her legs dangling over the back of the wagon gave the couple a condemning shake of the head and looked away. The stitching on her pack said *Shayla*.

A girl with a brown mohawk and filed teeth nodded toward Jayda. "Had to go far to find this one," she said to Ivy.

"All the way to the Valley," Ivy said. "How about you, Darcella? Meet your quota?"

Darcella nodded toward the wagon ahead of theirs. "Cleared out Fort Cypress's brig. One deserter was happy to come along. Figures it beats the firing squad. We'll see about that. I know, don't worry, I've got my eye on him."

Darcella stood and whistled to the mix of boys and girls in the cart ahead. She gestured that she was watching them, and threatened one in particular by sliding a finger across her throat. "Look at those faces. Half of them won't make it past the first week." She sank down and grabbed Jayda's knee. "How about you, young lass? You afraid of heights?"

Jayda jerked her knee away. "I'm not afraid of anything."

Darcella flashed her pointed teeth. "We'll see about that."

"Anyone hear what happened to Rykah?" Ivy asked.

"Deserted for sure," said Darcella.

"I don't believe that," Shayla said.

"You're right," said the girl cozied into Ivy, whose name tag read *Talia*. "I'd say she went to special operations. That Major Arcturus is running the show there, and they had a fling in Ranger school. Right steamy it was."

"That's a lie," Shayla snapped.

The other girls jeered.

"Don't like us talking about your crush like that?" said Talia.

Shayla pressed a blade to Talia's cheek. Ivy had her own at Shayla's neck an instant later. "I'm no dyke," Shayla said through clenched teeth.

"Sure," said Talia with a taunting smile. "Whatever you say."

Shayla retracted the knife and resumed her position staring off behind the cart. If not for her ill manners and hot temper one could mistake her for an Amyrian Beauty Queen. But this girl had no grace for such circles.

Ivy returned her knife to its scabbard. "Who's in charge of us now that Adarah's gone?"

"I heard Quella," said Darcella.

Shayla shook her head. "She's back at the Fort training instructors on melee fighting. Besides, you really think they'd make her an officer?"

Darcella smacked Shayla's back and said, "That reminds me. How'd you make out, anyway? Rumour has it you snagged an L.T."

Shayla peeled a chunk of apple with her knife. "That's him two wagons back." She fed herself a slice and waved. The young man eagerly returned it like a puppy wagging his tail. One could almost see the drool. "A highborn straight out of Military Academy. Said he recognized me from my pageant days in Amyria. I convinced him to volunteer."

"How'd you manage that?" Darcella said with a suggestive wink.

"Told him extraordinary lies," Shayla said, chewing. "May have made a few glass promises. Heard they stuck Songbird with us."

"That the wee little blondie who doesn't talk?" said Darcella. "How she ended up in an outfit like this I'll never know. Like this one." Darcella winked at Jayda and said, "Should get some sleep, little darling. You have a long couple weeks ahead of you."

The girls sprawled out and pulled their boonie hats down over their faces to shield the breaking sun. Snores rose as the cart rocked rhythmically down the twin tracks. Jayda did the same, though sleep did not take her so easily in present company, nor would her flustered mind submit to it.

At some point, however, she must have dozed off, because when she lifted her head next they were rolling across a wide open field. The girls were already in their gear and preparing to dismount the wagon. When Jayda looked ahead, past the front of the convoy, she caught sight of something that made her question if she were actually still asleep.

In many ways the camp ahead resembled other training sites Jayda had visited so far in her service. Except for one big irregularity, which floated three thousand feet over the field beyond.

She watched in awe as tiny blots fell in evenly spaced intervals from massive balloons. Each figure followed the one before it in a suicidal plunge toward the ground, until a silhouette bloomed above its head and formed a miniature half-balloon. The figures dangled and swayed beneath these descending canopies. Some crashed into the earth with little grace, but for the most part those who'd jumped from the balloons reached the ground with little apparent harm. Stretcher bearers rushed into the field to assist those who'd landed but not recovered.

So this was Jayda's punishment. Who would conjure such a mad idea? More surprising was Ivy's claim that soldiers were volunteering for this.

"Just a platoon-level drop," Ivy said flatly. "We did a battalion jump two weeks ago. Impressive sight."

"Will I be doing that?" Jayda said, trying to hide her angst. Would they force her onto a balloon right away?

"After five days of ground school," Ivy said. She smiled at Jayda. "Good thing you're not afraid of anything."

SIXTEEN

Toris bounced off the deck. The air blasted from his lungs and, as he gasped to replace it, a hand shot down to seize his collar. He grabbed the wrist and shot his legs up to wrap them around the assailing arm. Pulling the wrist to his chest, he thrust his hips against the back of the elbow.

Sweat dripped from Rykah's chin and onto his cheek as she struggled in his armlock. She was not getting out this time.

With her free arm, Rykah jabbed two knuckles into his outer thigh, striking hard and fast like a viper. The hit triggered a reflex that kicked Toris's leg straight, allowing Rykah to twist free through the momentary gap.

Nausea and dizziness struck as his legs flopped to the deck. Just when he thought he had her technique down...What sort of witchery was this? He'd been struck a good many times by the older boys at Lake Orion, but never could they induce such a hideous response. He rolled to his side and rubbed the knot out of his leg, fearing he may never walk the same again. How would crippling him help him rise above Atilus?

Rykah stood over him, flexing her elbow. "Good. Take a break."

She paced across the rocking rear deck in the shadow of *Polaris'* bridge.

Toris sipped from his canteen as the knot in his leg faded to a dull ache. As he lowered the canteen, his eyelids and head followed to the rocking of the ship. Rykah's rigorous training routine was hard to maintain over three days without sleep, which she called the 'sleepless seventy-two'. Though, now he was at the halfway mark and had already slipped away for four hours of rest. He suspected the stealing sleep part as being part of the curriculum. A test of its own. Rykah insisted this manner of training was the best way to ingrain the basics and is what gave Rangers the edge over regular soldiers.

Toris's hands loosened from around the canteen and dropped it to the wooden deck as his body tried to steal a minute of sleep.

"Fix bayonets!"

He jolted awake and scrambled to his practice rifle. His jittering hands and fuzzy eyes struggled to line the ring of the bayonet hilt over the barrel. Rykah was adamant he improve his timings, and would not hesitate to strike if he faltered. The hilt clicked into place as her bayonet drove at his side. He whirled about and knocked Rykah's rifle away with his, which he'd borrowed from Varcy, then jabbed at her to create distance between them. Her sheathed blade hovered before him like a wasp, searching for an opening—poking, prodding, taunting. Too many times the worn tip of her bayonet scabbard had bruised him. Not this round.

He lunged forward in a rush. Rykah swatted his rifle aside with hers and swung back at his head. He ducked, allowing the bayonet to glide freely through the air above, then slashed at her side. Wood clacked on wood as her stock blocked his barrel swipe. This parrying went back and forth until they developed a rhythm, their fight becoming a dance in the gentle breeze that blew from the peninsula's grey mountain chain to their right.

"Not bad for an Onero," Rykah said tauntingly, a tactic she'd adopted to stoke his anger. Another ploy he'd have to resist falling for. *Don't react emotionally to provocation,* she'd told him. "And a half-blood at that," she went on. "I must be a good teacher."

She slashed low at his leg, which he deflected with his borrowed rifle. She backed off and beckoned him to attack.

Toris held back. "There'll be no stopping us if we need to fight our way to the vault with bayonets. Think whatever trouble awaits us out there is inclined to such a primitive style of combat?"

When Toris had asked Rykah why she and Varcy used a single shot, bolt-action type of weapon when the other soldiers used automatic assault rifles, she informed him that firearms were a Ranger's last line of defence, used only when all other options fail. Carrying such a weapon was a mark of confidence. But Toris was not among this creed. He'd prefer to keep things less intimate when encountering an enemy.

"I'll teach you to shoot once we're in open water," Rykah said.

Toris would take her to her word on that. His and Jayda's fates depended on his ability to survive out there.

He stole a sweeping look down the grey peninsula toward the green mainland to the rear. There existed a strong possibility that he may next see this sight as a free man.

As if reading his mind, Rykah faked a lunge and drove him back into a stumble.

"Don't allow your lust for freedom to blind you," she said.

"What will you do with yours?" he asked, latching onto the dream tighter than he knew was good for him.

Rykah stopped mid-thrust. She backed off warily. "You assume too much. What makes you think we'll reach the vault first? Or make it back even if we have the seeds?"

"We'll make it," Toris said. "I found the vault reference for a reason. The stars chose me, and you made sure I got here." Seeing the skill of Rykah and her crew made all of this feel more than random. Without her, he'd be putting along on *Barnacle* with little more than rocks to defend themselves with. Ending up on *Polaris* was the work of forces higher than Ignatius. Much higher. "This is our destiny," he said.

Rykah lowered her rifle and gave a dim smile, then a satisfied nod. "Well, in that case, I suppose I'll go deep into the foothills and live off the land. Maybe seek out my old cabin on Lake Nichol if no one took it over already."

She stared longingly at the mainland. "I've often wondered what became of the home my father's father built. If it's hosting a family or fallen into disrepair." She smiled a bright smile, but only briefly before catching herself. "But that's getting ahead of ourselves."

"There's nothing wrong with dreaming. The promise of sunrise is what gets us through the night."

Rykah frowned. "It's a distraction we don't need right now. We must be willing to sacrifice everything to succeed, including any future that may await us."

"And you say I'm the serious one," Toris said with a smile.

"It's reality," she snapped. "You get caught staring at the mountaintop too much and you'll trip over something right in front of you. Then what good are you?"

"Sorry I asked," Toris muttered.

Rykah stopped and shook her head. "No, you're right. It's good to dream." She rested her rifle barrel over her shoulder. "So what will you do? I told you my dream - let's hear yours."

"Well, I've always—*Argh!*" Rykah's bayonet smacked Toris's wrist. His rifle clattered off the deck as he pulled his forearm tight to his chest.

"See," Rykah said. "You're already distracted and there aren't even projectiles threatening to rip your head off."

Toris cradled his throbbing wrist.

"Pull in the kite!" shouted Domlyn from the bridge.

Shaking the sting from his wrist, Toris left Rykah and wandered around the wheelhouse to the foredeck. He hadn't noticed the wind dying down, nor the decrease in *Polaris'* speed, but the kite that had been flying high ahead of the bow was now nowhere to be seen. At the bowsprit, Ike was instructing Atilus in how to reel in the fallen kite that had sank below the surface.

"Nazar! Jarik!" barked the Skipper from the bridge. "Get out there and help pull in that sail. I can't start the engines until I know it's clear of the propellers. Toris, wherever you're hiding, take a dive and make sure nothing gets caught up down there."

So this was the first perilous call of the crew canary. Well, this was one task he'd dive headfirst into. Literally. Toris had been dying to feel the water on his skin since leaving camp.

Splash.

Toris turned to see Rykah's clothes piled at the stern under the black Polarian flag, its white star rippling lazily in the whisper of a breeze. At the stern rail, he peered overboard to see Rykah floating in the water facing the sky, her body a pale blur below the surface. A quick inventory of her clothes lying by his feet revealed she'd taken effort to keep *all* of her garments dry.

"What's the hold-up?" she said, treading water. "They didn't teach you to follow orders in your civil service? Or do you expect me to do your job for you?"

Her closed-eye smile contradicted her scolding tone. Was this smile a glimpse of the real Rykah? That innocent girl who'd taken refuge way down deep when the authorities marched her into *Labour Camp V*. Or had she left that girl back in her cabin at Lake Nichol?

Toris's hand went to his heart. Did he have a softer version of himself hiding away below? Around Rykah, he was starting to worry that he may.

He stripped down to his undergarments, climbed onto the rail, and then dove headfirst into the sea.

The energy of the warm water woke every tired cell in his body, and he wasted no time getting to work. A quick look below the hull revealed that the boys had already managed to pull the scarlet sail up to the bow, far from the rear propellers or any other snag point. Hopefully his future tasks went so smoothly.

Toris returned to surface to catch his breath. He checked the water around him but saw no sign of Rykah.

A flash of panic electrified his nerves. Many mainlanders couldn't swim, and those who could overestimated their abilities.

Had she sank to the depths while he obliviously inspected the propellers?

No. A look above found her perched on the rubber raiding craft that sat horizontally on a rack extending from the stern. She straddled the black gunwale, already redressed in her tank undershirt and skivvies.

The rubber gunwale groaned as Toris climbed up into the landing craft.

"All clear!" he shouted.

A rumble and shudder declared the engines' awakening. Flurries of bubbles rushed out from under the ship, and a moment later *Polaris* straightened out and rocked forward.

"Mission accomplished," Rykah said.

She produced a carved wooden pipe from a leather pouch in her lap. She packed the bowl, then held the bit between her teeth and struck a match. Smoke filled the air as she took a few deep hauls. She exhaled a blue cloud and offered the piece to Toris.

He accepted the smooth handcrafted pipe and inhaled deep. On the first drag he coughed and sputtered, much to Rykah's amusement. His head swirled and his mind released all worry as he looked to the distant mountain peaks with a new appreciation. He never thought there'd come a day when he may miss this place.

He leaned back and swung his legs over the side, feeling somewhat like he'd found his place in the world among this band of misfits. Below, the wake grew longer and fanned out wider as *Polaris* picked up speed.

Sitting before Toris, Rykah's eyes glazed in watching the jagged tops of the peninsula's mountain range. Everything glowed with new light—her wet black hair hanging over her shoulders, the seemingly endless row of grey mountains stretching out behind her as far as could be seen, the glittering blue sea. The warm wind drying his wet skin could have put him to sleep if not for his racing heart.

Rykah's face glowed with a soft, dreamy smile. "A criminal

conscript and an exiled Onero, off to save Polaria. They'll be singing songs about us come next summer."

Toris closed his eyes and pictured the parade awaiting them in Abersali upon their return with the seeds—those tiny objects that promised to cure all of Polaria's woes. Famine and starvation would be little more than bitter memories, the very words eventually fading to extinction from disuse. The Artican would erect statues of each of the Agrinauts, with Toris and Rykah's names inscribed on the base of each, to ever be remembered together as heroes greater than even Odillian and his fearless warriors who drove the Ortarian hordes from Polaria three centuries ago.

After the celebrations, Toris would bring Rykah to Mintaka and show her where he spent his civil service. There they could buy buckets overflowing with oysters and crabs, and clams were cheaper than rice and you didn't need credit to deal with vendors. Every member of *Polaris'* crew would return with all sorts of curious spoils from the old world to trade, but no merchant would relieve the heroes of their bounty. That would seem too great a crime. "I bet I'll get a good deal on a catamaran," he said, thinking of one that he'd seen anchored off Mintaka last summer.

"Cata-ma-what?"

"It's like…a really wide sailboat."

Rykah nodded. "What will you call it? Every boat has a name, right?"

She took another drag from her pipe.

"The *Morningwood*," Toris said.

A plume of blue smoke exploded from Rykah's mouth, accompanied by the sweetest laughter Toris had ever heard.

He reached overhead onto the deck and, from his pile of clothes, pulled the tin case he'd pinched from Abersali's black market. Opening the lid, he exposed the oatmeal raisin cookie inside.

Rykah gasped and looked around conspicuously. "Where did you get that?"

Toris split the cookie in half and offered a piece to Rykah.

She accepted it with both hands, eyes wide in wonder as if he'd given her a fist-sized diamond. Almost ceremoniously, she took the first bite and closed her eyes. She breathed deep with each slow chew. When she finished her first bite, she said, "This is the best thing I've ever tasted."

Toris watched her break off tiny crumbs to ration it. Such delights should not be picked at, so he offered her his other half.

She looked at him in shock. "I couldn't…"

"It's okay - I have another." He didn't. But the look on Rykah's face was worth more to him than any piece of food.

Her hazy, euphoric eyes lifted from the two pieces in her hands and met his. "You are a gift from the stars, Toris Onero. Don't let men in golden collars ever tell you otherwise."

He stared deep into her eyes. Spending time with this girl was an experience beyond anything he'd ever known. She was starlight in his darkness.

He pushed a wet strand of black hair behind her ear and down over her ivory shoulder. Her lips called to him, inviting him in. He leaned forward to close the gap between them.

Four white knuckles rushed in to meet his advance. Toris's first kiss jarred his head and knocked him onto his back. He prodded his numb lips as Rykah stood over him, the dreamy look in her eyes replaced by alarm.

She squeezed the cookie pieces and tossed the crumbs out over the water. She gave Toris a disappointed shake of her head, then climbed up over the stern and ducked under the rail.

A whistle shrieked from above.

Toris stood and looked over the deck to the bridge.

Atilus stumbled down the wheelhouse stairs. "Arokya!" he shouted in delight. He laughed and carried on around to the fore-deck as Varcy, Jarik, and Nazar scrambled up from below decks. On the deck before Toris, Rykah pulled on her boots and ran ahead to join them.

Toris sank back into the landing craft. The sting on his lips was bad, but this throbbing was nothing to the deep stabbing in his heart.

The Isle of Arokya, home to the fair and gracious Rosaria, was little more than a wind-swept rock. The closest thing to a forest were sparse clusters of scrubby bushes.

Scattered across the island, however, stood structures of the most peculiar design. The tiered towers stood, in some cases, seven storeys high, with each level boasting its own eaves, the corners of which curved upward. Bright layers of orange and red suggested each building had received a recent paint coating, as no way could such vibrance survive the harsh winter weather out here.

Toris squeezed the port side rail at midship in the shadow of the wheelhouse. If *Polaris* failed to find the seeds first, this would be his new home. Rosaria herself would welcome him regardless of the manner in which he migrated there. He'd heard the offer from her own mouth. But seeing her home for the isolated rock that it was, that option didn't sound so appealing. What was it like out here during the six-month winter night? No doubt most citizens went to the capital for winter, which was not an option for Toris. It'd be him and fugitive Oneros left to fend for themselves.

A low-riding cutter of dark stained wood cruised out from around the island's northern point. Her course veered north as if to fall in ahead of *Polaris*. A purple ball launched from the ship's bow and bloomed into a kite twice the size of *Polaris'* scarlet sky sail.

Toris had witnessed the ship's departure from Port Abersali a few days ago. "That's the—"

"*Southern Zephyr*," Ike said. He stood at the rail nearby, looking rather unimpressed with Polaria's most remote and exotic territory, his expression surely a mirror of Toris's own disappointment.

"*Zephyr*," Toris repeated under his breath, certain he'd mispronounced it when he'd first seen her at Finn's Marina. Suddenly the name rang a bell. "That's Rosaria's ship," he concluded.

"Had to leave Abersali in a hurry last week. Rumour has it there was special cargo aboard that she needed to keep secret." Ike planted his elbows onto the rail and rested his chin against his palms. "They say her ship is as beautiful as she is."

One cannot compare the elegance of a ship to a person, but Toris took his meaning. In contrast to her home island, Rosaria's reputation was well-deserved and, in reality, failed to do her justice. But having met her in person, Toris could say without a doubt that the criminal conscript standing at the head of the port rail near *Polaris'* bow could challenge the Arokyan councillor for her title. Rykah didn't need a golden collar around her neck to glow. A black *V* tattoo suited her just fine.

The *Southern Zephyr*'s course, however, was cause to question. With only a Coast Patrol station beyond Arokya, a councillor had no business out at the peninsula tip.

"Where is the *Zephyr* headed?" Toris said to Ike.

Ike leaned sideways against the rail, nodding toward Rykah. "Just after you boarded, I heard her tell you we have a free pass through Point Bay Station. Well, that's it—our flagship for this mission."

Toris stepped back, this news hitting him harder than anything he'd so far had to digest. They were pairing up with another ship? One of higher status than theirs? If there was another civilian on this mission, for instance, the *Zephyr*'s captain, he'd not receive the full Accolade. "What are you talking about?" he said, hearing the distress rise in his own voice. "They're not coming all the way to Svalbard, are they?"

Ike leaned over the rail, eyes narrowed on Rosaria's ship. "Strength in numbers, my friend."

"Rosaria is a councillor," Toris said, refusing to accept this new development. "She could have whatever she wants. Why would she risk her ship to find the Accolade?"

Ike stood straight. "Here's the crazy part," he said. "She loaned it to that *special cargo* I told you about. Someone from the capital who needed to get far from the mainland. Someone who has the influence to talk Rosaria into loaning out her ship, and desperate enough to risk life and limb for the Accolade. A brother can't go against the Chancellor's wishes to protect his sister, but he can cast a wider net to ensure at least one crew returns to claim the Accolade."

Toris frowned. "Is Major Arcturus aboard *Southern Zephyr*?"

Ike's brow raised in amusement. "Wrong Arcturus. I'm talking about the Chancellor's daughter." He clapped his hands together. "Imagine if we got to see her? I bet we'll get close enough to at least catch a glimpse of her. They say she's so beautiful that when she skipped her wedding, the General was going to send troops to the capital to look for her."

Toris stared at the ship sailing ahead of them in pure shock. Could it be? No way. Though, Ignatius did go through a lot of trouble organizing this expedition for the sake of having Toris break Lex's engagement. Why throw all your seeds into one plot? Spread them out or, if you're searching for something as Ike had just said, cast a wider net. Was *Polaris* the only ship Ignatius sent as a back-up?

"There she is!" exclaimed Ike, pointing to the front of their flagship.

He was right. The figure fencing with an opponent on the *Southern Zephyr*'s foredeck held the same stance he'd seen Lex use on *Atlas*, moving with stiff yet calculated movements. In her violet longcoat, she appeared as magnificent as Ike had predicted. If they returned to Port Abersali together with the seeds, who would the people raise above their heads as their saviour?

He turned away from the rail and clenched his fists, his face blazing red hot. Lex's presence had jarred him so much that he'd forgotten about his disastrous attempt to kiss Rykah. Seeing her head disappear below decks reminded him, and his heart drummed a most dreadful beat.

When he went below to their berth and saw her hammock swaying empty, her rucksack missing, his swollen lips seemed to throb a little harder.

SEVENTEEN

Point Bay Station was a twelve-hour cruise from Arokya. Located at the tip of the peninsula, the Coast Patrol base provided battleships swift access to both sides of the peninsula, making it Anterra's forward line of defence against foreign threats.

Toris stood in the wheelhouse with *Polaris'* whole crew, nervously watching as a Coast Patrol ship raced out from the naval base to intercept the *Southern Zephyr*, which cruised a stone's throw ahead of *Polaris'* prow. Despite the closing battle cruiser, their flagship kept her purple kite high and made no signs of decreasing her thirty-knot pace.

Toris hugged himself and chewed his thumbnail as the patrol ship veered north to intercept the *Zephyr*'s course. His failed kiss attempt was now the least of his concerns. Though, he did remain to the far left of the bridge, opposite to Rykah.

The patrol vessel was similar to the ship that had shuttled Jayda away from Mintaka for the draft, the same ship that had brought Sallus to justice. Another encounter with Clavilla would bring no better luck out here.

Toris leaned close to Ike. "What makes you so sure they won't pull us in?"

"Whenever I was posted aboard a ship out here, our only place to go on leave was Arokya. Rosaria's people have always welcomed us. Even sent us emergency food when we got stuck out here on watch. Only a fool would dare harass her ship."

"And if they thought it was stolen? Say, by a crew of brigands desperate to win the Accolade?"

"Nah, she has a direct line of communication with the base out here. Pretty much runs the place. She could send word out well in advance."

Then Ike hugged himself and joined Toris in chewing a thumbnail, watching the patrol ship intensely. His demeanour didn't spell much confidence in his assurances.

"They're getting pretty close," Varcy said, pacing at the back like a caged tigress.

In the corner behind Toris, Nazar and Jarik were holding hands. Across the bridge, Rykah's face was stone hard, but the sweat dripping from her nose and chin offered a glimpse as to what was going on inside.

The patrol vessel fell in alongside the *Zephyr*. She angled to within shouting distance between both ship bridges. If any officer aboard spotted Lex they'd certainly have grounds to pull them in for inquiry, to confirm her father's authorization for his only daughter to join the most perilous expedition in Anterran history.

Toris felt as if he may choke on the sweltering air inside the bridge. The only breeze came from Atilus waving his wide-brimmed hat before his face, which was only blowing hot air around. Toris steadied himself on the forward panel and leaned out the window, but the air outside was no kinder. He instead settled for a few calming breaths.

"They're peeling away," Skipper Domlyn said.

Tension deflated from the bridge. Cheers erupted, hands patting backs and hugs going around. Toris embraced Atilus, who was bouncing in excitement. Atilus released him and turned to hug Varcy, who squirmed in his sweaty embrace. Swept up in the moment of relief, Toris turned and opened his arms to Rykah, whose eyes flared wide in alarm. He immediately backed away and wrapped his arms around his own torso.

Rykah double-checked to ensure the patrol ship was cruising back to base. With *Polaris* and *Southern Zephyr* sailing unopposed past the peninsula tip, she gave a satisfying nod. "We're on our own out here," she said. "Jarik, Nazar, help Ike mount the cannon above the bridge. Toris, Atilus, set up the *fifty* on the foredeck."

Toris looked to Atilus for clarification on what exactly a 'fifty' was, but saw a reflection of his own confused look on his partner's face.

"Ike will show you what it is," Rykah said. "Varcy, set up the balloons for target practice."

The weapons were not hidden so cleverly as one would expect of a smuggling crew. Pieces of heavy guns and small arms leaned in a storage closet with mops and brooms. Though, if the Coast Patrol had caught them, illegal weapons would be the least of this crew's concerns.

Ike explained to Nazar and Tarik which pieces belonged to the cannon, then showed Toris and Atilus what a 'fifty' was—a .50 caliber machine gun. Toris hefted the heavy weapon over his shoulder and wobbled up the stairs with it, Atilus's hand on his lower back for support. A tripod stood at the center of the fore-deck, upon which he set and secured the weapon with Atilus's help. Each took a turn swinging the long gun on its swivel, testing its maneuverability and range of motion.

Rykah arrived lugging a box of ammunition and slid it into the bottom of the gun. From the steel box she pulled a belt of linked rounds and draped it over the side.

Toris marvelled at the size of the bullets. They'd no doubt put a dent in any Coast Patrol ship.

From above, Nazar swore and flung a wrench overboard.

"Get down from there, you mongrel!" shouted the Skipper. "Toris, get topside and give them a hand."

Nazar climbed down the wheelhouse's starboard side. As he stomped toward the stern, Toris scrambled up the ladder to the bridge roof, where Jarik and Ike were struggling to set the cannon into a circular track. With Toris's patience and the help of a third pry bar, they managed to fit the gun onto the rollers. A test spin displayed a three hundred and sixty degree range of fire.

"Pretty handy," Jarik said, wiping his hands on his trousers.

Ike dabbed his forehead with a rag. "Let's hope we don't need to use it."

"Toris!" Despite the heat, Rykah's commanding tone sent a shiver down his spine. "Report to Varcy for target practice," she said from the foredeck.

A dozen orange balloons waved from the stern rail. Varcy stood before them with her arms folded, an assault rifle and pistol on the deck at her feet.

She greeted Toris with an amused smile. "Looks like you tried to kiss a cobra."

Toris licked his swollen bottom lip, tasting the tang of blood. So, to her soldier kin, Rykah had earned the reputation of a venomous snake. Toris wished he'd learned that earlier. Though, would it have made a difference in that moment? Probably not.

"Pick up the M4," Varcy said.

Toris hesitated. Seeing his uncertainty, Varcy rolled her eyes and nudged the bigger gun with her foot. Toris picked up the weapon. Its black polymer components differed greatly from the wooden bolt-action rifles used by the Rangers on his crew.

"That's an M4 Carbine," Varcy explained, "standard service weapon of the Polarian Defence Force. It switches between automatic and semi-automatic fire, but with a little practice you shouldn't need the automatic setting."

Varcy stepped aside to offer Toris a clear line of fire at the balloons. Beyond *Polaris'* wake, the grey mountains of Anterra's peninsula were rapidly sinking into the sea. Out here, the wind in the kite towed them at a speed greater than Toris had ever felt upon the water. With the sun shimmering bright off the waves, he pulled his goggles up over his eyes to dim the glare. It had become a habit of all on board to keep eye protection accessible by hanging them around their necks.

Varcy instructed him, very methodically, how to load, unload, and clear the weapon should it jam. She watched Toris run through the drills and dry runs several times before handing him a full magazine.

Toris held the loaded firearm nervously. At this point, Atilus and Jarik and Nazar rushed up to join the firing line for some recreational target practice. Varcy did not object.

"Watch and shoot," she said, then untied one of the orange balloons from the stern rail.

Deafening gunfire crackled around Toris until the balloon bobbing over their wake burst and shriveled to nothing. Brass casings clinked off the wooden deck at everyone's feet except for Toris's.

"Since Toris didn't fire his weapon, the next balloon is all his," said Rykah.

Toris turned to see her observing with crossed arms. He raised the carbine butt to his shoulder and squinted through the red lens of its optical sight.

Varcy released another balloon. Toris squeezed the trigger once and missed, then twice, and a third time, missing each shot. In his frustration he squeezed off several more rounds. None of them hit the distant balloon dipping and swerving over the wake.

"Varcy," said Rykah.

Varcy dropped to a knee and steadied her .303 on the rail, aiming carefully over its iron sight. *Crack!* The distant balloon disappeared in an instant. Varcy stood and gave Toris a taunting wink.

Rykah stepped in front. "Don't be too proud, Varcy. Your competition has never shot so much as a squirrel before."

Toris must have looked mighty uncomfortable for Rykah to have offered him that coded consolation.

"Ready," said Rykah, stepping off to the side.

Toris joined the others in raising their weapons. Rykah released two balloons, prompting her team to unleash a hail of bullets. Neither balloon made it far, but Toris wasn't sure who'd hit them, though it likely hadn't been him. But his effort seemed to appease Rykah.

"Nice work, everyone," Rykah said. "Safe out your weapons. Toris, pick up the brass casings. Nazar and Jarik, you're on first watch. Skipper Domlyn will tell you what to do. Atilus and Toris, you'll relieve them in four hours."

Toris kicked the rolling brass shells to the plate wall at the edge of the deck, where he scooped them into a burlap sack. The hot brass burned his fingers, so he wrapped his tunic around his hand to better handle the casings.

Atilus stayed back to help, his eyes frequently drifting to the hazy grey mountains sinking into the sea. "You ever know anybody who's been out this far?"

Toris shook his head.

"Think the Coast Patrol has?" Atilus asked.

"Maybe chasing pyrates."

Atilus straightened up in alarm. "Pyrates are real?"

"What do you think the guns are for?"

Atilus's gaze swept to the endless sea ahead, uncertainty plaguing his eyes.

Anterra sank into the sea on Toris's watch. Though Atilus was standing nearby, Toris's position in the captain's chair left him technically in control of the ship when the last mountain peak dipped under the choppy horizon to their rear.

The milestone lacked a monumental feel. With only sea in every direction, Toris felt no need to announce Anterra's disappearance to those sleeping below. Only Rykah stood at the stern, and the sudden vastness of the endless sea seemed to overwhelm her. She hugged herself and hurried below without sparing even a glance at Toris on the bridge.

He spun the captain's chair to face forward. Through the open window ahead, *Southern Zephyr* rocked over swells and was getting smaller with each nautical mile. Toris steadied *Polaris'* polished wooden wheel to keep her prow pointed at the *Zephyr's* stern, both ships cruising on a northeast course toward Africa. That should be the next land they encountered. If it still existed. They'd just crossed a line that, for all they knew, no Anterran had crossed in seven hundred years. Anyone's guess as to what waited beyond was as legitimate as the next person's.

The three hundred and sixty degree ocean horizon seemed to unnerve Atilus as it had Rykah. He sank to the floor, restricting his line of sight to the interior of the wheelhouse, and pulled his knees to his chest.

"Head below," Toris told him.

Atilus gave him a curious look.

"I can stand watch alone," Toris said.

Atilus seemed to give it some serious consideration. A moment later, he pulled his knees tighter to his chest and remained on the bridge like a loyal dog staying by its owner.

"I couldn't imagine getting it done twice," Atilus said.

Toris looked to Atilus for clarification, who in turn rubbed the *O* brand on his own deltoid.

"First time isn't as bad because you don't know how bad it's gonna be," Atilus said. He wrinkled his nose. "I still smell it sometimes - my own burning skin. If they waved that glowing red iron in front of me after I'd already known the burn, no way would they hold me still for a second go. No sir."

Toris's belly lurched at his own memories. Desperate for distraction, he leaned forward to observe the kite flying high beyond the prow, that scarlet fabric hauling them at a steady thirty knots. How many watch shifts must he endure with Atilus before seeing land?

But there he was making a big assumption. What if there was no land? Africa may have sank during the Decimation.

This doubt surfaced many times.

His belly twisted in knots, so he reminded himself of his purpose out here—for Jayda. Which was worse because any thought spared to her conjured the image of her screaming on a bayonet charge into Ortaria.

EIGHTEEN

Some asshole a long time ago declared the height of fear to be thirty-five feet. That's why the officers ordered the Aerodrome's jump tower built that high. The tower was the first stop to test your mettle on the road to becoming a paratrooper. Recruits rode a zip-line from the top of the tower to the ground. The scariest part was the sudden drop at the start before the slack tightened, but so long as you held on nothing could go wrong.

Jayda wished she could go back to those first five days of jump school, when everything was as simple as holding on. When the fear was only in your head.

Looking over the edge of the basket, to the ground three thousand feet below, she was glad to be fifth in line. The four previous jumps had built in her a resistance to the sensation of falling. Time leading up to the first jump had been managed with gear inspections and checklists so that the recruits had no time to worry. Nor had they truly known what they were getting into. Every time Jayda made the plunge her awareness expanded, drawing in all new considerations to fear. Would she land in that stand of trees? How long would it take for her to reach the ground this time? The instructors tied weights to her ankles to ensure her parachute deployed properly, but she remained in the air much longer than her fellow candidates. The possibility of an updraft or gust of wind delivering her to parts unknown became more real with each jump.

The fifth jump was the qualifier. You do this, you get your wings. The big worry was what happened afterwards. What plans did The Artican have for the Aero Insertion Regiment? In the last two weeks they'd doubled their numbers. Logically many assumed they intended to do something big. And soon.

The balloon pilot's voice announced the dreadful word: "Go!"

Lieutenant Valender, the young officer Shayla had persuaded to volunteer, was first out the door. Arla went next, then her sister Eris. The twins' bald heads dropped out of sight in quick succession. A boy whose name Jayda could never remember made it to the opening, took one look down, and shrank back into her. He unhooked his static line and stumbled away from the door.

The day was hot and bright, not a cloud in the sky, which made matters worse. Ideal conditions meant no excuses. Everything should go according to plan. And if it doesn't, it's all your fault.

Jayda shuffled forward to the opening, placed both feet together so that the tips of her boots stood flush with the edge of safety, looked below, and froze.

The soldier behind her pressed into her back, but her hands held the rails to either side of the opening. The three hundred and sixty degree horizon was dizzying. Below, three parachutes splayed out and shrank toward the ground. Humans weren't supposed to do this. Until a week ago fear was something she ignored or conquered. Now it was something that threatened to conquer her.

"*Go!*" cried the pilot. "Get out!"

Instructors had been present in the basket for the first four jumps, but remained on the ground for the qualifier.

Jayda looked to the soldier behind, a boy who stood two heads above her. He'd bruised his tailbone on the last jump and almost received a medical transfer for it. The petrified look in his eyes suggested he welcomed the delay of Jayda's hesitation. "Push me!"

His eyes snapped down to meet hers. "What?"

"Do it. Shove me out and jump right behind me. Don't think about it. Just—"

A force sent Jayda flying clear of the basket. The sudden drop made her insides seem to rise up into her mouth. Panic clouded her mind until a jarring deceleration indicated her chute deploying. She looked up and rejoiced to see that beautiful green canopy blossom into a full circle.

On the field below, four circular shadows appeared behind her own. Two of the ten hadn't jumped.

Jayda drifted straight to the ground this time, and for once she landed before those who'd jumped behind her. As her feet hit the grass her training kicked in. She rolled to her side as the canopy deflated and crumpled beside her. She unclipped her lines, pulled in her chute, loaded her gear, and hustled to join her cohort.

The baby-faced Lieutenant Valender greeted Jayda with a high five. When the eight jumpers mustered at the meeting point, the instructors unceremoniously handed each of them their AIR wings, then marched them back to the camp lines. Jayda thought the whole process quite anti-climactic.

At the hangar each jumper received their new platoon assignment. Ivy was waiting to escort Jayda, Arla, and Eris to their new home. Jayda harboured mixed feelings about this. In the last two weeks she'd heard many stories about *Adarah's Darlings* around camp.

Ivy showed the girls to their modular tent, where three empty cots sat ready for them. "Stow your gear," Ivy said, "then come with me. You can't sleep in here smelling like that."

At the riverbed, soldiers of various companies were lying in the sun while others fished or swam. The Borien Mountains sloped down to form the opposite bank.

Along the shoreline, a raven-haired girl took on three attackers with a battle axe in each hand. Upon seeing Ivy's approach, she quickly put an end to the sparring with three successive blows to each of her opponents, who she until now had apparently been toying with. She trudged across the stony shore to meet the entourage. Whatever had given her the white scar that mangled her upper lip had also chipped the top row of teeth and left her upper smile sloped.

"Ladies," said Ivy, "meet Sergeant-Major Quella."

Quella's ragged hair appeared as if she'd cut it herself with a dull bayonet. Her chestnut eyes flicked between the *III* tattoo on each twin's neck. "Do much fighting in camp?"

The girls crossed their arms and nodded.

Quella gestured to the rifle slung over each girl's shoulder. "Fix bayonets. Let's see what you got." She looked to Jayda. "We'll do one-on-one later."

Ivy draped her arm over Jayda's shoulders and said, "Make sure to go easy on her, Mama."

Quella jabbed her axe at Ivy's chest. "I'm not your precious Rykah. Don't ever call me that again."

Arla and Eris unslung their .303s, fixed bayonets, and charged at Quella in hopes of catching her off guard. Quella's dull blades swung in a blur and clacked off their wooden rifle stocks. Within a few seconds the twins were disarmed and scrambling to recover their weapons.

A familiar voice echoed from the riverbend: "Travarian twats!"

A *smack* followed as Shayla's fist connected with Corla's face.

Corla fell back but was quick to her feet and ready to strike. The redhead had recently reunited with the unit following a week-long stint in lockup. Darcella, her Travarian sister, hauled her back. "Come on," Darcy said. "She ain't worth it."

Corla spit blood and stormed off.

"The Darlings are a bit rough around the edges," Ivy said as she stripped off her uniform, "but they're who ya want by your side in a fight. We met in jump school, back in the experimental days. There were a lot more of us then. Lieutenant Adarah held us all together. We're hoping she comes back soon. Quella was Rykah's next-in-line, but I doubt they'll make her an officer."

Ivy stepped into the frigid river water and hugged herself.

Jayda joined, trying hard to silence her chattering teeth.

"When we get back to the tent you can write your letter," Ivy said, sinking down to her neck. "I have paper and ink."

Jayda shook her head. "Won't be necessary."

"I can help you if—"

"I know how to write," Jayda snapped. "I just don't have anyone to write to."

"You must have *someone*."

"I don't." Which couldn't be more true. Toris had run off and left her to endure his punishment. Lenus and Aster were dead. And any other Onero she grew up with would soon be too if they marched up the Valley into Ortaria.

Ivy drifted through the water behind and wrapped her arms around Jayda. Her soft skin pressed against Jayda's back.

Jayda's first instinct was to burst free from the embrace, but something other than Ivy's arms restrained her. She'd never allowed herself to cry in front of others like she did after Aster's death, but something about Ivy's comfort made her not care if people thought she was weak.

"The Darlings will be your family now," Ivy said.

Jayda watched Arla and Eris stumbling on the stony shore, struggling to land a strike on Quella. Nearby, Shayla's caustic stare watched the embracing bathers from the shoreline, oblivious to Corla watching her from a distance, who was likely plotting her revenge on the Amyrian beauty queen.

This was not the family Jayda wanted, but it was the one she got.

NINETEEN

Drake's Wrath had kept a good many sailor from venturing to Antarctica during the Decimation. So much so that they'd sooner burn to ash with the old world than risk that deathly dance on the merciless sea.

When *Polaris* encountered the first angry swells on that dreaded passage, Toris saw why those folk had decided to remain behind and endure the scorching heat and radiation during society's collapse into chaos. Thunder had cracked like a whip and woke him from his slumber. Not that he'd have slept much longer after that anyway. Swells rose so high that his hammock slammed into the steel bulkhead with each roll of the ship. This was the beginning of a long and terrifying ordeal.

When he went above, Domlyn ordered him to pull in the kite so he could tackle the waves with both engines. They'd lost sight of the *Southern Zephyr* in the toss, but Toris cared little for anything outside the confines of his own ship. The storm had reduced his world to *Polaris*. This ship was the only thing that existed in the purgatory of grey water and black clouds.

Back on the peninsula, the sun had started to set briefly every twenty-three hours. The farther north they traveled, the longer it stayed below the horizon, establishing a distinct night and day.

Out on the Drake, these increasingly long nights and intensifying storms merged into an endless nightmare. Thrashing waves pummeled *Polaris* so relentlessly that it was a wonder she'd not been ripped apart. Every bridge shift was a battle for the helmsman as they wrestled the wheel to keep them on their northeast bearing. By the end of each watch, Toris's arms felt as if the muscles had been stretched and weakened like cold elastic.

Adding to the dread was knowing every agonizing mile sailed forward was one they'd have to repeat coming back. Toris didn't fret about this as much as his watch partner, Atilus. At least coming back they'd be sure they weren't sailing into oblivion, that land was awaiting them somewhere beyond the horizon.

Between Toris's second and third watch, someone had the brilliant idea to post bets on when they'd see land. Everyone wrote which day in green marker on the bridge's starboard window. These optimistic guesses stoked anticipation every time the next watch came on, no doubt each crew member hoping, like Toris, to have the honour of calling *land* from the bridge. Six days after that first guess went up, however, having passed the most pessimistic estimate, someone scrawled *NEVER* across the whole betting window.

Gradually, the black clouds turned grey and eventually gave way to blue skies. But as the storm died away, the heat took over the task of tormenting *Polaris'* privateers. The temperature seemed to rise a degree every afternoon sailed north under that merciless sun, which rose higher and shone brighter each day. Toris could no longer walk barefoot on the main deck without risking blisters. So, with every crew member now experienced at standing watch, the Skipper ordered that each team split their watch into two hour solo shifts to limit heat exposure.

On a ship so small, Toris was surprised how lonely he'd become. When Atilus came to relieve him for watch each shift, neither bothered exchanging words. Things had obviously gotten bad when a growing part of him missed his partner's rambling.

Skipper Domlyn had brought enough *khat* for the crew for a

week. Once that wore off, so did all enthusiasm aboard. Toris went from rising a half hour early for each shift, to having Jarik come down shaking his hammock a few minutes after his start time. For this he didn't feel bad, because he'd become accustomed to dragging Atilus out of his rack and all the way up to the bridge at the end of his own shift. A few times he had to remain with him for the first half hour to convince him that they weren't all going to die on his watch.

This isolation became worse as the muggy days dragged on. It got so bad that Domlyn had to conduct headcounts every twelve hours to ensure that delirium hadn't lured the vulnerable overboard. Toris suspected this was in part to encourage crew interaction, but no one was having it. When Varcy failed to turn up for roll call one morning, a panicked search found her huddled in a cleaning closet stroking a mop head as if she were consoling a dog in a thunderstorm.

Was this the hell preachers of the old world raved so passionately about? Roaming across an endless sea under a blazing sun with waning hope and a crew who wanted nothing to do with each other did seem an apt punishment for the souls of killers like those Toris shared his ship with. He himself had never killed anyone, but his crime was worse. He was his mother's son. If he encountered her out here, then he'd know this was indeed hell. So he drafted a few choice words should they cross paths.

These mindless shifts and sweltering heat were turning Toris's brain to blubber. He hadn't had a meaningful conversation since sitting on the landing craft with Rykah, just before reaching Arokya. He didn't even know where most of his crew now slept.

Some days, while melting away in his hammock in the lonely V-berth, Toris endured hallucinations of sitting watch in the wheelhouse. Like the day he dreamt he was fighting sleep in the captain's chair, and land came into view. At first glimpse, the Africa of his delusion appeared in tiny brown bits over the wavy ocean horizon. It was land for sure, though. No doubt. He'd been staring at blue sea so long he was sure his eyes would soon turn to water and drain from their sockets.

Just ignore it, he urged himself. Getting excited promised a painful disappointment upon waking, so he sat there watching the bits of brown rise higher and solidify into a solid line.

The door squealed open behind him.

"Why didn't you wake me?" Atilus said as he shuffled in and patted his shoulder. "Did you fall asleep?"

Toris smiled. He was losing it. Even his dream was calling attention to itself by asking if he was sleeping.

Atilus threw himself against the forward window. He looked back to Toris with wild eyes, then punched Toris's arm and threw his hat back over his head. "Why didn't you say anything?!"

Toris sat up straight, feeling the sting where Atilus's fist had pummeled his bicep. So real. And if that were real, that meant…

He reached for the whistle hanging from the forward window. Atilus snatched his wrist and pulled the metal piece toward his lips. Toris threw him to the deck as Rykah had taught him, but Atilus dragged him down as well. They wrestled for control of the whistle, each man eager to deliver the news.

Toris twisted the small metal cylinder from Atilus's fingers and blew a wavering blast. He sat up and blew the whistle again, this time unleashing a shriek that was loud and clear.

Atilus heaved open the bridge door. From the top of the stairs he screamed the most glorious word in their mother language. *"LAND!"*

If you ever wanted to see the dead come back to life, scream that word on a ship whose crew thought for certain they were about to sail over the edge of the earth. By the time Atilus finished calling it for the third time, all hands had scrambled up from below.

Looking ahead, Toris watched the strip of land grow wide across the horizon. Some time passed before he realized he was alone on the bridge. Everyone else had run to the prow down below, each jostling for the ship's forward-most position at the bowsprit, everyone desperate for a closer look to convince their suspicious eyes. Some patted Atilus on the back. Others, like Rykah, pulled him in close for a one-arm hug.

Toris's chest swelled with envy. He'd blown the whistle, but it was Atilus's voice that had announced their salvation.

Rykah noticed Toris in the bridge window and waved him down with a smile.

The excitement between crew members was electric when Toris joined them on the foredeck. Despite being robbed of his moment, he couldn't contain his smile. He even offered Atilus a congratulatory shoulder squeeze.

Domlyn turned from the bowsprit to face his crew. The first time Toris had ever seen him smile was when he said, "I don't know about you lot, but I'd sure like to stretch my legs on solid ground."

Everyone, including the Skipper himself, looked to Rykah for approval. She offered a conceding nod. "Go gear up," she said. "Full battle rattle. We'll take the raiding craft ashore."

TWENTY

Africa sizzled under the merciless sun. The spirit of the paradise described in Sallus's illegal library had abandoned this place long ago, leaving behind a dusty barren carcass to forever remind survivors of the great catastrophe. Waves of heat radiated from the baking land, giving the horizon an appearance as fluid as the sea. One second there rose a mountain, the next it collapsed into a crater, though it could have been flat for all anyone aboard *Polaris* could tell.

Toris and Atilus watched from the shaded starboard breezeway beside the wheelhouse as *Polaris* crept closer to the dead continent. Even at late afternoon the heat was overwhelming. The crew should have stayed below to savour their last moments away from the sun's ferocity, but the foreign land had a magnetizing effect on Polarian curiosity.

Toris pulled his goggles down from his eyes and squinted at the undulating land. At first he thought it was the lenses causing the distortion, but they only dulled the glare with their green tint.

Jarik and Nazar joined them in full battle gear. Like everyone else, each wore his tactical vest over a poncho of near see-through olive material that blew in the breeze. Tan sleeves of thin cotton covered their arms and hands and, along with boonie hats on their heads, ensured the only exposed skin was their faces.

"This isn't right," Jarik said, wrapping a scarf around his mouth. "The lieutenant can't expect us to find anything in that wasteland. We'll fry out there."

"That's okay, Jarik," said Rykah from behind. "You can stay on board while we claim our place in history as the first Polarians to step foot on the old world."

The group turned to see Rykah in a similar outfit, her strapped webbing holding her poncho close to her body. Africa's reflection rippled across her green goggle lenses.

Atilus leaned over the rail, raised a hand over his goggles to shield the sun, as if it would make a difference, and shook his head. "Sorry, ma'am," he said, looking back to Rykah, "but it looks like someone beat us here."

A tabletop mountain had risen to prominence and became the focal point of all on board. At its base, a grey kite blew lazily up the sandy slope from the waterline. As *Polaris* eased closer, a ship came into view. She had run aground.

***

On *Polaris'* bridge, a debate erupted.

"What if they're pyrates?" Atilus said, squinting hard at the wreck.

Nazar hefted his carbine over his head. "Then that'll be one less pyrate crew our Coast Patrol has to worry about."

"And if they're ours?" asked Domlyn. "We don't have the provisions to take them to Svalbard. Are we just going to look them in the eyes and tell them we're leaving them there to die?"

"It's worth a look," Toris said, though he did agree with Domlyn. They'd be committing to a rescue if they did find Polarian survivors. But what if that were *Barnacle* smashed up there?

"Why?" said Domlyn, his face glowing red. "To appease a half-blood's curiosity?"

It'd be a lie to say Toris didn't want a look inland from that tabletop mountain, but this was a matter of obligation. "If the crew was killed in the crash, someone will have to perform their rites."

"Let the sea deal with them," said Domlyn, his grip on the wooden wheel pegs tightening. "Shouldn't be too long before the next storm roils up. That's the fate we all risked when we set out."

"Put it to a vote," Jarik suggested.

"This isn't a democracy," Domlyn snapped. "It's an expedition with a chain of command."

Varcy patted Rykah's shoulder. "And our sponsor placed her at the top. What do you say, Mama?"

Rykah had remained silent through the bickering, eyes staring intensely at the grey kite fluttering at the end of its cables. "Vote," she said.

"I say 'no'," said Domlyn. His forbidding look inspired Ike to vote the same.

"Yes," said Nazar, and of course Jarik followed suit.

Toris raised a thumb. "A 'yes' from me."

"No way," Atilus said, shaking his head vehemently.

It was a tie between landing and moving on, with only Varcy and Rykah left. Rykah nodded to Varcy. "What say you?"

Varcy raised both hands. "Don't care either way."

The tie-breaking vote fell on Rykah. She stared ahead at the grounded ship.

Toris stepped up beside her. "It's maritime law. We have to help a vessel in distress."

Domlyn spit out the starboard window. "Ain't no laws out here, boy. But you can bet the pyrates know ours. If they caught word of us moving this way, they'd employ the oldest trick in their chest: lure a well-intentioned ship in close, then hit them from all sides."

"It's true," Ike said. "They taught us all about it at the Maritime Academy."

"Have you ever seen a pyrate?" Toris said to Ike.

"Well, no, but..."

Toris looked to Domlyn. "And you?"

The Skipper frowned. "You don't need to see something to know it exists." To Rykah, he said, "Look at the dangers. They're smothering any benefit of going ashore."

"That depends how much weight you put into morality," Toris said, stepping up to challenge Domlyn.

"Look!" said Atilus, jumping and pointing out the wheelhouse door behind. "It's the *Zephyr!*"

Sure enough, appearing through the back of the port side window, a royal purple kite towed Lex's ship north. They must have fallen behind in the storm.

"Skipper Domlyn," said Rykah, "fall in with our flagship."

Domlyn gave a nod of approval. "Good call, Lieutenant. Boys, go launch the kite."

Though they remained on the sea, land still managed to spread its woes upon the Polarian flotilla. Easterly storm winds blew golden clouds of sand from the barren continent and peppered the *Polaris* and her crew. Domlyn ordered the kite down and switched to engines, fearing the sand may shred the fabric.

Toris kept his goggles tight and every inch of his skin covered as he and Atilus reeled in the kite. As Atilus packed it below decks, Toris joined the Skipper on the bridge. With the sun completely obscured by the sandstorm, lacking even a light spot to indicate her position, and their visibility limited to no farther than where the kite's cables had held her before the ship, they had only the compass to rely on.

They were sailing blind.

The storm raged for nearly an hour, though it felt more like a week. When the sun finally broke through the cloud over the ocean horizon to their left, its golden light revealed sand covering every surface of *Polaris*. Drifts had piled high along the wheelhouse at her starboard side. If not for the rocking motion of the ship, Toris would have thought they'd ended up on land.

Ahead, the *Southern Zephyr* sailed in the closest formation they'd managed since passing Point Bay Station.

"You know what to do," said Domlyn's muffled voice from under the scarf around his face.

Toris grabbed a broom and set to work sweeping off the foredeck while his crewmates did the same throughout the ship.

Cruising along Africa, with the safety and stability of land so close and security in numbers so close, Toris allowed hope to surge back into his heart. They'd survived Drake's Wrath, both ships, and *Polaris'* engines were humming only slightly harsher from the sand exposure, but not struggling by any stretch. Sea-belly from the rough crossing had left their food supply largely untouched, so they were doing better in that department than planned. Despite the battered feeling aboard, things were going well.

One dark cloud still lingered over the *Polaris*, however, but it was one Toris could clear away on his own. To do that required that he fix things with Rykah. If she saw him as one of her enlisted troops, then he'd crossed a line by making an advance on an officer. He needed to address that, to let her know he had since come to understand and respect her position.

He found her standing watch on the bridge while Domlyn helped Ike flush sand from the engine intakes. She remained seated in the captain's chair when he entered, her eyes trained on the *Southern Zephyr* through the forward window.

Seeing her sitting there, the wind blowing her hair and her skin glowing in the evening light, Toris's heart spun words that his head had not rehearsed nor approved. He stood at the forward window and joined her in watching their course along the continent of golden sand dunes to their right.

"You once told me that imaginary lines don't keep people apart," he said. "Does that not apply to the differences between officers and those they command? Is your lieutenant bar one line this Onero cannot cross?"

His heart issued a silent plea for an answer to that last question. He wasn't leaving until he got it.

"My rank has got nothing to do with it," Rykah said.

He turned to face her. "Then what?"

Her eyes remained fixed ahead, though her stare seemed to reach beyond the horizon and back through time. "I knew a boy once," she said. "We met in basic training, then were posted to the border together. We were inseparable. We vowed that no matter what happened, we'd never let anything keep us apart. Unit transfers or battle orders, none of those would separate us." She sat up straight in her chair, shifting uncomfortably. "Well, it turns out there is one line no one can cross. The border between the world of the living and the dead...*that* line is real."

So the fear of losing Toris was behind Rykah's distance. He didn't know what to say, so he turned to resume watching the sea.

The chair creaked behind, boots touched the floor, and Toris waited for the agonizing creak of the door to announce her departure from the bridge.

Instead, Rykah appeared at his side. "I'm glad you're here," she said.

Toris remained silent.

"I believe what you said before," she went on. "That this is our destiny. But I've seen what distractions like...Distractions of the heart, they can undo a person. We must be strong for the Polarians depending on us."

Toris agreed with Rykah's logic. He truly did. "You're right."

She smiled at him. "We'll stop at that wreck on our way back. If there are bodies, we'll give them a proper send-off. You have my word."

Thunder cracked in the distance. A second clap quickly followed, then a third. Then it was steady. Unnatural.

Rykah's eyes flared wide. She pulled the whistle hanging from the chain around her neck and blew an ear-piercing shriek through it.

Up ahead, the *Southern Zephyr* was cruising straight into a storm of a different sorts. Beyond her purple kite before the horizon, black sails bulged ominously from two ships, their course dead set on the Polarian flotilla.

TWENTY-ONE

Toris's heart seemed to expand wider with each thump.

When he leaned out the starboard window for a clearer view of the approaching ships, he heard drums along with rhythmic shouting—*"Hoo-ahh!"*

Rykah handed him her binoculars, through which he saw a row of oars from each ship's flank dip synchronously into the water, each movement timed with deep chanting. *"Hoo-ahh!"*

The black sails collapsed, leaving two giant masts rocking like metronomes as oars from each ship's hull worked like centipede legs to push the ships faster into the fray.

No longer able to hold the binoculars steady, Toris lowered them. The journey until now had been experienced like feverish delirium that at times had provided a blissful retreat. Those beating drums from the pyrate ships had just woken him to a reality from which there was no escape.

But this was one storm the Polarians could fight back against.

Footsteps clattered up the bridge stairs. "Pull in the kite!" Domlyn shouted as he burst into the wheelhouse. "Switch to engines - maintain course! Ike, signal the *Zephyr* to cut speed and fall into tight formation with us. *Now!*"

On the foredeck, Ike ran to the port signal light. Its shudders squeaked loud as he worked the steel flaps up and down to send Skipper Domlyn's message to the *Southern Zephyr.*

"Fine day for a fight," Nazar called down from the bridge roof. The slapping and clicking of metal revealed he was making the cannon ready for battle.

Jarik scrambled up the ladder to join him on the bridge roof, his vest and carbine hanging loose from his bare shoulders. "Ain't it!"

From the pyrate frigates ahead, two dozen skiffs swarmed out like bees from a hive and converged on the *Southern Zephyr.*

Toris stumbled down the bridge stairs, his hands gripping the rails tight to steady his legs that felt like jelly. He staggered around the wheelhouse to the foredeck.

Before the prow, Rykah stretched an ammunition belt across the machine gun and slammed the feed cover down over the linked .50 caliber rounds. She hauled back on the mighty cocking handle and swung the barrel toward a skiff rocking over the waves nearest the *Southern Zephyr.*

Toris fell in beside her. Gripping the machine gun handles with both hands, she gave him a scrutinizing look.

"You hoping to frighten them away with a mean stare?" she said.

Suddenly his hands felt empty. He darted down to his berth and grabbed his carbine, then slid into his vest that hung heavy with loaded magazines. He was back at Rykah's side within ten seconds. Varcy fell in on Rykah's other side.

Up ahead, *Southern Zephyr*'s kite remained high and her course set to run straight between the two pyrate frigates.

Ike quit flapping the signal light. "I don't think they got the message."

"They're not watching us," Toris said, noticing the skiffs zipping out around the *Zephyr.* If it were him first into the fray, he wouldn't be looking astern for orders either. The small craft buzzed around the lead Polarian ship like a dozen wasps, their motors rattling loud and spewing black smoke.

"We won't catch up to them so long as their kite is up and their engines roaring," Ike said.

"Well, we don't have a spare kite to waste," said Domlyn from the wheelhouse above. "We get holes in that one and we're running on engines the whole way to Svalbard. Then you better hope the Decimators stored plenty of hydrogen with those seeds, or we won't have enough fuel for the return trip. *Here.*"

The Skipper tossed a shotgun from the bridge window to Ike on the foredeck. Ike caught the pump-action gun and the sling of red shells that came behind it.

Watching the skiffs swerve in close to Lex's ship, Toris wondered what weapons she boasted and why they hadn't yet engaged the enemy that was now within even pistol range. Then, as a skiff made a broadside charge at the *Zephyr*'s starboard, Rosaria's ship burst into flames.

Toris watched the fire in horror. Only, the flames came in controlled blasts from the *Zephyr*'s flanks, long streams of fire spraying the skiffs in a bow to stern sweeping motion.

Standing behind Toris, Atilus cheered and whistled. "Have a taste of that, pyrate scum!"

Varcy gave him an ominous shake of her head. Seeing the skiffs break their attack on Lex's ship and zip toward the *Polaris*, coming for what they no doubt hoped was an easier target, Atilus's ovation died. He swallowed hard.

Polaris' engines revved as she lurched forward.

The figures riding low in each rusted skiff numbered from two to four. Mismatched rags clung to their faces, with looser fabric blowing in the wind as the skiffs maneuvered erratically over choppy waves. One pyrate stood, pointed directly to Toris standing on the foredeck, and slid a finger across his throat.

A lump formed in Toris's own throat and seemed to swell with each pump of his heart. He cocked his weapon, the metal cold in his shaking hands. The approaching targets were no practice balloons. But a good look around at his crew gave him all the confidence he needed. Not only did their enthusiasm for the swarming trouble assure him, but he himself embraced the adrenaline flood and welcomed the approaching fight.

Thud-thud-thud-thud-thud... Rykah's whole body shook behind the heavy machine gun as she blasted out rounds. Toris swore his teeth rattled with each shot. The red tracer of every fifth round streaked across the water, the spray of lead kicking up fountains from waves around the skiffs. Brass shells clinked off the wooden deck near Rykah's combat boots.

Several more skiffs fanned out from the two pyrate frigates ahead—a lot more. Toris reckoned three dozen buzzed over the water, spreading out as they skipped wide of the *Southern Zephyr* and on past *Polaris'* flanks to encircle the rear Polarian vessel.

Domlyn leaned out the bridge window. "Jarik, fire control! Everyone, shoot on Jarik's command."

Atop the bridge roof, Jarik took a moment to assess the circling skiffs, then pointed to his right. "Nazar, starboard quarter!"

The rooftop turret rattled. Green tracers zipped out from starboard side, blasting one skiff to splinters and following a second as she sped astern.

"Atilus, get back there and cover port! Toris, go with him!"

The ferocity in Jarik's voice when he yelled Toris's name frayed his nerves. He realized he'd so far been watching the enemy set up their battle pieces like a spectator. But he was in it, of that there was no doubt. Two lone Polarian ships facing down a pyrate fleet to save their people from starvation and war. This was the stuff he'd dreamed of as a young lad.

He put on his brave face and ran aft down the port side behind Atilus. To his right, a flicker arched from a skiff one hundred feet off port and streaked before his face. It buried with a clink into the steel bulkhead to his left.

He slid to a halt. His examination of the five-pointed star with edges sharp enough to slice steel was interrupted by six more flickers off port. He ducked behind cover of the rail plate.

Tink...tink-tink...tink-tink-tink.

He looked up to see one of the *sling-stars* had hit just above his head. His muscles tightened and threatened to lock.

Down at the back, Atilus put a foot up on the stern rail and snapped off a few shots. The skiff before him swerved away. Atilus swung his carbine barrel toward the next closest skiff and fired a few more shots, one round sparking off the metal hull.

"Are your fingers broken, Toris?" shouted Jarik from above. "Shoot!"

He didn't need to be told again. Toris had the butt to his shoulder, the forward grip slick in his sweaty left hand while the index finger of his right squeezed the trigger—*CRACK!*

Toris's first shot at a living target hit the water just behind a skiff's hydrocarbon motor. He shifted his aim ahead of its bow and squeezed off three quick shots. Two spurts of water erupted ahead of the skiff, followed swiftly by a mist of red above. A figure collapsed and disappeared below the boat's gunwale.

"Nice shot!" said Atilus with a nervous laugh.

Toris lowered his weapon in shock. He'd actually hit someone and they weren't getting back up.

A skiff roared in close, its toxic smoke almost enough to choke Toris. It was a wonder how these boat pilots tolerated it.

They are not like us, Toris told himself. *They're predators. Beasts.*

With that, he raised his carbine and pulled the trigger indiscriminately, sending twenty-six bullets beyond the port rail until the M4 clicked empty. He ejected the magazine and pulled a loaded one from his vest, then fed it into the housing, hit the bolt forward, and resumed rapidly pulling the trigger. It was easy. Anyone within range was there to kill him and his crew. This was kill or be killed.

He fired wildly. Despite the terror and noise and the possibility that these were his last breaths, Toris found himself smiling. Even if this were his end, what an end it would be. In a hailstorm of lead and steel on the high sea.

The rush was unlike anything he'd ever known. It sharpened his awareness, allowed him to perceive things he may not otherwise notice. Like, what seemed like a random swerving in of the skiffs actually had a pattern. The skiffs were working in pairs, with one rushing in close to draw fire from the star slingers in the rear, each boat taking turns distracting and slinging.

Atilus must have noticed this as well, because he joined Toris beside the wheelhouse. They knelt behind the rail plates.

"Watch each other's flank," Toris said. "Ninety-degree arcs. You watch left, I'll take right. Ready?"

Atilus nodded and together they stood side-by-side. Toris fired right while Atilus fired left.

One of Toris's tracer rounds struck a skiff pilot. Seeing the green light zip past his target, Toris initially thought he'd missed. Then the pilot flopped back into the sea and left his crew scrambling to regain control of the spinning boat.

He kept his aim trained on the crew and squeezed off a few more shots. A mistake.

Toris didn't see the glint of metal until it was within a foot of his head. A quick jerk brought him just clear of the *sling-star*'s path, with spinning points whirling a finger width past his right temple. A lock of black hair fell to his feet.

Atilus tackled him to the deck. Toris flinched as steel clinked off the other side of the rail plates and buried into the wheelhouse wall above him. When Atilus's eyes fell on Toris's head, he erupted with mad laughter. "Gotta watch that tunnel vision, brother."

Through a slit between plates, Toris saw a skiff speed straight in to hit *Polaris* broadside. A flurry of machine gun rounds blew the boat to splinters before it made contact.

Toris traced the line of fire to the prow, where Rykah swung the heavy machine gun to another target off the starboard side, oblivious to the steel stars whizzing all around her.

He bolted across the foredeck and grabbed the vertical webbing piece that connected Rykah's shoulder straps across her back. Her arms flailed as he hauled her back toward the narrow cover between the wheelhouse and the port side rail plates.

From here, as the *Polaris* entered the gap between both pyrate frigates, he was close enough to read the names painted across each bow. On the ship off port, sloppy white letters spelled out *Urchin* across rusted plates that overlapped like ill-fitted puzzle pieces, the armour clearly scavenged from a variety of sources. The ship off the starboard side was called *Salish Sweeper*.

The *Urchin* launched a ballista bolt the size of a birch trunk. A barbed head whizzed over Toris and Rykah and punched through the bridge's port side window with a gut-wrenching crash. *Polaris* heeled to starboard.

Toris and Rykah fell against the wheelhouse wall. Toris watched in horror as a slack cable of braided steel attached to the bolt's wooden base tightened. When the cable stretched tight, *Polaris'* bow hitched toward the *Urchin*. Below, the engines roared in their fight to maintain a straight course.

"Nazar, aim for that frigate!" Rykah said, trying to steady herself on the base of the wheelhouse as she made her way to retrieve her rifle from under the steep bridge stairs.

A steady stream of cannon fire zipped from atop the bridge and sparked off the frigate's armoured plates.

"Everyone else, shoot for that cable!" Rykah said from under the stairs.

Easier said than done. Trying to hit a finger-wide line between two moving ships was incredibly difficult, as Toris learned with ten missed shots.

The roof cannon above fell silent.

"Nazar!" Rykah shouted, popping off shots at a closing skiff. "Hammer that frigate!"

Jarik's head leaned over the roof edge. "Barrel is melted, ma'am! Damn heat!"

Small arms fire crackled from two assault rifles on the roof.

Rykah stumbled back to look at the cannon in shock. She shook it off. "Dom, spin us to port and slack that line! Varcy, get up there and unhook us! Everyone else, concentrate fire on those skiffs! Turn them all to scrap metal!" To Toris, she said, "Go help Varcy. I'm gonna help lay fire from the roof."

Varcy sprang up the bridge stairs two at a time, a battle axe rattling from each hip. Toris followed close behind.

On the bridge, Domlyn had the wheel spun all the way left, which should have spun the ship to port and slacked the cable. Yet the bow remained north under control of the spearhead's six-pronged hook that had sank into the steel below the port side window.

Domlyn pointed down to the foredeck. Through the forward window, Toris saw a second ballista bolt had anchored to the rail of the starboard bow from the *Salish Sweeper*. With both pyrate ships pulling *Polaris* in opposite directions, Domlyn had lost all steering.

"We need to ditch one of those hooks so I can spin us out," the Skipper said.

Varcy handed Toris a battle axe and set to work with her own, leaning out through the window to hack away at the thick wooden shaft.

From the skiffs below, canisters spewing clouds of smoke—purple and red—arched across the water and bounced onto *Polaris'* decks. Rykah kicked two from the foredeck, but firing at the skiffs took priority, and soon a crimson haze rose up and clouded inside the bridge. Toris and Varcy coughed and held rags to their mouths.

"Incoming!" cried Domlyn nearby.

Back through the bridge door, Toris noticed three pyrates climbing over the starboard rail before the stern. With anchor cables from both pyrate frigates stabilizing *Polaris*, skiffs were swinging in close in search of a gap to unload their boarding parties.

Varcy leaned out the door and fired her rifle three times, hitting two and sending the other for cover behind a crate. Below, Ike rushed from around the wheelhouse with his shotgun to flush out the surviving pyrate.

Toris looked back to the shaft protruding from the port side window, into which he and Varcy had only hacked out a tiny chip with her battle axes.

He leaned out the window. "Atilus, get up here! And bring a proper axe."

A moment later, Atilus arrived on the bridge with a red fire axe. He noticed the bolt shaft holding them steady and got straight to work. Three swings in, however, a flash of metal zipped over his head and forced him back inside.

Toris leaned out the port window and fired automatic bursts down at the nearest three skiffs. "Keep going," he told Atilus. "I'll cover you."

Behind, Varcy crouched beside the doorway firing single shots at the encroaching skiffs.

Atilus resumed hacking away at the wooden ballista shaft while Toris covered him with carbine fire. Each swing knocked out a deeper wedge.

By the midway point in his chopping, Atilus had worked up such a sweat that his hands could no longer grip the wooden axe handle. Toris ordered him to step back and drew his pistol, aimed at the wedge, and fired until it clicked empty.

The remaining sliver of wood could not withstand the pressure. It cracked, dropping the star-shaped head to the deck at Toris's feet.

Atilus gave Toris a nod of approval.

A crash echoed from the starboard. The ship nudged sideways as three pyrates rolled across the foredeck, away from the wreckage of their wooden skiff. One had boarded with an axe in one hand, then pulled a second from his belt. His partner drew a short sword and pointed it toward the bridge while the third, wearing a blue longcoat and wielding a scimitar, ran around the base of the wheelhouse and out of sight.

Ike charged out from around the bridge's opposite side and fired a blast into the axeman. He pumped the gun to eject the shell, then noticed it was empty.

The pyrate wielding the short sword charged at him, but Varcy rushed from behind Ike with a battle axe in each hand. Steel rang on steel as she met the attack, blocking with one blade while swinging the other into his neck.

Domlyn leaned out the bridge door, watching the pyrate in the longcoat descend the stairs below decks. "The engines!" he said to Toris. "If they disable them we're all dead."

Toris rushed down the steep bridge stairs with Atilus pounding down behind him. Atop the hold stairway leading below, Atilus held ground and fired at pyrate skiffs swerving in toward the starboard quarter. He looked to Toris with rattled eyes. "Get below. I'll cover you."

Emboldened by his success so far in the fight, Toris fixed a bayonet to the barrel of his carbine. He took a deep breath and was about to charge below when a skiff crashed into the port quarter. Two pyrates tumbled onto the deck and ate six of Toris's bullets. But there were many more eager to continue the rush, swarming aboard from all sides, any of which may overrun Atilus during a reload, so Toris remained above firing.

A canister spewing green smoke bounced across the deck and hit the back of the wheelhouse. Toris buried his mouth and nose into his elbow, picked up the smoke grenade, and dropped it down the steps below decks.

He snapped off a few shots at the remaining skiffs that were circling like sharks in search of an opening. He was reloading when the pyrate scrambled up from below while coughing up a lung. With hair in white dreadlocks and rabid eyes, she resembled the Ortarian archetype that had stoked Polarian fears for centuries.

Toris aimed his carbine at her. "Drop the sword," he said, though he knew full well she likely didn't understand a word of it. Her reaction suggested as much when she rushed him with her scimitar.

A pull of his trigger resulted in a weapon jam, so Toris threw his carbine up to block the blade—*TING!*

The pyrate pressed her attack, hacking and slashing while Toris put Rykah's training to use. He denied her at each turn until Atilus cracked her in the back of the head with his carbine butt.

The woman pyrate lumbered forward onto her face. Blood oozed up through the matted hair at the back of her head.

Toris was clearing his weapon to put a finishing shot in the pyrate when three long horn blasts echoed from the *Urchin*. It's sister ship to *Polaris*' starboard answered with three short blasts.

"We broke through," Jarik declared from above.

Toris noticed the gunfire had tapered to only Nazar's sporadic pot shots above. Both frigates had veered wide, slightly behind *Polaris* and with no sign of turning around. The nearest skiff hummed one hundred feet to port, headed hard south.

"Cease fire," Rykah said, almost casually, from the foredeck.

Metal rattled as the gunners cleared their weapons.

Toris assessed his shipmates. Watching everyone handle their weapons with such cool ease, as if they'd just finished another round at the shooting range, gave him a strong sense that made his hair stand on end. These Agrinauts were the stuff of legends.

Not only that, but he'd held his own and then some. He needed only to look at the notches from the scimitar blade in his carbine's black material as proof. Surely most of his crew had taken fire before and knew what to expect, an advantage Toris had lacked until now.

Did that actually just happen? Did he just face down a pyrate fleet off the coast of Africa? Jayda was going to have a hard time believing some of his stories when he returned home.

Atilus fumbled to feed loose rounds into his empty magazines. Toris patted his vest, felt that each pouch was empty, and realized his last magazine was in his weapon. He hadn't even noticed firing off nearly one hundred and fifty shots and was glad to have avoided the surprise of needing to reload only to find he was out of ammo. A novice move. He'd have to direct some awareness to that in their next firefight.

Cheers and howls erupted across *Polaris*' decks.

The excitement of another encounter stirred something new and unfamiliar in Toris, yet not entirely foreign. Watching the pyrate fleet shrink beyond their wake, part of him begged them to return. He wasn't finished.

As he squinted to assess the enemy fleet's damage, something beyond the pyrate ships caught Toris's eye: a grey kite. Red distress flares arched from the ship sailing north over the horizon, straight toward the pyrates.

Toris's heart drummed a dreadful tune. The pyrates had given up on them to pursue a weaker, more isolated target. Another privateer crew was about to earn their battle stripes.

TWENTY-TWO

Rykah rushed around the wheelhouse from the foredeck. "Nazar, Jarik, sweep below to make sure none are still aboard."

The two Travarians fixed their bayonets and rushed below decks.

At the stern, Toris watched as more red flares arched through the sky. Was that *Barnacle* begging for help? Were Drua and Antlia in over their heads, overcome with regret by embarking on this endeavour?

It didn't matter. They knew the risks. And the *Southern Zephyr*'s will to leave *Polaris* behind made it clear that every ship was on its own out here.

Nazar and Jarik returned from their sweep below. "All clear," Jarik announced.

"They's gonna eat yer friends," rose a voice from midship.

Everyone spun to see who'd spoken. Most figured it out at the same time as Toris, because they all drew their weapons on the pyrate woman who'd attacked him with her scimitar. Toris had assumed the buttstroke to the back of her skull had killed her.

The feral woman sat up, her head wobbling. Silver teeth glinted in the evening sun as she squinted at her antagonists. She pushed the white dreadlocks from her face and prodded the back of her head.

Rykah approached first. She detached the bayonet from her rifle barrel and pointed it astern. "How many more ships like those are north of here?"

"Shouldn't you be turnin' 'round to save them folk back there? What part a 'they's gonna eat yer friends' didn't you unnerstand?"

Toris crouched beside Rykah to level with the pyrate's eyes. "How do you know our language?"

"Ain't yer language, boy. They been speakin' it fer at least a thousand winters."

Toris crawled forward on his hands, lured by fascination. Rykah's hand on his shoulder stopped him from venturing within the pyrate's reach.

"Where are you from?" he asked.

"Pellington Grey."

Toris shot upright. He'd been expecting some unfamiliar name from the lands north of here, not a town located half a day's ride from Lake Orion Orphanry. Either this pyrate was using some form of witchery to inform herself of his homeland, or she'd grown up not far from where Toris had. Toris didn't believe in magic, which left only one possibility. "You're Polarian."

Nazar checked a body behind the pyrate wench. He pulled the dead pyrate's shirt down at the collar to expose his deltoid, where a raised *O* brand resembled Toris's without the slash.

"An Onero," Jarik said in shock.

For a long while all Toris could do was stare at that raised circle of scar tissue on the dead pyrate's arm. The brand that so many of his brothers and sisters received when they were old enough to run.

He drifted closer for a look at the dead pyrate's face, to see if he was from his orphanry or civil service. But the features under his blistered skin were as foreign to him as the dead land off *Polaris'* starboard.

"How does an Onero end up way out here as a pyrate?" Toris said.

Their captive pulled her collar down to reveal a faded black *III* on her neck. Varcy instinctively felt the numeral on her own neck, the number of the labour camp she'd called her home until the Defence Force conscripted her.

"You escaped?" Rykah said. Her impassive expression was betrayed by the amazement in her tone. Apparently breaking out of a labour camp was a feat of wonder. "Wait, you're—"

"Jorda," Toris said, connecting the dots at the same time as Rykah, "The Explorer."

Jorda cocked her head. "That what they been callin' me? Expected worse outta the mouths of Polarians."

The implication brought Toris's hair on end. "Are all you pyrates Oneros and criminals?"

Jorda's lips sealed shut, reminding them this wasn't a family reunion.

Atilus pulled off his hat and rubbed his scalp in distress. "That's what'll become of us if we don't find those seeds first."

Rykah shot him a scolding look.

Jorda sat up straight. "Seeds?"

Rykah crouched before Jorda. She brandished the bayonet before her face. "Tell me about your leader."

"The Divine Mother? What do ya wanna know?"

Rykah's jaw clenched. "That attack was well coordinated. Someone was giving orders, someone who knows what they're doing and has strong leadership."

"Oh stop," Jorda said, flashing her metallic grin. "You'll make a girl blush."

Rykah stood up straight, watching her dubiously. "A commander of a force that size wouldn't be cruising around in a skiff."

Jorda clinked both rows of teeth together. "Ya don't become queen of the sea by leadin' from a throne, m'dear. Which brings me back to yer friends there. I can see they go free."

"*If* they even survive that attack," Jarik said. "You came at us pretty hard."

Jorda spat. "You fired first. Think we recruited all them runaways by blowin' em outta the water? We'd be a pretty small fleet if we did that. We offer quarter and, if they's a good fit for our colony, make 'em proper citizens."

Toris grabbed Rykah's arm and pulled her away to speak in private.

"We don't have enough ammo for another encounter with them," Rykah said, her voice straining with regret as she watched the pyrates swarm the lingering ship.

"I know."

She met Toris's response with a look of surprise. "Then what?"

"The *Zephyr*, they left us behind without a second look back. We're just fodder to them." Hearing the words aloud dampened his spirit. Did Lex know he was aboard? Or had Ignatius assured her that *Polaris* was crewed by criminals, every one of them expendable, their only purpose to ensure she returned with the seeds? "If we lose our flagship, we risk losing our chance at claiming the Accolade with them. No matter what happens, we have to return to Anterra with the *Zephyr* in sight."

"Even if that means leaving a Polarian boat to the pyrates?"

Captain Antlia's ship was made to trawl fish. Not combat. They'd surrender pretty quick, and now that it was clear Oneros were among the boarding parties, Drua had a chance at brokering fair treatment for his crew.

"We all accepted that risk when we took to sea," Toris said, cringing at his own words. "The Coast Patrol's expedition ship will clean up that fleet and help whatever Polarian crew they come across. Those battle cruisers move a lot faster than this swamp boat, so we need to maintain as much of a lead on that military expedition as we can."

Rykah nodded, though hesitantly. "I'm glad you're with me on this." She looked up to the bridge. "Domlyn, get us moving north at top speed—kite and engines—everything we got."

"Wait!" Atilus marched to Rykah while pointing back at Jorda. "If she is who she says she is, they'll come looking for her."

Rykah glanced at Jorda. "We'll drop her off on land with some flares."

"No!" Jorda jumped to her feet, all her confidence crumbling away like dry leaves. Nazar and Jarik seized her arms to contain her writhing.

"Relax," Rykah said. She pointed astern. "Look, they're coming back around. You won't be there long."

It was true. Both pyrate ships had raised their black sails and swung north, leaving behind a ship billowing black smoke into the blue sky.

"No!" Jorda wailed, brows arched high in a plea. She sank low in her captors' hold like a child resisting her frustrated parents.

Rykah raised a hand and motioned for Nazar and Jarik to release her. She bent over and leaned close to Jorda's face. "What's out there?"

Jorda pulled her knees to her chest. "We don't go to land, no matter what." She rested her chin on her knees, head rocking while muttering that same phrase over and over. *We don't go to land, no matter what.*

Rykah stood straight. "Nazar, Jarik, lock the pyrate in Toris's berth. Toris, you'll have to find somewhere else to sleep."

Jarik and Nazar escorted Jorda below.

Toris returned to the stern and watched the burning ship. Part of him pitied the crew, but it was a burden he'd bear. He wasn't out here to do the right thing. He was here to save Jayda.

"Why aren't we moving, Dom?" Rykah said.

"Ike!" yelled Domlyn from the bridge. "What's going on down there?"

The strain in the Skipper's voice raised Toris's alarm.

Ike scrambled up from below, both hands black to his elbows. "Both engines are shot. All that maneuvering and force was too much in this heat. I'll need some time to get them going again."

Domlyn appeared in the bridge doorway at the top of the

stairs, face burning red as if he were about to lash out at Ike. Instead, he collapsed backward.

Ike was first up the bridge stairs. Kneeling at Domlyn's side, his greasy hands hovered warily over a slit in his father's shoulder. When Toris pounded up the steps behind, Ike pointed to a white box under the starboard window. "Wound kit."

Toris squeezed around Ike and stepped over Domlyn to retrieve the kit. In the wall beside the box, buried in the metal bulkhead, a *sling-star* dripped blood from one of its edges. Toris grabbed the wound kit and passed it to Rykah, who had just joined Ike. He watched as both ex-defence force officers patched the wound.

"You're going below to rest," Rykah said. When Domlyn made to protest, she cut him off. "That's an order."

Ike and Rykah each took an arm and helped Domlyn to his feet. The Skipper growled as he struggled to stand but, once upright, he required only a little help from Ike to descend the stairs. Halfway down, he looked back up to Toris standing in the bridge doorway and said, "Take the helm."

Then, on the main deck at the bottom of the stairs, the old Skipper's full weight collapsed into Ike. Both men toppled to the deck.

Toris grabbed both rails and skimmed down the stairs. Rykah had already removed the dressing when he arrived. Ike wiped away the blood for a better looked at the wound. The amount of bleeding was deceptively high considering the cut size. It appeared as if the star had only grazed Domlyn, which made his reaction seem exaggerated.

"All the stress of the attack and the heat," Rykah guessed, "it's making his symptoms much worse."

"He needs a physician," Ike said.

Jarik scoffed. "Where are we going to find one out here?"

"The *Zephyr*," Ike said, his voice rife with concern. "She's crewed with a full-time doctor. Anywhere Rosaria's ship goes, he goes. Especially now with the Chancellor's daughter aboard."

"Well then," Rykah said, looking up to Toris, "it's best we be playing catch-up."

Toris wasted no time. He looked to Atilus and said, "With me."

At the bow, Toris heaved the kite launcher onto this shoulder and deployed the sky sail. With Atilus's help, they adjusted the cables to fill the red sail with wind, and within three minutes they were cruising north again.

On his way around the wheelhouse, watching Nazar and Jarik carry the Skipper below to rest, Toris felt a tingle of pride in the fact that in his moment of incapacitation, the ship commander's instinct was to hand over control to him.

He sprang up the steps to the bridge. He paused before the captain's chair, felt the smooth handles of the varnished wheel in his hands and the mighty tug of the kite wavering in the sky before the bow, dragging them toward Polaria's salvation. And with it came the weight of it all. If they didn't reach the *Southern Zephyr* soon, the responsibility of this ship may remain entirely on Toris Onero to Svalbard and back.

TWENTY-THREE

Skipper Domlyn's life depended on catching the *Southern Zephyr*, and her crew wasn't making it easy. The *Zephyr*'s current speed suggested they were using both engines and her kite with no sign of letting up.

Toris stood before the captain's chair, both hands on the wheel and his eyes trained ahead at all times. The *Southern Zephyr* was his concern; the pyrate vessels in pursuit were Rykah's. The smaller Rosaria's ship shrank beyond *Polaris'* bow, the tighter Toris's hands gripped the smooth wheel knobs.

He loosened the goggle straps to relieve the pinching on his nose, but he dared not remove them until sunset. At least now the sun was at their service. If the pyrates wanted to catch them badly enough they could, but the equatorial heat kept their oars drawn in. For Toris, even trying to stay awake in the captain's seat was a struggle, so he remained standing. He could hardly breathe this humid air that was feeling more and more like steam.

As the sun rose higher than he'd ever thought possible, so that it was directly above the *Polaris*, its rays shimmered so bright off the water that he could no longer see the *Zephyr* ahead without his goggles. Their green-tinted flagship seemed to teeter on the horizon, so Toris kept his eyes fixated on that shrinking black dot in the green sea as if his life depended on it, because his skipper's did, and without their skipper they may all die out here.

At mid-afternoon, Atilus, Nazar, Jarik and Varcy began shuttling sandbags from the bow to the stern despite the blistering heat. When Toris turned to see what they were doing, he noticed the pyrate ships had slashed their separation by half. If *Polaris* were to stop right now, the pyrates would be on them in fifteen minutes or less.

At the bow, Rykah removed the .50 caliber from its tripod and heaved it over her shoulder. She lugged the machine gun past the wheelhouse to the stern and leaned it against the rear wall of sandbags.

Toris's heart drummed an ominous beat as he watched his crew set up a square perimeter of green sandbag walls at the stern.

Eventually the *Zephyr*'s speed eased and Toris was able to maintain pace with them. As she started to grow larger while pulling back from the northern horizon, Toris breathed easier. He even allowed himself to sink back into the captain's chair to give his feet a rest.

Finally, they were gaining on *Southern Zephyr*. Aside from offering a doctor, their flagship provided strength in numbers. Not to mention the deterrent of her flamethrowers. Because, though the pyrates had held off from attacking the night before, they were likely dealing with casualties and resting after their attacks on the three Polarian ships the previous day. There was no guarantee they'd show such restraint tonight after they'd recovered.

It took Toris until early evening, when the sun dropped down toward the western horizon and the shimmering glare of the equatorial afternoon eased, to see they had made considerable progress in their plight to reunite with their flagship. At this rate, *Polaris* would be alongside the *Zephyr* before sunset.

When he heard Rykah's light footsteps coming up the stairs, Toris was eager to share the good news with her.

She appeared in the bridge doorway, but before Toris could utter a word, she said, "He's getting worse."

Toris engaged *Polaris'* auto-pilot and followed Rykah down to the hold. He heard wheezing from halfway down the lower stairway. In the skipper's berth at midship, Domlyn did not look good lying upon his bed. Red blotches spread and swelled all over his skin, and the only hint of awareness came from the odd flicker of his eyelids to the sound of Ike's voice.

Ike knelt beside his father's bed, holding his hand and helplessly shaking his head. "I don't understand."

"I do," said Rykah. She turned and carried on down the passageway.

Toris backed out of the berth, eyes fixated on the signs of the Skipper's drastic decline, and then followed Rykah to what used to be their berth.

Jorda sat with her legs straight in front, her left foot chained to the floor, watching her captors in the doorway from under a mat of sun-bleached dreads.

Rykah loomed over the pyrate queen. "What poison do you use on those *sling-stars*?"

Toris rubbed his left temple, recalling how close one of those stars had come to him.

Jorda shrugged casually. "A carefully concocted mixture of venoms and toxins collected from 'round the world. It's th'only thing keepin' them Nordican mutts north a here from comin' after us."

Rykah crouched. "Crafting such weaponry is risky business. People make mistakes, get bit by their own devices. You must have an antitoxin."

Jorda smirked. "Course we do, but I ain't got none wit me."

"Where do we find some?"

"Me fleet has it a plenty. Bet they'd be willin' to trade a vile er two fer their leader. Send me back to me *Urchin*, and I'll make sure to send ya the antidote."

Rykah stood and looked down her nose at Jorda. "You take me for a fool? You'd tell them all about our defences and then attack."

"Wouldn't do that, m'dear." Jorda shook her head. "No, ma'am. Just wanna get off this boat before y'all goes too far north, is all."

Rykah crossed her arms. "What's north of here that you're so afraid of?"

"Nordicans," Jorda said, her gaze dropping to the floor.

"Which are…"

"People from Nordica. Ain't much of a civilized folk, if ya catch my meanin'."

"Where's the southernmost Nordican settlement?" Rykah said.

Jorda leaned back against the wall. "I'm givin' ya lotsa information for nothin' in return." She tugged at her leg chain. "Best be improvin' me accommodations before ya hears another word from me."

Toris left Rykah alone with the pyrate queen and returned to the main deck. Beyond the bow, *Southern Zephyr* appeared much closer. Behind them, the pyrate ships were falling behind. A few minutes ago he'd have rejoiced over this development. Things were a lot simpler then, more straightforward. All he had to do was keep his eye on the *Zephyr* and hope she lost speed enough for *Polaris* to catch up. But now, *Southern Zephyr* didn't offer Skipper Domlyn's salvation.

Rykah joined him at the stern rail. Her expression was grim. "Can you get us to Svalbard and back without him?"

Toris squeezed the rail. Perhaps Ike's Coast Patrol training had included navigation, but what good would he be mourning his father at sea? That was too much responsibility to put on a man who'd just lost his only family. It was too much for all of them. They were a carefully selected crew, the bare necessities. Without one, they all fall. It was clear what Toris had to do, and Rykah wasn't going to like it any more than he did. The very thought made him queasy.

"I need to go to them," Toris said, nodding at the lagging pyrate ships.

To his surprise, Rykah nodded as if she'd already come to this conclusion. "Take Nazar to watch your back," she said.

"You think it's a good idea?"

She gnawed on her lip. "No, but if you offered then that confirms my suspicions: without Domlyn, we're all dead out here." Her gaze fell on his shoulder. She forced a smile. "Besides, what better ambassador to send to a group of exiled Oneros?"

Toris smiled. That was true. Hopefully the brand on his shoulder was all he needed to establish trust with the pyrates. It should at least get him audience with the new leadership to present his offer—their queen for the cure.

"Okay," he said. "Let's get me out there before I change my mind."

A red sky over the western horizon welcomed the sun in its descent to the sea.

Toris prepared the rubber raiding craft suspended from *Polaris'* stern. Its hydrogen level was topped up and both paddles lay at the bottom, with a spare paddle as a backup to the backup.

Rykah leaned over the rail to hand him a bundle of six flares held together by two rubber bands. "Red is for trouble; green is for clear. If we see the green, we'll prepare Jorda for your return. Pop red if it goes sideways, and we'll do our best to come help."

Toris took the flares and pulled off a red cap to expose the launch striker. Both he and Rykah knew she couldn't turn around at a red flare. *Polaris* was at the mercy of the wind.

Rykah crouched behind the rail so she was eye level with him standing in the landing craft. "It's just a precaution," she said. "Nazar will be watching your back."

As if on cue, the Travarian brute approached from the foredeck with a vest bulging with what had to be half the ship's remaining ammunition, so much so that he couldn't close the pouch flaps.

Toris watched Nazar struggle to stuff a grenade into his already overflowing utility pouch. "We're going there to offer a trade, remember?"

Nazar used both hands to pull the flap over the grenade and forced the clip shut. "Yeah, well, they may have different plans when they see us coming. Best be ready for trouble."

Nazar jumped over the rail and climbed down into the landing craft.

Rykah squeezed Toris's shoulder. "If things go astray," she said, "you'll be glad he's there. Now, you best get going. I don't think Domlyn has much time."

Nazar sank down into the narrow bow alcove where the port and starboard gunwales met. "Let's do this."

Toris lowered the landing craft down its ropes until the bottom skimmed water, where he released its tethers from the ship. Because *Polaris* was still underway, the landing craft drifted quickly from her stern. Toris fired up the hydrogen motor, which sputtered and then hummed. He cranked the throttle and sent his envoy bouncing over white caps toward the two pyrate ships.

That's when it hit him. This was madness. But it was exactly that which may help them. Surely the pyrates would suspect some trick and exercise caution before engaging this lone raiding craft on its suicide mission.

The ships came up faster than expected. Toris debated which of the two to approach, and decided that the *Salish Sweeper* appeared less threatening than the *Urchin*.

When within rifle range, Toris ordered Nazar to raise their white flag. Nazar lifted a sheet tied to an aluminum pole and held it firm against the wind. Toris steered them far right of the flotilla's right-hand ship, past her bow, and then looped back to come along her port side. He released the throttle and waited for his speed to die, then stood.

Cupping his hands around his mouth, he shouted, "We have Jorda! We wish to make a trade!"

Four heads popped up from behind an uneven parapet of

rusted steel. A blood-soaked bandage revealed one of the leaders was among their casualties.

"What do you want?" responded a man's hoarse voice.

"A cure," Toris replied. "One of our crew is poisoned."

The heads dropped out of sight.

Nazar lowered the flag and gripped his carbine with both hands.

A few seconds later, one head popped up from behind the plates. "We have a new leader now. You can keep the extra mouth to feed."

The head dropped out of sight.

"Who are you?" Toris said. "Where are you from?"

Silence.

"Are you Onero?" he pressed.

Still nothing.

Toris cruised up to match their northbound pace.

"I grew up at Lake Orion Orphanry," he said. "Most of the kids from my childhood will be forced to invade Ortaria if we don't succeed in our mission out here. If any of you are Onero, then the same is true for you. Think of your brothers and sisters."

Toris awaited a response. Still, nothing.

"I know many of you made your decision to leave home out of desperation or haste," he said, "but all of you left with the hope of finding a better life. Many of you no doubt have regrets and wish you could go home. Well..." Toris hated lying, especially to his own kind, but to call them his own now seemed a stretch. "The Artican is offering a pardon to anyone who brings seeds back to Polaria. *Anyone*, including exiles."

"Liar!" came the response.

Progress, thought Toris.

He flashed his shoulder brand. "I'm an Onero in exile, and I'm out here looking for the same reward that's available to all of you." Now, to dress up the lie. "Anyone who aids in returning with the seeds shall be granted full amnesty from all crimes. I have a letter stating as much back on our ship."

Silence.

Nazar shook his head and gritted his teeth.

"We're not asking you to join us," Toris said, growing impatient. "We just need a single dose of the cure, that's it. When we return home, we'll tell The Artican of your assistance. We'll all get pardons so we can return home."

Toris expected laughter to accompany his offer. Instead, a half-minute later, a head rose above the *Sweeper*'s port side parapet.

"Jorda lied to you, brother," said the pyrate. "There is no cure for *spear spit*."

Toris sank to the floor of the boat, everything around him fading away. It took all his might for him to not slump back and give up right there. From here, *Polaris* seemed the same distance as *Southern Zephyr* when he'd last seen her beyond *Polaris'* bow.

Nazar kicked his leg. "Pull it together, man. We need to get out of here."

He was right. Toris grabbed the throttle, but he wasn't going back empty-handed. He stood once more. "If we return Jorda to you, will you abandon your pursuit?"

Over the port side defence plates, four heads bobbed in discussion.

"Send the wench back, Toris," a man growled. "Or she'll haunt me in hell until all the stars burn out, I'm sure of it."

Toris, the man had said! That pyrate knew who he'd been talking to the entire time. So who was he? Toris was dying to know. If the pyrate was from Lake Orion, then he might know Drua. Then he'd tell him if that were *Barnacle* burning back there. Or, if Drua and Antlia were alive, he could demand their release when he returned with Jorda.

He twisted the throttle and cruised forward, risking a close pass along *Salish Sweeper*'s port side for a better look at the crew without their rags on. A big mistake.

Hanging low on the forward mast waved a Polarian flag, its white star smeared red with blood. From the wire stays holding the masts upright, bones rattled in the breeze.

Without warning, Nazar lobbed a rock onto the *Sweeper*'s main deck. Only, the round pin curled in his index finger suggested it was something far more sinister than a rock.

A quiver of dread shot through Toris's heart.

Three seconds later, a blast of scarlet dust confirmed his fear. Before he could think or do anything, Nazar was kneeling against the gunwale firing his carbine on automatic. A hail of bullets swept wide across the port side, sparking off rusted steel plates and blasting splinters from the masts. When he stopped to reload, a cacophony of screams rose in the brief silence until Nazar resumed firing.

Smoking brass shells hit the floor beside Toris as he watched the carnage in shock. When Nazar emptied his second magazine, Toris had seen enough. He twisted the throttle and launched the landing craft forward ahead of the *Salish Sweeper*. When Nazar reloaded and stood to fire over the stern, Toris swung the tiller and cut the speeding craft hard left to fling Nazar overboard.

Toris swerved and straightened his course back toward *Polaris*. A look over his shoulder revealed Nazar's blond hair bobbing in the water, both hands flailing. Toris released the throttle. Then, just as quickly, he changed his mind and revved it again to continue his forward course. Nazar deserved to deal with the consequences.

Though, that wasn't how this worked out here. The pyrates would seek vengeance on the whole crew, and *Polaris* would need every trigger finger to face their wrath.

Toris swung back. Nazar's head had just sank for the last time, his left hand the only body part above water for reference. Toris cruised up and grabbed the Travarian brute's wrist and hauled him over the gunwale. Nazar rolled onto the raiding craft floor and coughed up water.

"You idiot!" Toris said. It took all his restraint to not kick Nazar while he was blowing out his lungs.

Ahead, the *Urchin* was mooring against the *Salish Sweeper* to presumably render aid.

Toris blasted the motor and sent the raiding craft launching over waves. A few times he almost flipped himself backward over the stern, but he didn't let up. Even with his engine screaming across the water, the tiny craft didn't seem to be gaining any distance on *Polaris*. The engine shuddered and sputtered. Toris prayed for her to hold up, regretting all the free time that he hadn't used to maintain it. If she died, he'd never reach his ship with the paddles.

TWENTY-FOUR

Toris crawled over *Polaris'* stern rail and was immediately swarmed by his crew, eager faces desperate for answers.

"We heard gunfire," Atilus said.

"Did they attack first?" asked Rykah, patting him over for wounds.

Toris sat on the rear wall of the square sandbag bunker. He looked to Ike, who bounced on his feet while wringing his hands anxiously.

"I'm sorry, Ike. There is no cure."

Ike's heels planted flat on the deck, though his expression suggested he'd already suspected this.

Jarik leaned over the rail. "You okay, Naz?"

"I'm coming up," Nazar grunted from the raiding craft below.

"The hell happened?" said Rykah.

Toris hung his head. "Nazar blew our chances," he said. *Literally*, blew their chances.

Jarik rushed to the ladder, where Nazar's wet hair rose higher above the main deck. Jarik helped him over the rail and collapsed with him onto the deck.

"What happened to you?" Jarik said, hugging Nazar close.

Nazar pointed a shaky hand at Toris. "He tossed me from the boat. Was gonna leave me to drown."

Jarik stood, eyes blazing and mouth twisting in rage. *"Bastard,"* he said, then spit.

Behind him, Nazar smirked up at Toris despite his struggle for air. What was supposed to be a taunt, however, Toris took for a warning. He spread his feet into a fighting stance.

Luckily Jarik's left hook resembled many of Rykah's during training along the peninsula, so Toris raised his arm into a triangle to block it. But Jarik's other fist was already in motion and pummeled Toris's belly.

He keeled over while spinning and stumbled a few paces. Jarik's footsteps announced his pursuit, and just before he came within swinging distance, Toris lunged into his torso and tackled him to the deck. All his life he'd been hit harder by boys at the orphanry, big lads like Drua, so Jarik's short-handed hit did little other than provide the aggressor a false sense of dominance.

While the two wrestled on the deck, struggling for top position, Toris awaited Rykah to step in to break them up. But a quick glance at the spectators revealed the crew with folded arms watching intensely, with Rykah chewing her thumbnail.

Toris was running the mill.

But to him this wasn't a game. Nor was it for Jarik. This was, for both fighters, about vengeance. And unlike his first run at the mill and his training with Rykah, Toris wanted to hurt Jarik. Bad.

Toris flipped Jarik onto his belly, grabbed his left forearm with both hands, then slammed his knee onto Jarik's arm. Though he'd heard worse noises in recent days, the snap still made Toris's belly clench.

Jarik didn't scream, only stared in shock at the angle in his forearm that looked like a second elbow below the actual one. When the initial shock wore off, Jarik's eyes bulged in pain. His lips sealed shut and folded inward to suppress his reaction, as if he could somehow convince Toris that he hadn't hurt him so bad.

That he'd lost only marginally and next time he'd come harder and win.

But there was no coming back from this, and Jarik knew it. He folded over onto his side. "*Argggg!*"

Nazar barreled toward Toris, and Toris raised both arms to brace for the impact.

BAAAAROOOOOOOOM!

Nazar slid to a stop before Toris. Everyone looked astern, where the oars of both pyrate ships lifted and dropped into the water, moving in unison to the vigorous beat of a drum, quickly chewing up precious distance between them and the *Polaris*.

"Stand to!" Rykah ordered.

Metal rattled as the crew readied their weapons, except for Jarik, who waved his good arm around in shock. Toris grabbed his carbine from the sandbag wall. This fight would be harder. This time he knew who he was shooting at.

Rykah pried the weapon from him. "At the helm," she said. "Keep us cruising north."

Toris nodded, relieved. He bounded up the steep stairway to the bridge and stood behind the wheel, watching the kite wave and flutter ahead.

Drums pounded louder from behind. Closer.

The wooden wheel felt cold under Toris's skin. He wiped his hands on his shirt to prevent them from slipping on the pegs.

Another horn blast sent a wave of terror through him.

He looked back and saw both ships five hundred yards behind and cruising up along either side of *Polaris'* stern. No skiffs this time. The course of each large ship suggested a plan to wedge *Polaris* in between.

Within the four sandbag walls of their makeshift bunker on the stern, four of *Polaris'* defence crew shifted nervously in anticipation. Behind the rear wall, Atilus sat cross-legged behind the .50 caliber, hunched over to line up the *Urchin* to his left through the machine gun's iron sight. To his right, Nazar aimed his carbine at the *Salish*

Sweeper cruising up off their port side. Jarik crouched beside Nazar with a pistol in hand. Varcy protected the bunker's left wall with her .303 rifle, a seventeen-inch blade extending beyond its muzzle.

Over the hatch leading below, Rykah slid a steel shudder over the descending stairway and fastened it shut with a padlock. She yelled into the metal door: "Good luck, Ike!"

Toris swallowed hard. He couldn't imagine being locked in the dark while a battle raged above. Though, as the *Urchin* cruised up into his peripheral, he realized Ike may be the lucky one. Or the crewmate the pyrates get to eat alive.

Footsteps pounded up the bridge steps. Rykah appeared in the doorway and passed Toris a black ball of silky cloth—the Polarian flag. She grabbed the door handle at the top of the stairs. "No matter what happens," she said, "you just keep looking ahead and you keep this door locked. Hear me?"

All Toris could offer was a stunned look. The door didn't even have a lock.

"Hear me?" she said, eyes growing wider.

"Yes," Toris said, seeing the pursuing ships now at four hundred yards. He could hear the grunting of the oarsmen with each stroke.

Rykah slammed the door shut. She wrenched on the outside handle, pulling this way and that until the metal lever snapped off. She flung it overboard and bounded down the stairs to join her team in the square sandbag bunker. Fixing a bayonet to her rifle, she joined Varcy on the left flank.

Toris stuffed the flag under the captain's chair and sat to watch the kite ahead, to focus on his job. To keep them moving north no matter what. But it was impossible to not look back. He sat sideways in the chair, left hand on the wheel while his right elbow sank into the armrest as he watched the hypnotic motion of the oars.

The *Urchin* came up on their starboard quarter faster, crossing the two-hundred-yard mark ahead of her sister ship, which was lagging off the port quarter either from lost crew or ship damage from Nazar's attack.

"Open fire!" shouted Rykah.

The second defence of *Polaris* began with the rattling thud of the .50 caliber machine gun. A seam of bullets sparked off the rusted plates along *Urchin's* port side as a long burst swept across the hull above the waterline. Atilus then broke into short but steady bursts, pausing only to clear jams which, from his swearing, happened more often than he'd like.

It soon became evident that the pyrates had designed the *Urchin* for an engagement against such weaponry. From where Toris sat, the hull plates were layered thickest near the waterline and withstood the machine gun bullets well. Atilus wasn't sinking the ship by that means. At Rykah's order, he raised his line of fire and encountered more success with the upper plates. Chunks of steel blew apart near the top, wearing down the parapet level and forcing the pyrates low.

On their right flank, Nazar popped off shots at any visible flesh aboard the *Salish Sweeper* as she cruised past *Polaris'* port side with a fifty-foot gap between them.

Across *Polaris'* starboard, the *Urchin* cruised up alongside undaunted despite the punishment to her port side armour.

Rykah and Varcy lobbed grenades onto the *Urchin's* decks. One bounced overboard a second later. A blast of debris on the foredeck revealed no pyrate could reach the second grenade in time. The dust of that blast hadn't yet started to fall when the girls sent two more grenades bouncing across *Urchin's* deck. One popped back out and exploded in the water. A disappointing silence exposed the other as a dud.

The thunder of the .50 caliber ended abruptly. This time, there was no metallic rattling or swearing from Atilus. Instead, two terrifying words: "I'm out!"

Toris gripped the armrests. Stupid Atilus for declaring that for all to hear.

And hear they did, for *Urchin* drifted in close to *Polaris'* starboard. Pikes and long axes poked up from behind the jagged parapet, swaying and bobbing as the pyrates lined up along the bow for the coming attack. With one loud grunt of the oarsmen on the other side, *Urchin's* prow swung and crashed into *Polaris'* starboard.

Toris steadied the wheel to keep *Polaris* from spinning. Instead, they rocked to port. As *Polaris* rolled back toward the *Urchin*, exposing her deck and Rykah's team in the bunker, a howling wave of pyrates vaulted across the gap between both ships and landed aboard *Polaris*.

POP! CRACK!—Rykah and Varcy opened fire from the front. Two pyrates fell backward between the hulls, but they were only two of two dozen. Rykah plunged her bayonet into the nearest pyrate and swung him aside. To her left, Varcy did the same. Both girls dropped to their bellies as Nazar and Atilus, who'd picked up a carbine, fired on automatic from behind. Those last bursts burned off the last of the carbine ammunition. Both lads tossed the weapons aside and drew their pistols.

Lying against the sandbag wall, Rykah fired her revolver while Varcy rushed into the open to meet pike shafts with her two battle axes.

A purple cloud blew back from the wheelhouse and washed over the combatants fighting at the stern. On *Polaris'* foredeck, Toris noticed a canister spewing the purple smoke. But worse than that was the *Salish Sweeper*. In Toris's fixation with the fight behind, he hadn't noticed the ship off his port side take the lead. Her crew hurled two more smoke grenades onto the foredeck below.

Through the thickening veil of purple smoke, Toris caught only glimpses of the close quarters fighting as it moved around the base of the wheelhouse. The absence of pistol fire suggested his crewmates were down to blades and fists.

Toris cringed as the *Urchin's* hull screeched along his starboard. When her bowsprit scraped past the front of his wheelhouse, Toris lost all steering. The *Urchin* swung left and pushed the *Polaris* into the side of the waiting *Sweeper* ahead.

Six pyrates jumped from the *Sweeper* onto *Polaris'* foredeck.

Toris flexed his trigger finger. Rykah should have left him a firearm. Those six would be dead on the deck. Instead, two released his kite while the remaining four rushed to join the melee around the wheelhouse.

Desperate, Toris looked ahead for help, but the *Southern Zephyr* was cruising far north without looking back.

But maybe the help he needed was below. *Good luck, Ike,* Rykah had said before the fight. At the time Toris thought she'd meant with his father, but the Skipper was a lost cause. That moment didn't warrant an expression of false hope, so maybe…

Toris turned the ignition switch. To his surprise, the engine rumbled to life. He pushed the thrust lever and sent *Polaris* surging forward into the *Sweeper*, spinning her straight.

If only Ike had worked his magic earlier.

"Kill the engine and open the door!" shouted a woman.

In the thinning purple haze on the rear deck, four of *Polaris'* fighting force—Rykah, Nazar, Jarik, and Atilus—kneeled in a line at the bottom of the bridge stairs. A dozen pyrates stood behind them, a blade resting on each of their shoulders. Nazar wobbled on his knees while nursing a flank wound. Two pyrates pulled Varcy's limp body from under the stairs and laid it before her kneeling comrades.

Behind them, the shudder barring access to the hold was curled back into a sheet of twisted metal, but Ike's absence from the line and the fact the propellers were still spinning meant he'd locked himself in the engine room.

Jorda paced before Toris's kneeling crewmates. She swept a saber over their heads and looked to the bridge. "Shut down the engines and hand me control of yer ship," she ordered.

Toris found himself standing before the rear door.

"Don't do it!" Rykah said.

A sword pommel to the top of her head knocked her onto her face, where she remained unmoving.

The metal door lever rattled in Toris's hand. Wedged between both pyrate ships, he couldn't maneuver *Polaris* enough to knock the pyrates off balance.

Jorda held a revolver to Nazar's head. "Open the door or I'll kill him!"

"Come on, Toris!" Jarik pleaded. "Listen to her."

"Yes, Toris, listen to her!" mocked an elder pyrate.

Toris released the handle. Rykah's last order before falling unconscious was to not open that door. He wasn't going to have her wake to disappointment on his part, so he sat in the captain's chair and stared out the forward window.

BANG!

Toris flinched. Much to his surprise, Jarik's wailing drew a single tear down his cheek. He quickly came to terms with it. They hadn't chosen Nazar at random. That was revenge. Now that they saw what Toris was willing to endure to keep this ship moving north, maybe they'd quit with Nazar and leave.

In a further display of his determination, Toris shoved the thruster forward and spun the wheel hard over to port to push *Salish Sweeper* away, then he spun hard to starboard to crash into *Urchin*. With this new space he went hard to port again and rammed the *Sweeper*. The momentum sent her veering far left, and when Toris pushed the throttle and broke forward, there weren't enough oarsmen on the high sea to catch up to *Polaris*.

Keep looking straight. That's what Rykah had told him. *Rykah.* The thought of her lying back there… At least she didn't have to endure this like the others. All Toris could do was ensure she woke to some good news. So he sat in the chair and stared intensely at the northern horizon. He could do it. Jayda and everyone else needed him to. That was all the reason he needed to keep the throttle forward and the wheel straight.

Jorda ran ahead to the bow. Two burly pyrates carried Rykah by her arms and legs to the prow.

"You listenin', boy?" said Jorda. She crouched beside Rykah's limp body. "I seen how you look at the girl here. I know that once me boys tosses her overboard, you'll be jumpin' in after her. So let's skip all the unpleasantness. Kill the engine and open that door behind ya."

Toris stared ahead, keeping his face impassive despite the storm raging inside him. If he fell into pyrate hands, that may be condemning Jayda to worse situations than this.

His resolve was easy to maintain until the two pyrates started swinging Rykah side to side, building momentum for an over-the-rail toss.

A knock on the bridge door behind had Toris on his feet and at the door in a single heartbeat. He placed his hand on the lever. Through the square window, Jorda nodded for him to continue, steel teeth flashing wide in anticipation.

From the foredeck, voices shouted the countdown to Rykah's demise. *"Three... Two..."*

Toris pushed the handle down and allowed Jorda to shove the door open. She pressed the point of her sword into his chest and forced him back to the captain's chair.

Smiling wide, Jorda said, "Looks like—"

An explosion from behind cut her off and blew her hair forward into his face.

Both Toris and Jorda looked into the blast wind coming from *Polaris'* stern, where the *Urchin* erupted like a fiery fountain of shredded plates and splintered wood. Black smoke whirled from the hull's remains as debris rained down onto *Polaris'* decks.

Buzzzzzzzzzzzz—a steady stream of blue tracer rounds zipped through the smoke and blasted into the *Salish Sweeper*, toppling her masts.

From beyond the *Urchin*'s remains, a solid hull plowed through the veil of smoke. Pink light from the setting sun outlined the curved edges of layered plates that gave the ship her scaled appearance. Rifle fire snapped from the battle cruiser's foredeck, picking off Rykah's captors and the other pyrates as it swept up along *Polaris'* port side at remarkable speed. Luckily, Atilus and Jarik had fallen flat onto their bellies to avoid the crossfire.

Jorda's stunned expression was priceless. It was even better when Toris kicked her backwards down the stairs.

From the bridge doorway, Toris watched with fierce pride as the Coast Patrol vessel fell in alongside his ship and matched their speed. Polaria's white, eight-pointed star never looked so good as it did now flailing from her stern.

Remembering *Polaris'* own flag, Toris grabbed the black ball of cloth from under the captain's chair and unraveled it outside the port side window. An officer on *Sea Serpent'*s flying deck, the open-air extension to the side of the battleship's bridge, slammed his heels together and saluted the flag. Several more officers joined him from the bridge, hands springing up in crisp salutes. The reaction was contagious. All along the battleship's starboard side, Polarian naval officers and sailors stood stiffly with arms raised to pay respect to their flag.

Toris smiled. They were saved.

TWENTY-FIVE

The *Sea Serpent* arrived along *Polaris'* port side and matched their speed. Floating at double *Polaris'* height, a heavy machine gun aimed down from her foredeck with several riflemen aiming at Toris in the wheelhouse.

"Unidentified vessel," crackled a voice through a speaker, *"this is the Polarian Coast Patrol. Heave to and prepare to be boarded."*

Toris killed the engine and was down at Rykah's side on *Polaris'* foredeck in seconds. He lifted her head onto his lap as she regained consciousness. Her unconcerned eyes rolled around as they took in the pyrate bodies strewn across the deck.

"You're okay," he assured her, swiping her hair back from her face.

"What happened?" she groaned.

"Coast Patrol battle cruiser."

Rykah's eyes widened. She sat up and would have smashed her head into Toris's face had he not moved.

"Don't worry," he said, "they're ours."

But this seemed to be Rykah's concern. She trembled as she watched the *Sea Serpent* draw closer, closing the gap. Clearly she feared being discovered as a deserter, but out here, a web of lies could not be unravelled by the Coast Patrol. Besides, anything was better than the situation they were in not two minutes ago. They were alive. So long as they were breathing, they could still succeed.

Grappling hooks bounced across *Polaris'* foredeck and stern. Their attached cables retracted to the port side rail, where the barbs bit steel and pulled *Polaris* toward the *Sea Serpent'*s gangway, which hung just above *Polaris'* main deck. Metal screeched as both hulls made contact.

Atilus arrived next to Toris and placed a hand on his shoulder to steady himself. Jarik sobbed from behind the wheelhouse, where he was no doubt hunched over Nazar's body.

Jorda and the surviving pyrates had gathered along the wheelhouse's starboard side, beyond sight of the Coast Patrol. Though, by their sluggish postures, they appeared as if they intended to surrender.

Atilus's fingers dug into Toris's shoulder as Captain Clavilla led his boarding party down the gangway and onto *Polaris'* foredeck. The sailors split up to sweep the bridge above and the hold below, rounding up the pyrates along with *Polaris'* crew and directing them at gunpoint to the stern.

With Atilus's help, Toris lifted Rykah to her feet. She wobbled a bit, then steadied and was able to walk unassisted to the rear. A sailor dragged Ike up from below. He landed on his knees and sank with his head hung low.

Captain Clavilla paced before the ragged group, assessing each detainee as he had during his conscription roundup on Mintaka.

Toris wished he could play dead. To join those lying on the deck, free of Clavilla's attention. The sight of the captain had that effect on him since every encounter with him ended in Toris losing someone he loved.

"Who commands this ship?" Clavilla said, his voice like sandpaper over Toris's eardrums.

Toris instinctively looked to Rykah, but she was kneeling beside Varcy's body, stroking her hair while whispering a prayer.

Toris pointed to the hatch leading below decks. "Our skipper—"

"Is dead," said Ike, sitting on the deck. He rubbed his eyes with the back of his hand.

A chill went through Toris. He knelt beside Ike and draped an arm over his shoulder.

Clavilla squinted at *Polaris'* wheelhouse. "From where does this ship hail?"

"Port Abersali," Toris said, "destined for Svalbard." He stood in front of Rykah, Ike, Jarik, and Atilus, separating them from the cluster of pyrates. "We're her crew. The rest are pyrates."

"He's lying," said an older pyrate from the group of eight. "They're the pyrates. We're Polarian citizens. This is our ship and they attacked us unprovoked."

"She's Jorda the Explorer," Toris said, pointing the pyrate queen out from the group.

Clavilla's jaw went slack. He composed himself and gave Jorda a smug smile. "That head of yours is worth a lot of credits." To one of his men, he said, "Throw her in the brig."

A sailor jabbed his muzzle into Jorda's back, prodding her toward *Sea Serpent'*s gangway.

Captain Clavilla returned his attention to Toris. He pulled a scroll of off-white paper from his slicker. "What do you call this piece of scrap metal?"

"*Polaris,*" Toris said.

The Coast Patrol captain unrolled the scroll and examined its text. "I have no record of a *Polaris* on the exit approval list."

"Then there's been a mistake," Toris said, mustering his courage. After all, how could Clavilla get to the bottom of a clerical error way out here? He couldn't. "Perhaps we're on the same permit as our flagship, the *Southern Zephyr.*"

Clavilla lowered the scroll. "There are no dual registrations - one ship per exit permit. Fetch me your inspection papers."

Toris shifted. They'd passed Point Bay Station with *Southern Zephyr,* avoiding the inspection by means of a special arrangement by Ignatius or one of his contacts.

"All our paperwork burned up in a pyrate attack," Toris said.

"How convenient." Clavilla stepped back to address the whole group. "We'll have the database sort this out." The captain held out his hand, and a sailor placed a reader pad in it. To the detainees, he said, "I.D.s."

The cluster of deserters exchanged wary looks. Toris offered his first. Out here, he wasn't breaking exile.

The captain punched in Toris's number.

While the database loaded, a flood of cold sweat covered Toris's body. Was there a note in there that said he was to be working his civil service on Mintaka?

The pad beeped. "Toris Onero," Clavilla said. "Status: Pending Transfer." The captain frowned at that, then moved on to Rykah. "I.D."

From Varcy's side, Rykah rhymed off her service number. The captain entered it into his data pad, read the screen, and smiled. "Rykah Adarah, Lieutenant. Status: Active Defence Force."

When he ran the IDs of Atilus and Jarik, he announced the same status as Rykah's.

As expected, no pyrate gave their number. Perhaps some had been out here so long they'd forgotten theirs. Or they were wanted for crimes that would earn them an instant bullet.

"Deserters, the whole lot of you," declared Clavilla.

Rykah kissed Varcy's forehead and laid her head gently on the deck. She stood to face Clavilla. "Captain, we received our releases not long before our departure."

"We updated our database before leaving Polaria," Clavilla informed, "which would have been *after* your departure."

"Then there's been a mistake," Rykah said, defiant.

"The same mistake happening to so many of you at once?" Clavilla mused. "Unlikely. Let's see your pardon card."

Rykah spread her hands. "I lost it at sea."

Captain Clavilla seized Rykah's hair and cranked her head to the side, exposing the black *V* on her neck. "Lost it along with your exit permit and inspection certificate, I assume."

He held her at arm's length and addressed the other detainees.

"I once found a shipwreck survivor on Thetis Island with not a stitch of clothing on him. Poor soul lost everything, crew and clothes and food, all but one polymer card—his pardon from The Artican. So, either you're fugitives from a work camp, or Defence Force deserters. Whichever the case, you're all now prisoners of the Polarian Coast Patrol."

Seeing tears well in Rykah's eyes as she struggled to remain calm in Clavilla's hold, exercising restraint for the moment, Toris stepped forward before she decided to break his arm and land herself in more trouble. He placed a hand on Clavilla's arm.

"You know me," Toris said to the captain. "Back on Mintaka, you drew your sword on me during the draft."

Clavilla's eyes narrowed on him, then opened wide with recognition. "Mintaka's fool."

Toris nodded despite feeling his face flush red. At least Clavilla remembered. "Yes. That was less than a month ago, so you know we're not pyrates. We're privateers conducting legitimate business on behalf of The Artican."

Clavilla untangled his fingers from Rykah's hair. "That very well may be," he said, nodding. "Of course, we won't know until we return home and hold a trial. Until then..." The captain looked to his boarding party. "Lock them up with the pyrate scum."

A lump swelled in Toris's throat. Going to trial was certain death for his crewmates, and threatened an unknown fate for him deserting his civil post.

"My father," Ike said, his eyes red and puffy, "his body is below. He deserves his mariner rites."

Clavilla ignored Ike's request and motioned for his men to escort *Polaris'* crew off their ship.

As the sailors herded *Polaris'* crew up the gangway, Rykah wrapped her hands around Toris's left arm and leaned her head against his shoulder.

On the *Sea Serpent'*s foredeck, two armed groups watched the prisoners board. One group Toris recognized as the sailors, their black slickers designed to cool them in the heat. The other group's camouflage fatigues resembled *Polaris'* Defence Force deserters, so he took these men and women as soldiers of the expedition security team.

One soldier of mid-twenties marched forward, the tail of his hunter green officer slicker flapping in the breeze. "What's the meaning of this, Captain? Are they not Polarian as their flag suggests?"

"Polarian deserters," Clavilla said. "See that they're locked below."

On the soldier's lapels, two wide yellow bars enclosing a single narrow bar marked him as a mid-ranking officer, but Toris wasn't familiar with specific insignias.

The officer singled Toris out. "Him…I've seen his face before. He's the half-blood, is he not?"

Clavilla gave Toris's face another look, then returned to his file on the data pad. "So he is."

"Then he's not a deserter," the young army officer said, and something about his eyes sparked familiarity in Toris. A square jaw and broad shoulders gave him the appearance of a national lacrosse player. "He's the reason we're on our way to Svalbard," the officer said. "He has every right to be out here."

Clavilla looked down his nose at the officer. "I'll not have a civilian unfamiliar with the workings of my ship wander unattended, so unless you're willing chaperone to him, he'll join the others for everyone's safety."

"Leave him in my charge," the officer said, much to everyone's surprise—from Toris to Clavilla.

"Very well," Clavilla said. "He's all yours, Major Arcturus."

Toris's breath caught. He took a step back to better appraise the officer, for this was the man who had scraped together *Polaris'* crew and sponsored their expedition. The man Rykah had referred to many times as 'Ignatius'.

Lex's brother ordered his men to escort the prisoners below, then motioned for Toris to follow him to the *Sea Serpent*'s stern.

Having spent so much time on *Polaris*, the length of the battleship was staggering. They seemed to walk three lengths of *Polaris* to reach the *Serpent*'s rear rail.

Major Arcturus's gaze flicked back to *Polaris'* crew disappearing down the stairs below. "There were more of you."

"A funny thing happens when you let a rabid dog off its leash: you don't control who it bites," Toris said, referring to Nazar. No way had he served in the Defence Force without signs of his explosive behaviour showing up on record, which Major Arcturus had surely combed through during his selection process.

The major jabbed a finger at Toris's chest. "You watch your tone with me, half-blood. Or I'll have you below with the others."

"No, you won't. You need me on this ship in case you reach the seeds first. I'm the only person aboard who can legally claim the Accolade, which you want me to bestow on your sister, so it's best you quit wasting your breath with threats. I'm done with it."

Toris's own tone shocked him. Never in his life had he spoken to authority with such provocation. But the major's insistence that Toris remain at large only bolstered his claim that Lex's brother still needed him. For now, anyway.

The major frowned. "The hell are you talking about? I don't need you. *Polaris* and the *Southern Zephyr* are both sponsored by Alexandra. She's guaranteed the Accolade so long as one of those ships returns with the seeds. And if we find the vault first? Well, I'll see that Alexandra ends up on this ship and you down in lockup if you don't start singing a sweeter tune."

Of course. Toris's face burned red with embarrassment. Clearly Ignatius had arranged the resources and put Lex's name on all the sponsorship documents. That part made a lot of sense. So that left one question: "Then why did you go through so much trouble to get me onto the expedition?" he asked.

Ignatius cracked a smile at what seemed to him an obvious question. "Because you deserve to be there to see the vault. My father had no right to bar you from participating."

This was far from the response Toris had been expecting. Never had someone done something for him because he 'deserved' it. All his labour in civil service was expected. Any favours or luxuries only added to the debt he had to pay back. Hopefully Ignatius's benevolence could help Rykah and the others.

"What will happen to my crew?" he said, his tone notably more docile.

"I'll get them pardons when we get home," Ignatius said. He nodded to *Polaris* tied to the *Serpent*'s starboard side. "Where's the *Zephyr*? You were supposed to stick together."

Toris clenched his fists. "Maybe you should have told them that. They left us behind without a second look back. Nice plan, making us the easier target."

Ignatius shifted uncomfortably. "If I could have spared your ship more armaments I would have."

"I get it, Major," Toris said. The *Polaris* crew consisted of expendable degenerates. No doubt *Southern Zephyr* was manned by highborns from Rosaria's personal circle. Though Toris did understand that, he didn't have to like it.

The major relaxed and, much to Toris's surprise, said, "Call me 'Ignatius'."

"And you can call me 'Toris'. No more of these 'half-blood' insults."

Ignatius smiled. "Got some fight in you. That's good. We may need all the help we can get up there."

"What am I to do?"

"Alexandra told me all about your exploits. You'll serve as the ship's backup diver. Until then, just stay out of everyone's way."

He dug a key from his pocket and handed it to Toris. "That's for my stateroom. Get some rest in there and keep out of trouble. If you manage to stay out of the brig before we get home, you'll get your citizenship reward."

"Major," said a man from the nearest stairway. Toris recognized the red-headed soldier from his orphanry. His spindly frame had earned him the nickname *Spinner*. "You're needed below, sir."

"Be right there." To Toris, Ignatius said, "Ask one of the sailors to show you to my room." He placed a hand on his shoulder. "Just relax and enjoy the ride, okay?"

Toris watched Ignatius follow Spinner below decks.

A sinking feeling took him as the *Serpent*'s crew released the mooring lines from *Polaris* to send her adrift. The pyrates shouted pleas from her foredeck.

Toris hurried below. He'd seen enough death to do him a lifetime. When the *Sea Serpent*'s machine guns rattled from the foredeck, he covered his ears to block out the screams.

TWENTY-SIX

Europe had plenty more to offer than its southern neighbour. It had started with a single dry shrub sprouting from a dusty hill. Variations of that tiny lifeform had since grown in size and frequency from the increasingly rocky land each passing day.

That was a week ago. Dawn had broken the darkness in Toris's heart at sight of that first brown plant. If such life could exist out here, then perhaps the vault and its seeds had survived as well.

Toris spent his time in a rubber raiding craft that hung from the *Sea Serpent*'s starboard side, grateful to be looking at a landscape other than Africa's golden sea of sand dunes. He'd witnessed two sunrises over the European land horizon, another over open water, and two more over the highlands to the north. If his memory of ancient maps served him right, then the mountains that now stood high before the eastern horizon belonged to Norway. On its southern shores, coniferous trees standing high as ten feet had greeted the Polarians. Though sparse in number, their presence had incited cheers.

Svalbard's shores were suddenly within reach.

A more temperate climate allowed Toris to lounge in the raiding craft almost all day and all night. From here, he watched the trees grow in height and frequency, thickening into dense clusters to eventually become forests. Unlike the mounds of dunes dominating inland Africa, the only sand here came in pale strips of white that traced small stretches of shore at the bases of steep mountains. Fjords surrounded by near vertical mountain slopes hundreds of feet high led inland, winding out of sight and ending who knew where.

Sometimes Toris sought refuge in Ignatius's stateroom, but only when he was trying to avoid attention from the crew. Surely his free ride to the Accolade may earn scorn from more than a few. Did anyone realize the implications of him being among their crew? That they were delivering him straight to the Accolade with all its honours? Because even if Rosaria's ship reached the vault first, Toris could sneak aboard at some point when *Sea Serpent* became her escort. If any of the military crew had figured this out yet, best not to rub it in their faces.

He'd slept in Ignatius's stateroom once, and his aching bones felt as if that had lasted a week. And perhaps it had. With no window it was hard to tell, and his fatigue and comfort had allowed him to ignore the outside world. Though Ignatius hadn't once visited his own room during Toris's self-imposed internment there, Toris had refused to sleep in his double bed, instead settling for the hard floor. So after that first long sleeping spell his entire body felt as if he'd been struck by a train. Now, he preferred the sunken floor and inflated rubber walls of the raiding craft. The shred of a spare kite he'd found stuffed away provided adequate cover from the sun.

The farther north they traveled, the easier it became to breathe. Unlike Africa's steam-like humidity, the northern breeze carried a slight chill. Or maybe it seemed that way after the equatorial oven they'd just crossed. Either way, Toris drank it in as if it were spring water.

Nights were the best. As if glittering starlight on the water surface wasn't enough, glowing rivers of blue bioluminescent jelly-fish was a spectacle no Polarian fisherman would ever believe.

As the *Sea Serpent* cruised past the mouth to an inland waterway, five distant waterfalls fell hundreds of feet from the mountains that formed a bend in the passage. A captivated Toris studied every detail of the green hills to accurately recount for Rykah the majesty of these northlands.

Rykah. Whenever he felt pity for her, Toris reminded himself of Ignatius's assurances. She was safe and getting a free ride to a pardon. As far as Toris could tell, Lex's brother was a man of his word. Even now, his troops cheered on the quarterdeck as their major wrestled with his men in a fashion similar to running the mill, only this was purely for entertainment and a show of strength to the sailors. A reminder that the expedition's soldiers had their uses.

It hadn't taken long for Toris to notice a division that bordered on rivalry between the sailors and soldiers. Clavilla's crew had taken to calling the soldiers *worms,* while the soldiers called the sailors *squids.* This tension led to a brawl in the passageway outside Ignatius's stateroom, when a soldier had accidentally stumbled into a sailor. Words were exchanged, backup flooded in, and both sides clashed.

Perhaps this was why the Defence Force had assigned Ignatius to lead the security team. If a good commander had foreseen the conflict between both elements, sending the Chancellor's son may inspire reluctance in even the ship's captain to abuse his position.

Still, the sailors refused to share their sleeping berths with enlisted soldiers, so the soldiers slept upon cots on the quarterdeck. In an act of solidarity, Ignatius slept with his troops, ate with them, stood watch with them. All of these signs reinforced in Toris the belief that Ignatius Arcturus would keep his word and secure pardons for *Polaris'* crew upon their return home.

Yet, in all likelihood, Rykah and the others did not know this. The whole time they'd been locked up, they may have been thinking they were doomed. This had actually kept Toris from sleep the past two nights. It was time to do something about that.

He waited until the change of watch bell rang, then rolled out of the raiding craft for another attempt. Below decks, he strode down the passageway with as much purpose as he could muster. Due to *Sea Serpent* lacking a proper brig, Clavilla had the prisoners locked in the seed storage chamber below the quarterdeck at the back, a room away from the heat of the engines and boasting its own refrigeration system. Perhaps when they needed that space for the seeds, Clavilla would allow them more freedom to roam the ship. After all, where were they going to run off to?

The guard at the end of the dimly lit passageway, a soldier girl with a short brown mohawk, leaned against the wall with one foot up under her buttocks. Good. Macey had grown up in the same orphanry as Toris until the Defence Force drafted her at age twelve.

"I'm here to check on the prisoners," Toris said, eyeing the door beside Macey.

"Piss off, half-blood" she said. When Toris carried on with his approach, Macey slammed him against the wall and pressed the point of a knife under his chin. She clenched her crooked teeth and leaned in close. "I bet if I tossed you overboard no one would care."

"Don't kid yourself," Toris said, forcing a smile. "You'd never be able to live with yourself."

Macey scoffed and pushed him back down the passageway. "Get out of here before I decide to test which of our theories holds true."

Toris rubbed his chin where the knife had poked and sauntered away from the brig. He'd made many attempts to check on his crew, but whatever guard stood watch always denied him. Only those on kitchen duty were allowed into the brig, strictly for the purposes of meal deliveries, which were meager quarter portions served twice a day by a kitchen hand.

It was time for Toris to concoct a lie.

He huffed as he entered the galley to take the evening meal trays, complaining of how this was above him and that Ignatius had no right to put him to work in this way. Seeing the extra help, albeit a bit early, the cook returned to his work without saying a word.

When Macey saw Toris return with a meal tray containing six bowls of oatmeal, she said, "Finally, Major got you doing something useful."

She unlocked the door and pushed it open. The hinges groaned as the steel slab swung inward.

Toris recoiled at the blast of heat from inside. The stench of unwashed bodies in the oven-like room was overwhelming, but he maintained his composure and entered to join his crew. Toris had no idea this was the condition they were in and felt guilt for his own comfort since they'd been picked up by the Coast Patrol.

The fear of that door shutting behind him suddenly rattled his fortitude. What if Macey decided this was where Toris belonged? That it wasn't fair for him to get a free ride to the Accolade. Would Ignatius even notice him missing?

He shook those thoughts from his head. It was hard enough to breathe the stifling air in here. He didn't need panic adding to it.

Against the far wall, Ike was on his back with an arm over his eyes to shield against the invasive light from the passageway. Atilus huddled in a corner muttering to himself. Jorda sat cross-legged, rocking back and forth while scratching what looked like calculations into the steel floor. She seemed to be tracking time, plotting their position, and likely her escape, however unlikely that was to succeed.

In the center of the room, Rykah sat with her back to the door, cross-legged and hunched over as if asleep sitting up.

"Where's Jarik?" Toris said, ever wary of an attack in revenge of Nazar.

Rykah's spine lengthened and her shoulders pulled back, but she remained facing the wall. "Toris, it does me well to hear your voice."

Her placid and unconcerned tone sent a chill through him.

He set the tray beside her. "Are you well?"

"Would you be, if it were you in here?"

Toris scanned the room, noticing vents evenly spaced across the walls near the ceiling.

"I'll get some airflow in here," he told her. "I promise."

"I wish you great luck in that," Rykah said with a profound listlessness in her voice.

"I spoke to Ignatius," Toris said. "He says not to worry—that you're all getting pardoned when we get home."

Rykah's shoulders sagged. "He means well."

"He does. And he'll come through. If anyone can, it's the Chancellor's son."

Rykah shook her head slightly. "There'll be no mercy for the Arrington food raiders."

"You spoon-feeding them in there or what?" said Macey from outside the doorway.

Toris stood and turned to leave. But there was something he needed to say first. He knelt behind Rykah, reached out to touch her shoulder, but held back. "I'm still with you," he said.

Her shoulders stiffened, but she remained silent.

Toris turned to leave.

"Until when?"

He looked back and saw Rykah's head cocked slightly toward him. "The end," he said.

Rykah lowered her head and hunched forward.

Toris stormed from the room and down the passageway. There was something he could do to ease his crew's suffering until Svalbard.

Around the corner, in a room adjacent to the seed storage, he found the refrigeration unit, which Ignatius had explained during his tour was to keep the seeds at a cool twenty degrees below zero centigrade. To preserve fuel, the unit remained off during the northward voyage and remained so despite the discomfort of the deserters. But a gentle flow of cool air would barely skim their liquid hydrogen levels, so Toris was delighted to find the door unlocked. He was about to wish he'd never entered that room.

For a long while all he could do was stare at the refrigeration unit. With a nest of split and twisted wires protruding from the large rectangular control box, not even the most skilled technician could salvage it without all new parts. Whether rats or sabotage, the cause didn't matter. Without cool storage, the seeds would not survive the journey across the blistering equator.

Toris prayed the engineers had spare parts to rewire it.

Footsteps thumped down the passageway outside, two sets, and stopped just before the door. Metal scratching from the other side revealed these new arrivals had expected the refrigeration room to be locked, and bought Toris time to hide.

At first glance there was nowhere to conceal himself. The shelving against the wall opposite the control box contained flats of canned beans that ran wall to wall, each shelf packed full. Except for the tops.

Toris was rolling to the back of the upper shelf just as the door squeaked open.

Through gaps in the polymer shelving unit, Toris saw two engineers in blue coveralls enter and shut the door behind them, locking it from the inside. They made straight for the refrigeration unit, pulled the front panel away, and gave a satisfied nod.

"Those guys weren't messing around," said one to the other.

"I can't believe the captain is really going through with it."

"You think he has a choice? That order came straight from Sydra, and you heard the way she gets on. If she wants that war, she'll get it one way or another. Even if it means a couple thousand need to starve to get support for it. Best to get on her good side now while you can."

His partner rubbed his chin. "Still, doesn't seem right."

"So long as the captain assures us our families will be fed, I'm fine with it. Anyway, what are you gonna do now? There's no way to fix this mess. Heard the boys tossed the spare parts overboard." The engineering tech pulled a rag from his pocket. "Now, let's make it look like the rats had a feast and get out of here. Heard Clay got some nice hooch on the go."

"Yeah, I could use a drink," said the other tech as he opened a rag of his own to reveal small brown pellets.

The technicians each flung a handful of rat feces under the shelving units, then left the room.

Even after the jiggling lock indicated the door was secure, Toris lay across the top shelf a long while, letting the words untangle in his head. He'd seen Sydra's lust for war firsthand in the Orichalcum, how enraged she'd become when he presented the Svalbard solution, and how she'd voiced disapproval for the expedition at every turn. And in the end it didn't matter, because she'd found a Coast Patrol captain who actually wanted the war like she did. No doubt Clavilla's list of privateer ships had come from Sydra, to ensure none slipped through his net. How many had he stopped south of *Polaris*, only to fabricate a reason to order their return home. An excuse like a 'defective refrigeration' unit to nullify their exit permit might work.

Toris wished he could go back to his sleeping spot in the rubber raiding craft and blissfully watch this new world grow and flourish before his eyes.

Too late for that.

TWENTY-SEVEN

"I think…she's trying…to kill us," croaked Arla as she shuffled beside her sister. Her twin, Eris, wasn't faring much better with sweat streaming down all sides of her shaved head.

Jayda's boots scuffed along the dirt path, adding to the trail of dust rising behind the soldiers struggling to keep pace with Quella in the Autumn heat.

"Quella doesn't *try* to kill," Talia pointed out as she trotted along, the soles of her combat boots barely leaving the ground with each step. "She wants you dead, you die."

Jayda huffed as she kept pace alongside Ivy. "With a name like that, what kind of girl did her parents expect her to become?" She knew what the name 'Quella' meant.

"Her parents didn't give her that name," Ivy said, whose face flushed red from exertion.

Jayda looked to her curiously.

"The guards gave it to her," Ivy explained. "Her labour camp had a fighting pit. Two inmates go into the ring, one comes out. Sometimes they gave them weapons—axes or daggers. Sometimes bare knuckle if they wanted to draw it out. The guards placed bets on it. Only those hoping to lose their money ever bet against Quella. Never lost once. Obviously."

Jayda ran in silence, letting the story sink in. Suddenly her orphanry days didn't seem so bad.

Quella slowed her pace until Jayda caught up to her. "Had enough?"

Jayda shook her head. She'd fallen for that trick twice in melee combat training and still wore the bruises from it. Quella thought you could beat the weakness out of someone.

When the bottom of the aerodrome hangar came into view, the activity there sent a commotion rippling from the front of the line toward the back.

"We just had a drill this morning," Darcella said of the paratroopers mustering before the hangar.

"Write a complaint to your local councillor," huffed Shayla.

Lieutenant Valender waited for his platoon in full battle gear at the edge of the tent line. He patted the top of his head to summon Quella.

She grunted and broke off from her troops. It was no secret she loathed answering to this rosy-cheeked urbanite who'd never seen a real fight in his life, but Jayda liked him. He was nice to her and sometimes gave her his chocolate ration. Though, she couldn't help but laugh when Corla joked that Ivy had probably been with more girls than he had.

"Go gear up," Valender shouted to his passing troops. His face was unusually red this afternoon. Maybe it wasn't a rehearsal this time.

At their modular tent, Valender's platoon encountered Dogwood's other two platoons already kitted up and filing toward the field. "Hurry up," ordered Captain Harwood, their company commander. "Chutes on in five."

Jayda shoved her way onto the tent through the throng of slick bodies. At her cot she peeled off her sweaty PT gear, dried herself with a towel, then pulled on a fresh uniform. She slung on her webbing and flipped her ruck onto her back, which she packed every morning upon waking. This had become the airborne routine, as the past week had seen them doing muster drills at random hours. She grabbed her rifle and hustled out as stragglers still stumbled in from the run.

Lines of soldiers strung out into the airfield and congealed before the hangar, where they formed up in their jump companies, which were further divided into platoons of thirty, which were halved into jump chalks since each balloon basket fit only fifteen jumpers with their gear. Lieutenant Valender commanded the first jump chalk of Dogwood's third platoon. Quella led the other half of his troops.

Quella emerged from the gaggle of bodies and joined her chalk in the field. She dropped to her knees and spread a map over the grass. The young men and women of her chalk crowded around. Ivy placed her hands on Jayda's shoulders and peered over her head to better see. This was the first time their leader had been issued a map.

"Our objective," Quella said, smoothing out the folds in the map, "is the Polis."

"Are you serious?" said Ivy, leaning in over Jayda for a closer look.

A black outline of an eight-point star marked the center of the map, presumably denoting the Polarian citadel that occupied the Southern Pole. Odillian's forces had left the citadel on the Ortarian side of the border after the war, under the guard of civilian militia to maintain. The savages had never tried to assail her walls nor accost its defenders, for what could spears and arrows do against stone battlements and firearms? The Polis was considered the spirit of Polaria—resilient and defiant.

Quella drew a circle around a field to the southeast of the citadel as marked on the map, though technically every direction away from the Polis was north. "That's Dogwood's drop zone," she said. She pointed to the other three quadrants and listed off the drop zones of Ashwood, Birchwood, and Cedarwood companies. "Each company will sweep their quadrant and converge on the Polis from four directions."

Talia crouched beside Quella. "Is this for real?"

Quella looked up and met the surprised stares of her soldiers. "At polar sunset, the border brigades will march up the Ardis Valley to seize Ortaria's western farmlands. By the time they cross the border, the dregs will have moved their food stores out of their reach. Our job is secure the recent harvest while operating out of the Polis. We'll use the militia's knowledge of the area to gather as much as we can, then secure the region around the citadel for balloon extract."

"This is a raiding party," Jayda said, more in wonder than fear.

Quella nodded her affirmation. Fifteen mouths murmured in excitement.

Jayda backed away from her cohort and surveyed the field for signs that this was not just another drill. She found many.

First Platoon troops of Ashwood Company were already emerging from the hangar with their parachutes as their Second Platoon comrades filed in to retrieve theirs. Though this element was occasionally included in rehearsals, the balloons inflating on the pads behind the hangar was a first.

Jayda watched with her platoon as the kitted Ashwood troops shuffled single file to the rear balloons and formed neat lines before their baskets. They continued to watch in silence as Birchwood, Cedarwood, and most of Dogwood filed into the hangar to retrieve their parachutes. Usually the drills stopped halfway through Birchwood, just so everyone had a chance to see how a battalion-level rig-up worked. This was the first time the last unit in the battalion, Lieutenant Valender's platoon, made the walk to the hangar.

As Jayda accepted her parachute from the jumpmaster, she felt herself crossing a line over which she may never return.

With the parachute occupying her back and rucksack hooked to her waist in front, Jayda waddled between rows of inflated balloons. Each oblong design resembled a predatory bird—some real, others mythical.

Quella stood at the basket beneath an inflated brown falcon, inspecting her chalk's kit before allowing them to board. The pilot at the back of the basket directed his passengers where to sit. Because the paratroopers wore their chutes on their backs, their rucksacks hung from their waists in front. This made climbing into the basket a feat of its own. Each jumper boarded with the help of the previous boarder, then turned to help the next in line before shuffling toward the back of the basket.

Arla climbed aboard with Eris's help, then turned to assist Jayda. Jayda grabbed both of Arla's hands and climbed up into the basket with a push from Quella, who climbed in behind. Jayda sat on the right-side seat beside the door. Quella sat directly opposite her, their rucks forming a bridge between their laps.

Colonel Marcellus made his rounds of the balloons, ensuring each chalk had boarded without issue. He'd never done this during previous rehearsals. As he passed Jayda's basket he gave her shoulder a squeeze and nodded to the troops sitting behind her. "I'll see you at the Polis," he said, then carried on to inspect the last three balloons.

Excitement filled the basket as reality struck. This was definitely not a rehearsal. Soldiers around Jayda rocked back and forth and jostled each other in giddy excitement. Some looked back toward the tent line as if suddenly realizing they'd forgotten something.

The excitement, however, fizzled after a half hour sitting cramped in the basket. Everyone was eager to lift off. The heat from the alcohol burner added to the sweltering day, but at least up in the air they'd get a breeze.

Then, with little warning, the balloons lifted off one by one starting with Ashwood Company, then Birchwood, on to Cedarwood, then Dogwood. The ground crew unhitched the ropes from Jayda's basket, sending the balloon surging upward.

Jayda's excitement rose with the balloon as their height surpassed the ominous Borien peaks. Exhilaration beyond comparison electrified her fingers and toes, which she could not keep still.

As the rush wore off the jitters took over. This was the most dangerous military operation in Anterran history. Odillian's boys had nothing on this when they drove the Ortarian horde back up the Ardis Valley.

From her shirt Jayda drew a folded piece of paper and a pencil. She spread the blank page across the rucksack on her lap and got busy scribbling the letter she'd spent the last week drafting in her head.

TWENTY-EIGHT

Grey clouds had swallowed the setting sun when Toris found Ignatius by the starboard bow. The major studied a map and compass, apparently comparing land features off the starboard side to his ancient map.

Toris slid in between Ignatius and the rail and got straight to it. "Clavilla plans to spoil the seeds on our way home."

Ignatius kept his eyes trained on his map. "Boredom getting to you, Toris?"

"Go check the refrigeration unit. Its controls are completely gutted."

"Did you not see the sign on that door?" said Ignatius absently while frowning at the shoreline. "That unit is for engineering personnel only. So unless you defied my one order, you shouldn't know anything about the condition of the refrigerator."

Toris huffed. "Fine, just order them to turn on the circulation setting for the prisoners. They're wasting away in there. You at least owe them that."

Ignatius lowered his map and met Toris's demanding stare. "This isn't a luxury cruise. It'll look mighty suspicious if I start giving them special treatment. It's bad enough I already went against Clavilla's order by raising their rations." He glanced at the bridge and leaned in close. "If you're caught snooping and the Captain orders me to punish you along with them, well, I'll have no choice but to obey. So, do us both a favour and stay out of trouble like I told you before."

Toris stormed off and took refuge in the raiding craft to clear his head. There had to be a way he could keep the seeds cool, or escape with a few, or… No, all that sounded too far-fetched. And even if he did find one of the ideas alluring, he didn't have time to flesh out the details, because a retched alarm frayed his already split nerves.

Braaaaaaam . . . Braaaaaaaam . . . Braaaaaaam.

Sailors and soldiers spilled up from below decks and raced across the main deck in every direction. Toris stopped one sailor, a young lad fumbling with his submachine gun. "What's going on?"

"Man battlestations," came the flustered reply.

On every deck, sailors manned the cannons and soldiers fanned out across the foredeck with their assault rifles.

Looking ahead, however, Toris saw the ship of their concern was not an enemy. For too long his eyes had fixed on the *Southern Zephyr* to mistake her for another vessel, even without the purple kite bulging out in the sky before her bow.

Rosaria's ship sat in a bay enclosed by forested hills on three sides. All around, coniferous trees stood as still as the glassy water surface upon which the *Southern Zephyr* spun slowly around her anchor. As the *Sea Serpent* slipped in alongside, the *Zephyr*'s crew gathered on the main deck, waving and cheering at the sight of the Polarian battle cruiser.

Toris watched from the rail at the starboard bow and, seeing Lex up close and well, he smiled.

When both boats moored together, Rosaria's ship floated at only half the height of the *Sea Serpent* above water. Coast Patrol sailors tossed ropes down to the lower ship, exchanged jovial banter with Rosaria's crew, and helped secure both ships together by tightening their ends of the dock lines.

On the battleship's foredeck, a boarding party comprised of a dozen sailors formed atop the *Serpent*'s gangway. Clavilla joined the line of armed sailors, but before he could lead them down the plank connecting both ships, Lex led her crew up the gangway and onto *Sea Serpent*'s foredeck.

Alexandra Arcturus marched aboard the *Sea Serpent* like she owned it, back straight and eyes steely. In her violet longcoat, with its high fastened collar, and a saber swaying from her hip, she appeared as magnificent as the Polarian legends of old. On her head, chestnut brown hair had grown thick enough to conceal her scalp.

Clavilla stepped up to block her way. "I didn't hear you ask permission to board my ship."

Lex's fierce blue eyes met the captain's in a manner only a highborn girl would ever dare. "Am I to expect The Artican's expedition would not welcome me?" she said.

"And who exactly would *you* be."

"My sister," said Ignatius. He stepped forward.

Lex's stoic expression softened at the sight of her brother. "Iggy!"

They embraced before the crews of both ships, and had it been another venue the affection would have drawn scorn from the officers. Out here, however, adherence to old customs had slackened.

When they released, Toris marched forward to make his presence known. He had to know if Lex knew he was aboard *Polaris* when she left him to the pyrates. Her stunned expression was all the answer he needed.

She threw her arms around Toris shamelessly, oblivious to the scrutinizing stares of soldiers and sailors alike. Toris embraced her awkwardly, painfully aware of both crews watching the Chancellor's daughter's affection toward a half-blood Onero. *This must be the servant who stole away the General's betrothed*, some must be thinking. A few appeared amused, others appalled. But something other than their stares bothered him. Was her surprise at the sight of him because she thought he was home on Mintaka? Or that he'd survived the pyrate attack?

Ignatius cleared his throat.

Lex released Toris and stood back, eyes shifting to her audience as if she hadn't noticed them until now.

Clavilla stepped forward. "Alexandra Arcturus, way out here. What a surprise. I don't suppose your father would know anything about you leaving home? Though, I suspect the good Major here might've known something about it."

Lex straightened and gripped the hilt of her saber. "As a free citizen of Polaria, I have every right to make a run for the Accolade." She looked to the soldiers and sailors gathered around. "In fact, I consider it my duty. Besides, I don't answer to you, Captain, or anyone else wearing a uniform, so you'll keep your inquiries to professional matters."

Clavilla rolled his eyes. "Why are you anchored here?"

"Water," Lex said. "Our desalination system sustained irreparable damage during a pyrate attack." She nodded to the forested shore two hundred yards away. "I sent a team to scout for a fresh source."

"When did they go ashore?" Ignatius said, touching Lex's arm.

She shifted uneasily, nervous eyes flicking to Toris briefly. Then she looked back to her brother and said, "Twelve hours ago."

"Twelve hours?" said Ignatius, eyes wide in despair. "They wouldn't need that much time to find water."

"That's right," Clavilla said. "At this point, it's best to assume they're not coming back."

"I'll send a party to search for the missing scouts," Ignatius offered.

Clavilla raised his chin. "This is a time-sensitive mission, Major."

"And you have a duty to help any Polarian in distress," Ignatius countered. "Especially out here."

Clavilla gave Major Arcturus a haughty glare, then smiled. "Very well. Your team has four hours to track down the missing patrol. In the meantime, I'll have my diver inspect the damage to the *Southern Zephyr* and make the necessary repairs."

As the gaggle dispersed, Lex remained with Toris.

"How is this possible?" she said in awe. "I thought you were back on Mintaka. I even ordered my ship to stop there on our way from Port Abersali, to take you with us."

"None of that's important right now," Toris said. He stepped close to Lex, but not too close. "Listen, I have something to tell you." Then he explained the problem with the *Sea Serpent*'s fictitious rat problem.

Lex looked to the bridge with a loathsome stare. To Toris, she said, "Show me."

TWENTY-NINE

It was Lex who led Toris to the refrigeration room. Apparently her claims about time spent at the Maritime Academy were not unfounded.

"I'm surprised Clavilla allowed a civilian to crew his ship," she said.

So Lex really didn't know. "I was on *Polaris*," said Toris, "the ship you left to the pyrates."

Lex stopped, her mouth agape. "Toris, I had no idea. Korvyn told me it was all criminals aboard that boat."

"*Fodder.*" To her they were criminals, but to him they were Varcy and Domlyn and Nazar. Toris would make sure she knew their names when the time came.

Lex grimaced. "Believe me, when Korvyn gets back he'll answer for that."

"How long have they really been gone?" Toris said in a whisper.

Lex looked up and down the passageway. "Twenty-four hours."

"Something went wrong." Toris recalled Jorda's warnings about the Nordican folk.

"I know," Lex said, "but we're not leaving without their bodies. They deserve their rites."

Toris would be lying if he said he cared. If this Korvyn guy was the reason behind leaving *Polaris'* crew to face both pyrate attacks alone, then he deserved whatever fate befell him on land and whatever awaited him in the next life.

At the refrigeration room door Toris tested the handle and, as he'd hoped, the door had remained unlocked following his departure. Inside, Lex stood before the control box of frayed wires, arms crossed and a hand rubbing her chin.

"You're sure it wasn't rats?" she speculated.

Toris wished that were the case. "I heard the engineering techs talking about it. Clavilla is working for Sydra, to see she gets her war."

Lex stormed out of the room. Toris followed, thrilled to see her taking him seriously.

They found Ignatius at the weapons vault preparing his patrol. Lex pulled him aside to speak in private. Ignatius listened impatiently, glancing suspiciously at Toris as she spoke, then nodded and broke away. "There must be some other explanation," he said, returning to his troops. "I'll look into it when I get back."

Lex snagged his coat sleeve. "You're leading the patrol ashore yourself?"

"I can't send my men where I won't go."

"But—"

Ignatius loaded his revolver. "I don't have time for this now. We need to find Korvyn's team and get moving again. Everything else can wait."

Lex shoved past Toris and exited the weapons vault.

Noticing the purpose in her strides, Toris ran to catch up. "Where are you going now?"

"To the bridge," Lex said, her gaze set intently on the stairs ahead. "I'm going to inform the Captain of his infestation and demand he fix the problem immediately."

For once, Toris was on board with one of Lex's radical plans.

As they climbed the steps side by side, Toris considered where he'd be better off during this confrontation. Would his presence at Lex's side distract from her concern? Perhaps, with Toris in view, Clavilla may spin a lie and accuse Toris of the sabotage. He *had* been in that room. Had anyone noticed him slipping in or out?

On the top deck, Toris stopped atop the stairs and lingered by the rail as Lex marched straight for the bridge. In the darkening twilight, fog had risen from the bay and thickened so that not even the *Serpent*'s bow could be seen from midship.

Halfway into her trek, something seemed to catch Lex's eye. She veered course toward the starboard side, where six sailors unhitched the lines securing *Southern Zephyr* to the battle cruiser and tossed them into the wall of fog.

"What is the meaning of this?" Lex said.

One sailor snapped to attention while the others continued their work. "Just following orders, ma'am."

Lex stopped before the sailors and planted her hands on her hips. "I gave no such command."

"I did." The fog must have carried Lex's voice all the way to the bridge, because Clavilla had stepped out of the doorway to address her queries.

Lex stomped out to meet him. Toris ventured closer to eavesdrop.

"Captain Clavilla," she said, "explain to me the reason for this."

"An inspection of your ship determined she's unfit to carry on."

Lex pointed to the outline of her mast in the fog. "Then make the necessary repairs."

"No time."

Lex recoiled, studying the captain carefully. "We still have men ashore and a patrol setting out to look for them. There is time a plenty."

Clavilla leaned his head back, annoyance clear on his face. "My hull techs don't work with wood. There's nothing they can do for your ship."

Lex smiled wide. She pointed to Toris. "We have a shipbuilder right here. I'm sure he'd love the honour of working on Rosaria's cruiser."

Clavilla gave her an indignant look. "We'll pick up the *Zephyr* on the way back, *if* she's still here. As for the men you sent ashore, your ship's doctor tells me they've been gone for over twenty-four hours. Something happened to them and we don't have time to wait around to find out what."

Toris broke away from the conversation and dashed down to the foredeck, to the rack of dive tanks that had been set out for the inspection. A quick look at the pressure gauges confirmed all were full. No diver had gone below to survey the *Southern Zephyr*'s hull.

When he returned to Lex and Clavilla on the top deck, he said to Lex, "They didn't inspect your ship."

"We didn't need to," Clavilla said. His cold eyes stared down Lex as he avoided sparing Toris even the slightest glance. "With no capacity to produce fresh water, that ship is good as driftwood."

"Arokya's councillor will not be pleased to hear you failed to make every effort to salvage her *Zephyr*," Lex said.

"A tragedy I'll have to live with," Clavilla said with a hint of sarcasm. To his men, he said, "Finish cutting the *Zephyr* loose and pull anchor. We're underway in five."

Lex raised her hand to demand the sailors stop working. "Send the patrol ashore," she said to Clavilla.

"Svalbard is the objective. I'll not have us delayed any further."

Lex's eyes narrowed. "You mean you won't have another ship find the seeds before you."

Toris watched her nervously, wary of what she might say next. An open accusation before the ship's crew would endanger her life and anyone else who knew of Clavilla's scheme. Allowing the Chancellor's daughter to return home with the knowledge of Clavilla's collusion to secure the war against Ortaria would be to sign their own death orders.

"What's going on here?" Ignatius led his patrol of eight soldiers to join the group.

"We're moving on, Major," said Clavilla. "Get your sister under control, or I'll declare her a security threat."

Lex marched to the sailors unhitching the ropes from her ship and stood before the last line, blocking their way.

"Please, Lady Alexandra," said the first sailor. "We're just following orders."

Clavilla gave an impatient sigh. "Playtime is over. Major Arcturus, have your men detain the Lady Alexandra."

Ignatius's hand went to his pistol, but it was unclear who he intended to use it on. The confused look in his eyes suggested he himself did not know.

With her right hand, Lex reached across her torso and grabbed the hilt of her saber, then yanked it from its sheath. The naked steel rang as she waved it before the sailors, the point of the curved blade keeping all at bay.

No, Lex! was Toris's first thought. This wasn't a game.

The determined look in her eyes told him she knew that.

Clavilla gripped his scimitar hilt. "Threatening a Coast Patrol officer is an act of pyracy."

The charge made Toris's short hairs stand at attention. But Lex remained firm, even when Clavilla drew his scimitar and the sailors backed away to make space between their captain and the accused pyrate.

Lex's eyes flared wide as they took in the wide blade. Then, much to everyone's surprise, her eyes narrowed as she adopted a proper fencing stance.

Clavilla held out his scimitar, the wide blade of curved steel twice as thick as Lex's saber, tilting it side to side for all to see her disadvantage. That to fight him would be folly. And yet Lex merely shifted her weight to her back leg to steady herself.

Toris's heart thumped loud in anticipation. Would Clavilla actually attack the Chancellor's daughter? What would her brother do? A quick glance at Ignatius revealed his hand on the grip of his revolver, its holster undone and pistol ready to draw.

Everyone knew Clavilla was a bold man who thrived on pushing limits, but it was still a shock when the glint of the scimitar's blade rose high and then swung down at Lex's head with enough force to split her in half. Luckily, Lex had been expecting the attack and lifted her sword to block the strike.

The ring of steel on steel rattled Toris's nerves. It was the first of many.

Clavilla jabbed at her navel, but Lex spun to his side and narrowly avoided the point. Then she went on the attack with a swing at his side, which he blocked with a deafening clang. He shoved her back to create space, then delivered a hard side swing, which Lex deflected gracefully.

With every cling of naked steel, Toris felt as if a hand were squeezing tighter around his heart, making it harder to breathe. But as the duel stretched on, he watched in delightful surprise, even feeling a measure of pride swell up. Lex could actually fight, and she could fight well. All those hours training for the Commander's Cup were paying off. She faced Clavilla's unrestrained attacks of brawn and might with calculated finesse, her shaky movements smoothing with each contact of steel, her confidence inflating at the encouraging shouts from the soldiers gathered around.

The fight had brought all hands on deck. Everyone, including Rosaria's Doc Cotterys, gathered on the top deck to watch the duel. Toris was afraid to blink. Many a drinks would be bought for whatever man recounted the tale in Port Abersali's taverns. Legends of the sword fight between the Coast Patrol captain and the Chancellor's daughter along the coast of Norway would echo through the centuries. Toris was witnessing history unfold on a level unimaginable to all who came before him. The stuff of legends.

That's when Toris noticed the bridge was completely empty, his for the taking. Control the bridge and the engine room and you control the ship. It was madness, sure, but what better way to get the expedition back on track and get those seeds home. Saving Jayda demanded that he do the daring, however crazy it was. And Lex's bravery inspired him to act.

He slipped behind the nearest sailor and wrapped an arm around his neck. The *squid* struggled in the chokehold as Toris dragged him back away from the gathered spectators. When the sailor stopped resisting and his body sagged, Toris lowered him gently to the deck and relieved him of his submachine gun and pistol.

Steel rang with the fight moving to the stern, and it took everything for Toris to pull himself away. Lex's brother had her back.

He ran below decks and followed the maze of passageways, weapon at the ready. But it quickly became apparent that word of the fight had spread, and all but the prisoner watch and perhaps the engine crew had remained at their posts.

Macey was talking with Spinner, who must have come to relieve her. She saw Toris approaching with the submachine gun and fumbled to raise her carbine.

Toris levelled his submachine gun with her chest and said, "Drop your weapons, both of you."

Spinner raised both arms, then slowly pulled the carbine over his head by its sling and set it at his feet. Macey hesitated, shooting Toris a rueful glare. Toris's finger went to the trigger, her eyes opened wide, and then her weapon clattered off the floor within two heartbeats. Toris motioned for them to drop their pistols. They did so without hesitation.

"Open the door," Toris commanded. Spinner obeyed, then he pulled Macey off to the side as directed.

The prisoners recoiled at the intrusion of light. Seeing Toris in the doorway holding two carbines by their slings with one hand, a submachine gun in the other, Rykah's eyes brightened. She sprang to her feet and accepted the submachine gun, removing the magazine to ensure it was loaded as Atilus and the others crawled from the shadows. Ike accepted a pistol while rubbing the sleep from his eyes.

"What's happening?" said Rykah, standing on tiptoes to see over his shoulder.

Toris nodded for his crew to join him in the passageway, then ordered Macey and Spinner inside the cell and slammed the door shut.

"There isn't much time," Toris said, and in fact they may have already been too late. "I need you to take Ike to the engine room," he told Rykah. "I'll lead Atilus and Jorda to take the bridge. Where's Jarik?"

"Infirmary, I think," said Rykah.

Toris forced the other carbine into Atilus's hands.

"Wait, take the bridge?" Rykah said in astonishment.

Toris nodded. "We're commandeering Clavilla's ship. But like I said, there isn't much time."

Without further ado, Rykah stumbled down the passageway toward the engine room with Ike trying to keep up. Her wobbling gait suggested her time in captivity had worn her down, but she did her best to not let it slow her as she bounced from wall to wall.

Toris led Jorda and Atilus in the opposite direction, toward the stairs leading up to the top deck, with Jorda stopping to pull a red fire axe from the wall. The irregular clatter of steel grew louder as they bounded up the steps two at a time. Halfway up, a collective gasp rose from the spectators above. Toris bounced up the remaining stairs.

Near the back end of the top deck, Toris caught a glimpse of Lex through the drifting crowd as she staggered backward, one hand gripping her sword, the other covering her left eye.

As Ignatius aimed his pistol, Clavilla slipped behind Lex and held his blade over her neck. With the sharp edge against her skin, Lex straightened, and that bastard Clavilla placed his free hand on the dull back of his scimitar to pull the sword closer to her throat. Blood streamed from Lex's palms as they resisted the blade, desperate to create space between the sharp edge and her throat. Clavilla arched his back and lifted her feet from the deck. Her boots kicked for solid ground but found only air. Blood trickled down her neck where the blade sank into her skin.

Ignatius charged forward, but a line of submachine gun muzzles levelled at his chest stopped him. In turn, the soldiers aimed their carbines at the rival *squids*.

Fury surged in Toris. Abandoning his plight for the bridge, he slinked aft toward the stern for a better angle on Clavilla. He dropped to a knee, took aim, and squeezed the trigger—*CRACK!*

The shot blew out the captain's knee and sent him lumbering onto his side. Silence hung heavy in the foggy night for a long moment. Then, all the Decimation's chaos broke out on *Sea Serpent*'s decks.

The next shot came from a sailor and punched through Ignatius's shoulder. His soldiers didn't hesitate to return the favour, snapping off shots while falling back to cover as the sailors did the same. The soldiers dragged Ignatius and their wounded to safety; the sailors left theirs where they'd fallen. Gunfire rattled loud into the chill night, stray tracers of red and green zipping through fog and high into the indigo sky as soldiers and sailors exchanged fire.

Toris was already dashing toward the bridge before Ignatius had hit the deck. Atilus and Jorda sprang up from the stairway to follow. Atilus's carbine clattered off the deck but he didn't stop to pick it up, instead crossing the threshold hot on Toris's heels. Toris slammed the rear door shut and pulled down the latch to lock it while Jorda shut the other. When that last latch squeaked shut, Toris smiled in relief. Polaria's mightiest battleship now belonged to an exiled Onero. With both Arcturus's on his side, he'd have them on course again.

If only Sallus could see this moment.

Outside, bullets clinked off the bridge walls and smacked its windows to little effect. This structure had been designed to withstand small-arms fire, so Toris ignored them like pestering wasps and grabbed the microphone hanging from a coiled cord above the captain's chair. He took a deep breath, pressed the mic button, then made his first address as *Sea Serpent*'s captain.

"Attention all crew." His voice echoed across the foredeck and faded down the passageways. "I've taken over the ship's bridge and engine room. All sailors will drop their weapons and surrender to Major Arcturus's soldiers, immediately."

The intensity of gunfire exploded, with a much higher volume of bullets rattling the bridge windows.

"Ah, guys," said Atilus from the front of the bridge, "you need to come see this."

Toris and Jorda joined him at the forward window, where the sight on the foredeck almost stopped Toris's heart dead.

Around the forward deck gun, a team of sailors had removed the safety block that prevented the cannon from rotating its firing arc to the ship's bridge, and were now swinging the cannon around, its massive barrel inching toward Toris.

"Are they crazy!" Atilus said, stepping back from the window while pulling his hair out. "They'll blow the bridge, too!"

Jorda grated her metal teeth. "Better than have their ship in the hands of a couple Oneros, I suppose."

As the large round opening of the cannon's muzzle came into view, Toris's panic flashed to a boil. He slid open a forward window wide enough to shove his carbine barrel through. He aimed at the rack of dive tanks that remained on deck from the inspection, clicked his weapon to automatic, then pulled the trigger.

The flash and boom were instant. At first the blast sucked the air from Toris's lungs, then it sent him flying halfway across the bridge and onto his back. The explosion rocked the whole ship backward. A moment later a fireball ballooned into the night sky, casting an orange glow over everything in sight.

Instinctively, half of the sailors abandoned the shootout with the soldiers and rushed below. Moments later they appeared on the foredeck dragging hoses. But they were too late.

Flames had spread to the ammunition magazine below the deck guns. A blast of fire erupted so intense that it burned off all the fog around the ship and left sailors strewn about the foredeck.

Another blast rocked the ship. Then another. The *Sea Serpent* teetered stern to bow from the downward force of the blasts coming from under the foredeck.

A Coast Patrol officer, Mr. Dempster, banged on the bridge's aft window, gasping for breath. "If this fire reaches the hydrogen tanks it'll blow this ship to the moon. Tell everyone to throw down their arms and meet me on the foredeck to fight that blaze!"

Splashes came from the starboard side as sailors jumped overboard to escape the heat and caustic black smoke. A few of the soldiers saw this and followed the sailors' lead.

"There goes your firefighting team," Toris muttered.

Jorda hauled open the starboard door and stepped out onto the flying bridge. "You can go down wit this piece a junk," she said to Toris. "I didn't last this long out here by accompanyin' ships to the seabed."

She climbed onto the rail and dove overboard.

Atilus stared at Toris with panic-stricken eyes, backing toward the door Jorda had just made her escape through.

"Toris! What's going on up there?"

Toris looked around for the source of Rykah's voice, which Atilus found first. He grabbed a curved black handle from the wall and handed it to him.

Toris pressed the talk button with his thumb. "Rykah, do you have control of the engine room?"

"Affirmative! What's happening?"

Toris lowered the handset and surveyed his surroundings. It seemed the *Serpent*'s crew would sooner destroy their ship than see an Onero at her helm, because through the aft window, a sailor planted a tripod at the center of the top deck. His partner arrived with a .50 caliber machine gun over his shoulder, which both sailors lowered onto the tripod and set about securing it to the base. A third sailor hurried up with a belt of ammunition draped over his shoulders and a steel box swinging from each hand.

Cold sweat covered Toris's body. That three-legged beast would inflict far more damage to the ballistic window than the dents from the small-arms fire.

Toris opened the bridge door and squeezed off several shots to scatter the sailors from the gun. A hail of small-arms fire forced him back from the doorway.

A second later, the bridge's rear window exploded inward. Heavy machine gun rounds sparked against the ceiling and ricocheted off the bulkheads, busting apart display screens and instrument panels.

Toris sprawled across the deck and covered his ears as a steady spray of machine gun bullets bounced around the bridge. Beside him, the receiver dangled from its curled cord.

Again, Rykah's voice graced the bridge, this time barely audible over the rattling gunfire. *"Toris! Do you need me up there? What's going on?"*

Atilius pried Toris's carbine from his hands and scampered to the flying bridge. Then, as Jorda had done moments before, he climbed over the rail and dropped out of sight to join the swimmers below.

Toris buried his face into his forearms. To hold out here risked the sailors blasting apart the bridge beyond function, and yet to give it up risked stalling the mission indefinitely.

"Toris? Answer me, please! Are you all right?"

He lifted his head, grabbed the receiver, and issued his final command as *Sea Serpent*'s captain: "Abandon ship!"

A long period of static followed, then came Rykah's dejected voice. *"Roger. Abandoning ship."*

Toris hit the talk button one last time. "Make sure to let Macey and Spinner out of the cell."

"Got it."

Toris crawled on all fours to the port side door, the side opposite of where everyone else had jumped. On the flying bridge, he checked the water below, careful to avoid landing near any drowning men, and saw everyone had instinctively jumped off the side nearest land, leaving this entire side clear. As the machine gun sailors rushed the bridge, Toris climbed over the rail and jumped feet first into the foreign water.

So ended his disastrous reign as captain of the *Sea Serpent*.

THIRTY

Toris crawled onto the rocky shore and collapsed. The stress of the blast and the shootout had called every fiber of his being into action, and now that he was out of the line of fire, at least for the moment, fatigue was seeping into his muscles. But he devoted little time to recovery.

He rose to a knee to survey his surroundings. Staggered rows of pine trees prevented a deep look into the forest ahead. Most of the sailors who'd jumped overboard clustered down the shore to his left, where they watched their ship burn. To his right, much closer, Atilus was on his knees stripping the carbine and drying each piece as best he could with his wet shirt.

Pistol fire popped from the forest ahead.

Metal rattled nearby as Atilus slapped his weapon back together and did a function test. Toris arrived at his side as he loaded a magazine and cocked it.

Atilus scanned the forest, the carbine shaking in his hands. "The hell are we gonna do?"

Toris peered through rising layers of tree boughs, trying to see any hint of what had held up Lex's scouts. Flashes from sporadic explosions on *Sea Serpent* offered brief glimpses of the hilltop outlines above. Flames from behind cast dancing shadows over the trees and through gaps in the fog, playing tricks on his eyes.

Hope burned strong in Toris's heart as he looked back at the blazing ship. The last of the crew were jumping into the water, and soon the *Sea Serpent* would be completely abandoned. Many of them would likely drown, or at least lose their weapons. But it wasn't the battleship he'd set his hopes on.

The *Southern Zephyr* had floated clear of the burning ship and so far remained unscorched by the flames. Once the ammunition on her neighbouring vessel burned off, she'd be safe to return to. But Toris would not be able to commandeer that ship alone. He'd need to rally his team plus a few soldiers.

"We need to find Rykah and the others," Toris said.

Gunfire rippled from the depths of the forest. Apparently not even a swim from their burning ship could quell the firefight between the sailors and soldiers. This was going to be a long night, and sitting here on the stony beach wasn't going to make it pass by any faster.

"Let's go," Toris said, nodding for Atilus to lead the way with his carbine.

Atilus gripped the weapon tight and shirked back. Toris wrenched the firearm from his hands, then pushed through the tree boughs and into the uncharted territory that had already swallowed Lex's team of scouts.

He walked nearly thirty paces over soft earth before Atilus scrambled after him. Together their feet squished into soggy ground. Water rose to Toris's knees, but he kept on. Above, pointed tips of coniferous trees disappeared into the enveloping fog.

Stepping lightly through the marsh, Toris felt as if he were being watched. He couldn't help but wonder if these trees had seen the world as it was before the Decimation. Were they the oldest lifeforms on Earth? Was their creaking a warning to retreat?

He ignored it and waded forward.

An eruption of gunfire nearby had Atilus gripping Toris's arm. They both sank low together. The exchange went on for another half minute, and was followed by a man shouting orders—something about forming a perimeter and coaxing a comrade to come join them.

Toris stood and crept toward the source of the voice. If the man was a soldier he'd be in luck, for he was clearly in the company of fellow soldiers. If they were sailors forming a perimeter, well, it'd best if he saw them first.

A slope rose from the marsh. As Toris led Atilus up the mountainside, the forest thinned and the ground hardened to dry dirt. He stopped beside a red alder tree to listen for more shouts or signs of movement. The only sign was footsteps fading behind.

He turned to see Atilus backing away from him. When Atilus caught himself and stopped, the crunching persisted for one footstep too long. Toris squinted at the darkness behind Atilus, and before Atilus could turn to follow his line of sight it was too late.

A javelin zipped from the darkness behind and struck Atilus's back. Its point punched through his sternum, the tip dripping blood.

Toris was on his belly before Atilus's knees hit the ground. A second javelin whizzed through the air over Toris's head and buried into a tree trunk with a thud. The shaft wobbled from the impact, and the white tip piercing the bark appeared to have been crafted from bone.

Atilus toppled to his side, eyes wide in agony and surprise.

Toris rose high enough to shoot over him. He fired on automatic into the surrounding forest, the flash of his muzzle blinding as he swept in a complete circle, spraying lead into darkness until the last round zipped off into the night. Then he dropped back to his belly.

Atilus's eyes were froze open in panicked agony, and his chest had fallen still. But there was no time to mourn him.

Footsteps pounded the forest floor nearby. Toris dug the spare magazine from his pocket and loaded it. Silence followed the clink of the bolt sliding forward. No chirp of crickets. No cracking twigs.

Just the sound of Toris's own pounding heart as he lay listening to the dark.

A *raaaaaap* like fabric tearing frightened him halfway to his grave. Over the rounded mountaintop above, a ball of white light flew straight up into the black sky. When it reached maximum height and fell back toward the ground, a small canopy deployed, from which the glowing white light hung and illuminated the forest. It cast shadows as it drifted slowly toward the ground, and revealed two solid figures standing with their backs to Toris.

As they watched the paraflare in wonder, Toris rose to a knee and shot each man in the back—quicker deaths than what they'd offered poor Atilus. He crawled over to check their bodies and, in the flickering white light, could not help but stand and stumble away.

The 'men', if they could be called that, wore red stripes of blood over their skin, which appeared to have been burned and stretched. Grey scales covered the back of one of these creatures, possibly the mutations of solar or nuclear radiation. And their weapons were reminiscent of primitive cave dwellers—blow darts, bows and arrows, and javelins of wood and bone.

Toris returned to his friend to close his eyes for the last time. Anger and fear swelled in his chest, but he kept a lid on it.

"Death is naught," he whispered, and swore to return for his brother's body.

The flare beyond burned out, leaving Toris in a darkness deeper than before. He blinked several times and strained to adjust to the dark.

Whoosh! A second ball of light rose like a star and pushed away the dark.

This time, Toris did not startle. Instead, he rejoiced.

He crept from the grove and sidelong across the slope, following that white beacon dangling from the parachute in its slow descent. Reaching other Polarians, whether soldier or sailor, was better than spending the night alone in the forest with these beasts. Hopefully his compatriots had realized that and launched the flare in part as a rally call.

Each paraflare burned for a short thirty seconds. Toris had started timing them at the launching of the third flare, after he found himself clinging to a tree in the suffocating darkness that made the ensuing five seconds feel like hours. Each time that white ball of light flickered out, Toris couldn't resist holding onto a tree to keep the void from swallowing him. What had at first seemed a saving light was actually ruining his natural night vision, plunging him into blinding darkness when each flare burned out.

The ripping fabric sound of their deployment that had at first rattled his nerves was now the greatest noise he ever heard. That and the defiant gunfire from his comrades beneath the drifting white light.

Gunfire tapered with each flare to fly. Toris watched shadows retreat up the mountain from the pervasive light until only the occasional shot shattered the night. Stumbling and muttering faded into stands of trees up the mountain.

Toris eased across the slope, comforted by the sizzling sound from the paraflare above. As he drew closer, that noise covered his footsteps while providing greater illumination. Each step toward the light was one step closer to safety. But the Polarians didn't possess a limitless supply of light. So he trotted faster, picking up his pace along the slope until a bullet nearly took his head off.

He felt the skin of his cheek tug as bark from a nearby tree exploded. Splinters impaled the left side of his face.

Fear provided a numbing sensation as he tried to sink lower into the ground, scanning the slope up and down for the source of the shot. Straight across to his right, the remnants of what looked like a stone watchtower was planted in the slope. A square base of crumbling stone walls shimmered like cracked platinum beneath the paraflare.

"I'm Polarian!" he screamed, his voice muffled by the sound of blood rushing in his ears.

"State your name!" came the reply from the tower base.

State your name? Did Toris hear that right? Did whoever was on that hill expect these primitives to know their home country by name? Now was not the time to bicker. "It's Toris Onero!"

"Toris!" A voice had never sounded so sweet as Lex's did now. "Get over here!"

Her voice was a beacon of light in the dark, brighter than any flare, and Toris ran to it without a second look around. His footsteps crashing over leaves and branches seemed to echo all the way to the sea, and his body tensed at the thought of one of those savages lining up his back with a javelin. Were these steps across this nameless hill on Norway his last? Would highborn children learn about *Toris the Agrinaut*'s last plight in history class, how he was so close but it was never meant to be?

No, they would not. He reached the Polarian stronghold and vaulted up the five-foot wall, the highest of the four sides, his hands clawing for purchase. Figures of half shadow, half light had stood to cover his arrival, and a few hands dragged him across the threshold and into safety. He landed on a pile of spent shell casings, some so fresh they burned his skin.

Lex wrapped her arms around him and squeezed so tight he could hardly catch his breath.

"Perimeter," hissed a soldier, a sergeant named Thane, and five defenders dispersed to their positions at the four walls.

Toris noticed a figure wearing a sailor's slicker. Nothing brings enemies together like a common foe.

"Welcome to Nordica," Jorda said from the far corner, her knees pulled tight to her chest.

When Lex released Toris, he noticed a bulky white bandage over her left eye. Whoever had dressed the wound had done so in haste, but her good eye fell on something behind Toris and widened with enough despair for both eyes.

He followed her gaze to a soldier slumped up against the wall, his head rolling in a semi-conscious stupor. An arrow shaft protruded from his belly, ominous black feathers as fletching at the exposed end. Ignatius.

"It's all my fault," Lex said under her breath.

Toris grabbed her shoulders and squared her to look him in the eyes. "You did the right thing, Lex. You always do." He forced a smile. "That's something about you that drives me crazy. To hell with consequences, right?"

She cracked a smile and wiped tears from her good eye. That's when he noticed both her hands wrapped in bandages and remembered her resisting Clavilla's blade against her throat.

He looked to the wall on the upslope side, where Macey and Spinner watched the high ground that rose toward the mountaintop.

"I saw them fleeing the light," Toris said to Lex. "We just have to hold out here until sunrise. We'll get Doc Cotterys to fix up your brother, then we can take over the *Zephyr* and go to Svalbard."

Lex met him with a smile, her good eye glowing bright with enthusiasm. It was doable, Toris's plan, and they both knew it.

"They'll attack at dawn," said Ignatius with a cough. His head drooped and swayed side to side as he tried looking up to see them straight. His eyes were sunken and his face pale with the look of a dead man. "These folk fight like Ortarians," the major said. "They'll come from the southeast, while the sun is glaring in our eyes. Right now they're gathering their forces to come at us in one good rush, and we don't have the ammo to push them back."

Toris noticed empty magazines scattered across the ground. Many of the hill's defenders were likely on their last shots.

"Best not to let 'em take ya alive," Jorda said, shaking her head gravely. "You'll be beggin' fer a bullet before they finishes wit ya."

Lex crouched beside her brother, wiping the sweat from his forehead and recounting stories of a childhood so different than this experience that it may as well have happened on a distant planet.

Toris fixed a bayonet to his carbine and peered over the crumbled wall, across the slope from where he'd just come, the image of Atilus still fresh in his mind. In fact, Atilus's agonizing death was all he could think about.

Jorda crawled up beside him. "You got a pistol for me?"

"So you can shoot me in the back?"

Toris wasn't about to forget it was her finger that had ended Nazar's life.

"Wouldn't waste a good bullet on you, boy," said the pyrate queen. "Khalid got a price on me head, so I intend to deliver it to 'em in pieces, if ya catch my meanin'."

"Who's Khalid? Is he their leader?"

"Leader of sorts. Right twisted he is. Into all sorts of research with genetics, tryin' to restore these folk back to whatever glory he thinks they once had. Lore says he owns a dragon even, so they do what he says. When they attack, it's best you be keepin' one of them bullets for yourself. And if you got any mercy in yer heart, you'll leave one for me too."

Sergeant Thane launched the last flare with a deafening tear. Its light was red, to give the Polarians a head start in adjusting their night vision. *Red*. How many shades of that color would the dawn bring?

THIRTY-ONE

Ignatius wasn't awake to see his prediction come true.

The Polarians defending the stone tower base had watched anxiously as a faint band of pink split the mountaintop from the sky. Anxiety turned to fear as the band spread upward and seeped into the clouds, painting them scarlet red like a foamy sea of blood. From below, fog had crept up the mountain and obscured their view of the downslope side.

When a sliver of that glowing orange disk pushed up from the rounded mountaintop above, a horn blew long and solemn. Then, all along the mountainside in every direction, the horns of death blew in response.

At half rise, with the sun glaring from the mountain crest, the Nordicans attacked not just from the east, but from all sides. Screams and howls and yelps rose up the hill like a flash flood of promised blood mirrored from the sky above.

"Hold your fire," ordered Sergeant Thane from the north wall. "Wait till they get close."

His order went unheeded. Macey snapped off shots uphill, and soon everyone was firing to the sides across the slope. Many soldiers shifted their fire to the eastern quadrant, up the hill, where dozens of howling voices rushed closer. Only Toris remained covering the downhill side, watching the fog with fifteen rounds in his magazine. His country-folk were lucky he was there.

Four primitive warriors, wielding spears and axes, emerged from the fog in a silent rush toward the west wall.

Toris waited until they were within spitting distance, then fired three shots into two targets before his weapon jammed. He sprang to his feet and greeted the nearest axeman with the butt of his carbine, sending him stumbling within their perimeter and into Spinner.

A spear thrust toward Toris's exposed side, but he was able to swing his weapon back and bat the shaft away. The spearman fell forward onto the carbine's fixed bayonet.

Toris didn't have time to look his opponent in the eyes as another spearman climbed over the wall to his right. He wrenched the blade free and pulled the cocking handle to clear the jam, then fired two shots into the spearman on the wall.

The last attacker in the rush, an axeman, was climbing the wall when Toris aimed and pulled the trigger. Nothing happened. Another jam. The warrior leaped and swung his axe down at Toris's head.

Toris raised his carbine horizontally with both hands, and the axe handle clacked against the forward handguard. Momentum forced him back against the north wall with the much taller warrior standing on a sailor's body for added height. The axeman pushed the back of the blade with his free hand, forcing the sharp edge toward Toris's face. Toris resisted by pushing up with his carbine. Sweat dripped onto his face and burned his skin. He turned his head from the advancing blade to avoid the smell of the man's breath, a stench so foul he gagged in disgust.

To his left, Lex rose from beside Ignatius. She fumbled a pistol in bandaged hands as she aimed at the axeman's head. She pulled the trigger. *Click.* The revolver was empty.

That's when Toris noticed all the gunfire had ceased, and a crowd of Nordican warriors had gathered atop the walls. Spears and arrow tips shifted threateningly between the surviving

Polarian soldiers—Macey recovering from a blow to the head, Spinner on his back with both hands up, and Thane sweeping his pistol aim across the beasts above them. Jorda held a blade to her own neck, hand shaking in anticipation.

The axeman before Toris was determined to carve out one last kill, pushing against Toris's shaking arms, black teeth clenched in animal rage.

And within the blink of an eye, the warrior's fighting spirit evaporated. He gasped and sprang back in alarm. He pointed to Toris's shoulder.

"Oshinga!" he wailed. He flung his axe aside and climbed the wall between two spearmen, disappearing over the other side briefly before reappearing in his retreat up the slope.

Toris cleared his carbine jam with shaking hands.

The warriors perched atop the walls ignored the threat of his wandering aim and craned their necks to better see the brand on his shoulder—the *O* dissected by a vertical slash.

"Oshinga?" a few muttered.

"Oshinga," came the responses.

Spears and axes clattered onto the ground, and the figures all scattered from the walls like a startled murder of crows, cawing and wailing as they ran for the hills.

Toris watched in astonishment as the attackers cleared out. Either the Nordicans somehow harboured an innate fear of semi-exiled Oneros, or the mark on his arm held other significance to them

This was not time to ponder the reason for this change in fortune. "We need to get back to the ships," he said.

The soldiers agreed, but before leaving they scavenged their fallen comrades for munitions.

That's when Toris noticed Lex leaning against her brother's chest and hyperventilating. A closer look revealed Ignatius's eyes wide open, but, like the many flares that had succumb to the night, his light had burned out.

Toris nodded to the soldiers gathered around to resume their watch positions, then sat against the wall beside Lex to give her a moment.

———

The sun had risen well above the mountaintop and burned off much of the fog when Lex finally stood and composed herself. The soldiers, Ignatius's men, had fashioned litters for their fallen using tree branches and their long sleeve shirts. Thane led them over the north wall and down the hill toward the bay.

Toris helped carry the remains of a sailor who'd been struck in the neck by an arrow. The zigzagged walk down the hill with the stretcher was slow and treacherous, with a dark shadow plaguing his mind the entire time. Were they walking toward an ambush by their own men, by sailors who'd perhaps been spared the attacks of these primitives and still saw the soldiers as their primary threat?

Luckily that was not the case when the party arrived on shore. The sailors greeted them as if nothing had happened, even ordering Doc Cotterys to check them for wounds. But the absence of Rykah and *Polaris'* crew was disconcerting to say the least.

The Chief Engineer wasted no time delivering the dreadful news. "Most of the *Serpent'*s operational systems were destroyed during the explosions. I need to go back for another look, but only after the hull team makes the vessel safe. Right now she's leaking hydrogen into the bay, so even if we miraculously get her going again, we're likely to run out of fuel."

"And the *Zephyr*?" Toris said, still clinging to some shred of hope.

The Chief frowned and glanced back at Rosaria's ship, which had drifted clear of the *Sea Serpent* during the blasts. "The hull sustained pretty heavy fire damage to her port side. Some sections are charred black, so you won't see me taking her north."

Every sailor standing on the rocky shore nodded in agreement. So that was that.

"Has anyone seen my crew?" Toris said.

Before anyone could answer, a voice from down the shore interrupted. "Lady Alexandra! You're all right!"

Everyone watched a man stumble up the shore from the forest near the far point. He looked like a dog just let out of its cage—a wary sense of freedom, half-smiles and half-frightened shoulder checks. And a cheek swollen to the size of a fist with two black eyes to match. Toris did not recognize this man, who he took for Korvyn.

Lex remained kneeling beside her brother's remains while combing her fingers through his brown hair. Korvyn made straight toward her, a relieved smile on his face at the sight of the soldiers and sailors gathered, a clear comfort in the security of numbers, but the sight of Ignatius's body stopped him. He continued his approach cautiously and crouched beside Lex.

"The time to mourn him has not yet come," Korvyn said in as gentle a tone his gruff voice could muster. "The locals...they wish to meet with our leadership to discuss a truce. They've summoned their overlord to speak with us."

Korvyn may as well have been talking to a tree for all the response he was getting from Lex. This he quickly saw, so he stood and turned his attention to the other survivors. "Who's in command here?"

This question drew many an awkward stare. With Ignatius dead and Clavilla's status unknown, a debate ensued. Though, it was going in the opposite direction that Toris had expected. Officers argued over which man should assume command, and each of those men in turn made a case against his own nomination. None of the bridge officers wanted to take charge of this mess, and the Chief Engineer rightfully claimed to have greater responsibilities. The charge even fell to Lex, the Chancellor's daughter, but only briefly, for her awareness of anything but her brother's lifeless body had already been noted.

Then, as if they actually needed more deterrents introduced, one of the sailors said, "They're probably trying to get us all in one place to butcher us."

"So we send a small delegation," an officer suggested.

"Are you volunteering?" said a colleague. "Didn't think so. If they don't plan to kill us outright, it'd be to at least get their hands on a valuable hostage. Oh, Mother! I bet that's what it is! Take away our leader and then attack."

This had apparently already been on many minds, as many heads were quick to nod their agreement.

"So we send someone without value to us," said Mr. Dempster, Clavilla's executive officer. "Like a messenger."

A few eyes drifted to Toris. He shrugged before he could allow fear and common sense to dissuade him. "I'll do it - I'll go parley with them."

His quick acceptance drew a mixture of looks. Some appeared relieved, others curiously grateful, but more than a few appeared reluctant to send a half-blood Onero to represent them at the treaty table. Plus, Toris was probably the last Polarian who should be heading a peace delegation. And someone other than himself quickly figured that out.

Macey pointed an accusing finger at him. "Maybe some of you have forgotten, but this is the son of Anaraxa Centaurus. I'm sure no one here needs reminding of her role at Anterra's only peace summit. It's because of her that Polaria still needs us soldiers at the border. She betrayed her country, and he's just as likely to turn on us to make a deal to save his own skin."

Resentful glares narrowed on Toris, but he was no stranger to such looks. He stood tall and lifted his chin, calculating a response in his head.

But Spinner stepped forward and jabbed Macey's soldier. "Come on, Mace, you were with him on the hill when they attacked. They'd have finished us off if not for his brand." He looked to the others. "It freaked them right out. Sent them running for the hills, *literally*."

Sergeant Thane nodded. "It's true. Saw it happen myself. That mark means something to them. They're a primitive type, you saw. Might be they got some superstition about it."

A heated discussion broke out, each taking a side for or against Toris, but he wasn't having this matter go to a vote. He raised his hands and said, "If any of you prefer to take my place, then I'll gladly stay back here."

Some looked to Korvyn, the only Polarian to have experienced the local hospitality while unarmed, but Lex's bodyguard hugged himself tight and stared at his bare and bloodied feet. His response ended the debate.

Toris only had one person to talk to after that. To the Chief Engineer, he said, "Make sure you have good news for me when I return."

THIRTY-TWO

To test the authority of his position as Polarian ambassador to Nordica, Toris ordered the soldiers to retrieve Atilus's body from the mountainside. A group of six set off without hassle. He then had the remaining soldiers fire green flares to summon survivors, with Rykah being his main concern.

When Macey insisted on accompanying Toris to the treaty table, threatening to kill him if he tried to betray the group, Spinner agreed to join. Toris did not protest. A show of their weaponry would remind the enemy of their effectiveness on the battlefield. Any organized attackers would now see their success last night had relied on surprise and catching the Polarians while they were fighting each other. Now that they'd consolidated their forces, an attack in daylight would be a fool's errand.

Still, when an unarmed Nordican arrived to guide the Polarian envoy, many of the soldiers and sailors recoiled at the sight of him. Seeing one of these locals in the light of day, with both of his flanks covered in what appeared to be indigo scales, everyone knew this was an enemy unlike any they'd encountered at their border with Ortaria.

Toris forced himself forward to meet the guide waiting at a bend in the beach. When he and his two-soldier escort were still fifty feet away, the creature turned to lead him to a trail that twisted from the beach up into the hills.

Apparently Lex had been listening all along, because when Toris walked to meet the escort she pulled herself away from Ignatius's body and fell in beside him at the trailhead. He gave her a smile, but her blank stare had fixed on the dirt path before her feet and remained there as they made the climb through sparse pine forest. A grumbling Korvyn soon fell in behind Lex like the dutiful watchdog that he was.

The guide led the party up a winding trail and through a pass between mountains. The sparsely wooded dip between peaks offered a view of an inland bay on the other side, where a cluster of huts sat sheltered by mountains on three sides. The village was nestled on a slope that seemed flattened from generations of funnelled foot traffic. Two neat rows of triangular wooden huts lined a wide dirt pathway from a dock up to a longhouse built into the hill, its doorway facing the dock. At the village edges, behind rows of pointed roofs, sat dwellings of stone walls and sod roofs from which puffs of grey smoke rose into the cool morning air.

As they zigzagged down the trail to the village, Korvyn grabbed Lex's arm. "You hear that?"

"It's the wind," Toris said absently as he compiled a list of possible opening statements in his head.

"No," Korvyn said, pulling Lex to a halt. "*Listen.*"

Toris stopped and turned an ear to the sky. He did hear it, a distant thudding from beyond the inland mountains across the village, like the flutter of giant hummingbird wings. It grew louder until not even Lex could ignore it.

The Polarians clustered together on the path as the silhouette of a monstrous black bird rose before the sun. Toris instinctively joined his comrades in a close huddle as they watched in shock as the beast approached at remarkable speed.

Atop the bird, massive dual propellers spun horizontally with enough force to whip the trees of the surrounding hills like the winds of a hurricane. As the bird swooped down over the village, a dust storm whirled up between the huts. A large grey hull glinted like steel in the morning sun, but it was impossible to fathom such a heavy vessel carried along by spinning propellers alone.

The flying machine landed on level ground beside the shore, its blurred dual blades spreading ripples across the inlet's still water. As the roof propellers slowed and the thudding faded, a ramp lowered from the back. Two dozen figures streamed out of the steel body and were escorted up to the longhouse by a group of locals.

Toris watched the envoy in terror. These bird men were a different breed than the locals he'd encountered last night. Not only did the new arrivals nearly match the Polarian strength by numbers, but their firearms resembled those of the *Sea Serpent*'s fighters back on the beach.

Toris's guide had stopped lower on the path and watched the stunned Polarians with appraising eyes. This arrival was a show of force, and Toris wasn't going to give them more than he'd already allowed, so he led his delegation down the hill as if a hulking steel machine hadn't just come down from the sky.

But as they entered the village, Toris couldn't help but study the machine in awe. To have a metal vessel float on water is one thing, but to make one soar through the air was most unnatural. Thick, armoured plates of steel with machine gun turrets made this mechanical beast a flying fortress.

Toris shuddered and walked on up the main dirt path between wooden huts.

Along the pathway, villagers dropped to their knees and lowered their foreheads to the ground at the passing Polarians. In Polaria, this was a sign of reverence; here, it could mean anything.

At the top of the village, triangular eaves covered a doorway that led into the hillside, which was flanked by walls of stone that cut the slope short. An honour guard of locals formed two lines facing each other, their spear butts in the dirt at their feet and the points tilted slightly forward. Toris would have preferred to walk around them, yet if they wanted him dead they could have easily set an ambush. And it wasn't these spearmen he now feared. It was the bird men who'd disappeared inside.

The guide stopped at the doorway and motioned for the Polarians to enter. Toris led his envoy into the longhall, where no locals or bird men were in sight.

A small fire crackled from a hearth across the hall. Smoke clouded in the wooden rafters above. Dividing the center of the hall, a long table stretched left to right, fifty feet in length, with flickering candles spread at even intervals. Masks of carved wood hung from the walls, the faces painted with expressions of taunting spirits. Twenty wooden pillars supported the rafters, each carved in the likeness of stacked animals believed to be long extinct.

Toris studied the carvings of spotted cats and hook-beaked birds. Did such beasts still exist up here? If humans had survived, why not the animals of ages passed?

The guide entered behind and gestured for the Polarians to sit at the table. Lex took the center seat on the side nearest the entrance, but Toris and Spinner opted to pace while Korvyn and Macey kept watch from the doorway.

At the far left end of the hall, the Nordican guide stopped beside a doorway and made an announcement that, much to Toris's surprise, came in his mother tongue. "The Village of Kalkadia is proud to present the Emperor Khalid, ruler of the resilient Nordican people, champion of the free mind and saviour of the human race."

A hulk of a man ducked through the doorway beside the guide and entered the hall. White slashes marring his ebon skin gave him the appearance of a fierce Ortarian warrior. Or how Toris had always pictured the enemies across Polaria's border, anyway. A large gold hoop hung from his septum and glinted in the firelight. A long purple robe with golden inlays hung to his ankles, under which a black ballistic vest held a pistol angled over his navel.

Seeing the small group of Polarians, he threw out both arms as if to embrace them from a distance. "I was expecting more of you," his voice boomed.

Toris could have said the same. He'd seen this Khalid arrive with two dozen armed soldiers. Where were they now? Somewhere that assured Khalid that the armed Polarians were no threat to him, no doubt. Or perhaps displaying his backbone in this manner was how he derived his power.

Toris stepped forward. "Our people elected us to represent them."

Khalid frowned and rubbed his chin. "*Elected*. Yes, I've read this word in the old texts." He gave Toris a knowing look. "You must be the Oshinga."

He strode straight to Toris and grabbed his shoulder with two massive hands, squeezing his deltoid to better examine the slashed O brand. Toris stood firm as the giant man, who stood two heads over him, leaned in for a close look at the exiled Onero brand.

The emperor released Toris's shoulder and scoffed. He waved a berating hand at the escort and said, "Fool, this is a mark set with iron. We've seen this before, on pyrate swine. I should have *you* branded for this foolishness." He returned his attention to Toris, smiled, then motioned for everyone to sit at the table. "Come, there are other matters for us to discuss."

Toris sat to Lex's right, Korvyn to her left while Macey and Spinner paced before the doorway.

Khalid walked around the end of the table to the other side.

"Welcome to my land," the Nordican Emperor said. "I hope the local reception wasn't too hostile for your kind. The people around here startle easily and, like wild animals, they bite when they feel threatened." Khalid sat in the chair across from Lex. "Where are you from?"

Toris hesitated. His home already had enemies on land. They didn't need flying machines coming at them from the sky as well. "It's south of here. I can't say more than that."

Khalid tipped his head in understanding. "What brings you to my shores?"

"We're just passing through," Toris said. "All we need is time to repair our ships and we'll be on our way."

Khalid steepled his fingers and leaned forward. "What interests do you have north of here?"

Several lies sprouted in Toris's mind, but he decided it best to be straight with this 'emperor'. "We're going to Svalbard."

Khalid's nostrils flared. He crossed his arms and leaned back in his seat, the wood groaning under his weight. "Still trying to convince me of the Oshinga story, I see. Well, this is a myth that I do not subscribe to, so you'd be wise to tell me the true nature of your purpose here. Or you'll find my hospitality far less endearing."

"It's true," Toris said. "There are seeds there that we need. If you help us get them, you'll be richly rewarded."

Khalid guffawed and held his belly with both hands. "I am not a man who seeks riches," he said. His laughter died and his smile levelled. "It's *order* that eludes me most, and allowing foreign invaders onto sacred soil will inflict more chaos upon my dominion."

Toris exchanged a concerned look with Korvyn, as Lex's blank stare had nothing to offer.

Khalid stood and turned toward the fireplace with his hands clasped behind his back.

"Though I myself do not believe in the Oshinga prophecy, many of my subjects do. They're a volatile bunch, and keeping them civil has vexed me beyond wits end. If I allow foreign devils to desecrate the tomb..." He shook his head. "Well, it will never happen." He turned to face the Polarians. "This is as far north as you may go."

As if his own words had sparked an epiphany, Khalid's eyes brightened. He wagged a finger at the envoy. "But your arrival here is a gift. I see this now." He paced the length of the table, looking to the rafters above. "For many years this tribe has made war with their neighbours over disputed land. For centuries there seemed no end, but now it's clear. You see, they're not fighting so much to acquire the land as they are to keep their rival from possessing it. If I give that land to you, to act as a buffer, then that would eliminate my biggest bane in this region."

Toris shifted uneasily in his chair. He didn't like the sound of where this was going. He looked to Lex, but even Khalid's insinuation failed to break her trance.

"I'll have a treaty drafted up," Khalid went on, excitement growing in his voice. "By signing it, you'll be agreeing to never venture north of here. Or south, for that matter."

"We'll be prisoners," Macey said from the doorway. She spat at her feet.

Khalid rubbed his chin. "More like…*esteemed denizens*." He pointed out the main entrance. "You see how they grovel for you? They think you deities, and I'll see that they always revere you as such. So long as you follow my rules, you'll walk these lands as gods."

Toris shifted in his chair. "If we refuse?"

Khalid frowned. "That would not be wise, young *Oshinga*. Do you think my offer unfair?"

Toris folded his hands on his lap, straining to maintain his calm. "My country is counting on us to return with those seeds. Many will starve if we fail."

Khalid's massive hands slammed down on the table. He leaned forward, scornful eyes burrowing through Toris. "Svalbard is off-limits to you," he said, a string of spittle dangling from his bottom lip. "You'll live the rest of your lives as subjects of my empire, or you'll not live at all."

Khalid frowned at his own words, seeming unsettled by his own outburst. He sank into his seat.

Toris thought of Jayda, of what life at the border would be like as food supplies withered. And that was the best-case scenario, if they weren't ordered to invade Ortaria. He crossed his arms and leaned back in his chair. He shook his head, but before he could verbally decline the offer, Lex spoke up.

"I'd like to inspect the land first."

Betrayal. That was all Toris felt in that moment. Not only had Lex contributed nothing to the negotiations, but she'd also just agreed to maroon every Polarian in Nordica.

How could she?

Lex stood from her chair. "Draw up whatever contract you need. I'll sign it on behalf of my country-folk if the land proves sufficient."

Toris grabbed her arm and dragged her to the doorway with Korvyn in tow. "What the hell are you doing, Lex? Do you know what you're committing us to?"

"This day has already claimed too many Polarians," she said, her good eye locked on the flying machine at the bottom of the dirt lane.

Toris looked to Korvyn for support, but all he offered was a shrug.

"Doesn't seem like we have much of a choice," Korvyn said. "Besides, we can play his game for now. Then, when he's not watching, we'll slip north to Svalbard."

Lex gave a faint nod to Korvyn's suggestion, but her distant stare suggested other matters occupied her mind. No doubt she was eager to start her brother's funeral process. Was this influencing her rash decision to settle on Khalid's land?

Yet, though Toris hated to admit it, they were both right. At this bargaining table the Polarians lacked leverage.

Khalid joined them in the doorway and placed a hand on Toris and Lex's shoulders. He nodded to the flying machine by the dock. "Shall I show you what my *chopper* can do? Perhaps a demonstration on your people gathered across the mountain might persuade you? I only need a few of you to occupy the land. With all guns blazing, she can spit out five thousand rounds in one minute. How long do you think they'll last under that storm of steel?" Khalid released Toris's shoulder. "But who benefits from such a waste of life?"

Toris nodded faintly. Khalid had made clear his desire, and

arguing would only waste time. He met the Emperor of Nordica's expecting stare.

"Show us to our new home."

"You agreed to this, Alexandra?"

Mr. Dempster's pale face resembled those of his crewmen gathered on the shore.

"She didn't have a choice," Korvyn said, stepping forward in her defence.

Toris folded the boundary map Khalid had given him, the acceptance of which had promised their submission to the Emperor of Nordica. "It's only for show," he assured them. "We'll play along with his wish and make it appear as if we're settling in. We can work on the ships under the cover of darkness, but for now…"

He gestured toward the headland to their south and the path leading over it, away from Battler's Bay, which was what the Polarians had taken to calling this pocket of water where their two disabled ships floated.

"This is madness," Dempster said, shaking his head in disbelief. He pointed forcefully at the path. "It's probably an ambush. Stretch our forces thin along a narrow trail and then hit us from all sides." He looked to the soldiers for support. "Am I right?"

The soldiers exchanged nervous looks with Sergeant Thane, the highest rank among them, exposing hints of their acceptance of the rival officer's suspicion.

"It's not an ambush," Toris said.

"How do you know?" Dempster pressed.

Toris thought of the guns he'd seen in the airship. *Chopper*, Khalid had called the metal beast, no doubt a reference to the damage its armaments could inflict from the sky. From his limited assessment, that machine possessed the means to have wiped them out hours ago if Khalid wished. Which was all the proof of Khalid's benevolence that Toris needed.

A landing craft emerged from behind the *Sea Serpent*. Two rowers straddled the gunwales, paddling toward shore.

Toris stepped away from the group and stood on tiptoes to better see. His heart beat with joy upon seeing Rykah on the rubber raiding craft's port side. Ike was paddling from the starboard. In Rykah, Toris at least knew he had someone as devoted to reaching Svalbard as him. She was all he needed, but he knew others would follow when the time came.

"They went to get heavier weapons in case we needed to make a stand," Thane said. He glanced at Lex. "Or go in for a rescue."

Rykah dismounted and gave Toris a curt nod. "From deckhand to captain of *Polaris*, and now lead Polarian delegate. Not bad for a half-blood Onero."

Mr. Dempster scoffed. "Yeah, wait till you hear the deal he got us."

Hearing the treaty terms sucked all the cheer out of Rykah.

"It's just to buy us time," Toris assured her. "We need some breathing room while we regroup."

"That being said, we have three days to strip what we need from the ships," Korvyn said to everyone gathered on the shore. "The rest will be salvaged by Khalid's engineers and taken inland."

"No way," said Mr. Dempster. "Our wounded need to be treated and monitored in our ship's infirmary. If that takes longer than three days, then Khalid is going to have to wait till we're well and ready to move them onto land."

"So we're really going to divide our forces?" said a sailor, gripping his submachine gun nervously. "What if there really is an ambush waiting for us?"

"I'll go scout it out," Rykah said. She slung her .303 bolt-action rifle, which she'd recovered from *Sea Serpent*'s weapons vault. "You just wait here."

Toris stepped forward to join her. "I'm coming with you."

Rykah leaned into the landing craft and pulled out a massive sniper rifle. She cradled the bulky weapon with the sling draped across her shoulders to help bear the weight. "I move better on my own," she said.

This was likely true. So Toris watched with his fellow Polarians as Rykah trudged down the beach to the headland that reached out to sea. At the end of the beach, she paused before the trail that ran up into the forest on the land point, looked back once, then disappeared into the pine forest.

THIRTY-THREE

Quella smeared cam paint across her face—black on the high, green in between. Unlike the other fourteen in her chalk, she didn't need a partner or a mirror to cover all the spots commonly missed, like around the eyes and in the ears. She spread the paint as naturally as Amyrian women applied makeup.

She stopped and stared at Jayda sitting across from her. Shaking her head, she reached over and smudged a thick blob from Jayda's cheek to below her eye. Jayda sat frozen as Quella moved on to her ears, rubbing the green paint into every cranny.

Jayda didn't know what to do other than sit still and hold her breath, fearful the slightest movement may anger Quella. Physical contact from the sergeant-major usually involved a lot of pain.

Quella sat back and gave Jayda's face a scrutinizing look, then offered a nod of satisfaction.

"How do I look?" Jayda ventured.

"Vicious," said Quella, with what could have been the hint of a smile pulling at the corner of her mouth.

Intimidating as Quella was, sitting across from her beat being anywhere near Darcella at the opposite end of the basket. The file scraping against the sides of her pointed teeth was enough to drive anyone mad.

Jayda turned her focus to checking her gear for the two hundredth time. Anything to keep her eyes from wandering beyond the basket rails, where the sun hovered frightfully close to the horizon. How many more days before it set for the six-month night? She'd lost track of time out here.

She ignored Talia's nudging at her side as she dug through her pouch for another piece of paper. The girl from Khartum had been writing Ivy poems to read since lift off, the contents of which drew disgusted looks from Shayla, who seemed displeased with her seat placement across from the lovers. The blond Amyrian's discomfort was the only thing Jayda had to smile about during the long ride over the Borien Mountain Range.

Waiting was the worst part. Emotions played tug-of-war between fear and excitement. Scenarios of all sorts ran through Jayda's head—of what could go wrong on the jump and, worse, what awaited them on the ground.

As the grey peaks below levelled to green coniferous forest, the pilots began communicating with their mounted lights. A green light flashed from the basket ahead, to which Quella's pilot responded by flapping the squeaking shudders of his own light. The pilot looked to Quella and said, "That's the Polis up ahead. We're twenty minutes out."

Nervous excitement shot through the basket like electricity as the balloons spread out toward their drop zones. The jumpers struggled to sit still.

Jayda expected the next twenty minutes to be the longest of her life, but, before she knew it, Quella was on her feet shouting, "Clip up!"

The sergeant-major hooked the static line from her parachute to the horizontal bar above. Fourteen others struggled to their feet and snapped their lines to the bar behind hers. "Equipment check!"

Jayda checked Quella's parachute before her. The possibility of Quella's equipment failure frightened Jayda more than the failure of her own, as she suspected Quella was the type who could survive such a fall and would hunt her down.

From behind, Talia squeezed Jayda's arm and said, "Good," in her ear. Jayda did the same for Quella.

A forest of golden leaves surrounded the Polis and was much larger than Jayda had been expecting. Somewhere toward the middle was a round field in which the eight-point citadel stood defiant in Ortarian territory. Surely the dregs had spotted their balloons by now and were mustering their defences.

"Anywhere here is good," said the pilot. The other balloons were not yet in position, but waiting offered Ortarian scouts a chance to pinpoint their drop zone.

Quella jumped without hesitation. Her static line pulled taut against her weight and drew out her chute. Jayda stepped up to the opening, her mind racing to remember every little detail of her training. She thought she'd been at the edge only a second, but Talia was screaming in her ear to jump. So she did.

The sickening freefall slowed as her chute deployed. She looked up toward the balloon and saw that glorious green canopy unfolding to obscure her view of the sky. She did her line checks like a pro while keeping her eyes on the ground, constantly scanning her landing site as it drew closer. Breaking a leg here was not an option.

She was so absorbed in watching the field below grow closer that she landed without having stolen even a glance at the nearby forest for enemy movement. As the canopy collapsed beside her in the grassy field, Jayda thought the whole thing to be anti-climactic.

This is only the beginning, she reminded herself.

Talia grunted as she slammed into the ground behind. Jayda had her chute pulled in and packed before Darcella—the last jumper—touched down.

Quella's chalk hustled to muster with Lieutenant Valender's troops, the nearest having landed two hundred yards away. Jayda and Quella arrived first and were met by much confusion despite the textbook jump. Quella shoved through the gaggle of soldiers in search of her platoon commander.

"Lieutenant Valender," she said. "Where is he?"

A corporal from his chalk pointed to the tree line. "Don't ask how," he said, shaking his head. "I was right behind him. Bad luck, I guess."

Quella bolted toward the forest with her rifle at the ready. The remainder of the platoon spread out and advanced in an extended line as rehearsed. Jayda caught up to Quella before reaching the forest, and together they discovered Lieutenant Valender a few trees in.

Their leader's feet swayed ten feet from the ground, his young face almost unrecognizable with its twisted expression frozen in a mix of fear and agony.

Dry leaves crunched as his platoon spread out into defensive positions. Surprisingly, the lieutenant's body attracted only moderate attention from his troops. Ahead, moss curtains hung from cedar trees, concealing who knew what dangers. As Second Platoon advanced to their left, Quella gave the signal for her platoon to move forward.

Jayda grabbed her arm and hissed, "You can't just leave him like this."

Quella's eyes flicked up to her former commander. "I doubt he'll complain."

Golden flakes fell from the tree crowns overhead, adding to the mat of dead leaves on the ground. As the paratroopers advanced, each crunching footfall sent a ripple of fear through Jayda's chest. Despite the crisp autumn air, her fingers were slick with sweat on her wooden rifle.

The company stalked through the forest unopposed until a clearing appeared ahead. The platoon found cover behind a line of trees at the edge of a poppy field. In the distance stood a twenty-foot stone wall with two forward points visible from this angle.

Jayda was awestruck. To most Polarians the Polis was only a

symbol, so to see it in person was surreal, as some even questioned its existence. Yet there it stood.

Jayda smiled. How many Polarians could boast seeing this wonder? But something was wrong. No sentries stood upon the citadel's ramparts. And instead of a patrolling Polarian militia, buzzing insects were all that greeted the paratroopers.

Jayda scooted up to join Ivy behind an ash tree. In the field ahead, Quella was snaking through high grass and red poppies that rocked gently in the cool breeze.

"Movement on the ramparts," someone said.

Everyone looked to Songbird two trees down from Jayda. The blond mute with comically large ears peered through the scope of her sniper rifle. Seconds later, she released a fluttering whistle.

"Ours," said Corla.

A green flare streaked high into the air from within the Polis's walls. Then another. And another.

Quella turned back and waved her troops forward. An extended line of legs swished through waist-high grass and poppy stems, each soldier holding their rifle at the ready, wary of any dregs lurking in the grass. But as they closed on the stone walls, it became evident this field hadn't seen foot traffic in some time. The grass leaned only due to wind, and the poppy growth was wild and unkempt.

The Polis's stone walls boasted only one entrance—a fifteen-foot-wide gap between two of its eight points. Rusted hinges implied a missing gate. Six silhouettes with rifles above oversaw Dogwood Company funnelling into the entrance corridor.

Major Milora, battalion second-in-command, waited just inside the gate, recording each unit as they arrived. Quella informed her of Lieutenant Valender's death. The Major needed reminding of who he was. Jayda was about to suggest a party return for his body when the state of the citadel drew her attention away.

Many paratroopers had been expecting their arrival to incite a victory parade from isolated militia inhabitants and their families, but Jayda saw only familiar faces. Had the dregs sacked the citadel?

Unlikely. Everything seemed pretty well intact.

Colonel Marcellus emerged from the housing in the far wall and marched toward Major Milora, who immediately informed him of Valender's death.

Marcellus pursed his lips. The day's first known casualty, clearly. He looked to Quella and said, "I'll send a squad to collect his remains. Ready your Rangers for a reconnaissance patrol."

"How long?" Quella said.

"Leave momentarily. Prepare for a week out." To Milora, he said, "Set up a casualty collection point in one of the supply magazines below. I want lookouts on every rampart point. Whoever has an axe, get them chopping. Everyone else will hustle logs. I want a picket line around these walls as soon as possible." He surveyed the ramparts above. "There's a lot about this place I don't like."

The jump companies wasted no time getting to work on their defences. That eerie silence of the abandoned citadel was replaced by the knocking of wood in the surrounding forest, the crunch of falling trees, and the grunting of soldiers shouldering logs across the poppy field to the perimeter walls. No one required motivation to keep a hustle in their step. Whatever happened to the Polis' previous occupants seemed to come quick and without a fight. A search of the fort had failed to turn up a single spent shell casing, and the mystery of the missing gate left even the Colonel scratching his head.

Jayda swung a machete into the wood, creating a notch deep enough to snap the branch from its trunk by hand. She moved along the felled tree to the next branch. Colonel Marcellus had offered her to serve as his orderly, but de-limbing kept her mind busy.

Having seen a map of the area, she understood the Colonel's

reason for dispatching Quella's patrol. Aside from the eight-point star at the center and contour lines denoting elevations, there was nothing. Information on the area was to be gained from the Polis's inhabitants.

"What do you think happened to them?" said Shig as he hacked away at a trunk with his axe.

"Mighta gone on vacation," replied Omar.

The two soldiers were in Quella's platoon, with whom Jayda sometimes shared meals.

"I mean the dregs," Shig said.

"Why would there be dregs here if there's no Polarians?" said Jayda. She swung her machete into a branch.

"Wouldn't the Ortarians want the pole for themselves? You know, like a trophy er somethin'."

A thought stopped Jayda midswing. She stared at the stone walls across the field. Maybe the Polis' defenders weren't killed by Ortarians. Perhaps they'd abandoned the citadel on purpose.

"Stand to!" rose a cry from the citadel. "Riders coming in!"

Shig and Omar ditched their axes for rifles. Jayda crouched low and checked to ensure her .303 was loaded, then joined her comrades on the lookout for the intruders.

Troops on the ramparts converged on the gate to the left. From the far left tree line emerged three riders on horseback, their robes draped over the rear of their galloping mounts.

Omar leaned against a tree to steady his aim. Jayda slapped his barrel down. "Wait, you idiot."

She ran hard across the poppy field, not caring if she broke their stems. As an Onero at home that would have earned her the whip, but she was a long way from Lake Orion. And whoever held the rights to these plants wasn't around.

By the time she reached the gate, Colonel Marcellus had emerged alone to meet the envoy. Major Milora watched from safety above the gate. Jayda dropped her rifle and fell in beside the Colonel, who welcomed her with a nod. Commanders often brought orderlies to meetings as a second set of ears and for memory's sake.

He stopped and allowed the riders to close the remaining distance.

The three Ortarian riders dismounted and continued their advance on foot. A large white mare identified the middle man as the leader. His shoulder-length brown hair was neatly cut and combed. As he drew closer, he flung his purple cloak over his shoulder to reveal a burgundy leather jerkin underneath. No weapons.

"Oya," he said, extending a hand. Marcellus's arms remained at his sides. The man reached in and grabbed the Colonel's hand anyway, forcing a most awkward handshake. "I'm Ardis, you know, like the valley. I'm a distinguished member of the Ortarian Grand Councilry. And you're Colonel…"

"Marcellus Arcturus."

So the man knew Polarian ranks. Perhaps from campaigning against them at the border.

Ardis released his hand and stepped back. "Cool trick, coming from the sky like that." He wagged a finger. "*Very* sneaky." His accent was clipped and harsh, with exaggerated *a*'s, but flowed well enough to suggest this was his first language. He looked admiringly at the walls, nodding and squinting with a high smile. "I was telling the boys she needed a facelift."

He suddenly seemed to notice Jayda for the first time. "Oya," he said, and reached out to pet the top of her head. Jayda recoiled. Ardis raised his hands apologetically. "Shy one. That's okay."

"What's your business here?" Marcellus asked.

"I could ask you the same, though I think I know the answer. Our scouts say your country has fallen on hard times. Bet you come looking for food and medicine. Am I right?"

Marcellus shifted uneasily.

Ardis smiled warmly. "Well, you've come to the right place. But I must say, your arrival is a bit extravagant, and somewhat concerning. All you had to do was ask."

Marcellus smiled skeptically. "And you'd have just give us what we wanted?"

Ardis shrugged innocently. "It's the neighbourly thing to do. I'm sure you'd do the same for us."

Jayda watched the Colonel squirm.

Ardis drew a folded letter from his pocket and handed it to Marcellus, who accepted it and read. When he finished, Marcellus looked to Ardis. "You'd give us all of this…for nothing?"

Ardis spread his arms wide. "The Mother was kind to us this year. She must like what we're doing on this side of the border to have blessed us with such a bountiful harvest. But this offering is not for nothing. Your presence here makes some of our people a bit uneasy, what with our history and all. So, willfully evict yourselves from our lands, and I'll have all the food on that list waiting for you at the border."

Marcellus looked back over his shoulder to the Polis. "Where are the residents?"

"On this side of the border we are all one people. They integrated with our society many years ago."

Marcellus frowned. "Our government received regular reports from the Polis stating all was well and secure. Nothing of this *integration* you speak of."

"Yes, well, the residents knew how much you lowlanders coveted this claim to the South Pole. They feared news of its abandonment may elicit a dramatic response from your army." Ardis studied the Colonel's face. "Still not convinced?"

He held a hand out to the side. One of his attendants passed him a scroll, which he in turn offered to Marcellus. The Colonel warily accepted the document and read it silently.

"You can keep that," Ardis said.

"How do I know the signature is authentic?"

"Because it's mine." The attendant standing to Ardis's right stepped forward. A snow-white beard, stained yellow around his mouth, covered half his weathered face. Grey eyes watched from under a wide-brimmed hat.

"And you would be?"

"Tarlin Canopus—Warden of the Polis."

"Why haven't you introduced yourself until now?" Marcellus said. His thinking seemed in line with Jayda's. This man was likely a hostage. "And where are the rest of your people?"

"Neighbouring tribes have adopted them," Tarlin said. "You didn't think we survived so long out here by killing our neighbours, did you? We have more in common with them than with you lowlanders. If The Artican cared so much about their precious Polis, then why did they ignore our requests for help all those years? We'd have died if not for Ortarian generosity."

Jayda suddenly felt awkward. Tarlin's contempt toward The Artican seemed genuine. As did his gratitude toward Ardis. The Aero Insertion Regiment seemed unwelcome from both sides. An unfortunate situation for any military force.

Ardis clapped his hands together once. "Well, that's enough chit-chat." He took a good look around at the soldiers standing visibly in the forest. "Vacate these premises immediately and march straight home, and no Ortarian will bother you. Take my confidante here. He's widely known and well respected. Tell your Chancellor the Polis is neutral ground now. Next Polarian seen here with a firearm will die. You have one hour to gather your belongings and leave."

Marcellus held up the letter. "How do I know you'll keep your word?"

"Colonel, we have many children inhabiting these nearby settlements. We don't want their blood shed by your soldiers any more than your soldiers want to spill it."

Ardis gave an exaggerated bow, then turned to mount his white mare. Tarlin shook his head at Marcellus, his face rife with disdain.

Jayda and Marcellus stood in silence as the two riders galloped off. Ardis's confidante remained behind as offered, likely to oversee the evacuation. "Wait out here," Marcellus told him. "I need to confer with my officers."

Jayda followed the Colonel through the gate. The battalion's officers met them in the courtyard. "Get ready to move," Marcellus said.

"Whatta ya mean, sir?" Jayda said. "The Darlings are still out there."

Marcellus rubbed a hand through his hair in distress. His surprised expression revealed he'd forgotten about the long-range patrol.

Major Milora stepped in close. "What happened out there?"

Marcellus explained everything, ending with his acceptance of the offer.

"We take our orders from the General," Milora said, "not the Polis commander—if that really was him."

"Our orders were to fortify the Polis for food extraction. If Ardis makes good on his promise, we'll have accomplished that end while avoiding a war. Captains, get your companies ready to march. We move out immediately."

"And the Darlings?" Jayda said. "If they come back here the dregs'll skin them."

Marcellus rubbed his chin, deep in thought. His eyes were grave when they met hers. "This is strictly voluntary… I need someone to stay behind, out of sight, to await their return."

"I'll do it," Jayda said without hesitation.

"Good. When Sergeant-Major Quella returns, take the quickest route to the border. Now, go find a good hiding spot for when we leave."

THIRTY-FOUR

The first Polarian from the *missing in action* list arrived shortly after Rykah had set off. He washed up fifty feet downshore from the band of soldiers and sailors, and his sailor comrades rushed to drag him out of the water and cover his face with a slicker. Seeing his body riddled with bullet holes, the sailors split from the soldiers and gathered at the forest edge, watching the soldiers distrustfully.

The soldiers, on the other hand, formed a semicircular perimeter with their backs to the water, monitoring the marsh and hills beyond for the real enemy.

Toris paced between the water's edge and the tree line, watching the trailhead that snaked up the headland where Rykah had disappeared nearly an hour ago.

"Walkin' straight into the bear trap yas are." Jorda sat cross-legged on the rocky shore nearby with her elbows tied behind her back. "Worse, even. Khalid's gettin' ya to build yer own prison."

Toris sat beside her and offered her a drink from a canteen he'd found on the beach.

"You're saying Khalid can't be trusted?" Toris said, realizing her words had piqued the interest of some nearby sailors. "I know many who'd say the same of you."

Jorda gulped the water down, then licked the stream from her chin. "This is self-preservation, boy. My fate is locked wit yers, and I don't like where this is goin'. No matter what you heard of me er my folk, it ain't nothin' to what people says of Khalid. He ain't the givin' type—not unless you have somethin' he wants in return."

"We're helping him solve a dispute."

"Believe me, that ain't what he really wants. If the folk 'round here was causing him trouble, he'd grind 'em all to mincemeat and feed 'em to his dogs." She looked over her shoulder and eyed the mountains suspiciously. "No, it's some trickery he's got goin' on."

Toris held the canteen before Jorda's face. When she leaned forward to drink, he pulled it away. "So what does Khalid want?"

"Same thing as you, kinda. Gene stuff, but not the kind ya find in plant seeds. No sir." Jorda shook her head, face twisted in disgust.

The sailors at the forest edge bristled at her words. Doubts were rising, and they threatened Toris's plan to get everyone to play along with Khalid's offer.

"How would a pyrate know the business of the Nordican Emperor?" he said.

Jorda nodded for the canteen. Toris held it to her lips, and she'd have gulped the whole thing down had he not pulled it away.

Jorda caught her breath, then said, "Ever hear stories of pyrates stealin' away youngins and island folk from back home? Well, that Khalid used t'offer a fair price fer fresh blood fer his research—the price of lettin' us live. When I rose to leader, though, and I learned what he was up to—the things he was doin' in those camps to good Polarian folk—tryin' to use our blood to undo all the wrongs this world did to their Lord's creation… Well, let's just say they wasn't gettin' anythin' else from us. So we stuck 'round the equator, where no Nordican's got any desire to venture, and that's where we stayed till you went and dragged me back up here."

Toris let the claims sink in. He weighed each word with the tongue it rolled from. A pyrate queen who'd lied to him already, promising him a cure that didn't exist. Someone desperate to make an ally by turning him against her enemies.

Jorda lifted her chin toward the scorched battleship in the bay. "That *Serpent* is scrap metal now. Too high maintenance for us anyway. The *Zephyr*, though, she's our ticket outta here. You and me could sail that on our own. Take a handful of yer folk if ya want—not them Coast Patrol scum, though—and we'll build our own fleet. Have a ship slip back home to pick up some loved ones if ya wants. You'll never know freedom like the kind ya find on the high sea."

Had Toris heard such a pitch before setting off on this expedition, he'd have seriously considered the offer. But he'd seen the pyrate life. It wasn't what he wanted for Jayda or himself.

He stood and was brushing the sand from his bottom when a crack echoed from afar. Five soldiers rushed to join Toris on the shore. Their eyes scanning the forested headland confirmed the gunshot had come from where Rykah had stalked off to.

Toris sprinted down the beach toward the trailhead at the end. Several sets of footsteps crunched the shore rocks behind him, fellow soldiers eager to come to Rykah's aid. At the end of the beach, he scrambled up the dirt trail and started across the forested headland toward the next beach. The path zigzagged through clusters of pines, climbing and dropping in elevation, and seemed to go on forever.

Toris ignored the stabbing branches and twisted roots assaulting his soles. He didn't even look behind to see if any soldiers had followed him onto the trail. The farther from Battler's Bay he ran, the louder the blood rushed in his ears, drowning out any footsteps that may be in pursuit. He should have been more careful, but all he could think of was Rykah facing an enemy on her own.

The first glimpse of the beach appeared two miles down the trail through the thinning forest. Toris slowed to take in the view. A crescent of white sand held his attention until he stumbled upon a bloodied Rykah.

He buried his mouth into the crook of his elbow.

Kneeling on the path before him, Rykah hunched over a deer on its side. Her arms were sheened with blood up to her elbows, and her chin glistened red from where she'd bitten into the deer's eviscerated heart.

The soldiers who'd accompanied Toris to Rykah's rescue watched in silence as she performed the hunter's ritual. She raised the heart above her head and acknowledged her Polarian 'saviours' for the first time.

"A welcoming gift from the Mother," Rykah said. She then placed the heart into a small hole in the ground, then swiped dirt over top to bury it. She placed both palms onto the carcass and smiled wide, her teeth stained red. "When we bid farewell to our dead, we shall feast."

"Nice work," Toris said, clutching his roiling belly. Seeing a large animal gutted like this reminded him of his own delicate innards.

Rykah stood. With the back of one hand, she wiped the blood from her chin while pointing a knife in her other hand to the nearby beach. "Come," she said. "We are home now."

The land Khalid gifted to the Polarian Agrinauts was Toris's worst nightmare. The white crescent beach stretched for one mile at high tide, two miles when the sea retreated and gave access to another beach beyond a distant headland of sheer off-white rock. To make matters worse, the sun happened to be shining bright in a clear blue sky, its rays glittering off the inviting Atlantic water.

But it wasn't so much the land itself that defeated Toris. It was the reactions of his kin. When Rykah told them she'd scouted the beach before shooting the deer and deemed it clear, the soldiers who'd joined Toris on the run from Battler's Bay stripped off and swam in the surf until the next group of soldiers arrived.

Toris sat atop a dune at the beach entrance, his hope sliding away like the sand beneath him.

From around the near headland, Korvyn piloted a raiding craft with Lex and Macey and Spinner to the beach.

Toris hurried down to meet them. In the bottom of the craft lay Ignatius. Macey, Spinner, Toris, and Korvyn lifted him on a stretcher and carried him up the beach to the forest edge. As Lex followed her brother's procession to the tree line, a soldier ran in front to stop her.

"This is all ours, Lady Alexandra?" asked Thane.

Lex didn't respond.

"It is," Macey said with a grunt from the foot of Ignatius's litter. "Heard it from the Nordican leader myself. We'll be doing that king of theirs a favour by occupying this land. If he wasn't sincere, he'd have wiped us out with his airship."

That was all the expedition teams needed to hear. Soldiers dropped their weapons, stripped off their uniforms, and ran to join their comrades in the sea.

Toris helped set Ignatius's body in a grove at the forest edge and left Lex to him. From the beach berm, he watched the cheering soldiers play in the surf.

Rykah emerged from the tree line behind. "It seems they approve."

Unfortunately, Toris had to agree. It would be a great task to get his country-folk back into their uniforms when the time came.

Playtime lasted for half an hour. Then the soldiers got to work stripping both ships of their provisions and shuttling everything to the beach in raiding crafts. There, they planned to divide everything by thirty-nine—the number of remaining Polarians in this new colony. The rest was a free-for-all. Soldiers stripped *Polaris'* sleeping racks and set the mattresses at the forest edge beside the beach. *Sea Serpent's* main and spare kites hung overhead for shade.

Toris sat on one of the many driftwood logs along the beach berm before the tree line, the winter in his heart growing darker and colder with each boatload of scavenged gear to arrive. At least it made a good show for Khalid. Perhaps he'd take these efforts at face value and abandon his plan to have his own men dismantle the Polarian vessels. So long as no one shredded all the kites, Toris could recover enough gear to continue north.

When a raiding craft full of food arrived, Toris helped carry a crate of canned soup to the pile growing in the forest under the shade of a black kite. Singing on the Battler's Bay trail grew louder as soldiers arrived carrying stretchers piled high with bags of rice and flour.

Spirits were high. And rightfully so. Few of these men and women had ever been called 'free' before. Plus, food was pouring in from everywhere—over land, by boat, and the deer carcass Rykah had strung up without any help. A few possible names for their new colony already sprouted up—*Norland, Serpent's Landing, Onero Flats, Alexandra's Bluff*.

Toris slammed the crate of soup cans onto the pile, his fingers stiff from the weight, then found a shaded spot under the trees at the edge of the beach.

Laughter rose as soldiers ran with empty stretchers back toward Battler's Bay for more pillaging.

Toris knew this cheerful banter would die off when the crews realized they were never allowed to return home. Ever. That they were the buffer between warring tribes of savages worse than Ortarians. All he had to do was wait and watch to see who emerged as leader. It was bound to happen. Someone was going to start giving orders, and the men and women who'd worn the uniform since they were twelve years old would dutifully obey. That was the person Toris would need to convince to carry on to Svalbard.

At mid-afternoon, heavy fog rolled in from the sea and was the strangest weather phenomenon Toris had ever seen. The white screen reduced his field of vision to twenty feet all around, enough to obscure his comrades down the beach, but their laughter and yelling assured him they were near.

Rykah had gotten her hands on one of *Southern Zephyr*'s spare kites. She cut the purple fabric and fashioned the strips into a long dress. Toris watched from the tree line as she twirled and delighted in the silky fabric flaring out from her waist. She walked barefoot in the sand, the first time he'd seen her without boots since swimming off the Polarian peninsula. Then she tested her balance on huge driftwood logs piled at the beach berm lining the forest. She disappeared into the fog thirty feet away.

An hour later she rematerialized in her approach, running skillfully across a long pole, arms out for balance. At the end she leaped across a gap to the next log.

Toris didn't blame her. If he'd been locked in that oven for over a week he'd be stretching his legs too, so he let her have her moment. Soon it would be time to plot their way out, and she was the one person he needed to help raid the vault.

Finally, after hours of exploring the beach—long enough for the fog to dissipate—she plopped down beside Toris in the sand. She looked like a different person than the Rykah who'd stumbled down the passageway with Ike to seize *Sea Serpent*'s engine room the night before. Sitting cross-legged, the silky fabric of her purple dress stretched tight between her knees. A raven feather protruded from her hair at an angle, its black sheen matching the color of her own wet hair.

"I'm glad to see you're enjoying this little holiday," he said.

Rykah brushed a strand of Toris's hair from his face. "Holidays have an ending, Toris. This is life for us now. We're free."

He recoiled from her touch. "Take a good look around and then tell me you think that's true, that we're actually free. We're wedged between hostile tribes in a land that none of us know how to make a living from. We don't know the seasons or the customs…"

Rykah stood, her fists clenched at her sides. "You're the one who needs to take a look around." She pointed to soldiers playing football on the beach in their undergarments, then to rocks leading out into the sea, where sailors cast fishing lines scavenged from the *Sea Serpent*. In the shade of the nearby trees, a few soldiers lounged on an island of mattresses with not a care in the world. No one giving orders. No one training to run the mill. The only competition on that stretch of beach involved two teams trying to keep a ball out of their invisible nets. No one had issued a command since Korvyn declared it Lex's will for the food to be split evenly, and that all belongings should be accessible to the community. Toris doubted Lex had said this, as she cared little for anything other than her brother's lifeless body, which she knelt beside in silent vigil with Korvyn standing watch over her. It was reassuring to see her bodyguard use his proximity to the only status Polarian for good.

Toris rested his elbows on his knees. "You once asked me if I'd just abandon my country-folk," he said to Rykah. "Now you're doing just that."

Rykah stared wistfully at the orange sea beneath a golden sunset. "This is different. Right now, I don't have a choice. None of us do. We're stranded on the other side of the world, yet we're living the life we've been dreaming of our whole lives." Her face darkened as she pointed to the *V* tattoo on her neck. "It doesn't get better for people like us. Clavilla was going to bring us home to hang as deserters. Any chance I had at avoiding that fate died with Ignatius." She squeezed Toris's hand, her rough fingers soft on his calloused skin. "You deserve better than the life they gave you," she said softly. "We all do. Up here, we have a chance to do something great. We have a chance to actually live."

"My sister—"

"Is lucky to have had a brother like you, and I'm sure she'll mourn you deeply. We can't save the world, Toris. All we can do is try to find our peace in it. That will never happen on Anterra."

Toris avoided Rykah's pleading eyes. Yet everywhere his gaze wandered, he saw her truth clear as crystal. Brothers and sisters kicking a ball on the beach. Sailors and soldiers helping each other build shelters. None were wedded. None had children awaiting their return. For them this truly was paradise.

Yet Toris could not enjoy it. He'd never breathe easy knowing his sister was fighting a war he knew he could have prevented. If the others on this beach could, then shame on them.

Toris stood and crossed his arms, frowning at the fun being had. It was as if they were on an island surrounded by nothing, free of time and responsibility. But this was an illusion. Time did exist. And the sand in Polaria's hourglass was running out.

"You want to be stuck on this land for the rest of your life?" he said to Rykah.

"Would it be so bad?"

Rykah stood before him, cupped her hands over the back of his neck, and pulled his forehead to hers. "If we get bored here then we'll roam the midlands. Together we'll see all the sights, wander to places that even Khalid hasn't heard of. Rediscover lands and wonders long forgotten."

A scene took shape in Toris's mind: he and Rykah cruising the Nile on a boat of his own design, their eyes the first to take in the ancient pyramids in seven hundred years.

Rykah's hand slipped up into Toris's hair. "We'll settle somewhere in Asia. We'll dine on game we never even heard of before, with no one to bother us. We'll rule whatever world we walk across." Her smile grew wide, her turquoise eyes shining bright. "We'll forget about the rest of the world, and that world will forget about us."

Toris opened his mouth to tell her she was mad, but he couldn't release those words. Because she was right. As crazy as her proposal sounded, at this point transporting the seeds from Svalbard to Polaria seemed more the fool's endeavour.

He sighed deeply and summoned a smile for Rykah. "You're right," he said, then stepped back from her embrace. "People shouldn't be forced to fight battles they don't believe in."

He walked down the beach toward the Battler's Bay trail. If he allowed himself to walk in Rykah's heaven while Jayda endured hell in Ortaria, he'd never be able to face her in another life.

"Where are you going?" Rykah said.

Toris stopped and contemplated his response. Looking back slightly, but only enough to see her in his peripheral, he said, "Stay here, Rykah. You've done enough for Polaria. This is where you belong now."

THIRTY-FIVE

Toris spent his first sunset in paradise following the two-mile path to Battler's Bay. Streams of golden light cut diagonally through shadowy forest until he reached the north end of the headland, just as the sun dipped below the horizon.

He hid at the forest edge and watched the two Polarian ships in the bay while waiting for twilight to darken. On *Sea Serpent*, red lights flashed from the sailors who'd remained aboard to 'care for the wounded', but it was not the battle cruiser Toris was interested in.

Two hours after sunset, he slipped into the black water and swam out to *Southern Zephyr*. He found a mooring line hanging from her starboard side and used it to climb aboard. On the main deck, he spent only enough time to locate the nearest ladder.

In the cabin below deck, the ship was everything he'd expected of the Arokyan councillor. The entire quarterdeck at the back consisted of a king bed with red sheets of silk and a matching canopy overhead, all of which had survived the pillaging parties. Even out here it wasn't worth risking the scorn of a councillor. The crew cabins, however, had been ransacked. Yet even stripped of their amenities, the berths exhibited more luxury than any space aboard the *Sea Serpent* or *Polaris*.

Toris was painfully aware of his body dripping water onto the dark wood floor. He resisted the urge to dry himself and crawl into Rosaria's bed, which Lex had no doubt been using during her journey. If she declined to accompany him north to Svalbard, he'd deliver it to her on the beach as a parting gift.

Making his way toward the front of the ship, a blue light glowed from a floor hatch at midship. A short ladder led to the bottom of the hull, where the engines sat silent. The light shifted and shook as if someone were holding it.

Toris leaned over the hole. "Who's down there?"

A wrench clanged off metal and thudded onto the floor. Ike appeared at the bottom of the ladder and shined his light up through the hatch. Toris shielded his eyes.

"Are you spying for the Lady Lex?" Ike said.

"I've come to assess the ship."

"Why?" Ike asked warily.

"I'm going to Svalbard. I assume you're here for the same reason."

Ike shined the light at Toris's face for an uncomfortable few seconds. Then he climbed the ladder to join him in the passageway. He sat at the edge of the hatch, his feet dangling below.

"You're serious?" Ike said.

Toris nodded.

"Good." Ike winced. "Because I won't have my father's death be for naught. He was doing this to clear our family name. I'll see that through even if it kills me."

Toris crouched to peer through the hatch. "How's it looking?"

"Starboard hull got a bit scorched from *Serpent*'s fire. Not sure if it's just superficial or if she runs deep. I'll leave that assessment up to you now that you're here." Ike aimed his light beam below. "The desalinator is a different story. Her heat exchanger coils took a blow from a ballista bolt that punctured the hull. Apparently they didn't get through the first pyrate attack unscathed like we thought." He cocked his head for a better look below. "We'll never make it home without it, but I think I scavenged enough spare parts to get it going again."

"How long?"

Ike hunched his shoulders. "Two hours before we can fire it up for a test."

Not bad. The tension in Toris's chest loosened. "Okay. I'll have a look at the hull, then come give you a hand."

A bump against the outer hull jerked the ship to port. Boots clunked over the deck above, then pounded down the ladder below deck. At the end of the passageway near the bow, two beams of white light cut through the dark and grew brighter as they bounced toward the engine hatch.

Toris squinted in the light and saw two sailors armed with submachine guns approaching.

"Well, look who it is," said one of the sailors. "The Prince Onero. Nice piece of land you got yourselves out there. Beats any beach I ever saw along Polaria's shores."

The sailor bumped Toris's shoulder.

"Everyone is welcome to it," Toris said, growing edgy at the sailor's aggression.

"What are you doing here?" the sailor said.

"I should ask you the same," said Ike from the hatch. "You're supposed to be tending the wounded on the *Serpent*. Anything else violates our treaty with the Nordicans."

The sailors exchanged amused smiles.

"We're here to salvage some critical equipment," said the second sailor. "Our medical equipment require a lot of power, so we need our engines running tip-top. Now, get your arses out of our way."

Ike huffed and climbed up through the hatch and stormed down the passageway. Toris followed him above deck.

Up top, a second raiding craft moored along the *Zephyr*'s port side next to the first. Three sailors disembarked and rushed below.

Toris sat on the wooden stern rail over the quarterdeck while

Ike wandered toward the bow cursing under his breath. He returned a minute later with a bottle in hand.

"Found Rosaria's wine stash when I was scavenging parts," Ike said. He popped the top and smelled the opening. "After me and the old skipper got busted for smuggling, I swore that when I got out I'd never touch the stuff again."

Sailors returned from below carrying engine parts to the landing craft. They shuttled gear up under the cover of darkness, which confirmed Toris's suspicion. The sailors were stripping the *Southern Zephyr*'s engine to repair the *Sea Serpent*'s.

Ike raised the wine bottle. "To same mistakes."

Toris watched as Ike took a long pull from the bottle. When Ike offered it to him, he eagerly accepted. He'd never even eaten a grape before, let alone experienced the taste of red wine. The drink was sweet and bitter at the same time. He and Ike passed the bottle back and forth, watching sailors grunt and cuss as they loaded heavy parts into their raiding crafts.

Toris took a small drink of wine, then handed it to Ike. "We're screwed, aren't we?"

Ike snatched the bottle and squeezed the neck as he gulped down a few mouthfuls. He wiped the runoff from his chin with his sleeve. That was all the answer Toris needed.

The sailors spent nearly two hours gathering what they needed. As they secured their last load into both landing crafts, Toris and Ike were savouring the last few sips of their third bottle of wine. Toris's head was spinning, and Ike's face glowed red like a bad sunburn.

"They're going to limp home in *Sea Serpent*," Ike said, gritting his teeth. "I know it."

"Clavilla accomplished his mission," Toris said, noticing the slur in his own voice. "So long as no seeds cross south of the equator, Sydra will get her war. My sister…" A lump swelled in his throat. Tears blurred his vision, and it took everything for him to keep from breaking down.

"My father…" Ike sniffled. "I should've been there when he passed. Instead, I hid in the engine room like a coward."

"You sacrificed your last moments with him for the mission," Toris said. "Nothing cowardly about that." He'd have offered more, but he was too tired.

Snoring rose from Ike, who'd slumped back against the stern's flagpole and passed out.

Toris hunched forward and stared at the patches of silver starlight rolling over gentle waves. He was dozing off, nearly falling forward and overboard, so he slid around onto the main deck. The trek back to the beach in the dark seemed too daunting, so he retired below.

He flopped onto Rosaria's bed, where silk sheets and a cushy mattress carried him into the deepest of slumbers.

THIRTY-SIX

Jayda dropped her shovel onto the mound of fresh brown dirt. The hole beside it was deep enough, she decided. Given the heat of the day, Lieutenant Valender would understand. Not like his family could come visit anyway.

She dropped to her knees and, in the shadow of the Polis' walls, set about the ugly task she'd been delaying since realizing the Colonel had forgotten the body in the storage magazine below. Understandable, considering he'd forgotten a patrol of nine roaming the countryside in his haste to evacuate the citadel. Scavenging dead men for belongings seemed a foul act, but this dead man didn't need the pipe and pouch of leaf in his breast pocket. Nor the knife strapped to his boot.

Water spattered onto his ashen face. Jayda wiped the sweat from her brow, but the dripping persisted. Tears, she realized. But why? Perhaps it was because Valender was nice to her when he shouldn't have been.

She should have stopped her search then, because the next item turned the trickle of tears into a river. In his hidden pocket was a photo of him holding an infant. This officer with the boy face had a boy of his own awaiting a return that would never come.

She returned the photo and stood. That was enough.

Grabbing his webbing straps, she dragged his body into the hole. Determining the center of the Polis for his grave wasn't easy. She'd paced out the distance between each wall to determine the center, a task that required many adjustments and repacing, along with a fair bit of frustrated swearing.

The dirt went in easier than it came out, forming a displeasing mound. No matter how many times Jayda smacked the dirt with the shovel, the lump remained. She flung the shovel aside and paced around in frustration. Looking to the Polis walls, she realized the isolation was making her mad. She needed to get out of here.

She whispered a few parting words from the foot of the pile, then gathered her gear. Before leaving she turned back and stared at the fresh dirt. "Some day I'll tell your son all sorts of wonderful lies about your bravery," she said.

With that, Jayda marched out the Polis gate feeling she'd done Valender right. Even Polaria's most famous heroes couldn't claim a grave in the center of the world. That had to be worth something.

She found a shaded glade in the tree line with a good view of the citadel's open gate. All she had to do was wait quietly for the Darlings' return.

Easier said than done.

She loaded Valender's pipe with leaf and struck a match. Skunky smoke filled the air as she took a few hauls. She coughed and sputtered for half a minute, which left her head spinning, so she dropped onto her back and stared at the golden leaves fluttering under a pink dusk sky. For the first time since arriving here she heard the cheerful banter of birds.

So peaceful.

She was nodding off when voices roused her. She vaulted upright and looked around to get her bearings. Instinct warned these voices were not those of the Darlings. Army Rangers made quieter entrances than this.

She fumbled for her rifle and peered around the nearest tree trunk. Nothing. Maybe she'd imagined it.

A baby's cries rose from a distance. Or was it a deer whining?

Jayda didn't have to wait long for the source of the noise to reveal itself. From around the point of the Polis' wall appeared a few frail-looking men garbed in shabby shendyts. They watched the ramparts warily as they traced the walls toward the gate. Women and children followed. Mothers kept their young ones close, the men their scythes and axes at the ready. At the gate the men spread out and guarded the entrance while a few went in.

Barking rose from the field.

A young girl broke away from her mother. "Here, Shelby!"

"Rhea, get back here!"

Shelby the dog ran past the girl called Rhea and charged across the field—straight toward Jayda.

Jayda scrambled to her feet and aimed the rifle at the charging German Shepherd. She squeezed the trigger but it moved only half a hair before locking solid. She fumbled with the safety switch, but by the time it released the dog was on her.

The beast plowed Jayda onto her back. Its snout went straight for her neck, a wet tongue sliding up over her jaw and across her cheek. Panic turned to elation as the dog licked her face and nose. Jayda couldn't help but laugh in relief.

"Mama! Soldier!"

Jayda shoved the dog aside and aimed her rifle at the human intruder. The little blond girl raised her hands and stumbled back. Jayda lowered the weapon and stood.

The child rushed forward and wrapped her arms around Jayda's waist, squeezing with all her might. "I knew it," came muffled whispers against Jayda's belly. When Jayda pushed her away, Rhea stepped back and looked around. "Where are all your friends?"

Jayda stood silent, dumbfounded at this child's brazenness.

"Well?" said Rhea.

Jayda refused to reveal she was alone. And she had questions of her own, like, "Who are you?"

"Rhea," the girl replied. Then she pointed to the Polis and, with a big smile, said, "That's my home."

The women of the Polis each greeted Jayda with a hug and kiss on both cheeks; the men shook her hand, but their eyes lacked any warmth. Instead, their stares drifted to the walls nervously. A woman carried a crate of bottles filled with vodka from below and passed them around.

"We were expecting more of you," said a man tugging nervously at the thick black collar around his neck. He'd introduced himself as Sam. Jayda noticed everyone else, including young Rhea, sported a similar collar. "No offence, but when word of a liberation spread, we hardly thought that amounted to one little girl."

"There were more of us," Jayda said, "but your leaders made us an offer. Now my battalion is marching to the border."

Sam's eye twitched. "What are you talking about?"

Jayda pointed to the gate. "Tarlin. He came with Ardis and offered us food to leave. Said you're all Ortarians now."

The man rubbed a hand over his mouth and turned away. That's when Jayda noticed strips of raised skin over his back. Moans of despair rose as the Polisians broke up their cluster around Jayda. Family members consoled each other.

"They may not have noticed we left yet," said a woman. "If we head back now—"

"You're dreaming."

"Well, we have to think of something!"

Jayda was confused. "You do know Tarlin, right?"

"Of course we know that old drunk," said Sam. He pointed to his deltoid, where what was probably supposed to be a branded eight-point star resembled more of a starfish. "We exiled him last winter for his numerous indecencies. Ardis recruited him to convince the local Ortarians that we were plotting an attack on them. He managed to raise a big enough force to storm the walls. All of us survivors were sold off as slaves."

Jayda ran her hands through hair, pulling the skin on her forehead taut. So Ardis had lied.

"Most Ortarians ain't so different from us," Sam said. "But Ardis…he's the Ortarian of your nightmares. Men like him are the reason for the border. When Tarlin's claim rallied a bunch of extremists to his cause, the Grand Councilry of Ortaria put a bounty on his head. But his *Rogues* number in the thousands now. When they marched on the Polis, Ortaria's Grand Councilry sat back and let it happen. But this all seems like news to you, so what brings you here?"

"Food," Jayda said, feeling the walls close in around her. "Ardis promised to have some waiting at the border. That's why my battalion left."

"Why are *you* still here?" Sam pressed.

"I'm waiting for my unit. When they return we're heading straight home."

"Take us with you," a young woman said.

Jayda expected protest from the men. Instead, she got eager stares from them. This lot really had their hopes up when they returned. And they'd risk their lives by coming from the sound of it. Could the Darlings do it? How many were here? Fifty or so. Their retreat relied on discretion. A row of crying babies didn't offer much of that.

"Do you have eight spare dresses?" Jayda said.

From their bags the women pulled robes and shawls, a few tattered gowns. Jayda picked out eight that could conceal a rifle with each of the Darlings in mind. Quella wouldn't like what they offered in her size, but she'd have to tolerate it to make their escape.

"Be ready to move at a moment's notice," Jayda said. "And stay off the walls and out of sight."

A voice echoed across the citadel: "Stand to!"

Jayda stomped into the center of the courtyard, scanning the ramparts for the culprit. She swore she'd told them to stay off the walls.

"Stand to!" came the voice again.

This time, Jayda's heart shuddered. The order had come from outside.

She climbed the walls and stayed low on her belly when crawling to the outer edge.

A soldier raced across the poppy field, turning to check the forest behind every few steps. Jayda squinted and saw strands of orange hair hanging from Corla's boonie hat. Redder than her hair was her face as her legs pumped in a full sprint.

Jayda jumped down and met her at the gate. "What's going on?"

Corla continued into the center of the courtyard and surveyed the walls. "Where is everyone?"

"Marching back to the border."

Corla stared at Jayda as if looking at her own ghost. "No, no, no..."

Jayda grabbed Corla's shoulder straps and shook her. "Where's the rest of the patrol?"

"Quella sent me ahead with word of..." Corla placed her hands on her knees to catch her breath.

"Word of what?"

Corla's wild eyes met Jayda's. "Enemy. Coming here."

"How many?"

Corla hung her head in despair. "Hundreds. Maybe thousands. So spread out...too hard to count."

Jayda offered her canteen. Corla snatched it and gulped it dry.

Arla and Eris stumbled through the gate. Their shock at the empty citadel resembled Corla's.

"What happened?" Jayda said, nodding to the blood on their uniforms.

Darcella staggered in next. "Lookouts," she said, swinging her arm wide to indicate the surrounding area. "They been watching this place. Where is everyone?"

Talia and Ivy arrived at the same time, with Quella and Shayla not far behind. Quella scanned the empty courtyard, then her eyes locked on Jayda. She grabbed Jayda's collar with both hands and leaned in close, teeth clenched. "Where are they?"

"Gone home," Jayda said, and the dreaded words were barely a whisper leaving her lips. "We gotta leave, now."

"Why?"

Jayda sputtered everything she recalled of Ardis's parley.

Quella shoved Jayda away and looked to her troops. "Who else saw scouts in the woods?" Every girl raised a hand. "Any get away?"

Ivy nodded. So did Arla and Eris.

Songbird stumbled in through the gate while pointing erratically around her, then to the far walls in shock.

Shayla pointed to the cluster of Polisians emerging from the magazines below. "Who in the fuck are they?"

"Our Polisian militia," Jayda said.

Sam climbed atop the wall opposite the gate. He took a quick look outside, then looked back to those gathered in the courtyard. "They're here."

Shayla leaned close to Quella. "They haven't completely surrounded us yet. We can slip out if we make a run for it now."

"We can't leave them behind," Jayda said, nodding toward the Polisians gathering nearby.

"Did the Colonel order us to take them with us?" Quella said.

"Well, no," Jayda said with a frown, "but he thought they were safe. You know he wouldn't leave them behind like this."

Quella sized up the Polisians, then their walls.

Jayda grabbed Quella's clammy hand. "If you leave them here they'll die."

Shayla shoved Jayda back. "So will we if we take them," said the blond Amyrian. "How far you think we'll make it with this many? They'll slow us down and make us easier to track."

Jayda shoved Shayla back, and Shayla wrestled her to the dusty ground as the remaining Darlings erupted into debate. Bickering turned to shoving. Fists clenched and arms cocked back. Quella remained quiet through the turmoil. As Jayda struggled in Shayla's guillotine choke, she followed Quella's gaze to young Rhea sitting with a machete in her lap. The little girl was warily examining the blade's edge.

"I want a lookout on every point," the sergeant-major finally said. This put an end to the squabbling, with Shayla immediately releasing Jayda. Quella's word was not to be contested. Ever. "Report all movements," Quella added, "however insignificant. A bird doesn't take a shit without me knowing. And don't shoot unless I say. Maybe there's a chance we can still talk our way out of this."

Quella's hope for diplomacy was as shocking as her empathy. Was the ruthless sergeant-major afraid?

Sam stepped forward. "We appreciate you staying and all, but I don't want you getting any illusions. Ardis *seems* the diplomatic type, but it's just a tactic to feel you out. They don't call him the Borien Butcher for his conversational skills."

Knocking rose from the forest. Jayda recognized the noise from felling trees with Omar and Shig as they'd prepared defence stakes. Trunks cracked and leaves swished. Sawing rose into the still air, interrupted by more knocks and thuds.

The Darlings and the Polisian fighting men hurried to the ramparts, where across the field they saw patches of golden canopy shake from the feverish hacking below.

"They don't waste any time," said Sam.

"What are they doing?" Jayda asked.

"Building ladders," Sam replied. "That's how they overran us last time. They waited till sunset, then rushed us in force."

Jayda noticed only a sliver of sun above the tree line. This year's polar sunset was not far off.

Quella's grinding teeth rose above the woodcutting. She leaned over the wall's edge to examine the freshly-planted stakes jutting out at angles below. "Pile them in front of the gate," she ordered. "No one gets in or out unless I say."

THIRTY-SEVEN

The funny thing about sleep is: the more you get, the more tired you become. Toris's life circumstances had never allowed him to experience this phenomenon until he encountered Rosaria's bed. His eyelids had remained heavy long after waking, so he slept through the rest of the night and most of the next day. Only when a sliver of evening sunlight slipped through the curtains covering the rear window did Toris wake fully. He pinched the gap closed and would have returned to sleep if not for the one eye watching him from across the room.

He sat up with a heavy head and rubbed the sleep from his eyes.

"They pulled anchor," Lex said, slouching deep in a chair beside the doorway. She took a sip from a clear glass. "The *Serpent* is gone."

Toris threw aside the crimson curtains and saw an empty bay from this angle. He jumped from the bed and sprinted down the passageway, then climbed the ladder above deck to confirm Lex's claim. She was right. The *Southern Zephyr* sat alone in Battler's Bay.

Ike was nowhere in sight. Only Korvyn, who leaned against the starboard rail watching the red evening sun hover just above the ocean horizon.

Toris returned below and shuffled back to the quarterdeck. He fell face-first onto Rosaria's bed with a pounding head and a quivering heart.

"Worked out pretty well for them," Lex said from her plush red chair. "Clavilla won't have an Arcturus to dispute his account of what happened out here. Father won't even know where I ended up. Might think I'm living as a common girl somewhere. Not that he'd be wrong in that."

She tipped a deerskin flask over her glass to fill it with water. Toris grabbed the skin and took a mouthful, but immediately spit out the burning liquid.

"Where'd you get that?" he said.

"An offering from the locals. They think us gods." She raised her glass in salute. "To the dead gods."

She shot the whole drink and winced hard, then leaned back and stared at the ceiling.

Toris sat at the edge of the bed, where he buried his face into his hands.

"There's a funeral tonight," Lex said. "Our dead deserve their send-off. It's past time."

"The pyres?" Toris said.

"We're sitting in it."

Toris dropped onto his back. Without a functioning refrigeration unit the seeds would spoil on the return trip, but Rosaria's ship could still sail back to Anterra if Toris recovered at least one kite from the beach. "How will we get home?" he said.

Lex's laughter turned to a hiccup. She took another drink, then wiped her mouth with her sleeve. "They took a vote at noon," she said. "Ninety percent in favour of staying." Lex swivelled in her chair to stare out a porthole in the starboard wall. "If you try to stop them, they'll shoot you and add your body to the fire."

Toris covered his eyes with his forearm. So that was it. He could try to fight it, to persuade them to take another vote, but it was folly, and he was too tired to fight nature. It seemed this outcome had been written in the stars all along. Between Clavilla and Khalid, the vault was never meant to save them.

He wiped tears from his eyes. Returning without the seeds was not an option. And though Rosaria would protect him on Arokya, he couldn't live there while Jayda served at the border. Best for her to think he'd died out here trying to save her than living in peace at home.

"You're fine with staying here the rest of your life?" he asked.

Lex sagged deeper into her chair. "I voted 'no', which was more say than I ever got with my father."

———

Two hours after sunset, with only a faint glow of mint green light over the ocean horizon fending off the night, twenty Polarians gathered around a bonfire on the shore of Battler's Bay.

Toris stood at the back rolling an arrow shaft between his fingers. The night chill from the mountains behind tickled his nape while the fire before him warmed his face. Though he disagreed with burning their only ship, the dead spread across her main deck deserved to hear his goodbye.

In front, Rykah stepped knee-deep into the water. In her right hand she carried a bow. A flame danced from the head of an arrow in her left. She nocked the arrow to the bow that had been gifted to the colony by the local tribe.

Rykah raised the bow and drew back the arrow.

"Kadrina Onero," she said, then released the string to send an orange ball of light arching into the indigo sky.

"*Hail Kadrina!*" shouted the Polarians as the flaming arrow landed onto *Southern Zephyr*'s main deck.

Rykah held her left hand to the side. Spinner offered her another fire arrow and said, "Pyke Onero."

Rykah loosed the second arrow onto the funeral ship as everyone shouted, "*Hail Pyke!*"

She held her hand out for another.

"Hail Stagg!"

When the tenth fireball streaked across the bay's black water, Toris stuck the tip of his arrow into the bonfire and watched the alcohol-soaked rag burst into flames. He walked into the water and handed it to Rykah, whose turquoise eyes remained fixed on the burning ship. Atilus's flame danced before her face, glazing the thick strip of black paint across her eyes from temple to temple in orange light.

Toris retreated to the group as Atilus's arrow arched from the shore and landed on the glowing ship deck.

"Hail Atilus!"

Flames now climbed the mast and had spread from bow to stern.

As Rykah held her hand out for another arrow, Toris noticed that two Polarians were missing. He'd watched Lex and Korvyn walk back up the trail and assumed it was to prepare Ignatius's body. It'd be highly improper for his own sister to miss his farewell, which suggested Ignatius's remains weren't among those burning on *Southern Zephyr*'s main deck. In highborn fashion, she likely planned to give him his own service.

The fire had already engulfed the ship when the last funeral arrow flew. Sixteen sparks for sixteen lives lost. Toris closed his eyes and felt the heat from the blaze on his face.

Rykah turned to face the Polarian soldiers on shore. "Death is naught."

"Death is naught!"

When the main deck bearing the sixteen dead Polarians collapsed into the hull, whispers of the feast rippled through the group. The colonists were hungry for Rykah's deer meat and thirsty for the ale left as offerings by the neighbouring tribes. They peeled away in groups of two to five, patting Rykah on the back for her expert archery.

Only Toris remained to watch the ship burn. He waited there on the shore, listening to the roar of the blaze devour the crackling wood, until the *Southern Zephyr* sank in the bay. In that moment, the Polarian Agrinauts had officially marooned themselves on the other end of the world.

The party was well underway when Toris arrived at the Polarian colony. He'd smelled cooking meat, heard a fiddle sawing, and noticed the orange glow of a fire from over a mile away. If any Nordican settlements hadn't yet heard of their new gods, they would after tonight.

Toris plodded across the sand toward the bonfire at the center of the beach, where a mix of nearly twenty boys and girls danced to a cheerful song from two fiddles. Spinner had managed to salvage his from the *Serpent*. Macey had claimed Rosaria's violin from the *Zephyr*, which she now played in tune with Spinner in the firelight.

Following the tree line, Toris noticed driftwood arranged in triangles or stacked in patterns that marked each soldier's personal piece of the beachhead. Many had set up hammocks and stretched tarps overhead. Wet clothes hung from lines, uniforms to never be worn in service again.

A soldier staggered from the fire toward the forest, chugging from a deerskin flask. Seeing Toris, he threw up both arms. "Smile, brother. We're gods now!"

Toris watched Thane stumble into the forest and fall face-first onto a mattress. Toris shook his head and carried on. Before reaching the bonfire at center beach, he encountered a smaller fire concealed inside the tree line. Across that campfire, Rykah sat on the edge of a hammock fashioned from one of the *Zephyr*'s purple kites. Each corner of the doubled fabric stretched out to four trees, with an excess flap folded over top to form a canopy. She held a chunk of brown meat in one hand while slicing off a sliver with a knife.

Toris stopped before her fire.

"Your drunk brother is right," Rykah said. "You should smile and claim your place among the gods."

"There are no gods here," Toris said.

Rykah folded a cloth around the knife and meat, then set it aside. "Look above and tell me what you see?"

He didn't need to look up to catch her meaning. "You think this was written in the stars."

Rykah leaned back on the hammock and stared out over the ocean at the night sky, resting the back of her head on her hands. "Maybe we were never meant to find the seeds. Anterra's days may be done. What if the purpose behind you finding the vault reference was to draw us here, to spread our civilized ways to these Nordican folk? To build civilization anew up here, for when it falls down there."

Toris looked up at the specs of light dazzling the moonless night sky. "All I see is a million stars that don't give a damn about what happens to us."

"That's what I saw whenever I looked at Amyria." Rykah leaned up on her elbows. "Did you find yourself a place to sleep?"

He leaned against a tree and shook his head. "I wasn't planning on staying."

Rykah ran a hand across the purple silk upon which she rested. "My hammock can sleep two. Will you join me?"

Toris's face burned. He turned to face the beach, felt the cool sea breeze on his face. His whole life he'd swore to never risk cursing an innocent child with the blood of his mother and his last name of Onero. But now, here, things were different. They no longer lived in the world he grew up in. And yet, to submit to that urge would be to give up all hope of ever seeing home again. He wasn't ready to physically accept this new reality yet.

He cleared his throat. "I have to check on Lex."

As he walked away, Rykah said, "Is that a 'no'?"

Toris kept walking.

He found Lex in the forest beyond the roaring bonfire. She was sitting on her knees facing the dark forest, with Korvyn standing guard over her.

The veteran bodyguard placed a hand against Toris's chest to block his way. "The lady doesn't want to be disturbed."

"Tell her it's me—Toris."

Korvyn shoved him back. "She's grieving."

"Lex," Toris said.

She didn't flinch to her name or his voice. "Lex, Iggy's gone. He deserves his rites."

Korvyn shoved Toris back with both hands and got in his face. "Major Arcturus *is* gone. She sent his body back with Clavilla."

Toris instinctively looked to the sea. Lex had sent her brother home to be buried while she remained here for her father to think dead? Toris peered around Korvyn to Lex, who still hadn't shown any signs of acknowledgement. So he let her be.

Rykah was still sitting on the edge of her hammock when Toris returned. When she noticed him approach, she sat up somewhat eagerly and watched him expectantly.

Toris mustered his courage and met her stare. "It wasn't a 'no'," he said.

She slid over to make room for him on the kite hammock. He sat beside her and leaned forward, resting his elbows on his knees. Rykah's fingers traced up his spine, and every hair on his body seemed to wake with a life of its own. Both her hands slid over his shoulders and pulled him down to lay beside her. She wrapped her arms around his neck and pressed her nose to his. He felt her warm breath on his lips, felt his skin prickle like static. She reached up and pulled the silky canopy down around them. Toris ran a hand down the exposed skin on her side, stopping above her hip. Somehow her body felt softer and more inviting than the silky cocoon enveloping them.

Rykah touched her lips to his, at first gently. When he pushed his mouth out to meet hers, she pressed her whole face into his, breathing loudly. In that moment, with fiddles playing and fire blazing on a nameless beach in Norway, Toris Onero died. No one from Polaria would ever hear from him again. He'd have to learn to forget about Jayda, but perhaps that really was written in the stars all along.

And in time, if he became a good father and used his status as a god to spread civility to the Nordican folk, he might forgive the failures of his youth.

Hopefully he'd make a better god than he did a man.

THIRTY-EIGHT

"Rider!" yelled Shayla from the ramparts. "White flag!"

Quella raced across the courtyard to the gate. Everyone had been on edge since the hammering in the forest stopped, which happened to coincide with the polar sunset twenty minutes ago. The recent sunset had left a pink dusk sky in its wake, along with a feeling of impending doom to those inside the citadel.

Jayda joined Quella and Shayla on the rampart above the gate. "That's Ardis," she said, noting his white horse and purple cloak in the twilight. "I bet he just wants a closer look at our defences."

"Let me shoot him," Shayla said. "Bet I could nail him first try."

Quella dropped her rifle and pistol at her feet.

"You're not going out there?" said Talia, who'd just arrived.

"Should at least hear what he has to say," Quella said.

Jayda dug the epaulette she'd taken from Valender from her pocket and handed it to Quella. "He knows ranks. If he sees a sergeant leading us he'll know we're in rough shape here." The thick lieutenant bar suggested at least a platoon-size presence, which beat their current strength threefold.

Quella stared at the rank with wistful eyes. How long had she waited to receive that promotion? She slid the epaulette onto her shoulder strap, then climbed down the ladder Sam had just slid down the outer wall. She didn't protest when Jayda followed. Instead, she waited for her at the bottom.

Together they marched to where Ardis stood holding the reins of his white mare. He started marching to meet them, a squinty smile raised in greeting. Quella stopped and waited for him to close the remaining distance. "That's close enough," she said before he could enter reaching distance.

Ardis stopped and nodded to Jayda. "Nice to see a familiar face. You been enjoying the weather?" Jayda remained silent and stone-faced, so he moved on to Quella. "Do you have everything you need in there? Food? Water?"

"Offerings aren't necessary," Quella said. "If you're here to plead for your mens' lives, you needn't bother. We'll let you leave if you do so at once."

"It's not our lives at risk here. But let's make a deal to avoid unnecessary bloodshed."

"We've done well enough without your help."

Ardis looked around. "It seems you've miscalculated your situation. The sun just went down and you're alone in enemy territory. I have three thousand warriors in that forest, with more on the way, plus a little surprise we've been working on. I hope all that banging didn't keep you up."

"Stick and stones," Quella said. "A hundred of us will hold these walls against ten thousand."

Ardis gave a solemn shake of his head. "You don't have that many, Lieutenant."

"Maybe not. But you'll pay a heavy price to find out for sure."

Ardis spread his arms. "Listen, I'm a reasonable man, and you're a…you're a…" Ardis struggled for a quick compliment. Quella didn't offer much to work with. "Well, we can both avoid a lot of unpleasantries here today. I can see your presence here is a misunderstanding. Bad timing more than anything. So, being the forgiving gentleman that I am, I'm willing to let you leave and join your unit at the border."

Quella's hands squeezed her webbing straps. Her eyes flicked briefly to Jayda. "What of the others?" she said to Ardis.

"They've become an integral part of our society. This is where they belong now."

Quella rocked back onto her heels, then forward. Jayda saw the temptation in her eyes, but her decision came quick and as a surprise to both Jayda and Ardis. "No deal," Quella said.

Ardis's eyes narrowed, his jaw bulging from clenched teeth. "You're making a terrible mistake."

Quella shrugged. "I didn't end up here by making good life choices."

Ardis smiled and nodded. "You know, you're a lot smarter than you look."

He hopped onto his horse, but before riding away he reached back into his saddlebag and withdrew a ball. He tossed it at Jayda's feet, then rode hard toward the forest.

Jayda stumbled back and fell onto her bottom, where she began hyperventilating. On the ground a few feet away lay Colonel Marcellus's severed head, his face offering her a look of agony.

Quella dragged her to her feet and toward the wall. "Come on," she said under her breath. "Don't lose your shit now." She stopped at the bottom of the ladder and squared Jayda to face her. "You don't say what you saw to the others. They don't need more bad news."

Jayda's shaking arms climbed the ladder. She waited for Quella on the rampart with the Darlings. With the possibility of reinforcements gone, what hope did they have?

"Well?" said Talia.

"He doesn't have enough men to take these walls," Quella said as she recovered her weapons. "His best chance is to draw us out."

It seemed Quella had gone to this meeting with more than the intent to hear Ardis's proposal. She wanted to size up her enemy, as Ardis was surely doing with her. What did that monster take away from his encounter with Quella?

"The Red and Blue Brigades will be marching up the valley

soon," Ivy said. "All we have to do is hold off until they make it here."

"Who knows how long that'll be?" Shayla said. "The dregs won't let them just walk in."

"He may try to starve us out," said Talia hopefully.

"I don't think Ardis has the patience for that," Jayda said sullenly, the image of Marcellus's face stuck in her head. Ardis had a thirst for Polarian blood.

Quella stared hard at the tree line. "Shoot anything that comes out of that forest."

The Darlings spread evenly across the grassy ramparts facing the tree line where Ardis had disappeared. Jayda found a spot on the inner crook between the two points which the other girls had spread out across. She lay prone with her webbing piled in front, on which she rested her rifle. Several clips of ammunition lay within reach to her right. Quella directed Sam to set civilian watches on the other points.

Ardis didn't wait long to show his hand. Drums echoed from the forest ahead, at first slow, but gradually speeding up the rhythm. Men groaned and grunted. Wood creaked. Through a gap in the trees a wooden platform emerged, a dozen men to each side carrying it. In the front, a shield of logs angled like a plow offered them cover.

"Catapult!" someone cried.

"Take it out!" Quella shouted.

Deafening gunfire thundered from the ramparts. Splinters of wood exploded from the onager's mechanisms and its forward shield, puffs of dirt kicked up from the surrounding field, and tree branches fell from stray bullets. Soon, the smell of smoke and sulphur polluted the fresh twilight air.

Jayda lined the shuffling platform in her iron sight, took two steadying breaths, then squeezed the trigger—*Crack!* The butt slammed back into her shoulder as a chunk of wood splintered from the forward shield. It was the first time she'd fired a weapon at a real target, and it came easier than she'd been expecting.

She continued in earnest, sliding the bolt back to eject the spent casing, returning it forward, squeeze the trigger and then repeat. The sequence quickly became routine.

Strange how much of a day at the range it seemed, with shooters lying prone to either side of her, casually putting rounds on target. Only, this time her heart raced with fear and excitement as her bullets dented the face of the catapult and shredded splinters from its sides.

Despite the havoc around them, the Ortarian battery continued their forward shuffle undaunted. Jayda had put her first ten rounds into the shield, hoping to blow a hole in it, but so far she'd only managed to leave the logs pockmarked, because hitting the same spot seemed near impossible. As she reloaded she noticed Darcella and Corla scampering down the ramparts to her right. Ivy and Talia did the same on the left to widen their arc.

The volley from the wider angles dropped two dregs from the right and one from the left. The catapult shimmied to a stop. Its handlers hurried to wind back the arm while six men rushed from the forest behind carrying a boulder in a sling.

Jayda stood and fired at the dregs loading the catapult. Her height offered a better angle, but her instability decreased the accuracy significantly as each shot rocked her backward. It didn't matter. She fired wildly, not noticing if she took out anyone or not. Just get rounds down range. Let them have it. With each shot the ringing in her ears grew louder than the gunfire.

The catapult banged and lurched forward. A boulder flew from the sling and arched through the air.

"Incoming!"

Arla and Eris scrambled out of the way as the boulder hit dirt a hundred feet away. It bounced across the field and crashed into the stone wall with a thud. The impact dropped Jayda onto her behind.

The crackle of gunfire resumed as the catapult advanced, their three fallen comrades replaced by more from the forest. A few more fell until the catapult once again wobbled to a stop. A crew wound the arm back as six men lugged a second boulder from the forest. Gunfire dropped a dozen dregs, but for every one to fall another was waiting to take his place. They hooked the sling to the arm and sought cover.

The arm banged forward and the platform lurched. Another boulder arched through the air toward the wall. Panic spread as Shayla and Quella scrambled out of the way, tripping over Ivy and Talia as the boulder bounced off the ground fifty feet away and crashed into the wall. Chunks of stone and mortar exploded high into the air.

Jayda aimed but could not see the catapult through the dust kicked up by the impact.

Another projectile immediately followed. This was bright and flew farther, brushing Jayda with heat just before it exploded behind her. She looked back to see the courtyard stable in flames. Polisians hurried about with pails of water to put out the fire.

"We gotta do something better than this!" said Ivy.

She was right. Jayda's arm and collarbone ached from the amount of lead she'd sent into that catapult, yet it still moved forward.

"Shayla, keep watch," said Quella. "Everyone else, on me."

Quella jumped down to the courtyard. The remaining Darlings, excluding Shayla, gathered around Valender's grave. Sam shouted orders for the civilians to keep fighting the fire as he hurried to join the Darlings. Everyone looked to Quella expectantly.

"I need a volunteer to go outside the walls with me," Quella said as she stuffed ammunition clips into her pockets. "We'll do a two-person rush, one going wide on each flank to get a better angle on that catapult. Our attack should interrupt their firing, so the rest of you will be safe to cover us from the walls. Target their archers first."

Sam held up his hand. "Hold on, now. There's gotta be another way."

"There isn't," Quella said. "Who's coming with me?"

Ivy stepped forward. "I'll go wherever you go, Mama."

"And she ain't goin nowhere without me," Talia said.

"There's no way I'm letting you have all the fun," said Darcella.

The others nodded in agreement.

Quella gave a satisfied nod. "We'll need cover from the walls," she said, dropping a bandolier at Songbird's feet. Jayda pulled the bandolier from her webbing and tossed it onto the growing pile.

"Incoming!"

Shayla's voice preceded a fiery explosion from the top of the wall, where Jayda had been shooting from. Flames, dust and rock rained down into the courtyard. Shayla emerged from the smoke to join the girls.

Jayda bolted down to the magazine. Calls of cowardice chased her but she continued her descent underground. From a stack of stashed crates she pulled five bottles of vodka, stuffing two into her ammo pouches, another in her shirt, and carrying one in each hand. When she returned to the courtyard the Darlings were already climbing through the jumble of logs blocking the gate.

Outside the wall, they kneeled behind a section of remaining picket line in freshly-tossed dirt and stripped their webbing of unnecessary gear—flashlights, wound kits, rations. Quella handed Jayda her pistol.

Shayla watched her cock it and said, "Thought you tucked tail in there."

A fireball streaked overhead and exploded in the courtyard behind.

Jayda uncorked a bottle and took a long drink of vodka. It burned all the way down and lit a fire in her belly.

Shayla snatched the bottle, took a swig, then passed it down the line.

"How many you think there are?" asked Arla, squinting toward the distant tree line.

"Don't worry," said Jayda, embracing the burn in her gullet. "You'll get your share."

Her words drew a mixture of looks from her sisters.

Jayda pointed to the catapult. "See that beast out there? There'll be a statue that looks just like it in Shackleton's Square come next Spring. They'll engrave all our names on its base, with a stroke for every Ortarian we're about to send to the afterlife."

Another fireball streaked overhead and exploded behind the wall.

"Fix bayonets!" Quella said.

Steel rattled as bayonets clicked into place.

"Time to show these mangy mutts who they're dealing with," Jayda said, her blood running hot. She looked down the line to where Arla and Eris watched her expectantly. "They think Odillian's lot were a hard bunch, but wait till they meet Adarah's Darlings. I see twenty dregs out there destined to become strokes under Arla and Eris's names."

The twins growled and banged their rifles off the picket before them.

Jayda continued down the line. "And Mother help those who tempt fate against Corla and Darcella, pride of Travaria, who knew fear only through the look in their enemy's eyes.

"And their sisters from Khartum, Ivy and Talia, whose biggest mistakes turned out to be their greatest blessings. For if they'd played it safe in life they'd have never discovered a love hotter than the stars themselves.

"And you can bet Ardis has been warning his men about Lieutenant Quella. Soon they'll see they've been right to fear her fury."

Jayda looked to her left. "And last but not least, Shayla the Unshakeable, who mounted that catapult like she owned it, and held it until the great fire set the Polis free."

The bottle of vodka made its way back to Jayda. She took another long drink and paced along the back of the line, the fire burning bright in her. "Together they came from the sky. Together they fought back the shadows that prey upon the hearts of the innocent. Not for flag nor country or honour, but for the duty bestowed upon the enlightened to keep humanity's light shining bright… To keep woman and man from falling into darkness once more. For dark clouds may block out the Sun's glory, but nothing can deny the star burning inside each of us unless we let it. And so none of us shall. Not on this day or any other. For it's in the darkest hour that our lights shine brightest. And on this day they'll remember the eight points of Polaria not as the stitched corners of a flag, but as eight howling bitches from hell!"

Jayda smashed the empty bottle off a rock at her feet and cocked her pistol.

Quella squeezed through the pickets first. The others shoved their way into the field to join her in an extended line. Together they marched across the poppy field, bayonets glinting from fireballs streaming overhead, footsteps falling heavy upon the ground, no effort to conceal their approach. They wanted this enemy to know they were coming.

CRACK! Quella fired her rifle into the air. This shot demanded not a forfeit of life, but attention. *We're coming,* it warned. Run or die. The choice is yours… For now.

The Ortarians quickly decided. A dozen fanned out from the catapult and charged. Another thirty spilled from the forest behind. Arrows arched under the pink sky and found soil ahead of the Polarians. Too soon.

With rifles raised to their shoulders the girls marched forward. *Pop! Crack! Crack! Bang!*

Dregs wielding axes and short swords dropped. Others dove for concealment in the tall grass. Newcomers emerging from the forest ran as far as the catapult, then sank low into the grass to continue their advance.

At the jagged seam of slanted arrows protruding from the ground the Darlings picked up their advance to a trot, firing from the hip and zigzagging to avoid an archer's aim. *Pop! Crack!* Cries of agony rose from the shifting grass around them. Onward pressed the girls, firing at the swaying grass and the bold chargers until the inevitable clash.

First blood was Shayla's. The spear thrust at her belly was easily deflected to the right with her rifle. A leftward backswing delivered the long edge of her bayonet to the spearman's neck and unleashed a spray of red mist.

As Shayla turned to double-check her kill, an axeman sprang up from the grass behind her and charged. He cocked his arm back to swing his axe, but Ivy jumped from the side and thrust her bayonet into his chest to drive him to the ground. As she struggled to pull her blade free, Shayla gave her a pat on the shoulder and carried on past.

Howls and cries and shrieks rose as both forces clashed in melee combat. Bayonets pierced flesh. Butts cracked skulls. Sharp steal knocked off wooden rifles. Gunshots rang out intermittently nearby and pattered steadily from Songbird's rifle on the walls behind. Despite the chaos, the Darlings managed to hold their line and press forward toward the catapult.

One may have thought these girls invincible until a crossbow bolt found Arla's chest. Eris cried in despair and ran to where the grass had swallowed her sister, only to have three dregs swarm her with axes.

"Keep moving!" screamed Quella.

Jayda levelled her pistol with the catapult and marched toward its splintered shield. So far she'd managed to keep her hands clean, her main priority to transport the bottles, but the loss of the twins meant she'd soon have to earn her strokes on the monument.

Shayla drew her pistol and swept the left side of the onager. Corla tossed her rifle and unslung the twelve gauge from her back. Jayda followed Corla as she swept the right side.

BOOM! A hail of pellets ripped apart the first dreg cowering behind the shield. She pumped the shotgun—*chick-chick*—and fired again—*BOOM! Chick-chick. BOOM!* Merciless the Travarian redhead was, pumping and firing until all four enemy became a mash of one.

She loaded shells into the empty gun and nodded for Jayda to do her thing while the remaining Darlings formed a semi-circle around the back of the catapult to fend off the Ortarian rush.

Jayda wasted no time. She crouched beside the catapult where the firing mechanisms sat vulnerable. She canted the first bottle back and forth to soak the rag stuffed into the bottle's mouth, then set it down to strike a match.

Footsteps thumped over the ground behind. Jayda whirled around and aimed her pistol at the charging axeman. *BOOM*—a shotgun blast tore open the dreg's side. He stumbled to the ground and bled out a few feet from Jayda.

Corla pumped the shotgun and fired at another target in the rustling grass. Jayda nodded her thanks, and Corla nodded back and smiled.

And from atop the catapult an Ortarian leaped high into the air, both hands swinging his axe down at Corla's head. The blade buried into her skull with a sickening crunch. Her knees buckled and her body shrivelled to the ground.

The axeman struggled to wrench his blade from the mess of bloodied orange hair at his feet. How he'd slipped in undetected was unbelievable. He was the biggest man Jayda had even seen.

Furious, Jayda aimed her pistol and pulled the trigger. *Click.* A jam. Her anger turned to terror at the weapon's failure. Shaking, sweaty fingers slipped on the steel slide as she struggled to eject the stuck round.

Corla's killer freed his blade and marched toward Jayda.

Ivy noticed and charged from the side, screaming loud to announce her attack and draw attention from Jayda. The axeman swung wide to meet the charge. His axe would have earned another notch on its handle had Ivy continued her course, but at the last second she slid onto her bottom. The axe blade glided free through the air while Ivy drove her bayonet into the brute's side. The crimson tip punched out his flank.

The impalement only stoked the axeman's ferocity. He raised the axe above his head for a downward swing at Ivy on the ground. Ivy pulled her .303's bolt back and slid it forward to load a round into the chamber. *Crack!* The shot sent Corla's killer spinning to the ground.

Seeing the Darlings wither away put the urgency in Jayda to

finish her job. She grabbed another match to light the rag, but found her focus drawn to Ivy, who rose and immediately found herself faced with another axeman. She raised her rifle horizontally to block a downward swing, then smashed his face with her butt. As he hit the ground, Ivy raised her rifle high and brought the butt down upon his skull to finish him off.

Without warning, a short sword jabbed straight at Ivy's head. Even with a last-second recoil the tip came within an inch of her face. The swordsman followed swiftly with a second swing and sliced a notch into her wooden rifle. He pressed the assault with furious swings and skillful jabs. Yet despite the Ortarian's skill, Ivy's rifle was there to block his blade at every angle. But Ardis, the Borien Butcher, was if anything persistent. He hacked and slashed at his comrade's killer. Ivy denied him his vengeance by blocking the blade, until a lucky swing clipped off two of her fingers.

The momentary shock was all Ardis needed. A hard swing batted Ivy's rifle to the side and left her wide open for the back-swing. Her rifle hit the ground as both hands clamped over the gaping gash across her throat. She dropped to her knees, eyes wide in terror, and instinctively crawled from her enemy with one hand on the ground, the other fruitlessly attempting to contain her gushing wound. Her mouth worked as she struggled to scream.

"Ivy!" Jayda hardly recognized the squeal of her own voice. Her hand worked the pistol slide feverishly until the skin scraped from her fingers.

Talia heard the cry and turned to see her lover sputtering blood through her fingers. She screamed and rushed forward, but didn't make it far. A spear soared through the air behind and punched out through her navel. She stumbled forward and landed on her side.

Ardis returned his attention to Ivy. With eyes blazing in fury, he swung his sword down hard at the back of her neck to seal his vengeance. But instead of biting flesh, the blade smacked off an axe handle. He turned in time to see Quella's forehead smash into his mouth. Blood gushed from his lips as he stumbled back.

Quella stepped forward to follow through, but a spearman rushing from the side summoned the axe in her right hand to bat the spear away. She swung her left hand and buried its axe into the spearman's neck. She twisted the blade free and turned to see Ardis wielding two short swords while squaring off with her. Quella glanced at Ivy's lifeless body on the ground nearby and her lips twisted in rage.

Her axe blade came down from high and rang off Ardis's forward sword. He ducked her second swing and thrust his sword at her belly, which Quella deflected with her free axe.

A symphony of ringing steel echoed across the field as Quella pressed forward with violent grace, swinging both axe's with such overwhelming speed that Ardis struggled to keep up. She was relentless in her rush and grew faster as she drove him straight back toward the catapult, where he'd be cornered. Twice she caught him in the chest with a blunt jab of the flat axe top. Then, with one slick outward swing of both axes, she slapped both of Ardis's swords apart, exposing his torso for the kick that sent him crashing onto his behind.

Quella walked a circle him, then raised one axe high for the finishing blow. Her blade was halfway to his skull when a black arrow skewered her left shoulder. She stumbled back, arm dropping until the wooden handle slid from her grasp.

Ardis jumped to his feet and came swinging with both swords. Quella did her best to block the whirlwind of steel, but one axe wasn't enough. One of Ardis's blades slipped through an opening in her defence and buried into her belly.

Quella grunted and dropped her remaining axe. Ardis twisted the blade and then pulled it free. Quella hit her knees, both hands covering the gaping wound in her belly. Her eyes drifted absently toward the ground as her head lowered, blood streaming from her mouth and onto her lap.

Jayda slammed into the side of Ardis's legs, her shoulder

connecting with his knees. Both swords flew from his hands as he flipped onto the ground. Jayda clawed her way up his body and mounted his chest, where her fists rained furious strikes upon his face. Within seconds Ardis's nose was busted and gushing blood. Yet he still managed an amused smile, so Jayda grabbed a rock and swung down at his face. Ardis's hand caught her wrist before she could smash in his teeth.

He flipped Jayda around and ended on top. His hands wrapped her neck and squeezed so hard her eyes felt as if they may pop out of her head. She glanced left and right, desperate hands feeling through the wet grass for a weapon. She saw Shayla in a similar position thirty feet away, a dreg mounting her with both her hands pushing back against the dagger inching toward her face.

Darcella was nowhere to be seen, but a dreg wandered in a daze wearing the imprint of her brass knuckles on his cheek.

Jayda's mouth opened futilely to draw air. Through her spotted vision, she saw Darcella appear behind Shayla's assailant. Darcy balled his long hair tight in one hand while the other dragged a serrated knife across his throat. Shayla fussed as blood cascaded onto her face. Darcy shoved the limp body aside and helped Shayla to her feet.

Darcella met an attack as Shayla's eyes fell on Jayda, who'd just started shaking and convulsing. Shayla grabbed her rifle and charged at Ardis, her bloody face screaming like a madwoman.

Ardis jumped off Jayda and grabbed both swords to meet Shayla. But their weapons never touched. Shayla stopped a few feet away and circled her opponent, her madness checked by the bodies of her sisters at her feet.

Gasping for air, Jayda's shaking arms barely supported her as she crawled to Corla's body. Her wheezing blocked out even the ringing in her ears. She pulled the shotgun from under Corla, aimed, and squeezed the trigger. The *BANG* brought back the ringing to her ears and the recoil sent her sprawling onto her back.

The blast hit Ardis's side and sent him spinning to the ground. Shayla stuck her bayonet into his heart for good measure.

Darcella and Shayla fell in around Jayda, who remained seated on the bloody ground as a dozen Ortarians surrounded them.

Jayda's hands shook as she struggled to pump the shotgun. She placed the butt against the ground, wrapped both hands around the fore-end, and put all her weight down to pump it. A *chick* ejected the empty shell, and the upward motion loaded another. She struggled to her feet and took shaky aim as she wheezed loudly, the world around her spinning out of control.

The dozen dregs seemed poised to attack, the only thing stopping them the Polarian firearms. Jayda would squeeze off one shot. She had no idea if Shayla and Darcy held loaded weapons, nor did the Ortarians, though Jayda was confident each girl could take down at least one more with her fixed bayonet. The cluster was too far and tight for Songbird to risk a shot from the citadel walls.

Barooooooom!

The horn blast sent a shiver up Jayda's spine. Every combatant looked across the field to where a row of mounted Ortarians emerged from the tree line. Hooves thundered over the poppy field as a calvary unit of one hundred abreast and double thick charged straight toward the foray.

Jayda wished she could shrivel up and disappear. Shayla and Darcella struggled to steady their rifles. Even at full strength they'd hold no chance at defeating these howling, blade-wielding reinforcements.

As the lead rider drew closer, scimitar extended in front, it became obvious she was a girl with long black hair. In her crimson and black cape, black leather corset, seamless leather breeches and knee-high boots, she looked absolutely magnificent. And terrifying.

"Raven," one of the dregs declared.

Jayda faced her impending death with surprising calmness. For the first time since seeing Marcellus's severed head, her mind was clear. And she knew what had to be done.

With steady hands she grabbed a bottle of vodka, lit the rag with a match, and tossed it at the catapult. The fiery cocktail exploded off the stop bar and sparked a blaze. She watched the fire spread with a twitchy smile. She'd just made their deaths worthwhile.

As the calvary drew closer the circle of Ortarians around the Darlings broke and fled into the woods. The riders pursued them, cutting down Ardis's *Rogues* with swords and spears.

Jayda watched in shock and confusion as the leader, Raven, peeled off from the vanguard and approached the catapult. Haughty eyes assessed the carnage as she circled the remaining Darlings. Black swirls decorated her olive skin, with similar ink patterns painted on the two male riders who joined her.

"Find Ardis," Raven told them. "I want him dead or alive."

The girl couldn't have been older than twenty, but the Ortarian men obeyed her as if she were a Sage. She looked to the Darlings. "Have you seen their leader? Is he here?"

Jayda pointed to Ardis's body on the ground nearby.

"Who killed him?"

Shayla and Darcella looked to Jayda, who then reluctantly raised her hand.

"Ortaria owes you a bounty," Raven said. "Though, I'm not sure how well our method of payment will serve you in Polaria. Perhaps an armed escort to the border will suffice. When you get home, you'll tell your leaders that what happened to your Polis was condemned by our Grand Councilry. The rest of Ortaria does not believe in slavery."

Jayda exchanged wary looks with Shayla and Darcy. The clang of steel and howls of battle echoed from the forest, signifying Raven's riders were not the same as Ardis's fighters. She was their best chance to leave this place alive.

"I assure you," Raven said, "your actions against Ardis's *Rogues* will have earned you notoriety among our kind. No Ortarian will challenge you outside the Valley."

Jayda realized her two companions had wordlessly appointed

her as negotiator and were awaiting her decision. She looked to Raven. "There *is* something you can do. Something that will spare both countries a lot of suffering."

Jayda crouched beside Ardis's body and dug the letter from his jerkin. She handed it to Raven. "Our people need this food. Can you deliver?"

Raven read the list. "I'll bring this to my father. See what he says. In the meantime, give your dead a proper send off. Leave Ardis for the crows."

THIRTY-NINE

Toris woke with an unfamiliar feeling. Suspended in a hammock four feet above the ground, with Rykah's face burrowed against his neck, her breath hot on his skin and her warm body stuck to his, he felt at peace.

She flinched and groaned, her nails digging into his side. He squeezed her tight and wondered what scenes of war haunted her dreams. What had she been forced to do to survive in this world? In his arms she felt small and frail, but it was the heart of this Ranger that made her dangerous.

He flipped up the canopy to peer out into the predawn light. The party was long dead. A blue haze from the neglected communal fire hung over the beach, its smoky smell heavy around Rykah's campsite. A few soldiers slept on the beach.

Toris dreaded the prospect of getting up. The mere thought of pulling himself from under the weight of Rykah's warmth to step out into the chill morning air made him hold her closer. If only they could lie like this forever… And that's when it hit him.

He didn't have to get up.

He had nowhere to be.

No one to serve.

This was *his* time. Time to spend as he saw fit. If he wanted to lounge in this hammock all day, then no one could stop him.

His heart fluttered, glowing with the warmest feeling he'd ever known. This warmth radiated from his chest and spread down his arms and legs to his fingertips and his toes.

He closed his eyes and caressed Rykah's shoulder. Matching his breathing with the rise and fall of her belly against his, a peace rose up from deep within his heart and smothered the worries of his mind. He smiled. Sleep was taking him again, the rolling surf of the receding tide and the occasional snapping from the dying fire soothing him into oblivion. He was nearly there when a new sound joined the ambience.

Putt-putt-putt-putt-putt-putt-putt...

Toris strained to hear. The putting noise was steady, almost mechanical, and was growing louder. His heart raced to match its rhythm.

He slid from under Rykah and out of their cocoon of purple silk. She shivered and pulled the flap back over.

The sand was cold beneath Toris's feet, almost painful as the chill shot up his calves. He hugged himself as he scanned for the source of the noise. It sounded like an echo travelling over water, so he looked south just in time to see a boat cruise past the point of the southern headland.

Toris rubbed his eyes, because there was no way he was seeing the *Barnacle* chugging north along the coast of Norway. He stomped forward and squinted for a better look. The trawler's hunter green paint was worn and peeling, and her mast swayed off center.

Toris jumped and screamed. "Hey!"

A soldier lay passed out on the sand nearby clutching a drink flask. Toris wrenched the deerskin container from him and dumped it on the fire at center beach.

Whoooosh!

The flash was bright but not bright enough. *Barnacle* stuck to her northbound course toward Battler's Bay.

Toris raced to the salvage pile in the forest. He rummaged through the mix of food and clearly marked water containers in search of something volatile. A green cannister wedged between two crates stopped him. Its label read: *'Warning: Liquid Hydrogen'*.

Hugging the cold steel cylinder to his chest, he sprinted back toward the dim fire on the beach, stopping to grab a polymer mug from the sand. He wanted to get *Barnacle*'s attention, not blow himself to dust, so he knelt a good distance from the fire and filled the cup with hydrogen, then flung it onto the flames.

Though he shielded his eyes with an arm, he still saw the flash and felt the heat on his eyelids. The flames jumped high and burned bright. Toris laughed at its warmth until he saw the trawler maintain its northern trajectory.

Of course. Why would they assume it to be Polarians?

A quick look around revealed a soldier sleeping with a blanket of black silk wrapped around him. Toris grabbed a loose corner of the flag and hauled backwards. The soldier moaned as he rolled out of the flag's embrace. He rose to his knees to protest, but Toris was already racing toward the sea. His cries gave way to splashing water as Toris sloshed out into the bay waving the flag. When up to his knees, he looked back to the fire and then ran left to position himself between the flames and the ship, so that crew would see the white eight-pointed star glowing in the firelight. A northerly wind lifted the flag and spread it wide.

It worked. The *Barnacle* swung out to sea and then looped back around toward land.

Toris waded out to a rock with the flag above his head, laughing hysterically.

A figure leaned over *Barnacle*'s bowsprit. Toris recognized the outline of a rifle barrel aimed his way. The figure's head turned back toward the bridge.

"Captain!" rose Drua's voice through the predawn air. "It's Toris! It's Toris!"

Toris wrapped the flag around his waist and cupped his hands around his mouth. "About time you showed up!"

Drua's laughter roared over the water.

Toris looked to the sky above, where only the brightest stars remained in the cobalt sky. It seemed they did have a plan for him after all.

While Antlia dropped anchor one hundred feet from the beach, Drua jumped down into the water and swam to Toris. The journey had leaned him out, but that didn't stop him from throwing Toris into a headlock and roughing his hair when he joined Toris on the rock. Drua released him before Toris could display Rykah's teachings on him.

Drua pushed him at arm's length for a better look. "Man," he said, shaking his head in disbelief, "I never thought I'd be glad to see *you* of all people."

"Likewise," Toris said. He jabbed at Drua's belly. "Looks like you've been eating well enough."

Drua pushed out his abdomen and patted it with both hands. "I'm a stress eater."

"Toris!" From *Barnacle*'s bowsprit, Captain Antlia gave two thumbs up along with the biggest smile Toris had ever seen. "Good to see ya, lad."

Drua's gaze shifted over Toris's shoulder to the beach. His smile faded.

Toris turned to see Rykah standing at the water's edge with her rifle in hand. The last time she and Drua had seen each other, Rykah had nearly broken his arm. Toris smiled at her, but she about-faced and returned to her campsite.

Drua draped an arm over Toris's shoulder. "Come. It's been too long since I've walked on land."

Drua's legs laboured through the water to the beach.

"Saw a Coast Patrol ship anchored for repairs south of here," he said, stomping out of the shallow tide. "How'd you get here before your own expedition?"

Toris shook his head and tried to think of where to begin.

Drua placed a hand on his chest and recoiled. "Wait, did they get the seeds already?" His head tilted back in despair. "And they marooned you so you couldn't claim the Accolade. Dammit!"

Toris placed a hand on Drua's shoulder. "They didn't get the seeds. Their mission was to make sure nobody did. You're lucky their weapon systems are offline." Toris then told him about the clash between the expeditionary forces.

Drua's laughter at the ordeal was most inappropriate, but Toris was in too good a mood to scold him.

From the tree line, seven soldiers stomped toward the water. Toris stiffened at the sight of their weapons in hand, the first time they'd carried them since arriving on this beach.

Drua held both arms out wide. "Greetings, siblings."

Thane emerged as leader. He wagged his pistol at *Barnacle* and said to Toris, "He needs to get that boat out of here before Khalid gets the wrong idea."

Toris held up a hand. "Just give us a few minutes. If the locals decide it's worth angering the gods over, *Barnacle* will be long gone before they get word to Khalid."

Thane's expression softened slightly. He waved his pistol at Drua. "You got one hour to be out of my sight."

He led the half-dozen soldiers back up the beach, their shoulders slumped and heads heavy from the night of drinking.

Toris returned his attention to Drua. "How are *Barnacle*'s systems?"

Drua faced the ship and planted his hands on his hips. "Wouldn't call everything tip-top, but she runs the same as when we set off from Abersali. Antlia knows that vessel better than I know my own body."

"The refrigeration unit?"

Drua cocked his head. "A bit chilly."

"Desalination system?"

"Never leave home without one."

Toris fell onto his back and breathed a sigh of relief. "You have room for a few more on board?" he asked.

Drua nodded. He glanced down at Toris. "There is one thing we need, though."

"What's that?" Toris said, sitting up.

"A kite."

Toris looked back to the purple blot in the tree line, where he'd spent what he thought would be the first of many nights with Rykah.

"Ours blew away," Drua explained, "ripped clean from the cables in a storm. If we burn any more hydrogen we won't have enough to power the freezer on the way home."

"Take a walk and stretch your legs," Toris said, his eyes fixed on Rykah building a fire at her campsite. "I'll get us a kite."

Rykah crouched and prodded the burning logs with a stick. Her gaze remained on the fire when Toris arrived.

"Did you wish Drua luck with the rest of his journey?" she said.

Toris's heart burned with a sensation he'd never felt before.

"I'm going with them," he said, "and you're staying here. When we get the seeds, I'll come back for you. I swear upon every star in the sky. You'll get your freedom."

Rykah stared at the flames, unmoving.

"Then go," she said.

Toris turned to leave, fearing to upset her any more. But this was about something greater than her feelings. He turned back. "I need your kite, Rykah."

Without hesitation she tore down her hammock, their haven. She balled it up and threw it at Toris's chest. "Something to remember me by."

Toris's throat swelled like a balloon. He couldn't swallow, let alone form words of comfort or reassurance. All he could manage was a weak, "Rykah…"

"Leave!" she said, thrusting her poker stick toward the *Barnacle*. Then she turned her back to him and crouched by the fire.

Toris walked on trembling legs toward the sea, clutching the bunched-up kite to his chest. Rykah's smell radiated from every fiber of the silky fabric. His heart felt as if it had slid up into his throat and was choking him with each beat. But that was a phantom sensation, because he felt his heart inside his chest pull as he walked away, stretching thin from its invisible cord attached to Rykah's. How could he do this to her? To himself?

Jayda. That's how. He thought of his little sister in uniform, and he forced his legs forward toward the water.

Down the beach to his left, Lex walked alongside Drua toward him. Korvyn lingered behind like the loyal watchdog he was. Rumour had it he'd taken a blood oath from Ignatius to protect Lex with his life, but it was Lex's stand against Clavilla that had earned her bodyguard's fanatic loyalty. If she'd have allowed Clavilla to abandon him, he may have ended up as the main course at the next Nordican feast.

Toris reached the tide line when Drua's new entourage arrived.

"Nice kite," Drua said. "She'll do just fine."

"My family colour," Lex pointed out.

Drua and Lex stopped before Toris. "The good lady here says the vault might be heavily guarded," said Drua. "If that's true, then we'll need more things that go *bang* than what we've got aboard *Barnacle*."

Lex looked back to Korvyn. "Escort Drua to the salvage pile and take whatever he needs."

Korvyn led Drua up the beach with Lex trailing them. Toris watched nervously, expecting the colony soldiers to protest. A few gathered around to watch, but none spoke up. Korvyn's reputation in the Defence Force had carried a lot of weight. Anyone who had reported directly to the Chancellor knew how to take care of belligerents effectively and without raising alarm. So it was no surprise when he and Drua walked away from that pile unopposed, their arms overflowing with munitions.

But it was more than gear they'd mustered on that short stroll. Macey and Spinner followed with their rucksacks and rifles, along with Ike, too. Though no big surprises among that lot, Jorda was an unexpected addition.

"You're really keen on seeing she ends up on trial back home," Toris said to Lex.

"She knows more about Svalbard's defences than anyone here," Korvyn pointed out.

Lex ordered Korvyn to bring the gear straight to *Barnacle* with Drua, then she waded into the water behind. Toris followed.

The new crew gathered on *Barnacle*'s rear deck. In addition to firearms, Drua had gathered six more crewmates. Captain Antlia weaved through the tight group, greeting each new member with a handshake and a friendly hello.

"Just sit back and enjoy the ride," the captain said. "I need you rested up to handle any trouble. Hopefully that won't be until Svalbard."

Toris joined Antlia on the bridge. The captain pointed to the engine button on the forward control panel. "Care to do the honours?" he said.

Toris pressed the red button and felt the engines below shiver to life.

"Just to get us into deeper water," Antlia said. "Then we'll fly that kite of yours."

As Antlia swung the bow toward the open sea, Toris avoided stealing a glance at the beach behind. He didn't need a reason to jump overboard right now and swim back to that haven.

The engines rumbled as Antlia pushed the thruster forward.

"Wait!" Korvyn shouted from the stern. "We got one more!"

Toris's heart raced. *Rykah!* he thought with a sense of dread and relief. When he looked out the rear window, the figure he saw wading out from the beach was carrying a rifle in one hand, his other arm in a sling. Jarik.

Toris sank low against the wheelhouse wall and pulled his knees to his chest. The crew outside clapped and hailed the last-minute recruit as they helped him aboard. Toris kept his head hung, awaiting Antlia to get them cruising from the bay. It seemed a few minutes had passed when Toris lifted his head to see what the hold-up was.

"Just waiting on one more," Antlia said, squinting at the shore behind.

Toris leaned into the doorway and looked astern to the beach. The sight of Rykah holding two rifles above her head as she waded toward *Barnacle*'s stern had him on his feet and down onto the main deck in a single heartbeat. He waited back as Korvyn and Drua helped her aboard. Her camouflage pants matched the uniforms of the other soldiers who'd joined.

Antlia wasted no more time. The engine roared and sent them rocking toward the sea.

Rykah sat behind the stern rail, staring wistfully at the shrinking beach. Toris knelt behind her.

As if sensing him near, her shoulders hunched. "Not now, Toris."

His heart squeezed tight.

"Toris!" Drua waddled past the wheelhouse with the purple kite. "Give me a hand setting this up."

Toris left Rykah at the stern rail. Hopefully she'd forgive him before they reached Svalbard. The last thing he needed during the vault raid was her scorn hanging over him.

FORTY

After Toris had 'volunteered' to join Rykah's expedition back in Port Abersali, Drua managed to recruit a replacement. An urbanite from the capital in search of adventure, young Marlin hadn't seen the frailty of human life when pitted against nature the way his rural counterparts had. *Barnacle*'s lack of safety rails didn't help matters when the young Amyrian wandered above decks during Drake's Wrath and the waves swept him off to a briny grave. So, when the *Barnacle* left Norway's north coast behind and ventured into the rough open sea, Captain Antlia ordered that everyone remain below.

Toris's time in the ship's hold, however, was not idle. The security force had appointed Korvyn to lead the landing party. Rykah's Ranger qualifications rivalled his experience, but when Toris had nominated her, she withdrew her name despite his protests, which had resorted to personal attacks against Korvyn for his willingness to abandon the *Polaris* and her crew to the pyrates. Twice.

So Toris found himself cleaning weapons in the engine room, failing inspection after inspection as he tried to scrub every grain of sand from every nook and groove. Whenever he did satisfy Korvyn's eye, his success earned him another dirty gun to clean. But Toris was in no mood to fight with his own at sea after what had happened aboard *Sea Serpent*. He'd seen how tempers could flare in close quarters with these military types. Best to save his fighting for Svalbard.

His first break came for the planning discussion at Drua's invite. In the seed storage room, he joined everyone on the dusty floor around a map of the Svalbard archipelago. Everyone but Rykah sat cross-legged in a circle, knee to knee. Toris squeezed in between Lex and Drua. Blue light glowed from a lantern hanging from the ceiling. Its swaying sphere of illumination revealed glimpses of a reclusive Rykah sitting in the room's forward corner.

"This is our most recent map of Svalbard," Korvyn said. "Unfortunately, it's over seven hundred years old. Luckily, our meeting with Khalid confirmed the vault is still intact and above water. That's the good news. The bad news is that entrance is possibly guarded by Khalid's private army." To Drua, he said, "Khalid is our friendly local warlord, by the way."

"What does he want with the seeds?" said Drua.

"It's not the seeds that interest him," Korvyn said. He looked to Jorda. "But I'm afraid my knowledge on the specifics is limited, so I'll not burden you with secondhand information. Jorda, enlighten the group about Svalbard's significance."

Jarik jumped to his feet and pointed his good arm at Jorda. "We can't trust that pyrate scum!"

Toris pulled his knees to his chest to stifle his own outburst, as he was inclined to agree. She'd led them on that wild chase for an antidote that had provoked the second pyrate attack.

Korvyn gave Jorda a wary look. "In exchange for her cooperation, Lady Alexandra has promised her a pardon upon her return to Polaria, so it would be unwise for her to betray us."

Jorda clinked her teeth at Jarik. "Aye, but it's about more than that, me love. We southern folk is all the same in Nordican eyes. Now that you dragged me along, my fate is tied to yours. This is about self-preservation. If I lies to you, you're just as likely to toss me overboard than take me home to trial. This much I knows."

She stood. "Besides, from Polarians you'll not find a better scout for your mission than a pyrate. Me fleet once had free range up here," Jorda explained, walking around the outside of the circle, "till we had a fallin' out with Khalid. Only can tell ya what I heard, and it ain't pretty." Jorda shook her head. "They think that vault is the tomb of their sleepin' saviour, and truth be told, until I met your lot, I assumed the same thing. Only that he was long dead."

"What defences are we looking at?" Drua asked, squinting at the map as if it may hold the answer.

"Can't tell ya much about them except that the vault may be guarded by a big gun called the 'can opener'. Not sure if that's what the Nordican folk wanted us pyrates to believe so we'd stay away, or if there really is one. If the vault is important enough to his people, then Khalid probably set somethin' up to protect it."

"Why would he do that?" Macey asked with a frown. "I heard him say he doesn't believe in the sleeping saviour myth."

"You can split the Nordican folk into two groups," Jorda explained, stepping into the circle. "For our purposes, we'll call em…" She rubbed her chin in thought. "Let's call 'em the *Keepers* and the *Seekers*. Yeah, that should do."

Crouching before the map, she pointed to Norway and traced her finger along northern Russia. "See, not long ago, Nordica wasn't an empire at all. Khalid was just one of a good many warlords. People was fightin' over all sorts a things, but nothin' caused more trouble than this vault." She tapped a finger on Svalbard's main island—Spitsbergen. "It started out with everyone wantin' to wait for the saviour to wake in his natural time. Then a younger generation started gettin' impatient. Started talkin' about goin' in and wakin' him up."

"The *Seekers*," Drua guessed, watching Jorda like a kid listening to stories of the Decimation around a campfire. "Did they try?"

Jorda nodded gravely. "Aye, they tried."

Toris's belly twisted. What if they'd succeeded and Khalid had erased that part from the lore in a cover-up?

"A big group of 'em set sail north," Jorda said, tracing the coasts of northern Europe to Svalbard. "Word travelled fast, but not fast enough. *Keepers*, the lot committed to seein' the vault stays sealed, they mustered a force to sail after 'em. But the closest war party was a day behind. Only thing between the *Seekers* and the vault was a group of pilgrims who went to make an offerin' for first sunrise after the long winter night."

Around the room, the faces watching in the pale blue lantern light reminded Toris of huddling around the fire on Mintaka during the six-month night, when his young Onero kin listened to stories from the seniors, everyone desperate to hear what happened next.

"Did they stop them?" Toris asked, squirming in suspense.

Jorda's eyes met his and darkened. "When the *Seekers* got to the vault entrance, the pilgrims bought some time with a parley. But those *Seekers*, they wasn't in much of a talkin' mood, and they wasn't leavin' without seein' the inside of that vault. So when the pilgrims made a human barricade a hundred people thick in front of the door, the *Seekers* butchered 'em—men, women, and youngins—all dead."

Drua leaned forward. "And the vault?"

"That's where Khalid comes in." Jorda tapped lower Norway on the map. "See, he had this mighty flyin' ship that he thought would scare everyone into followin' him. But fear don't work on all types of folk, and the ones it don't work on is the ones that will cause ya the most problems. Khalid spent years tryin' to bring em under his control, with not much luck. So, when some of them *Keepers* set sail for the vault, a few more went to Khalid to beg for his help, to put that air ship to good use.

"By then, Khalid figured out there was way more Nordicans who was *Keepers* than there was *Seekers*. Way more, actually. He saw this was his chance to win the loyalty of almost every Nordican between both great oceans." Jorda nodded. "And he did. Those tribes who went to meet with him took a blood oath on the spot. So long as he swore to protect the vault from that moment till the day the saviour walked out its door on his own accord, those tribes there promised to convince the others to submit with either words or blood."

Jorda paused to assess her audience while licking her lips. Clearly she enjoyed having these Polarian folk captivated, and was dragging it out.

Toris played into it. He had to know. "Did he make it on time? Is the vault really still there?"

"Well," Jorda said with a shrug, "if you can believe the stories, then, just as them *Seekers* finished their slaughter of the pilgrims, that's when Khalid's air machine came swoopin' in to save the day. Brought some prisoners back to his capital and gave each a gruesome death for the satisfaction of his new loyal subjects."

"So now the Nordicans owe him their allegiance," Rykah said from her dark corner.

"Most of 'em, you bet. But his obligation didn't stop there. Always could be another force that slipped north without anyone knowin' in time, so Khalid had to put in place a solid measure, to show his ability and commitment to deny anyone entry to the vault. So he built a fort that overlooks the entrance."

"With a gun called the 'can opener'," Toris recalled.

"Aye," Jorda said with a shiver, "the 'can opener'."

Korvyn crossed his arms. "So we need to disable that gun before *Barnacle* can come in for the pick-up. First take the fort, blow the gun, then secure the vault entrance below."

On the map, Drua pointed to a smaller fjord south of the waterway accessing the vault. "We can land a team here and move north over land to the vault. Once we take possession of the fort and disable the gun, we'll signal the *Barnacle* to come in for the seeds."

"A word of warnin'." Jorda pointed to an island to the east. "Some say there's *Seekers* in hideouts here, waitin' for an opportunity to make their move again. So you can bet they got scouts watchin' that fort for weaknesses. If they hears a fight, they'll assume you're *Seekers* and come join ya. Just don't expect 'em to stay friendly once they figure out you're foreign invaders."

"So whatever we do, we do it quick," Korvyn said.

"What if there are pilgrims there," said Ike. "Like the ones the *Seekers* slaughtered? They'll slow us down."

"Then we don't waste any time talking like those *Seekers* did back then," Macey said.

"You'll kill innocent civilians?" said Toris.

Macey shrugged, too casually.

"What if we slip in among the pilgrims?" Toris suggested, before Macey's idea gained any traction.

"From what I hear," Drua said, "we don't blend in very well."

"We won't be trying to blend in," Toris said.

A shadow rose in the forward corner. Rykah stepped forward to give Toris a look of caution.

Jorda nodded and wagged a finger at him. "Aye, Oshinga is said to be a foreigner."

Drua's brow scrunched. "O-who?"

Toris stood and recited what he'd learned earlier from Jorda. "The Oshinga prophecy predicts that one day a man or woman will seek out the vault, yet side with neither *Seeker* nor *Keeper*. Nor even pilgrim, for that matter. His purpose will be to summon the saviour from his rest in the tomb."

"So the Keepers will grant him access to the vault?" Drua said.

"Might allow him close enough to touch the door and do a ceremony," Jorda said.

Behind her, Rykah's eyes locked onto Toris with a forbidding look.

"And they'll be fooled by that brand?" Drua said suspiciously. "Why hasn't a *Seeker* used such trickery before?"

"Heard they did," Jorda said.

"What happened?"

Jorda bit her lip. "The *Keepers* clipped off their heads."

Rykah broke into the circle. "No way. It's too risky."

Having just heard the fate of his predecessors, Toris agreed. Nordicans were territorial and impulsive.

"If he can talk the *Keepers* into openin' the vault, it'll save everyone a lot a trouble," Jorda said.

"We don't mind trouble," Rykah said, stroking the pistol grip at her side.

"So long as you's the ones causing it," Jorda pointed out. "The lad Toris here is different than the other frauds."

"How?" Rykah said, challenging.

Jorda turned her back to Rykah to address the room. "Remember, the prophecy says Oshinga is a foreigner. The *Seeker* imposters couldn't disguise their Nordican identities. His untainted features gives a credibility that no Nordican could ever fake. He'd be like…"

"A Trojan horse."

Everyone looked to Lex, who'd just spoken her first words since leaving the Polarian colony. Even she appeared surprised by her own interruption.

"A what?" said Rykah.

Lex stood to address the group. "It's from a war before the Decimators' time. They used a wooden horse to smuggle troops into a fortified city."

Rykah folded her arms and chewed her thumbnail in deep contemplation.

"And it worked?" said Korvyn.

Lex gave Toris an apologetic look. "They sacked the city."

Toris now wished he'd kept the Oshinga idea to himself.

Rykah shook her head vehemently. "I don't like it. Too much can go wrong."

Korvyn stood. "It's a good idea. The Oshinga ruse will get him close enough to the entrance to deploy his hidden troops, which in this case will be a block of plastic explosives. It'll blow the door right off and scare away the pilgrims. Our assault teams will use the confusion to sweep in."

Lex's wide eye fell on Toris and the colour drained from her face as if just realizing what she'd volunteered him for.

"I still don't like it," Rykah said.

"You don't have to like it," said Korvyn. "You're not the leader here. If I need to sacrifice one hundred half-bloods to accomplish this mission, then so be it."

Macey jumped into the mix. "It sounds like a fair trade to me. He's one Onero. Bigger sacrifices have been made for Polaria."

Spinner grabbed Macey's wrist and tried pulling her back down. "Take it easy, Mace. We'd still be at the border right now if it wasn't for him."

"Are you kidding me?" Macey said, her eyes wide in disbelief. "We're *all* still at the border because of him! If his mother's blood-line died off stopping this war, that'd be a good start to make up for that."

Toris sat and listened, relinquishing his fate to the group. So long as Jayda got his reward he'd do whatever it took to get into that vault. Still, hearing his own kin fight for the right to do away with him hurt. He'd die for any one of his brothers and sisters, but it was clear the sentiment wasn't mutual.

Rykah stepped toe to toe with Korvyn. "Everyone aboard *Polaris* saw how quickly the hero of Dagger Ford fled a pyrate attack to save his own skin. Why were you the only survivor of that battle? Did you leave your comrades behind to cover your solo retreat?"

Korvyn clenched his fists at his side. "Don't test me, Adarah."

"Korvyn, stand down," said Lex.

Her bodyguard held his stare with Rykah, who also wasn't backing down.

"Both of you, *sit,*" Lex ordered.

Korvyn broke out of the circle and paced the back of the room.

Lex remained standing in the middle of the circle. "We stick to the first plan. If the firefight from taking the fort isn't enough to scare off all the pilgrims, we'll fire warning shots. If they insist on becoming martyrs, then so be it. But we'll not force one of our own to become one."

Toris breathed a sigh of relief and praised Lex's logic.

Rykah nodded enthusiastically. "A fine plan, Alexandra." She looked to Toris with imploring eyes. "Right?"

Toris nodded.

Korvyn didn't look so convinced. His rueful glare remained on Rykah a long while, even when a debate over the finer details broke out between the other Defence Force veterans.

The general plan, however, quickly garnered favour with all involved. A team of eight would land in the fjord south of the vault and travel north on foot to the fort. There, they'd employ heavy firepower and the element of surprise to overrun the fort and disable the gun. A flare would signal the *Barnacle* 'all clear' to enter the fjord. While one team descended to the vault entrance, another would cover them from the fort. Then they'd load the seeds onto the *Barnacle* and head home.

When everyone had their input and the consensus was made, Korvyn folded up the map and said, "We board the raiding craft at first sight of land."

FORTY-ONE

The handle of an idling hydrogen motor vibrated in Toris's left hand. His right hand held the hemp cargo net hanging from *Barnacle*'s starboard bow to steady the rubber raiding craft against the hull. Waves slapped against the boat from the open sea and soaked him. Already his feet were in water to his ankles.

Above, a silhouette climbed over the rail onto the net in the predawn light. From the foredeck, eight heads watched the first vault raider descend to the small raiding craft. From his bottom viewpoint in the dark, Toris couldn't tell who was who until they joined him in the craft.

Korvyn boarded first and slid straight to the front. Next came Rykah, who crawled up to Korvyn's left to make room for her spotter, Jarik, who climbed down shakily with only one arm. Macey and Spinner descended the net side by side and jumped into the boat together. Then Ike climbed down with his father's shotgun slung across his back. Last to board was Drua.

Jorda lowered two patrol packs containing pieces to Rykah's disassembled AS50 sniper rifle. Then came baskets of ammunition—belts and boxes of linked machine gun rounds. Drua piled them into the center of the boat.

The cargo net lifted as Lex and Jorda pulled it up onto the foredeck.

When the loaded raiding craft drifted clear of *Barnacle*, Toris twisted the throttle and steered east toward the scarlet band of light lining the horizon. The hydrogen motor hummed through the dark and revved over swells toward black mounds that rose higher from the sea under a navy blue sky.

All seven members of the landing party before Toris leaned against a gunwale—three on each side and Korvyn at the front— watching for trouble. Everyone wore different styles of uniform, but all wore one common piece—a thick band of black paint across their eyes from ear to ear. Markings for a funeral.

Toris followed the compass on his lap due east, occasionally corrected by Korvyn, who sat hunched over the prow with his own navigation set. When they drew nearer to Svalbard's west coast, pink dawnlight over rippling water led him into the Lower Fjord. Before Toris knew it, the black mounds were rising around them as they entered the waterway and followed its north coast. Hills loomed high all around, amplifying the humming motor, so Toris eased off.

Black hills softened to grey as the red band of sunlight rose higher from the horizon. Silhouettes of evergreen trees prickled the rounded hilltops against the indigo sky.

Toris's jaw went slack as he took it all in. He was actually here. A few weeks ago it had only been a dream.

He skirted the north shore to his left up into what was once a dry valley, which invading sea levels had claimed as an extension of the fjord. Beyond the bow, half a mile away, Toris noticed a line where the ripple of soft pink light on water ended and ranks of towering black poles began.

He gave the throttle one last twist to run the boat aground. Rubber groaned over rocks, the landing party dismounted, and together they carried their raiding craft beyond the tide line, setting it in the shrubs at the base of a tree.

Toris joined his team in a defensive semi-circle as rehearsed. On the left flank, he aimed his carbine at the forest rising up a mountain slope, but couldn't keep his gaze from wandering directly above to the treetops spreading in the orange glow of dawn. Redwoods.

A lump formed in his throat as he adjusted Atilus's hat on his head. If only his brother from Khartum could have seen this forest, touched these trees. He rubbed the rough bark of the nearest trunk, Arctic life that had defied certain death, just like his people. Resisters of the same great catastrophe. Allies in their struggle to survive.

Lapping waves and creaking redwoods filled the still dawn air.

Toris pushed a silicone bud into his ear canal. Enough of these short-range radios had been salvaged from *Sea Serpent* to supply half the raiding party.

For five minutes they remained in the semi-circle, still as stones, until the swish of frosty grass announced Rykah's advance. She carried her bolt-action rifle at the ready, with the barrel of the larger AS50 sticking up from the pack on her back. The heavy weapon had to be broken down, with Rykah carrying half of the pieces and Jarik the remaining parts.

The other seven raiders returned to the boat to gather their gear. Toris grabbed two boxes of machine gun ammunition along with Ike, whose torso was wrapped in belts of the linked rounds.

Korvyn gave Rykah a one minute head start to scout ahead, then led the two teams to the intersecting Longyear Valley. Eight Polarians strung out single file through the forest valley of pine and redwood, boots crunching over twigs and occasionally sloshing through a stream or puddle. Drua covered the rear with his heavy machine gun with Ike in front of him. Toris followed third from the rear, behind Macey.

Every ten minutes they each found a tree to hide behind while they stopped to let Rykah scout a blind area ahead. After two hours of this, sweating from nerves and then shivering in the crisp morning air, her precautions were becoming tedious. All Toris wanted was to reach the vault and get this over with. But he dared not object. Rykah knew what she was doing. Instead, he distracted himself by planning his approach to reconnecting with her on the return voyage. There'd be plenty of idle time and not much room to avoid each other.

The Polarian raiders slinked through the quiet forest valley until the swish of lapping water once again rose louder than the creaks of swaying redwoods. Both teams clustered at the base of the western mountain while Rykah and Jarik scrambled up its slope. Jarik's swathed arm limited his shooting ability, but he could still spot for Rykah. Even a guardian angel needed a watcher when in Nordican territory.

Toris closed his eyes and listened to the shifting scree fade above.

Several minutes had passed, maybe fifteen, when Rykah's voice whispered in his earpiece. *"Adarah - in position. I have visual on the fort and the objective below. Fort defences are twenty-foot stone walls on a plateau mountain eight hundred yards west of me. A cleft separates that mountain from my position on the ridge above you. This will be a good firing base for Drua, and if you double back, Korvyn, you can slip down the cleft from the south. But there's a problem."*

"What is it?" said Korvyn over the radio.

"I count a large crowd gathered around the vault entrance."

"How many?" asked Korvyn.

The radio remained silent for a long ten seconds. Then, Rykah delivered the damning news. *"Three hundred unarmed. Looks like they're performing a ritual."*

"We expected this," Korvyn said, giving his team a look of resolve.

"I see little ones," said Rykah. *"Lots of them. Like…half of them are children. Must be some sort of pilgrimage for the younger generation, like when we visit Amyria at age eleven."*

Toris's belly roiled so loud he feared even the Nordicans may hear.

Ike groaned. "Shooting stubborn adults is one thing, but kids?"

This was bad. The group huddled close enough to whisper.

"If we make enough noise," Korvyn said, "the shootout with the fort will scare them away."

"If it doesn't?" Ike said. "Who's eager to shoot up a bunch of children for some seeds? This isn't how I want to get my family name back."

Macey extended both arms to Drua. "Give me the machine gun, Dru. We came too far to lose our nerve now."

Spinner gave Macey an incredulous look. "Shooting pilgrims in a place of worship is bad enough, but children too, Mace?"

"It might be our only way," Korvyn said. He looked to the ridge above and swallowed hard. "Once we secure the high ground, we'll fire warning shots to scatter them. If that doesn't work, well…"

"We got it," Drua said, stroking his machine gun.

Korvyn nodded and pinched the radio switch clipped to his collar. "Adarah, no change to the plan. I'm leading my team into position now. Drua will take his team to set up a firing base on the ridge near you."

Another long silence hung over the radio. Then came Rykah's tense voice. *"Roger."*

Korvyn led Macey and Spinner back the way they'd just come. Drua nodded up the slope to where Rykah and Jarik had disappeared through dwarf conifers. "Let's go, boys. Grab those ammo boxes and follow me."

Ike froze. He gave Toris a bewildered look.

Toris grabbed Drua's vest and pulled him back. "They're *people*, Drua. You're going to shoot a bunch of kids?"

"If it comes down to it, I'd shoot the Sage Abelia herself if it guaranteed to save Polaria." Drua winced at his own claim, but Toris didn't doubt that he'd do whatever he needed to accomplish their mission.

Seeing Toris's reluctance, Drua grabbed both his shoulders. "Think about Jayda, man. If we don't get inside that vault, she'll be kicking in Ortaria's front door a few months from now. No one will ever find out what happens up here. Let whatever you do in these next few minutes haunt you for the rest of your life, but you carry that burden for Jayda. Okay?"

Toris thought about it. Though he loved Jayda more than anyone, could he commit mass murder for her? Even if it was to save her life?

Drua gestured for Ike to start up the hill.

"There's another way," Toris said, trying to stifle his dread. But sitting here now, looking back, it seemed it had been the only way all along.

He handed Drua his carbine and stripped off his vest.

Drua stepped back and gave him a head-to-toe appraisal. "The hell are you doing? We need to get in position to cover Korvyn."

Toris yanked on the seam at his left shoulder to rip the sleeve from his tunic.

Drua's eyes fell on Toris's *O* brand and flared wide. When he opened his mouth to speak, Toris was expecting protest, but instead, Drua pulled a clay block from his vest. Identical to the blocks he'd taken from *Atlas* to trade on the black market.

"You know how to use it?"

Toris accepted the explosive block and nodded. Sallus had shown him in case they needed to turn the *Atlas* and her evidence into splinters.

Drua passed him three stick flares and a green cylinder with a purple cap. Toris recognized the smoke grenade from the pyrate attacks.

"Go make some magic," Drua said. He pinched the button on his collar. "Change of plans, everyone. The Trojan horse is going in."

"Toris, no!" Rykah didn't try to hide her distress.

"It's our only option," Toris said into his mic. As Rykah continued her protest, he yanked the radio receiver from his ear.

As Toris neared the Upper Fjord's shore, soft chatter wafted over the water from the direction of the vault entrance. His heart hammered harder inside his chest, his hands shaking uncontrollably. What if they were impulsive warriors like those who'd killed Atilus?

Though he could sense Rykah watching over him, Toris felt very alone, so he pushed the silicone earpiece back into his ear. "Oshinga is back," he said into the mic. "I hope I didn't miss anything."

Korvyn's voice whispered in his ear. "*Assault Team is in position.*"

"*Firing Base is standing by,*" said Drua. "*You did miss a fair bit of Lieutenant Adarah swearing at you.*"

"*I'm over it,*" she said. "*Everyone stay focused.*"

Rounding the slope in the direction of the vault, Toris said, "I'd welcome a good distraction right now."

A long pause ensued. Then came Rykah's voice. "*So, here we are - at the end.*"

"What happens after the end?" Toris said in his mic, desperate to pull his mind from the danger around the hill ahead.

"*We go home and find a beach,*" Rykah said, "*just like the one we left on Norway. Your cata…cata…*"

"…maran."

"*Right. Catamaran. We'll use it to explore beach after beach until we find one just right.*"

Toris sniffed at the cool morning air. "The sea is a harsh place in winter."

"*Then we'll spend the long night at Lake Nichol. Plenty of game to keep us fed and fat until sunrise. Then we'll hit the water.*"

"Okay," Toris said, his heart beating lighter.

"*Okay.*"

Murmuring grew louder with each step forward. Toris resisted the urge to turn back. The impulse to retreat swelled with each step until he spotted the vault entrance protruding from the mountainside to his left. Then he found himself wandering forward beyond his control as fear yielded to wonder.

Years of rummaging through the Decimators' graves had fostered the expectation that the vault entrance would have fallen into severe disrepair. Seeing a remnant of the old world above water as intended by its creators left him awestruck and lured him closer for a better look.

The tall rectangular entrance remained much like the photo in the reference Lex had discovered, no more than a few decades old. The mass of shifting bodies ahead and their predecessors who'd come before them had no doubt played a role in its preservation. An homage to their sleeping saviour.

"Show time, Oshinga," said Korvyn. *"Just keep your cool."*

As Toris treaded lightly from the rocky shore toward the pilgrims up the slope, his heart thumped harder than it ever had before. A storm raged inside his belly, his heart, his mind. It took great focus to keep his feet moving in a straight line along the slope.

Children playing on the fringe noticed the newcomer first. Squeals of fright erupted, and their retreat into the mass sent a ripple of alarm through the pilgrims. Heads turned to face the intruder approaching the vault.

A brawny Nordican in a goatskin cloak stepped out to meet Toris. Swirling tattoos of faded blue ink covered his face where his white beard did not. His left shoulder hung much lower than the right, at midchest. The elder man stopped to block Toris's way. He stared deep into his eyes, a challenge or an assessment, who knew.

Toris twisted his left shoulder toward him. "I am Oshinga." He cringed at the cracking of his voice, but mustered his courage. "I've come to summon the saviour."

A few from the crowd ventured forward for a closer look, but the elder waved them away. He leaned in to appraise Toris's brand. Skeptical eyes from the crowd watched Toris as the elder conducted his assessment, rough hands feeling his face and working his way down his neck to his chest.

Toris steadied his breathing as unwelcome fingers slid down his belly toward his waist, where the brick of plastic explosives sat in a pouch strapped to his front. Toris grabbed the man's hands and stopped him just before it was too late.

Gasps rose from the crowd. The elder straightened and gave Toris an indignant look. Apparently Toris's actions were some slight to the Nordican culture. Was interrupting an appraisal taboo? Or was it the touching of an elder without permission that jarred them? Whatever the reason, Toris didn't care. He wasn't here to make friends.

"What's going on here?" A man sporting a black longcoat forced his way through the crowd. Aside from rotted black teeth, he was otherwise 'untainted'. Upon seeing Toris, he halted his advance and unslung his rifle. "What's your business here?"

Toris stared at the assault rifle with trepidation. "I've come to see the vault."

"Well, you've seen it," said the gunman impatiently.

Toris shifted uncomfortably. He cleared his throat. "I'm here to see the *inside*."

The guard clicked the safety lever on his rifle. "Emperor Khalid made it clear your type aren't to step foot on this island."

The pilgrims watched nervously, some translating to the non-English speakers.

Toris's heart pounded against his chest wall. He straightened his arms at his sides and stuck out his chest. "I am Oshinga," he said proudly. The guard frowned. "The Summoner," Toris clarified.

The guard nodded knowingly. "Ah, another tribal prophet. Been a while since we had one come around." He lowered his weapon. "What do you need to do? Throw some dust on the door? Chant some nonsense and dance in circles?"

It hadn't occurred to Toris that the Oshinga Prophecy might be regional, possibly restricted to the small stretches of coast that Jorda's fleet had once traded with. Which explained the skepticism on so many faces before him.

Toris patted the pouch at his waist. "My ceremony involves the placement of a talisman at the base of the doorway. Then I'll need everyone to step back while I recite the sacred words, words meant only for the saviour's ears."

The guardian stepped closer for a better look at Toris's face. "Where are you from?"

"A far away land. You wouldn't have heard of it."

The guard looked over his shoulder to the fort above. Toris had been so captivated by the vault that he hadn't noticed the grey walls crowning the flat mountaintop until now.

The crowd grew restless. The guardian looked back to Toris and said, "Make it quick."

Toris wasted no time. As he walked forward, the crowd parted to make a path for him. The rectangular entrance loomed nearly twenty feet above his head. He stopped within arm's reach of the double doors, upon which a giant red line slashed a red circle, similar to the brand on his arm.

Keeping his elbows tight to his sides, he pulled the clay block from his waist pouch. The entrance did not appear as fortified as he'd been expecting, so he twisted the block in half. He crouched at the seam between both doors and fixed half the block against the sill, then jammed a blasting cap into the plastic explosive, from which a cord strung to the detonator in his waist pouch. With everything set, he stood and stepped back from the doors while gently unspooling the line. To the onlookers it hopefully appeared as if he were praying with both hands at his belly.

A glance over his shoulder revealed the crowd standing firm, so Toris threw both hands into the air and yelled, "Back away! Make way for the saviour who stirs now from his slumber!"

Pilgrims tripped over each other as the crowd edge peeled back.

Toris continued his backward shuffle, inching his way to a safe firing distance.

"Couple more feet to go," Rykah said through his earpiece. Her voice soothed Toris's nerves. With his world reduced to the vault

door and cord before him, he'd forgotten she was there watching over him.

"Stop!"

Toris froze.

Shale crunched under the guard's boots as he circled to Toris's front. Once again Toris found himself staring down the barrel of that assault rifle. The guard kept the weapon aimed as his gaze traced the firing cord back to the block on the door. His furious eyes snapped back to Toris. "Hands up!"

Toris felt the detonator through his waist pouch. One squeeze promised to turn this guard's whole world upside down. But he'd not be the only casualty. The crowd stood only feet away, with curious children making up their forward ranks.

"Toris, you're in my way," Rykah said. *"I don't have a clear shot."*

The guard thrust his rifle forward. "Hands up! Now!"

Toris raised his hands and stepped aside to open a clear line of fire for Rykah. The guard shifted with him, eyes scanning the surrounding hills nervously. Khalid's vault guardians were well trained.

"Still don't have a shot," Rykah said. *"Korvyn, you're up."*

The ground shook as an explosion rumbled from atop the mountain. A steady rattle of machine gun fire shattered the morning calm as green tracer rounds zipped from the ridge on Toris's left to the fort above.

The guard watched the firefight in shock. Toris snatched his rifle and butt stroked him with it. He then stripped the weapon down as best he could and tossed the pieces aside.

He rushed at the edge of the crowd, who paid him little mind as they shuffled backward, eyes fixed on the spectacle above. Tracer rounds of blue, green and red lit up the mountaintop as gunfire zipped in both directions between the stone walls and the ridge to the east of the plateau mountain. Somewhere in the cleft between both slopes, Korvyn was leading his team in a rush toward the fort.

Toris faced the crowd and threw up both arms. "Behold, your saviour awakens!"

He crouched with his hands over his ears and squeezed the detonator. The blast was instantaneous, rocking the ground and launching a wave of debris at his back. When the pelting stopped, he looked over his shoulder to where a cloud of smoke obscured the vault entrance.

He bolted toward the fountain of debris. Both doors lay crumpled and smoking on the ground to both sides of the entrance. Toris gagged from the sulphur smell as he crossed the dusty threshold.

Inside, he dropped the smoke grenade to the floor. A purple cloud filled the corridor and spilled out the entrance, a supernatural fog that should deter any pilgrim from following. He struck a stick flare and tossed it into the abyss of the rectangular entrance hall. The orange glow in the purple haze produced a mystical effect. *Magic.*

Toris wiped his brow and rejoiced. He made it.

FORTY-TWO

Whoosh—a fountain of sparks sent the darkness retreating down the tunnel as Toris held a newly-struck flare before him. He treaded carefully into the abyss, veering left toward a curved wall of rusted tin to avoid a mess of cable trays and broken lights littering the concrete floor.

Clattering gunfire faded as he advanced deeper under the mountain. He held the flare out as far as his arm allowed, pushing the darkness farther ahead. If memory served him right, the reference had described this tunnel as over four hundred feet long. With a floor sloping deeper into the abyss and a battle raging above, it seemed as if the passage led all the way to the underworld of the Old Greeks.

Toris pushed the darkness from his mind and advanced.

Through a doorway, the tunnel of rounded walls became a rectangular corridor. A few hundred feet down this passageway, the forward edge of the flare's orange glow crossed through a doorway and expanded across a void beyond. Toris stopped in the threshold of this cross tunnel. In the flickering light, three doorways stood facing him from the opposite wall—one to his right and two to his left.

Feeling the heat from the shortening flare on his hand, Toris flung the stick to the floor.

Static crackled in his ear. He thought he heard his name but wasn't sure. It didn't matter. He was at the end. No turning back.

He struck his last flare. Fifteen minutes of light was all it offered, so he hurried to the far right doorway. The door fell forward at his touch and slammed onto the floor. Inside the room, steel racks standing twice his height stretched across the chamber to the far wall. Orange flare light washed over their empty shelves.

Toris's throat tightened.

He moved on to the middle chamber and found the same— empty shelves from front to back. He stopped outside the third and final vault on the far left and took a deep breath. This was Polaria's last chance.

He stepped into the doorway and held the flare stick out before him.

Empty.

That's when it hit him. That red paint on the entrance doors wasn't the prophetic symbol of a saviour. He'd seen it during trade school. A circle cut by a forward slash meant *empty set*. Whoever withdrew the seeds must have marked the door to denote an empty vault.

He wandered inside anyway. Drifting between rows of rusted steel, he scanned the shelves for even a single seed.

Nothing.

At the end he leaned back against the rough cavern wall and slid down to the floor, all hope crashing with him. For a while all he could do was listen to his own breath mocking him in the cavernous space. Then it was more than his own.

Across the room, Jarik appeared hunched over in the doorway catching his breath. "Rykah sent me," he gasped. "*Seekers*...lots of them...getting close."

Toris pulled his knees to his chest. He couldn't muster the courage to leave this vault empty-handed. How could he tell Lex her brother died for a few rows of dusty shelves? This was his fault. Good Polarians gave their lives for his fool's errand.

Jarik wandered inside, his eyes taking stock of the empty shelves. "It was all for nothing," he said. In a frenzy, he aimed his pistol at Toris. "You led us here for *this*?"

Toris hung his head, undaunted by the threat of the pistol. Part of him welcomed the swift end.

Seeing Toris's apathy, Jarik leaned against a shelf and slid to the floor. His sobs echoed loud in the chamber. A few minutes of this passed. When he had enough, he stuck the pistol into his mouth and feathered the trigger.

Toris's instinct was to sit up straight and try to stop him, but why? Die in here or out there, or starve to death back home, it was all the same outcome except with less suffering.

The pistol shook in Jarik's hand. Toris considered what words to say, but only lies could offer comfort. They were doomed. What right did he have to try to prolong Jarik's misery?

Gunfire snapped in the corridor nearby, crisp and sharp. As if jolting from a trance, Jarik crawled to the doorway and aimed outside, but his pistol remained silent. Gunfire persisted, but who were they shooting at?

A tremor shook the wall behind Toris. Dust stirred from the shelves. He stood and pressed his ear to the wall. Blasts from above shouldn't vibrate so far through the mountain. Nor should the muffled gunfire he now heard.

He held the flare before the wall, sweeping its light in search of inconsistencies.

Seamless.

He leaped over Jarik in the doorway and returned to the middle chamber. At the back of the room he held the flare to the wall. From floor to head height, a dark patch marked the rockface. This section that stretched double arm width across was not part of the original construct.

From his waist pouch he pulled the leftover explosive. Jarik's demands to retreat faded into the background as Toris stuck the block onto the middle of the discoloured patch. He drove a blasting cap into the clay-like surface and joined Jarik outside the doorway, where he covered his ears and squeezed the detonator.

A deafening boom blew dust and smoke into the cross tunnel. The blast left Toris's ears ringing worse than ever, but he didn't let it faze him.

Toris was first in. A swirling cloud of smoke and dust smothered his flare light and devoured Jarik's flashlight beam. He pressed forward blindly, mouth and nose buried into the crook of his elbow to avoid choking back too many particulates. He stumbled over piles of rubble until reaching a hole in the false wall. A threshold. Here, his foot landed on something soft.

He lowered his flare to illuminate a hand sticking out from the debris.

The remains were shrouded in a black longcoat similar to that of the guard outside. It lay between two shelf rows, though not those of the chamber where Toris had placed the explosive.

A rock wall three feet thick divided the shelving units of this chamber from that of the newly exposed cavern. Both had a similar layout with the exception of one striking difference: every shelf in the next room was packed with boxes.

A hand grabbed Toris's shoulder. He turned to see Jarik smiling, eyes absorbing the marvellous sight before them. His expression of wonder must have mirrored Toris's own.

Gunfire cracked from the far end of the cavern. Jarik aimed his pistol over Toris's shoulder, and Toris wished he'd kept the entrance guard's assault rifle.

Two vault guardians rushed into the chamber before Toris. Upon seeing the Polarians in the blown-out wall, one levelled his assault rifle with Toris's chest.

Jarik pulled the trigger but his pistol jammed. Toris raised both hands as Jarik shrivelled behind him.

The nearest gunman pulled his trigger. Toris jumped at the *click*. As the guardian reloaded his rifle, something behind drew his partner's attention. He stuck his head back out the doorway they'd just come through—*CRACK*—and lost it in a bloody explosion. His body toppled forward into the corridor.

The remaining guard finished reloading and swung around to aim over his fallen partner's body.

Through the doorway, green beams of light cut through the smoky corridor—two overlapping each other in erratic movements. Then came the source of these lasers, black figures stalking silent as shadows past the doorway, heads tilted over their firearms and knees bent slightly to soften their steps. One turned left into the vault.

The guardian opened fire—*pop-pop-pop!* One shot slammed into the intruder's torso.

Toris tackled the guard to the floor, slipped his forearm in front of his foe's throat, and pushed down into the back of his neck to crush his trachea as Rykah had taught him.

He recovered the enemy's rifle but, when he looked up, he was faced with a black figure standing in the doorway behind his fallen comrade. A green dot slid across the shelves and settled on Toris's chest, where it danced like an excited wasp, ready to sting.

"It's Toris!" gasped Macey from the ground. It was she who'd taken the guardian's bullet. She pulled off her cap to reveal her short mohawk.

Korvyn lowered his weapon in the doorway and relaxed his shoulders. Seeing Jarik and Toris must have brought him to the same conclusion as them. To protect the seeds from the *Seekers*, Khalid had them transferred to a new facility and sealed up the old, creating a new entrance accessible only from the fort above.

Korvyn knelt beside Macey, who remained slumped against a bottom shelf. "You hit?" he said.

She waved the dust from before her face. "Just catching my breath," she said, then pulled a broken magazine from her vest. "How's Spinner?"

"Looks like he stopped the bleeding. Good thing we don't need to get him back up those stairs." Korvyn stood and pointed to the doorway beyond Toris. "Our extraction point is at the end of that tunnel."

"That's a problem," Jarik said. "You get Adarah's report about the swarm of armed Nordicans moving toward the entrance?"

"How many?"

"Fifty, I'd say."

"Won't be the first time we shot our way out of a corner," Macey said. She grabbed a shelf and pulled herself to her feet.

"Go keep lookout," Korvyn told her.

Macey squeezed between the gathered Polarians and staggered toward the vault entrance.

Korvyn swung a duffle from his back and zipped it open to reveal several more bags folded inside. "Everyone grab two. Whatever is on the list takes priority, then stuff whatever else you can fit. Each bag has a copy of that list.

The three men worked their way down the shelves, comparing the names on their lists to the writing on each plastic tote and wooden crate.

Spinner limped through the doorway. A red blotch stained a white bandage around his knee. He slumped down against a shelf and cried out in agony.

The seed team continued down the shelves, stuffing the bags until they required two sets of hands to close each zipper. When each bag was bulging with seeds they piled them all together—twelve in total—between the shelves of the original storage chamber.

Korvyn gave the bags a satisfied nod. "Nice work," he said. He turned an ear toward an escalating firefight echoing down the tunnel. "We turned the 'can opener' to scrap metal. Drua stayed up top to keep a lid on the fort. All we have to do now is clear the entrance and summon *Barnacle*, then come back for the bags. Spinner, you're good to guard the stash?"

Spinner smiled and raised a shaky thumb.

A fierce firefight raged at the vault entrance. The deafening roar echoed down the tunnel as Macey exchanged fire with *Seekers* hiding in the entry hall. Though she had the advantage of darkness on her end, plus the silhouettes in the entrance presenting easy targets, her muzzle flash gave her location away. So she lay on her belly, shooting and then rolling across the tunnel to change her firing position.

Toris followed Korvyn up the tunnel into the fray. When Korvyn opened fire nearby, the noise became way past too much, but it didn't hold Toris back. He joined Korvyn in kneeling beside Macey and together their three assault rifles, along with Jarik's pistol, blasted the silhouettes at the entrance, chipping away their hiding places beside the doorway. This volley of gunfire erupting from the darkness forced the surviving *Seekers* back outside, where machine gun fire from the fort above cut them down.

As the gunfire tapered, the ringing in Toris's ears grew louder in its place.

Korvyn crept forward with his weapon trained on the jagged rectangle of light one hundred feet away. Toris followed to his left with Macey on their right and Jarik bringing up the rear. The glow from the rectangular hole of light at the end of the tunnel grew larger and brighter in their advance.

At the entry hall, Korvyn directed Toris to the left wall with Macey against the right, each kneeling and aiming crossways out the front door. Korvyn knelt in the corner before Toris and pinched his collar.

"Adarah, we have the package," said Korvyn into his mic. "Are we clear for extract?"

Rykah's response was muffled in Toris's ear. *"Looks like Drua swept away the last of the* Seekers. *Might be a few hiding in the hills among the pilgrims, but they shouldn't be a problem. I'd call it clear."*

Macey lowered her rifle and stood, prompting Toris to do the same. In a most shocking turn of events, she offered him a thumbs up along with a hint of a smile.

"Any casualties?" Rykah said.

Korvyn smirked at Toris and pressed his ear. "Toris is fine. Drua, send the signal."

Toris imagined a green flare streaking high from the fort above to summon Captain Antlia.

"Toris, Macey, go fetch the seeds," Korvyn said.

Macey punched Toris's shoulder. "Race ya!"

Toris and Macey sprinted past Jarik down the tunnel. From inside the deeper vault, Spinner watched as they each loaded a bag onto their back, strapped one to their front, and carried one in each hand for a total load of eight bags between them. Jarik arrived and loaded what he could with his good arm.

From the entrance hall doorway, Korvyn tossed three smoke grenades out onto the shore. In addition to guiding the *Barnacle* to their exact location in the Upper Fjord, the screen would provide Korvyn's team cover between the vault entrance and the shoreline. But this seemed a bit premature to Toris.

As Macey's footsteps faded down the tunnel to gather the last load of seeds, a humming over the water drew Toris to join Korvyn at the outer doorway. Through fleeting gaps in the smoke screen, he saw a small boat skimming top speed over waves.

"That was fast," Toris noted.

"You won't hear me complain," Korvyn said, hefting a duffel bag onto his back and setting one to either side of him in the doorway.

Toris leaned out for a better look at the approaching rubber raiding craft. The boat was to shuttle the seeds back to the *Barnacle*, but the trawler was nowhere in sight.

Toris pressed his radio talk button. "Drua," he said into his mic. "Do you have a visual on the *Barnacle*?"

"Negative, but your smoke is blowing in my way. I can't see much of the fjord west of here."

Korvyn stood and frowned at the raiding craft speeding toward shore. As it drew closer it failed to slow even the slightest. Instead, it ran aground at full speed. A figure flew through the red smoke and rolled several feet up the slope. Undaunted by the impact,

Jorda scrambled across the remaining ground to the vault entrance. She dove for cover into the vault entrance despite no opposition.

Korvyn helped her stand. "Where's the *Barnacle*?"

Jorda pointed west toward the fjord entrance.

"Are they close?" Toris said.

Jorda shook her head. "Coast Patrol! Lady Lex sent me to warn ya."

Toris's whole body went numb.

Korvyn leaned out the door, then immediately recoiled. "Fall back!"

Toris snapped out of it. He risked a peek out the door and saw through the thinning red cloud the *Sea Serpent* cruising toward the vault. That was all the fright he needed for one day.

He dragged two duffel bags back into the tunnel. Jorda did the same, with Korvyn and Jarik right behind her. Korvyn dropped his bags and ran back to the entrance for the remaining two.

A familiar thudding thundered outside. As Korvyn bent to pick up the duffels, fountains of dirt kicked up the shore outside in a line that swept toward the entrance. A stream of .50 caliber rounds exploded through the concrete walls before Korvyn's face.

Toris stumbled backward over two flailing bodies as the vault entrance collapsed, sealing out the light and leaving them in total darkness.

FORTY-THREE

Hands patted Toris's body in the dark. He swatted them away in a coughing fit.

"You okay?" asked Macey.

"I'll survive," Toris said, hacking up dust from his lungs. Had he been unconscious? In the dark it was hard to tell if he'd missed time between the entrance collapse and Macey's hands prodding him through the void.

"I'm fine, too," said Jorda nearby. "In case you were wonderin'."

A man coughing behind suggested Jarik was at least still breathing.

The four huddled close, warm bodies a comfort in the smothering abyss.

"Korvyn," said Macey, her voice cracking. "He..."

Muffled machine gun fire rumbled like a ceaseless thunderstorm from outside. No doubt Clavilla had all his guns now trained on the fort above.

Toris stood. In the dark he wasn't sure if he was falling or standing straight. A soft white glow suggested the direction of the vault.

"Everyone grab two bags," he said. "We need to join Drua up top."

"What if the *Sea Serpent* blew them up already?" said Macey, panic swelling in her voice.

"I think they lost all their big guns off Norway," Toris said. Though that was merely a guess, entertaining Macey's fear was not the best action to take right now.

Toris felt the ground blindly. When each hand located the double straps of a duffel bag, he bunched them in his hands and lifted, then staggered down the corridor toward the soft glow of artificial light. Footsteps and dragging followed. He bumped into the left wall and corrected himself, thinking he was running straight until he tripped over cable trays. The clatter was deafening.

Beyond the doorway ahead, dim white light grew brighter and beckoned them deeper under the mountain. Toris followed it to Spinner inside the center vault, whose muzzle flashlight had served as their beacon in the dark.

"What happened?" he said. His bewildered expression suggested Toris looked worse than he felt.

Toris dropped the bags. "That way is a dead end," he said. "We need to get these seeds topside. I'll send a stretcher down for you and the rest of the bags."

Spinner glanced nervously into the darkness down the tunnel. Macey knelt and squeezed his hand. "I won't leave you," she said.

"I'll help him," Jarik offered. "You can still put weight on one leg?"

Spinner nodded and accepted Jarik's help in standing.

As they'd done to shuttle the bags to the entrance, Toris wore one over his back and another on his front while carrying one in each hand. Jorda and Macey did the same.

Outside the room, Toris stepped over bodies. Dry blood stuck to his feet as he moved toward a set of silo stairs. The ring of boots on steel rose steadily up the spiral stairwell. From below, Spinner's groans and protests echoed up, growing louder despite he and

Jarik obviously falling behind by the look of their flashlight beam below.

A steady thunder grew louder the higher Toris climbed until he could hardly hear his own laboured breathing. At the top of the stairwell, three walls of polished stone welcomed Toris to surface, with an opening that faced a courtyard surrounded by similar grey walls.

Toris squinted in the daylight and rejoiced in its warmth on his face.

In the open air the thunder sounded close, but not close enough to be coming from the fort. Toris was relieved to see Drua atop the northern rampart overlooking the fjord. On the opposite wall, Ike kept watch to the south. A hole in the east wall revealed where Korvyn's team had breached the fort.

Drua howled and fist pumped behind his machine gun. "Yeah! Give 'em hell, Rykah! Pour it on them! Sink those slimy snakes!"

Behind Drua, a set of stairs rose diagonally up the wall to the rampart lining the top. Toris was up there before the rest of his team arrived from the silo stairs. Piles of spent shell casings and links littered the ramparts all around.

From atop the wall Toris saw red tracers zip toward the fjord from the ridge to his right. Below, the *Sea Serpent* took a beating from Rykah's AS50 with little grace. Incendiary rounds from the heavy sniper rifle had already punched through the bridge's bulkheads and left the roof slanted toward the foredeck so that anyone inside could not see forward. But Rykah didn't stop there. Now she blasted away plates at the starboard bow with a steady pounding of single shots—*BOOM, BOOM, BOOM*—blasting devastation into Clavilla's ship.

Toris joined Drua by breaking into a cheer. Everyone on that ship was here to see that Polarians back home starved. They'd come to force Anterra into war, so they deserved the punishment Rykah was delivering them. And punish them she did. She unloaded on them until the Polarian battleship listed to starboard, tipping toward land and exposing her top decks to the fort.

The *Sea Serpent* was dead.

The echo of Rykah's last shot travelled far over Svalbard's mountains in every direction. When it faded, a welcome silence settled over the seed vault.

The calm did not last.

Moaning rose from the courtyard below. Toris turned to see Spinner limping from the silo stairs, sagging against a struggling Jarik. Macey dropped her duffel bags in the center of the courtyard and rushed to help Spinner sit. He flopped onto his back, barely able to lift his head.

"There are more seeds below," Toris said to Drua.

Drua nodded absently and pinched his collar. "Nice work, Lieutenant. Jorda's landing craft still looks good to go. We'll use it to shuttle the seeds out to *Barnacle*."

"*Agreed!*" yelled Rykah into the radio. Clearly the gunfire had rendered her near deaf. "*Can you give me a casualty report yet?*"

"Korvyn is dead," Toris told Drua, who passed on the message to Rykah, adding a wounded Spinner to the record.

"*And Toris? Have you seen him?*"

Hearing Rykah's voice say his name, her concern for him, made his heart swell. Had anyone ever been so concerned about his well-being?

"He's right beside me," Drua said into his radio.

Rykah sighed into her radio. "*Get those seeds ready to move. I'm coming over!*"

Drua cast a sweeping gaze all around. "Roger. Looks like you have a clear lane to us."

"*Make sure it stays that way!*"

"Give us a minute to shift our firing positions," Drua said into the radio. "Macey, Ike, Jorda, get below and bring up the rest of those seeds. Jarik, load what's there onto a stretcher." He unslung Toris's carbine from his back and handed it to him. "Take Ike's spot on the south wall. If any *Seekers* are out there, that's the only other angle they can hit her from."

Drua lugged his machine gun toward the east wall with Toris

in tow. "When she gets here," Drua explained, "you'll take that landing craft back to the *Barnacle*." He planted the machine gun's bipod on the east parapet to cover the ridge at Rykah's back. "Tell Antlia not to worry about the *Serpent*. If any survivors dare stick their heads up, we'll see they lose them. Once he's here, you'll shuttle the seeds over to *Barnacle*, then come back for us. I'll have everyone up here keeping watch over you."

"Got it," Toris said, checking to ensure his carbine was loaded and ready to fire. He continued around the wall to cover the south.

Drua's voice whispered in his ear: *"You're clear to move, Lieutenant. We got you covered."*

Kneeling among Ike's spent shotgun shells behind the south parapet, Toris scanned the forested hills south and west for movement, for someone who may mistake Rykah for an easy target. But he couldn't keep his gaze from wandering left, to where an exposed Rykah slid down into the cleft with her massive sniper rifle cradled in her arms.

His heart fluttered in his ears in a way it never had before. His hearing must have been coming back full force, because the fluttering was getting louder. Oddly enough, it was out of rhythm with the beating in his chest. Then it hit him. His heart stopped dead cold, long enough to hear the flutter was actually rapid thudding, too fast for any creature's heartbeat. He had heard this noise before. Back on Norway.

He squeezed his radio mic. "Rykah! Take cover!"

Rykah slid to a stop midway down the slope across the cleft. Her head swivelled in all directions in search of the reason for Toris's warning. Then she must have heard it, too, because she looked to the southern hills just as a black mass appeared in the clear morning sky.

The *chopper* swept straight toward the fort, unleashing a maelstrom of bullets onto its walls. Toris dropped to the rampart floor and rolled close to the parapet. Drua fired a long burst until the hail of bullets forced him onto his side.

The thudding grew to pounding as the metal beast flew overhead.

Toris rolled onto his back and fired at the steel belly on automatic until the magazine emptied. His bullets clattered off the *chopper*'s plated exterior to no effect. Down the wall, Drua lay on his back firing upward until the machine gun belt jammed.

Toris tried to keep a lid on his terror as the flying beast swept brazenly over the fort. At least he had cover.

Through a slit in the rampart, he saw Rykah had fallen onto her bottom on the slope. She levelled her AS50 barrel with the thudding skycraft, resting the butt into her hip, and released three carefully-aimed shots. The rounds zipped wide, her aim clearly inhibited by the weight of the weapon and the high angle of her target.

The chopper circled the fort counter-clockwise. Machine guns roared from its port side flank and blasted away chunks from the ramparts over Toris and Drua, whittling down their cover. As the thudding sky machine looped around the north wall, Toris lay exposed on the opposite rampart.

His whole body tensed in anticipation for the burst of hot lead that would tear him to pieces. And that's no doubt how his life would have ended if not for a red streak sparking off the *chopper*'s tail and sending it into a spin.

Smoke streamed from the machine's hindside. The beast steadied itself but bobbed and listed at random. Gunfire continued to rain from its flanks but was more chaotic than accurate. It settled into an eastward course over Rykah and beyond. A tail of black smoke strung out over the ridge and circled down toward the Longyear Valley.

Toris listened for a crash. Instead, the thudding slowed and tapered as it had upon arriving in the Nordican village. The *chopper* had landed safely.

"Rykah, get over here," Toris said into his radio mic. *Come to me*, he wanted to say.

Rykah had watched the chopper descend beyond the trees above her, to where her gaze now remained.

Toris's heart drummed an ominous beat. He squeezed his radio mic. "Rykah..."

She yanked out her earpiece and charged up the hill, much to Toris's dismay.

"She's going to finish off that...that flying devil!" Drua said in awe.

But Rykah was not the only person racing to that hilltop. Just as she reached eye level with the ridge crest, a black-clad figure appeared among the trees above her. Both already had their weapons at the ready, but the enemy soldier pulled his trigger first. The bullet struck Rykah in the chest.

Toris clutched at his own heart as if the bullet had hit him. He watched, breathless, as Rykah rolled back down the slope.

Rage. That was all Toris felt toward the soldier lining up another shot at Rykah rolling defenselessly toward the cleft bottom. Blinding and all-consuming rage took over. At the east wall, he shoved Drua away from his machine gun and fired a long burst at the ridge line, thirty shots at least, before the weapon jammed. Toris ripped back on the cocking handle to clear it and then resumed firing with a longer burst.

Drua grabbed his shoulder. "You got him!"

It was true. Toris had witnessed two bullets punch into his target's torso. Though, someone should have told the soldier that, because he was back on his feet a second later.

"Body armour," Drua hissed.

Toris sent another burst across the cleft. This time the soldier found cover behind a tree. As Toris aimed, waiting for a clear shot, more black figures appeared on the ridge sporting similar armour. Khalid's elite shock troops.

Muzzle flashes sparked from the tree line atop the ridge, half a dozen spread above Rykah.

Toris abandoned the machine gun and rolled down off the wall into the courtyard. As he wobbled to his feet, Drua landed on top of him and pinned him to the ground.

"The hell happened here?" said Macey at the entrance to the silo stairs. She dropped two black duffels and surveyed the long seams of bullet holes that scarred the inner stone walls.

Drua pointed to the east wall. "Macey, get up on the machine gun and put some fire on that ridge. Watch out for Adarah. She's on the slope."

Macey scampered up the rampart stairs. A second later, the machine gun was ripping away in controlled bursts.

"Get off me!" Toris said, struggling to no avail under Drua's mount.

Instead, Drua pinned both of Toris's arms to the ground. "You go out there and you'll end up dead like..." Drua caught himself. His jaw went slack.

Toris exploded upward, but not enough to knock the mighty Drua off balance.

"She's moving!" said Macey from above.

Drua crawled off Toris to the crumbled edge of the blasted-open east wall. Toris joined him, leaning over his shoulder for a better look outside the hole.

On the slope across the cleft, Rykah dug under her vest and prodded where the bullet had hit. Toris pulled Drua's binoculars from around his neck and watched as Rykah winced in pain and withdrew her fingers. No blood. Hopefully just a broken rib at worst. It appeared a magazine in her vest had absorbed the brunt of the force as had happened to Macey.

Drua punched Toris's shoulder. "See, she's okay."

Gunshots crackled from the ridge above her. Tracer rounds zipped from the fort in response. Rocks exploded on the slope above Rykah, prompting her to shield her face from deflected debris.

She grimaced as she rocked herself to a sitting position.

"Rykah, are you okay?" Toris said into his radio.

She sat up straighter. She stuck her earpiece back into her ear and pressed the radio key. *"Just got the wind knocked out of me. Tell Drua to cease firing on the crest above me."*

"Cease fire!" Toris yelled up to Macey.

The machine gun fell silent.

"There's half a dozen soldiers there, Rykah. They're a different breed than the *Seekers* and fort guards. They have body armour and heavy weapons. I think they came from that aircraft."

"Roger that," she said. *"I'll take care of those pricks."*

She stripped her AS50 and flung the pieces in different directions, stuffing the bolt into her vest. She unslung the .303 bolt-action from her back, fixed her seventeen-inch bayonet to its muzzle, and crawled up toward the snapping gunfire.

When thirty feet from Khalid's shooters, she pulled two grenades from her vest. Holding one in each hand, she used the index finger of the opposite hand to pull both pins simultaneously. She lobbed the first grenade over the crest and the second immediately after, then tucked her chin to her chest and covered her ears.

A double blast launched splinters and smoke into the air. Before the debris cloud reached its full height, Rykah was charging into it. She plunged her bayonet at the ground. A black-clad arm clawed at her leg, then flopped back down. Rykah twisted her bayonet free, swept the ground before her, then fell against a tree. She slid down the trunk and sat upon its roots facing the fort.

Toris breathed a sigh of relief. "Okay, Rykah," he said into his radio. "Get over here and I'll go fetch the *Barnacle*." He wasn't leaving until she was safe inside the fort.

Rykah leaned her head back against the tree trunk. *"Negative,"* she said into her radio. *"That landing craft is out of action."*

Toris clambered up the rampart steps and leaned over the north parapet. His heart sank upon seeing shreds of black rubber strewn about the beach, no doubt courtesy of the *chopper*. To further diminish their victory, the shock troopers Rykah had just elimi-nated were not alone in the hills. Gunfire crackled from south down the ridge. Bullets cracked the fort's stone walls and blasted bark from the trees around Rykah.

Toris dropped to his knees. It seemed Svalbard's seeds were never meant to leave the sacred tomb below.

"Toris, I need to speak with Drua."

"I'm here, ma'am," came Drua's voice. He watched anxiously from the hole in the east wall. *"What do you need?"*

Rykah keyed her mic. She breathed heavily into the airwaves for a few seconds, then said, *"Take the seeds and the wounded to the alternate extract."*

Drua frowned up at Toris in confusion before responding. "Alternate?"

"The raiding craft back at our landing site - it's our only way out of here. I'll meet you there."

Toris squeezed his radio mic to speak but, as if anticipating his protest, Rykah beat him to it. *"There are too many shooters up here. I'll lead them away and meet you at the boat. Call me when you get there. Adarah, out."*

Toris watched in horror as Rykah removed her earpiece and flung it aside.

Drua peeled himself away from the hole in the wall. "Load those seeds onto stretchers! We're moving out!"

Risking rifle fire from the hills, Toris stood atop the east parapet. He cupped his hands over his mouth and yelled, "Rykah!"

She either didn't hear him over the surrounding gunfire or was ignoring him as she stripped her vest. Through Drua's binoculars, Toris watched as she rose to a knee, slung a bandolier of .303 ammunition over each shoulder so they hung in an X across her chest, then scooted along the ridge in a crouched run.

"She's on the move," said Macey from behind the machine gun.

Watching Rykah charge at the enemy, firing single shots which drew exponentially more fire in return, Toris had only felt so helpless once in his life: when the Coast Patrol drafted Jayda for Defence Service.

FORTY-FOUR

Distant gunfire pattered, not a single shot meant for the fort.

Toris leaped from the ramparts and bolted for the hole in the wall. Drua snatched his collar and hauled him back. Toris whirled about and wrapped his arms around Drua's waist, then flipped him onto his back as Rykah had taught him aboard the *Polaris*.

Drua's shocked expression struck Toris with what he'd just done. No Onero had ever taken down Lake Orion's toughest fighter. Toris remained over him, hand clutching his vest, anticipating Drua's retaliation to restore dominance.

Drua, however, remained flat on his back. "Come on, Toris. I need my brother with me on this."

"Rykah needs me more."

Drua glanced at the surviving vault raiders in the center of the courtyard. "Look around, man. I can't get these seeds out without you. Then all this'll have been for nothing. Think of Jayda. Think of *all* our brothers and sisters gathering at the border to invade Ortaria. When the sun sets this winter, that'll be the last time many of them ever see the light of day."

Toris assessed the remaining team in the courtyard. They were in worse shape than he'd assumed. Jarik and Jorda were each still catching their breath from the exhausting second climb up those silo stairs. Spinner lay on a stretcher, oblivious to anything going on around him. Ike was trying to stack all the bags onto one stretcher and failing.

Toris offered Drua a hand and helped him to his feet.

"It's working," said Macey from the rampart. "She's got a big fan club on her ass."

Toris rubbed the back of his neck in distress. Of course it was working. Khalid's shock troops didn't have a chance at taking the fort by force, so their best shot was to capture a hostage.

"Who's got smoke?" asked Drua.

Ike pulled a bandolier of smoke grenades from a dropped pack on the ground.

Drua nodded. "Get up on the wall and lay a smoke screen over this whole mountaintop."

"We can't fit all the seeds onto one stretcher," Jarik said. "We need another."

Spinner rolled off his stretcher with a groan. Seeing this, Macey jumped down from the wall and slid on her knees to his side.

"You won't make it to the Lower Fjord with all the seeds *and* me," Spinner said.

Macey wasn't having it. She lifted his legs and tried dragging him back onto the stretcher. His wailing stopped her, so she dropped to his side and clasped both his hands in hers. "If you stay I'm stayin' too," she said, tears streaming down her cheeks.

Spinner's eyes glazed with tears. "Don't do this, Mace. Not now."

"I ain't leaving ya, Spin. And without me they won't have enough hands to carry out the seeds anyway, so what difference does it make? Now get your stubborn arse on that stretcher so we can make a mile."

Spinner's expression suggested he held no doubts about her will to follow through on her threat to stay. So, with Macey's help, he slid back onto the stretcher. She hurried to strap him on before he could change his mind.

Toris didn't need to see such devotion right now. Not when he already felt sick at allowing Rykah to run off alone.

"Everyone, marshal up," Drua said from the head of Spinner's stretcher. He directed each member to their place in the marching order. Ike was to help Drua carry Spinner. Toris and Jorda were assigned the stretcher piled high with bags of seeds—six in total. Whoever carried the back of a stretcher also had to carry a black duffel on his back. Even their point and rear guards, Jarik and Macey respectively, were not spared this burden.

"Everyone ready?" Drua said.

Toris lifted his stretcher with Jorda at the front end. The top-heavy load of bags wobbled, but they got it under control for the moment. Luckily the pile had been strapped in.

Jarik waited at the hole in the east wall, shifting the bag on his back while practicing aiming his pistol with his one good hand.

"Move out," Drua ordered.

The smoke screen outside was so thick that Toris became disoriented when they charged from the safety of the fort. Jarik immediately disappeared into the swirling haze of green, purple, and red, so Toris kept his focus on the hulking black bag rocking side to side on Drua's back.

He lowered his head and hunched his shoulders despite the weight of the loaded stretcher, awaiting the crack of nearby gunfire. But as they crossed the plateau mountaintop, all he heard was smoke *hiss* from the canisters and Polarians grunting under the burden of their heavy loads.

And of course the crackle of Rykah's distant firefight, which faded by the minute.

The smoke cloud thinned at the edge of the mountaintop. As they descended diagonally down the slope into the valley, the snapping of gunfire and bark exploding from nearby trees signified they'd been spotted.

Macey's machine gun rattled from behind. She held position midslope, returning fire until she yelled the dreaded words: "I'm out!"

She tossed her machine gun and grabbed the carbine from Spinner on Drua's stretcher. She snapped off single shots until they reached the valley floor, where their retreat through the forest became eerily quiet.

Aside from their burdensome loads, the fallback was too easy. Rykah had chewed off the brunt of Khalid's shock troops. Clearly the besiegers weren't expecting an escape attempt from the fort and had devoted more men to capturing her for leverage. And she was making it easy for them by firing frequently and yelling so that even Toris knew where she was in her escape to the eastern mountains. As the Polarian envoy drew closer to the Lower Fjord, the sharp cracking of distant gunfire faded to distant echoes. When shimmering water came into view through the trees ahead, the shooting stopped altogether.

Toris dropped his end of the stretcher and turned to watch the mountains through the tree canopy to his rear. Rykah had either killed all her pursuers or settled into a hiding spot. Toris refused to consider the other possibility. But she couldn't hide up there forever.

Macey jogged past. "Keep going. We're almost there."

Jarik, who'd fallen behind, stopped beside Toris and traced his gaze.

"Bet she's hauling ass to catch up to us right now," Jarik said. "Those louts never stood a chance against her."

Jarik's reassurance served the opposite effect. Sure, Rykah had a better chance than all of them at making it out alive, but the fact that a veteran such as Jarik felt the urge to console him revealed the depth of her peril.

A volley of gunfire erupted from the mountains, more intense than before.

Toris grabbed his carbine from the stretcher and sprinted toward the shooting. The coast was only a two-minute hustle for the rest of his team, and they hadn't taken fire in a good while. Drua and the others could make it without him.

Toris was gasping for breath when he reached the mountain slope nearest the sporadic gunfire, but he began his scramble up without stopping. He followed the loud cracking up a gully, to a horizontal cleft that cut across the slope, which three of Khalid's troopers were using for cover while firing up the bare mountain. Their tracers led Toris's eyes to a boulder just under the peak, from behind which a wooden rifle barrel emerged and snapped off shots.

Toris threw a grenade at the back of the farthest trooper, then lowered his head to his knees and covered his ears. The blast shook the ground and silenced the nearby gunfire. But there was more, across the slope to his left.

Toris crawled into the cleft with the three smoking bodies. He swept down the natural trench, squeezing off shots until six more of Khalid's finest lay dead. No more gunfire crackled from this side of the mountain, but silhouettes were moving along the far side to angle a shot behind Rykah's cover.

"Rykah!" he called. "I'm coming up. Watch your nine o'clock!"

With that he scrambled up the slope, feet sliding under shale rock. Tracer rounds zipped between Rykah's boulder and the silhouettes moving on her flank to Toris's left. All he had to do was reach her and together they'd obliterate the remnants of Khalid's boys.

That plan, however, crumbled when he slid around the boulder to join Rykah. She was sitting with her back to the rock, rifle shaking in her lap as her trembling hands worked the bolt to clear a jam. But her firearm was not the only thing faltering.

For a long moment, all Toris could do was stare in shock at her bloody fingers slipping on the cocking handle. A tourniquet cinched around her thigh and a vertical streak of blood on the boulder above her shoulder suggested she'd been hit at least twice. The band of black eye paint had crept down her cheeks from sweat and tears.

Her wheezing hung up as she met his stare. The determination in her eyes softened as her eyebrows arched high in despair. She clutched a stuffed rabbit to her chest, her blood staining it a darker shade since Toris had last seen it on *Polaris*.

He leaned her forward to examine her back. Frothy blood bubbled from a hole in her shoulder, which he quickly covered with a dressing from her wound kit. She gasped in an effort to speak.

"*Shhh*," Toris said. "I'm getting you out of here."

Bullets shattered the rock face behind and chipped away at the boulder.

Rykah shook her head fiercely. Her hand grasped his arm. "Not…s-s-safe."

Gunfire snapped from the cleft below, where Toris had taken out Khalid's men with a grenade. His heart went cold. That was their escape route.

They were trapped.

Rykah squeezed his hand and forced a twitchy smile, though the fear in her eyes betrayed her.

"Toris! Adarah! You up there? We can't hold them off all day!"

Rykah's eyes lit bright with hope.

Of course! How could Toris have not noticed? None of the shots had come near since the new arrivals sealed off their left flank. He risked a peek at the new shooters and saw Drua and Macey exchanging fire with Khalid's men across the mountain.

"We're gonna be okay," he told Rykah.

She nodded and wrapped her arms around his neck as he scooped her up and left cover. He slid down the slope with her cradled in his arms, bullets whizzing overhead and kicking up rocks around his feet.

Drua and Macey increased their rate of fire to suppress the enemy, even standing tall before their trench to draw fire onto themselves. Toris focused on running to their left, behind them, until the crevice lip collapsed under his weight. His feet fell out in front and he landed on his back with Rykah on top.

"Get out of here," Drua said as he reloaded his carbine. Macey fired wildly beside him. "Don't stop until you reach the boat."

This order Toris would not protest. He continued down the gully with Rykah in his arms. When the ground levelled into the valley floor, he heaved her over his shoulders to rest his arms and make available the use of the carbine hanging from his vest.

Rykah shuddered and gasped. She pressed a hand against his back in an attempt to lift her chest from his shoulder. Feeling her laboured breathing, Toris laid her gently onto the ground and cringed at the blood streaming down her chin.

"A little rest," he said, stroking her sweaty hair. "It's not much farther." He'd carry her to the end of the earth if she needed him to.

Gunfire echoed louder down the mountain.

"Sit me up," she said as she fumbled to draw her pistol. "I'll hold them off."

Toris grabbed the gun and tossed it aside. "I need you to make it home with me. You know how hard it is to sail a catamaran solo?"

Her eyes snapped from the mountain to meet his.

Toris went on. "We'll get rich fishing tuna and herring, because we'll brave waters no fisherfolk would dare venture into. Unica has a beach where we can dig for clams and mussels. We'll drop anchor wherever we want and no one can tell us to leave. Not that they would anyway. We'll be Polarian heroes." His heart swelled at the memories to come.

Rykah winced in pain. "You'll have to do it without me. Besides, you'll have Alexandra. You and her, you'll have to stay together after all this. No one will ever understand what you've been through out here. You'll need each other. Believe me."

"I want you, though."

Rykah's eyes softened. She brushed his cheek. "I know."

Toris hung his head. "Besides, Lex is highborn. We don't belong together. So you can't leave me." He forced a weak laugh. "You're not allowed."

"Remember what I told you about borders?"

"The Great Lie." Toris held back his tears. If only Polaria had more people like Rykah. "Don't die," he said, his chest heaving with sorrow and his eyes threatening to spill tears.

Her fingers combed through his hair. His scalp tingled to her touch. "Death is just another border," she said, "one we must all cross." Tears of black paint streaked her cheeks. "Make the world good, Toris. See that your kids get the chances we never had."

"We'll do it together."

"Maybe in another life." Her eyes flashed wide in alarm. "The seeds…"

"They're safe, thanks to you."

She began to smile but ended up wincing in pain. "In case you're wrong…In case I don't make it much farther than this patch of dirt, I'd like to trade my citizenship reward for a wish."

"Name whatever you want," Toris said. He'd see she got whatever she asked for. After doing the impossible, she couldn't ask for anything he couldn't deliver. He'd come to the other end of the world for momentos the Decimators had left behind over seven hundred years ago. Together they fulfilled a prophecy the originators didn't even know they were making when they built that vault. Their legacy was Polaria's saviour. What he was doing now, what they all did here, had been part of some bigger plan to save the future.

"I want you to live long enough to experience what we all paid for up here," she said, her breath crackling. "Live for all of us who can't. Make what we gave up all worth it." She brushed his cheek. "I hope your children grow up eating strawberries and food we only ever heard of in stories. The only thing I'd wish for more than that right now is my own dear life, but I know that some things can't be undone, some lines we can never cross and come back from."

Her hand clamped his wrist as she gasped, short of breath. With her other hand she grabbed the back of his neck and pulled his forehead to hers. She closed her eyes and wheezed, trying to speak words that drowned in her lungs before they could escape.

And there, on an island that couldn't possibly be farther from their home, Toris Onero felt Rykah Adarah's last breath on his lips.

Gunfire drew closer to the valley floor. The enemy had Drua and Macey on the run.

Toris didn't care. He sat with Rykah's head on his lap, his tears dripping onto her face. His heart squeezed so tight he thought he might die. He wished for it. Let the heathens send him into that great unknown. Let him die with his fingers laced through his love's ink-black hair.

Crunching rocks accompanied gasping and wheezing. Toris didn't look up.

Macey fell to the ground beside him. "Let's go," she grunted. She struggled to her feet and grabbed Toris's vest. "Toris, come on."

Macey's cracked voice caught Toris's attention. He looked to see her holding her belly, blood seeping through her fingers, face scrunched in pain.

"Drua?" Toris asked.

Macey shook her head.

"Get back to *Barnacle*," Toris told her. "They'll fix you up."

Toris returned to brushing Rykah's hair. Her last wish be damned. She had no right to abandon him with the burden of all that. He'd deal with an eternity of consequences if it promised an eternity suffering them with her.

Macey gave Rykah a good look over. "Come on. She wouldn't want you dying here."

"Why do you care?"

"You're my brother."

Toris looked up. The pleading look on Macey's face was no different than when Spinner had requested she leave him at the fort.

"We kill for each other," she said, then looked back toward the mountain. "We die..."

Toris's heart somehow squeezed tighter. Drua had given his life to come back for him. It didn't seem right to make it for nothing.

He stood and heaved Rykah's body over his shoulder, then followed Macey.

An idling hydrogen motor hummed from the Lower Fjord's north shore where, hours before, the Polarian vault raiders had disembarked as one. When the empty black raiding craft came into view, Ike jumped out from a tree nearest the shore with a pistol in hand.

"Hurry," he said.

Toris set Rykah's body gently into the rubber raiding craft and fell in on top of her, then turned to help Macey board while Ike watched the forest. With the crew settled in, Ike pushed the boat belly-deep into the water and then clambered aboard with Toris's help. He crawled over Rykah's body, faltering briefly at the sight of her, and took the helm.

The *Barnacle* was only a nautical mile away, cruising into the fjord to meet them. Ike piloted the craft to the cargo net hanging from the starboard bow. Both he and Toris reached out and grabbed the net to steady the craft.

Jorda lowered a cable from the foredeck. Macey looped it around her chest and allowed the winch to hoist her aboard. When the cable fell back down, Ike helped Toris slip the loop around Rykah's lifeless body, but the winch remained immobile as Toris and Ike climbed from the raiding craft onto the cargo net.

At the top, Lex grabbed Toris under his arms and helped pull him over the rail. She fell to the deck with him, her arms wrapped around his neck and nearly squeezing the life out of him. When she pulled away, her eyes were bright with joy. "You did it."

Nearby, the winch squeaked as it raised Rykah from the raiding craft. Toris watched with a profound emptiness as Antlia lowered her body onto the deck.

Seeing his distress, Lex sat back with a look of shame on her face. But Toris didn't blame her for her excitement. Instead, he pulled her close and buried his face into her shoulder. She squeezed him tight in return, holding him as the *Barnacle*'s engines rumbled and the bow swung about. He gave himself permission to release enough tears for a lifetime, but a numbness had settled over him and he could not shed a single drop.

By the time Toris lifted his head, Svalbard was a green rock beyond the *Barnacle*'s wake. Then he realized how selfish he'd been, wallowing in his own despair. He held Lex's shoulders.

"Korvyn..." he said.

Lex nodded and rubbed her good eye.

"We couldn't have done it without him," Toris said.

"I'll make sure father knows," said Lex, watching Svalbard sink lower into the horizon behind. "I'll make sure everyone knows the names of every Agrinaut who set out from Anterra."

Toris took a measure of comfort in that.

EPILOGUE

"They could barely hear the bells over the cheering when *Barnacle* cruised into Port Abersali," Toris said.

He sniffled in the chill air of the Spring dawn.

"Word from Point Bay Station had reached Amyria in time for the Chancellor to join the welcoming party at Finn's Marina. He tried to award Captain Antlia the Accolade on the spot, but Antlia wouldn't accept it. See, *Barnacle* did have a sponsor after all. It was Toris Onero who provisioned the expedition, so that was the name Antlia had marked in the sponsorship field on his exit permit."

Large flakes of snow gathered on the wool blanket around his shoulders. He pulled the blanket around his torso and read on.

"The Chancellor waited until Winter Solstice to hold his son's funeral. A crowd in the thousands gathered in Shackleton's Square to attend the ceremony. Many wonder what happened to Alexandra after that, but Toris got his sister back. Some actually say the Chancellor's daughter accompanied them both to the foothills, but no one really knows because her father granted her emancipation."

Toris closed the book. "What do you think?" he said. It'd only taken him five months to write. Not bad considering he could hardly read when he started, and the hold-up of Jayda's reluctance to tell certain parts of her side. A long dark winter huddled around the hearth was plenty of time for Lex to help him perfect his letters. She was a good teacher when it came to words, yet it seemed Jayda had her beat at their current pastime.

Steel rang over the lake, where a thin layer of ice reflected the orange dawn glow. Jayda howled as she brought her axes down onto Lex's saber in a manner reminiscent of Varcy's style of fighting.

The blades sang as the two parried along the lakeshore. A winter of hiding from the cold in the cabin had turned them feverish and eager to flex something other than their minds. The time for reading and writing had passed. The time for fighting had returned. And a fight was coming, whether any of them knew it or not.

"Maybe I'll leave that last part out," Toris said. "Don't want to be giving people clues about where to find us, being that we're famous now and all."

He rubbed a hand over the polymer book cover. "Lex thinks The Artican will make everyone read our story. May even make it part of the curriculum. I think she's right. The Chancellor will want every Polarian to know what his children did out there."

He looked to Venus glowing bright in the indigo sky over the mountains. "I'd give a million Accolades to have you back," he said. "I'd do anything to be where you are, but I have a life to live. For all of us. I'll see your wish comes true."

Jayda tackled Lex to the ground. Lex's laughter echoed across the field as she struggled under Jayda's mount.

"You were right about her. About us. She's not you, but she's got her own way about her."

Lex gave up her back to Jayda so she could stand. Jayda wrapped both arms around her neck as if to choke her out, though not tight enough, because Lex was able to walk up the hill to the bare willow under which Toris sat. As they drew near, Jayda jumped off Lex's back and set about clearing dead weeds from around the dirt mound nearby.

Lex took her place beside Toris but said nothing, only centered a stuffed rabbit of stained cloth over the eight-pointed star carved into a square stone.

"When can we plant the flowers?" Jayda asked.

"Soon," Toris replied. Polaria didn't need more roses or tulips, so whatever flower seeds they'd salvaged from the vault he took here, to plant upon this fresh patch of dirt beneath a willow tree that stood near a cabin that had served as Rykah's home for the first eleven years of her twenty-year life. Rykah Adarah didn't get a funeral attended by thousands of Amyrians, but she'd have the prettiest grave in all of Anterra.

Finding the vault was worth that alone.

ACKNOWLEDGMENTS

The biggest lesson I had to learn on the journey to publication is that writing a coherent book is not a DIY project. Without my family, friends, and editors who offered me advice and encouragement when I needed it, I doubt any reader would have made it this far into the book.

Thank you to my mother, for always believing in me and for supporting me since my first breath. It was this backing that not only helped me see this endeavour to its end, but also kept my feet pedaling across the windswept prairies during my cross-Canada bicycle trip in the many moments where I'd seriously entertained the idea of giving up.

To the first fan of my writing: my father, who managed to sneak in a read of my first story about WWII paratroopers from Margaree before it ended up in the trash. He has read everything I've written since, and his eagerness to dive into the next chapter while I revised this book was enough to keep me plodding along during the times when it was hard to make the words go. His keen eye for spotting errors has also saved me a fair bit of money on proofreading.

To my brother, Mitchell, for sharing the dream.

I'd like to thank my former mentor, Pearl, for helping me build the foundation that eventually led to the creation of this book.

Thank you to Mica Scotti Kole, for providing me with guidance that helped improve my writing, as well as teaching me to manage my words. Well, she tried.

This story has seen countless revisions and has been in many forms throughout the six years it took me to write it. A special thanks goes out to my beta readers who offered feedback in all stages of development: Scott McGuigan, Nikki Boccelli, Mitchell Devoe, Cate, Eric, and Corey. And to Jim Thomas, for steering me toward new beginnings.

I am also grateful to the friends who helped me out along this journey. I'd not be the writer I am today if not for Colleen House and Paul Bailey allowing me to take over their kitchen table for the countless hours it took me to develop my craft, and for also forgiving the occasional missed rent payment. And to Alfie, who was always there to cheer me on and provide the periodic necessary distraction.

Some honourable mentions go out to my cousin Tony, who showed me the path and then gave me the fuel to drive it. As well as Leon and Brigid, for always being in my corner and reaching out to offer words of wisdom when I needed them.

Many aspiring authors have to face not only doubt from themselves, but also from their family and friends. As evidenced by the paragraphs above, I am not among those writers. Everyone in my life has offered me unwavering support in my pursuit of this dream, and for that I am eternally grateful.

PLEASE LEAVE A REVIEW!

If you enjoyed this book, please consider leaving a review on Amazon or Goodreads, or both!

Emerging authors rely on reviews to help their books gain visibility and spread word about their work to other readers.

ALSO BY J. R. DEVOE

The Dark Monarch Series

Book 0.5: The Light Ones
Book 1: Dust
Book 2: Ashes
Book 3: Sparks

For exclusives, updates, and other information, visit
www.jrdevoe.com

ABOUT THE AUTHOR

J. R. Devoe grew up on Cape Breton Island, Nova Scotia, in the town of Sydney Mines. He has since travelled to six continents—including Antarctica in 2013 to research elements of this book. He enjoys folk music, pizza, and the occasional cross-country bicycle ride.

At the time of publication he was living in Victoria, British Columbia, Canada. At the time of reading, he may be anywhere.

www.ingramcontent.com/pod-product-compliance
Lightning Source LLC
Chambersburg PA
CBHW050850210726

48290CB00004B/1162